KILLING EVIDENCE

"The photographs are incredibly sharp," the General murmured. "They are a disaster—their existence endangers us all."

The General pushed the prints aside, leaned back in his chair, and with great deliberation placed a cigar in his mouth. Something would have to be done, and done quickly. But he would not involve New York. They had placed him in command. *He* was the arbiter of life and death, the ultimate responsibility was his, and he welcomed it. He lit up the cigar. Ruthless decisions had to be made for the safety of the mission, and for all involved. He took the cigar from his mouth and studied the ash for a moment.

"No one else has seen the photographs except Berger and the girl?" he asked.

"I'm sure of it," Lupane said. "They're alone in this."

"Then kill them."

THE RAID
The Blistering New Thriller by
ARTHUR MATHER
author of *Deep Gold*

Also by Arthur Mather

DEEP GOLD

THE RAID

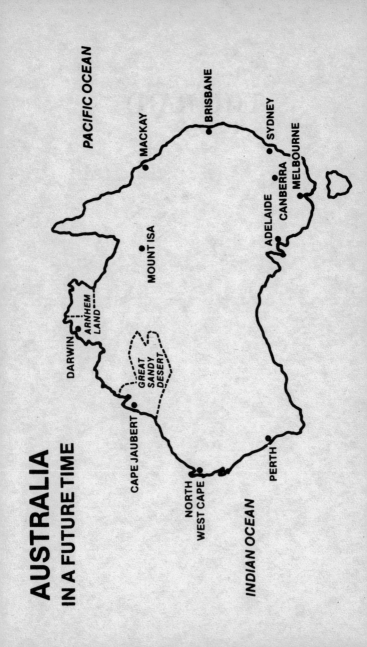

AUSTRALIA
IN A FUTURE TIME

PACIFIC OCEAN

INDIAN OCEAN

DARWIN
ARNHEM LAND
CAPE JAUBERT
GREAT SANDY DESERT
NORTH WEST CAPE
PERTH
MOUNT ISA
MACKAY
BRISBANE
SYDNEY
CANBERRA
ADELAIDE
MELBOURNE

I

Prelude to the Raid

1

Alexei Karsov liked the relaxation of a walk after dinner. Some of his colleagues at the Russian embassy thought it a trifle odd, when the after-dinner period was the time to make points with the ambassador over vodka. Even wheedle some home leave. In truth Alexei was bored with his colleagues. He had been at the embassy in Canberra, Australia's capital city, for three years now, and the work was tedious monotony. Perhaps at a higher level where invitations were received to Canberra's various social functions, life could be a little more stimulating. He was too far down the pecking order to obtain such invitations, and likely to remain so. He had six months to go before his next home leave, and he longed for the sights and sounds of Moscow, even the frosty bite of winter. At twenty-eight, with his dark Georgian good looks, he considered himself too young to waste away in this far-off embassy, with its limited career opportunities. He had studied hard for his degree, had a fair mastery of English, and believed he deserved better than this posting.

He had decided to wait another three months, then summon up courage to ask the ambassador for a transfer back home. It would mean a demotion in grade, but it was better than remaining in this isolated exile. And he longed for the feel of a woman. There had been no one since Tanya on his last leave in Moscow, and God, that seemed an age away now. The ambassador should be more understanding of his single staff. Celibacy was scarcely an aid to efficiency. His pace quickened at the memory of Tanya, trying to contain his yearnings.

He liked to walk by the lake along Parkes Way, past the green picnic grounds. The sharp night air was ideal for brisk walking. The traffic was light, passing with an intermittent murmur, headlights flickering over the trees. He always came this way, and that was another concern. Everything was becoming stale routine, even his personal habits. The thought reaffirmed his determination to return to Moscow. He needed to make a fresh start, even if it meant beginning all over again in another department. And he desperately wanted to be with Tanya. He was so preoccupied, he failed to notice the car pulling into the curb beside him, until the voice called, "Excuse me, sir. I wonder if you could help me locate a street?"

He recognized an American accent, smiled tolerantly, and stepped across to the car. Getting lost in Canberra was one of the constant tourist irritations. It took time, and occupancy, to learn to find your way around the unusual design of the city. The rear window was wound down, and a youngish man in a casual shirt offered him a friendly grin. Alexei crouched to the car and smiled pleasantly in return. "Of course. What street are you looking for?"

"Alexei Karsov?" asked the man.

The Russian looked at him in surprise. "Why, yes . . . I'm Alexei Karsov. Do I know you?"

The smile disappeared from the man's face, and he shook his head solemnly. "No."

Alexei cast a puzzled glance to the back of the driver, but that told him nothing. When his eyes returned to the man in the rear seat, he found a handgun pointed directly at his head. The sight was so unreal, so unexpected, he experienced more surprise than fear.

"Get in the car, Karsov," demanded the man coldly. "Or I'll kill you where you stand."

Karsov stared at him incredulously, and wondered how much chance he would have if he ran. The gun was only a few feet from him, and if the man was serious, he would be dead before he took two paces. There had been no one else along the sidewalk before he stopped. It was possible to feel the loneliness of the desert traveler in the middle of Canberra. Cars sliced along the road with the indifference of the blind.

"I have no money with me . . ." Karsov faltered. "So it's useless trying to rob me."

"You've got five seconds between getting in the car and a bullet in the head," threatened the man, with ugly intensity.

Fear shouldered Alexei's initial surprise to one side, and chilled his body. He had never been confronted by a criminal before, neither in Australia nor in Moscow.

The man pushed open the door and motioned with the gun. "Inside," he ordered, in the same tone.

Alexei had no alternative but to obey. He stumbled through the door with hesitant, shambling steps and lowered himself fearfully into the seat. He felt very afraid.

"Shut the door," directed the man.

He complied. The metal handle had the touch of ice under his perspiring fingers. "What do you want from me?" he asked hoarsely.

The man didn't answer. He settled down in the opposite corner, the gun never wavering from Alexei's head. "Go," he muttered to the driver.

"I told you I have no money," the Russian quavered.

Again he drew no response. The ticking sound of the traffic light was the only answer. The driver gunned the engine, and the car swung smoothly into the anonymity of the Canberra traffic.

From the office window Leo Starker watched the setting sun create twin pillars of gold from the World Trade Center. Past the shimmering towers, the honeyed light sweetened the waters of the Hudson, and beyond, the New Jersey shoreline was fuzzed with a warm glow. Those golden spires symbolized everything he loved about New York. About the entire country. Strength. Power. Courage. Dominance. Everything except leadership. To give all this marvelous country to inept politicians in Washington was like giving a child a precious gem as a toy. It was a depressing reality. Spineless nitwits, conning a gullible public into granting them power, then proceeding to bumble and fumble this great country into a state of impotence. Allow it to be ignored and humiliated by tinpot governments around the world. Such men betrayed the country. Well, no more. If the voting rabble were too preoccupied with instant gratification to elect a man who would enforce respect for the most powerful country in the world, then he would take that responsibility away from them. Christ, someone had to lead the country out of the morass, someone whose every decision wasn't formed by the number of votes it would win. He sighed, shifted his weight about on the deep carpet, and clasped his hands tightly behind his back. He knew Halmen was waiting for his answer, but the man would have to be patient. Just watching the golden light embracing the city was close to a religious experience for him, a reaffirmation of faith. In himself. In the fact that he had found a sense of mission again. His life had floundered since Vietnam, but to be heading the committee was like a rebirth for him. Some men looked only toward retirement in their sixties, but he had too much vigor to even contemplate sinking with senile content into a swamp of past memories. He had time to make his mark again. He had been an army man all his life, but until the committee he had felt like an efficient fighting machine left out in the weather to rust into crumbling junk. But it was like the beginning of life again. Army had been with him since birth, the only son of a high-ranking staff officer and a doting mother. Memories of exchanging infantile salutes with his father. From birth his life had been an undeviating, prepared program. He had loved it all. Doubt, insecurity, confusion were excised from his learning process, for such emotions could only be saboteurs of one born to lead. Such words were never part of his vocabulary until Vietnam. He failed to grasp how it all went wrong, had been left with only an overwhelming sense of betrayal by the Washington traitors. It finished him. Transformed him into a military leper. Untouchable. There was an incomprehensible son to add to the burden, but even a loyal wife failed to breathe life back into him. He had even attempted to write a justification once, until he realized it would only be more fodder for the Washington jackals, so he had destroy the manuscript.

But that was all behind him now. He would use the committee like an army, to resolve the political failures. He would be a good front man. It required no ego-inspired judgment to know he was still a good-looking man. The vague reflection staring back at him from the window was ample reassurance. It was a strong face. Good jawline, good nose. Deep-set gray eyes demanding obedience from beneath shaggy brows. Thin, stern mouth used to crisp words of command. Craggy lines and close-cropped gray hair added to a portrait that suggested distinguished achievement rather than age. There was a time he couldn't have walked the streets of New York without stares of recognition, but that was long past. The politicians saw to that. There were no votes to be won associating with a symbol of a lost war. Now he had the anonymity of the pathetic bag woman who prowled the night alleys of New York.

He sighed again, ignoring the impatient rustle of papers behind him from Halmen's desk. It wasn't the time to be swayed by bitter memories, because it would only sour his new dedication. Now he would do for this country the necessary things of which the feebleminded politicians were incapable.

He unclasped his hands, turned from the window, and brushed fastidiously at the impeccable suit clothing his lean six-foot-two frame. He held himself well. The army had given him a spine the envy of a man half his age, that would hold him erect into old age. He had been long out of the army, but he still liked to be addressed as General.

After the Vietnam debacle, it was one of those small things that helped him to retain self-respect. When he spoke, his clipped voice matched the aura of physical authority.

"The prisoner needs to be kept like a Christmas turkey," he stated firmly. "Fed well, treated well, kept in perfect health right up to the moment of execution."

"Yes, I think we all understand that, General," said Halmen.

"Yes, I know we do, Simon," answered Starker. "Just as long as our friends in Australia understand it equally well."

"They're your friends, General. You spoke to them. The plan may have been conceived in a comparatively short time, but I'm sure because of its danger and importance, everyone involved grasps every detail by now."

Starker nodded slowly, lapsed back into silence, and his hands went automatically to the clasping position behind his back again. The sun struck the window at a fresh angle, daubing the side of his face an orange hue as he thoughtfully studied Halmen. He wasn't too sure he completely understood Halmen, but they shared much common ground. An equal contempt for a political system that reduced the country to impotence. An equal determination to redress the situation by action, with or without the consent of the politicians. An equal patriotism. An equal dedication. But there the resemblance ended. Halmen had never experienced Starker's frustration. His betrayal. Physically he was at the other end of the scale from the General. His chair was necessarily kept at a distance from his desk, to make allowance for his obese bulk. His pudgy hands folded over his rotund belly like a child embracing a balloon. He was completely bald, small eyes, button nose, wide thick-lipped mouth. A succession of chins slagged into his shoulders, obliterating his neck. Starker had heard much of his appetite for food and women—almost parallel to his appetite for wealth. And that was insatiable. He had seen newspaper columnists and television commentators attempt to gauge Halmen's wealth, but inevitably the figures would reach such gargantuan proportions as to challenge credibility. The man's financial resources had the depth of the mythical bottomless pit. He was in everything: oil, transport, banking, whatever made money. He had achieved the American dream, with a Midas touch that produced one bountiful money crop after the other. He had more power than any political figure, but he made no ostentatious display of his wealth. Even this office, while tastefully designed, could have been the center of operations of a moderately successful lawyer.

If the General observed with distaste his undisciplined obesity and the rumors of his bizarre sexual preferences, they were canceled by an exhilarating shared view of the world. Halmen believed, like him, that the most powerful nation on earth should lead, even coerce if necessary, and the rest should follow. The democratic process merely got in the way, a disease that reduced politicians to inertia, their blood to water. That's why he had formed this secret Committee of Concerned Americans, as an act of survival for all the things he believed. There were members of the committee kept secret even from the General, people like Halmen, the real power in the nation, with similar wealth, similar ideas, and a common determination to force the country in the right direction. Pull other minuscule governments into line. People who take our money with open arms, then deride us when we ask for unquestioning support. Yes, he had much in common with Halmen.

After many meetings, much cautious probing, Halmen had asked him to be operations commander for the committee. The General had never ceased to be grateful. It had the scale of a rescue mission for him, to be lifted from soul-destroying retirement. To be offered unlimited financial resources to convert impotent dreams into reality.

"Has there been any publicity in Australia concerning the disappearance of our . . . prisoner?" asked Starker abruptly.

Halmen shrugged. "No. His embassy has kept it very quiet."

"Doesn't that seem strange to you?"

"Not at all. What else could they do? The man has vanished without a trace. Their first instinct would be to believe the man has gone into hiding, to emerge later and ask the Australian government for political asylum. Such things have happened there before, and caused the Russians acute embarrassment. No, they'll be very, very cautious. They'll say nothing until they're absolutely sure of the reason for his disappearance. It suits us admirably, General. It's the way we want it."

Starker inclined his head in hesitant agreement. "It makes sense, I suppose. My friend Martin Blandhurst has vouched for the Russian's security. He'll be transferred to the ship when the time's right."

"Just as long as he has no idea why he was kidnapped."

"He has none whatever. Like I said, he'll be fattened like a Christmas turkey. The moment of execution—when it comes—will be a sudden and rather unpleasant surprise for him."

There was another short silence, as the General turned again to the window. The golden walls of the Trade Center had faded to watery yellow, and the half-light that precedes dusk sharpened the city with eerie detail. The drum of traffic along Broadway was like the finale to a closing curtain. Halmen hadn't framed the question yet, but Starker knew what his decision was going to be. It was time. He had weighed all the data, and action had to be taken before the Australian elections. This was the committee's first operation outside America, and everything had to be absolutely right.

"The next meeting for the committee is set for tomorrow night, General," prodded Halmen cautiously. "They're expecting a firm recommendation. I need hardly add they're eager to make a start. The Australian election date is drawing close."

Starker nodded irritably. Halmen was capable of using a patronizing tone at times, and it annoyed him. "Then I recommend we draw up a schedule and go. We should move as rapidly as possible now."

"The committee will be delighted," exclaimed Halmen.

"The raiding party will need some practice exercises first, but if we move now they'll have sufficient time."

"They need to be dedicated."

"I've spent a long time selecting them," said Starker tardily. "Handpicked Vietnam veterans. With a need for vindication I understand. Men who fight an unpopular war have deep seeds of bitterness. And they'll be paid extremely well . . . those that survive. Don't worry, Simon, they have more than enough dedication." He stared morosely into space. "They know that the American bases in Australia like North West Cape, essential to our security, are under threat because the party predicted to win the Australian elections intends closing them down. They agree vehemently with the committee's point of view that it's imperative to this country's security that those bases remain where they are. At all costs." He glowered across the room at an unseen enemy. "And that the mealymouthed politicians in Washington will sit on their asses and do nothing about it, except make bleating sounds." He smiled with lofty confidence. "Have no fears about the men, Simon. They'll do well."

Halmen nodded with satisfaction. The General's confidence seemed to provide him with needed reassurance. "You'll go to Australia, General?"

"Of course. That's essential. I intend to use Darwin as a liaison base."

"And you'll be in touch with your friend Blandhurst?"

"Only if it's necessary. I don't want to risk compromising him in any way, when we have such a long personal friendship. Without his cooperation our entire plan would have been much, much more difficult."

"But then, he has a lot to gain from our success," said Halmen tartly.

The General shrugged. "Let's say success is to our . . . mutual benefit. When it's over, and I feel it's safe, then I'll probably see him."

"Then you must pass on the committee's thanks," said Halmen. He pushed his chair away from the desk and stood to his feet, breathing heavily. He was approximately the same height as the General, but his obesity created the illusion of a much smaller man. Starker compressed his mouth tightly to conceal his distaste. He admired the man's achievements, but it was a crime against nature to allow the body to degenerate into such an appalling condition. But he knew Halmen's weight was a sensitive subject, and he went to great pains to conceal his disapproval.

Halmen waddled to the bar and poured two Jack Daniels. He retained one glass and offered the other to the General. His gaggle of chins jiggled with a broad smile.

"To our success, General," he wheezed. "To the committee's success . . . to America's success."

Starker moved from the window to accept the glass. His body in motion personified the military image, erect, arms swinging in time to a parade-ground stride. He raised the glass to answer the toast. "Yes . . . to unqualified success, Simon."

"And a good trip for you, General," Halmen added.

Starker sipped cautiously, surreptitiously watching the way Halmen gulped at his whiskey. Even the small things the man tackled with ferocious enthusiasm. He dropped his eyes to his own glass, thinking of Australia with pleasure. It would be good to see his old friend Martin again. The way the plan for the raid had dovetailed with Martin's own ambitions had been a delightful surprise. And Martin had proved invaluable for them in Australia. He knew who could be trusted, who could be bought. He had helped to make success inevitable. There would be no public kudos for any of them afterward. No one would ever know they were responsible for altering a small portion of history. And there would be many more operations for the committee after this one. Anywhere in the world where American prestige or power was under threat by some minuscule government, that's where they'd be. In a way it was unfortunate the democratic process had failed, but someone had to demonstrate this country's muscle to enemy and allies alike. God, someone had to put the nation back on the right track.

Mark Berger had set the alarm for three-thirty, but he was unprepared for the darkness inside the Land Rover when he woke. An impenetrable blackness that for a moment disoriented him. He rolled over on the camper bed, fumbled for the flashlight, and checked the time. It was just after three-thirty. He snapped out the flash and lay for a moment listening to the steady drum of the Indian Ocean surf beating against Cape Jaubert. Up until now he hadn't minded the isolation of his photographic assignment around Australia, but he seemed to have been traveling forever. Maybe it was the girl in Darwin who had instilled a longing to be static for a while, to come to a halt and just enjoy life with someone like her. He shrugged. Darwin and the girl were a long way behind him now.

He flicked on the flashlight again, propped it amid the photographic equipment in the corner, and shrugged into his denim jacket. Even inside the vehicle he could feel the sharpness of the early morning, and he needed warmth until the sun rose. He congratulated himself now on making sure he arrived at the cape yesterday afternoon with enough remaining daylight to select a good position on one of the dunes for the sunrise shot. To be able to take a compass reading for the correct direction where the sun would rise, and to have the ninety-millimeter lens fixed ready on the camera. Better than fumbling guesswork in the darkness.

He was a young man of twenty-six, lean and brown from

long exposure to the sun. What he considered an embarrassingly youthful face was camouflaged by a heavy dark beard, a color match for his curly hair. He observed the world from intensely curious brown eyes. When he laughed, which was often, his mouth was a startling flash of white against his beard. To girls he resembled a handsome, swashbuckling adventurer from another age—although there had been precious little female company since he'd started this around-Australia project. With the exception of Darwin. That had been pleasant. Not particularly sexual or passionate, but pleasant. When the project was finished, he'd go back and see her like he'd promised. There was something about her that would take a lot of forgetting. And he didn't want to forget.

He opened the thermos flask, made himself some coffee, then balanced the cup in his hand as he clambered out of the Land Rover. The chill felt raw against his bare legs, and he pondered a moment about changing his shorts. He let it be. They'd be more comfortable when the sun climbed to a scorching height later in the morning. He would need the flashlight for operating the camera, but it was unnecessary for walking about in the open. The entire universe seemed on show in the sky. A vast canopy of uncountable stars, accompanied by a gleaming full moon, coated the landscape with a cold, luminous glow. Everything from the Land Rover to the smallest sliver of grass had its own sharply defined shadow.

He strolled across to the cliff edge, sipping at the coffee, his feet squelching in the sand. The Indian Ocean shimmered like wet plastic in the night light. The vast, desolate coastline of Western Australia stretched infinitely north and south from where he stood. He could have been the only mortal on earth. He always made a point of first reading the history of any place he was going to photograph, and to be here, where countless ancient ships had foundered, stirred his imagination. Crude navigation had failed so many of those seventeenth-century sailors, head-

ing across the Indian Ocean en route to the Spice Islands
in the north. The journey had ended for so many in a
horrendous nighttime collision with this coastline. The
surf, the cliffs, the arid land, must have made it a fear-
some place for the unfortunate Dutchmen stranded thousands of miles from home. Even to survive the sea would
have been no guarantee of salvation. To the south, only
the long stretch of the eighty-mile beach. To the north,
only more isolation. To the east, where he would point his
camera, the immense reaches of the Great Sandy Desert,
just sand, spinifex grass, and scattered kanji trees, where
the heat would drop a man in an hour. If there was a place
for ghosts, it was surely here. If one listened hard enough,
and long enough, imagination would convert the shrill
cries of the gulls to the long-ago screams of drowning
sailors. He shrugged the mournful thoughts aside. He
couldn't allow the isolated location to play games with his
mind, shadows to assume threatening forms, sounds to
haunt his imagination, when he had work to do. He drained
the cup, urinated in the sand, and retraced his steps to the
Land Rover. He checked over the Cambo by torchlight,
just to make certain nothing had been forgotten in his
preparation of the camera yesterday. He picked up the
thirty-five-millimeter Nikon and hung it about his neck.
He'd decided to have a second camera in readiness, just in
case he wanted to take some hand-held shots when the
desert was flooded with sunlight. Then he picked up his
camera case and trudged back across the sand to where he
had positioned the tripod last night. He removed the
cover from the tripod, laid it out on the sand, and placed
the Nikon and the camera case down on top. He plugged
the legs of the tripod deeper into the sand to minimize the
risk of any movement; then, fumbling awkwardly with the
flashlight, he attached the five-by-four Cambo. He decided for a warm filter, to give the shot that extra glow. If
he could just get some long stretches of cloud along the
horizon to reflect the sun, it would give the picture an

added dimension. He wanted this shot to be the same high standard as the others. He was delighted so far with the shots he'd taken around Australia, and he was sure the publishers would share his enthusiasm. The shots around Darwin had been so dramatic, the only difficulty he anticipated was in selecting which one to use. And he wanted this picture to have equal drama. The first rays of the sun exploring an endless expanse of desert, everything rendered magical with dawn light, the feeling of mystery and loneliness of the great Australian emptiness. He threaded the cable release into position, then checked and double-checked to make certain it was operating correctly. He couldn't risk a last-minute technical fault once the sun began to rise. Then he waited. Maybe three-thirty had been too early, but he couldn't afford the chance of some unforeseen hitch that would have him scrambling frantically to catch the light. He stood there silently, a sea breeze flicking the grass about his legs, thinking of home in Sydney, of Darwin, of Lisa and the wonderous smile she had left in his memory.

Reminiscence dissolved time, until a smudge of light along the horizon warned of approaching sunrise. He knew it would come quickly out here. He checked the camera position again, took an anxious peek through the viewfinder, slid a film into place, and snapped the lens shut. The light along the far reaches of the desert bloomed into the sky, revealing the hoped-for streaks of cloud parked just above the horizon. He checked the meter reading. He would start with fifteen at eleven, and probably work down to a second at sixteen as the sun rose higher. It was like a curtain coming up on the desert, the sun sculpting the landscape with dramatic starkness. He began to shoot as the first rays probed over the horizon, working with the unhurried speed of the professional, taking a shot, sliding a new film into place, dropping the exposed film into the case, checking for a new reading, adjusting the exposure, then shooting again. The only sounds were the click-click

of the release cable and the rumble of the surf. He was
working to a short time schedule, because once the sun
was well clear of the horizon, all the eerie light quality he
wanted would be gone. It was going perfectly, just what
he wanted. It would fit beautifully with the rest of the
portfolio.

When the sun had climbed to a position where he
considered the shot had exhausted its potential, he stopped
shooting, dropped the final film into the case, and lit a
cigarette. The Nikon lay unused by the case. Well, it had
been comforting insurance to have another camera in case
of mishap, but the Cambo had operated perfectly. He was
well satisfied. He dragged at the cigarette, absently watching the breeze whisk the smoke into the desert. He would
make some more coffee, cook some eggs and bacon on the
Primus stove, and then drive leisurely down to Port
Hedland. There was a sunset shot he wanted to get
there, then he was finished with the west coast. He didn't
know what made him look out to sea. He was kneeling in
the sand, stacking the exposed film in the case, when he
glanced out and saw the ship. It was only a small freighter,
but he was surprised to see it anchored so close inshore. A
black vessel of no great style, floating motionless like a
dead whale. It must have anchored there before first light,
and he'd been too preoccupied with shooting to notice.
He closed the case, stood to his feet, and idly studied the
ship for a moment. It made a nice scene in the early-
morning light, rock-still on a calm sea, hot spots of sunlight flashing off the superstructure. On impulse he swiveled
the Cambo around on the tripod and tried to focus on the
ship. The ninety-millimeter lens was too wide, shrinking
the image of the vessel, making it an uninteresting shot.
But he was sufficiently impressed to believe another lens
could turn it into a good shot. He decided, for speed, to
use the Nikon. He strode briskly back to the Land Rover,
fitted the five-hundred-millimeter lens to the Nikon, then
paced rapidly across to the cliff edge. He knelt in the

sand, positioned the camera on a ledge of rock to keep it
steady, and checked the meter reading. The sky was bright-
ening so fast, five-hundredth at eight was already possible.
He squinted through the viewfinder, focusing on the ship.
The lens was just right, and the image swelled into extreme close-up. There was nothing about the ship that
appeared unusual, except for the helicopter standing on a
small landing pad at the stern. Perhaps it was used for fish
spotting. He could see men fussing about on the deck, and
ropes dangling down amidships to a large rubber landing
craft floating by the side hull. He didn't know if the shot
would be any use, but he had the usual photographer's
eye for anything that would make an interesting picture.
He decided to shoot off a roll or two, just for the hell of it.
He took several shots of the ship, without bothering to
vary the angle, just trying different exposures. There were
black-dressed men clambering down the ropes into the
rubber launch. Ten, maybe twelve of them. The splutter-
ing buzz of an outboard engine came sharply over the
muted roll of the gentle surf; then the launch broke free of
the ship and headed inshore. He focused on the launch,
shooting swiftly, using the rock ledge like a steadying
cradle. Click, click, click. He grinned to himself. It looked
like navy guys practicing early-morning commando tactics,
and he wondered how surprised they'd be to find their
pictures in a glossy photographic book on Australia. Maybe
it would fit in the portfolio after all. The launch turned
away from him, heading for a small sandy strip of beach at
the base of the cliff. He stopped shooting, checked the
exposure, and waited. It was only a slight surf, but it
might make a dramatic shot if they caught a wave and
went rushing shoreward in a surge of white foam. They
certainly looked like navy commandos, the black garb,
crouched in tense attitudes like men preparing to attack
an enemy base. It appeared slightly theatrical. They drove
hard at the beach, throwing a white trail like an attacking
shark. The craft lifted easily on a small wave, accelerated

through the foam, and ground to a halt on the sand. He
was shooting again, and he caught it all. The rubber
launch surrounded by surging white water. The black-clad
men leaping out and dragging the craft up the beach. He
glanced quickly at the exposure counter. He had only a
few shots left, and he was debating if he had either the
time or the inclination to insert another roll of film, when
he became aware of the chutter-chutter of the helicopter.
He glanced quickly back to the ship, at the now empty
landing pad; then he saw the helicopter heading toward
his position on the cliff, skimming low over the sea, all
black like the men in the launch. And somehow menacing,
coming like a hawk with a fix on its prey, the canopy like a
gleaming eye spraying hot spots of sunlight. For the first
time he felt a quiver of unease. Maybe he was inadvertently photographing some secret navy maneuver. It hadn't
occurred to him he might be seen from the ship, but he
guessed it would have been easy enough for someone
checking the shoreline with binoculars. He didn't want to
get involved in any tangle with the authorities, not when
his project was still uncompleted. The hell with them, he
wasn't in any classified secret area, so they couldn't confis-
cate his camera. But he was alone, and people liked to
play rough sometimes to assert their authority. He decided to play safe, at least until he found out if he had
anything to answer for. He pushed the camera hastily into
a cleft in the rock until it was hidden from sight, then
returned swiftly to the tripod. There was no time to conceal the Cambo; the helicopter was coming fast, zooming
up from sea level in a sharp-angled climb. Then it was on
him, the landing skids almost brushing the cliff edge, stirring the grass into frenzied movement. Sand whirled into
the air like a miniature cyclone, and he buried his face in
his arms, tightly shutting his eyes. He groped toward the
camera, hunching over it in an ineffectual attempt to ward
off the rain of sand. Aggravation replaced unease. Fucking
maniacs. He would probably have to take the camera apart

and clean out the sand before he could risk using it again. The sound of the chopper receded, and he lifted his head as the swirling sand began to settle. It was banking around in a tight turn above the fringes of the desert, a blurred black pod against the sun. It came in slowly, maneuvering toward him, then it was down with scarcely a bump to the right of the Land Rover. He could see two figures in the cabin now, white faces watching him, garbed in black like the others.

He didn't move from his position, hands still resting protectively over the camera. The chutter of the engine faded, and the blades slowed in whistling accompaniment. He rehearsed scathing words in his mind. If the camera was badly damaged, then these gung-ho idiots were going to have to foot the bill.

The two men clambered out of the helicopter and moved briskly toward him, the leading man partly concealing his companion. Maybe they considered him fair game, an inquisitive civilian who needed to be taught a lesson, because everything about them suggested aggression. Like the men in the landing craft, they wore a black overalls, peaked black caps. The leading man's face told him nothing. Fortyish, nondescript, devoid of emotion. It was impossible to make a comparison with the second man, he was so completely blocked from view. Angry words spilled out of Mark's mouth, too volatile to be held back any longer.

"You stupid bastards," he shouted furiously. "What the hell do you think you're doing?" He raised his hand from the camera and raked the air with angry gestures, as if to emphasize the potential damage to the Cambo. He made no effort to restrain the aggression in his voice, determined to take the offensive. "All the bloody sand you stirred up could ruin my camera." Hearing his anxiety converted to words only inflamed his resentment further. "What sort of fucking James Bond act was that supposed to be? Haven't you got any bloody brains at all? Who the hell do you think you are?"

He had raised himself to boiling point. The entire photographic trip around Australia had gone without a hitch, and it was infuriating to think he might have to replace a camera at this late stage.

Neither of the men answered him. The leader abruptly halted a few yards away and gestured briefly to his less visible companion. The second man moved immediately to one side, into full view. He had a small submachine gun in his hands, the muzzle pointed toward Mark. The photographer's anger dissipated like a doused flame, replaced by the acrid taste of fear. It enveloped him in a form of paralysis, locking his limbs, stilling his tongue. His hand fluttered from the camera like a falling leaf.

"Now . . . now, wait a . . . minute—" he began hoarsely.

It was too sudden to inflict pain. Just the overwhelming power of the bullets hammering into his chest, then his body hurtled back from the camera, one flailing hand bringing the equipment down with him in a grotesque tangle of twitching limbs and metal legs. The sand formed a soft, resilient cushion for his body, absorbing his blood like a sponge. Then he was still.

The assassins walked slowly toward the body, the sand scrunching beneath their boots, and stared down at the corpse for a moment. The one with the machine gun prodded Mark roughly with his foot. "He won't take any more photographs," he muttered tersely.

The other nodded with satisfaction. "Just as well. Jesus, what incredibly lousy luck. You wouldn't believe it possible to have someone like him appear out of nowhere in a place like this and start taking photographs of our practice operations. It's unreal."

"Maybe. But bad luck for him."

The leader silently contemplated the body for a moment. Then he stared thoughtfully out at the freighter. The rubber launch was on the way back to the ship, loaded with the men. "It didn't take them long to get out of here," he grunted.

"Blucker was probably in touch on the radio. They must have got a hell of a fright. Blucker too." He jerked the gun toward the body. "It might be just coincidence this bastard being here, but we'll have to try to make sure. There might be some identification on him . . . or in the Land Rover." He shook his head. "If he's a plant, if someone sent him here to photograph us, then Blucker's in real trouble. We all are. The whole plan's gone down the chute. We may as well all pack up and go back home."

The leader scratched thoughtfully at his chin. "Maybe, maybe. Don't let's panic yet. It could still be coincidence. Let's see what we can find out about him."

They were fast but thorough, expertly dissecting the personal items and photographic equipment in the Land Rover. A driver's license with the name Mark Berger and a Sydney address. Credit cards and a checkbook with a bank in Sydney. Letterheads and business cards with the words "Mark Berger, Commercial Photographer." Clothing and traveling equipment, but nothing of significance. They had what was wanted, an identification that could be checked out.

"One of our people can get this verified in Sydney," said the leader. "It should tell us what this guy was doing here right at this exact moment. Maybe it's coincidence, maybe not. Blucker's going to have to suspend any more practice runs for a few days, until we get an answer." He stared morosely out to sea, where the men were already reboarding the freighter. "If this man was here deliberately, then there's a bad leak in the organization somewhere. That would be a bastard of a thing to happen, after all the work. All the planning. The General isn't going to like it. Not any of it."

His companion stirred the body with his foot again. "Maybe we should have asked him first," he said sardonically.

"No. It's better this way. We haven't the time to grill anyone, and we'd only get a lot of crap answers anyway. I mean, he was here, and he photographed us—that's all that matters. Deliberate or not, he had to be blown away. Those were Blucker's orders."

The other man nodded slow agreement. His eyes moved over the body, the camera equipment, then to the Land Rover. "We can't just leave it like this," he said.

"Right. We'll dump the body and all the gear into the Land Rover, lock it, and shove it over the cliff. I noticed a deep gorge from the air, on the other side of the headland. It'll sink like a stone."

"We'd better move fast. They'll be as edgy as hell on the ship to get out of here as quickly as possible."

"I can understand Blucker being edgy. It's his neck. A few of the guys on board thought using Cape Jaubert for a practice exercise was risky. The General's going to hold him responsible for the foul-up." He bent foward and clasped his hands about Mark's ankles. "You know, Blucker didn't have any trouble picking up this guy with the binoculars. He wasn't making any attempt to hide himself. That's why I figure it probably is a coincidence." He shrugged. "Let's get rid of him anyway."

They moved with speed, lifting the body from the sand and dumping it in the Land Rover, together with the camera equipment. A few empty film cartons were scattered about, but they ignored them, believing the wind sweeping in from the ocean would soon carry them into the desert.

The leader started up the Land Rover and drove it cautiously across the sand to the cliff edge, the other man trudging in his wake. He took the vehicle dangerously close to the edge, facing out to sea, then slammed on the brake and clambered out onto the sand. The force of the wind was rising, darting into the crevices in the cliff face with an eerie moaning sound. He left the door open and checked to make sure he could reach the hand brake. The

body was sprawled on the seat, propped against the opposite door, the dark beard matted with blood. The man
ignored it, as if it were an irrelevant piece of baggage. He
balanced on his toes, readying himself to spring clear
when the Land Rover began to move. Below, the wind
had pushed the waves higher, and the sound of the surf
smashing against the cliffs boomed up from the gorge.

The second man trekked to the rear of the vehicle and
put his weight against the tail. "Ready," he shouted.

"Right . . . now push," called the leader. He snapped
off the hand brake, slammed the door shut, and leapt
backward as the wheels moved sluggishly through the
sand. The vehicle gathered momentum, teetered on the
edge for an instant as if reluctant to accept destruction.
Then the front wheels went over, carrying the body into
free fall. It turned in a slow circular motion, striking a
craggy outcrop on the way down, smashing open one of
the doors as it bounced clear, then plunging into the sea
with a whoosh of exploding water. For a moment it bobbed
on the surface like a metallic cork before the sea gushed in
and dragged it under, leaving only a bubbling wake. Then
that was just as quickly gone.

The two men watched in silence until it had disappeared, then retraced the route of the Land Rover, scuffling their feet in the sand to erase the wheel marks. The
man who had done the actual killing worked at a slower
pace, the muzzle of the submachine gun trailing in the
sand, as if murder had inflicted him with a strange lassi-
tude. But he said nothing. They stood for a moment
examining their handiwork; then the leader nodded with
satisfaction. He glanced briefly toward the ship. The men
were all on board, and there was no sign of the rubber
launch. "Okay, that'll do . . . let's go," he said curtly.

A ray of sunlight explored a small cleft in the rocks
along the cliff face as they passed. The lens of the concealed Nikon threw off darts of reflected light, but neither
man noticed.

2

The terrain of central Australia, seen from an altitude of thirty-five thousand feet, presents a mind-numbing expanse of infinite vastness. An unchanging panorama that unfolds mile after mile, with little change. To the keen observer, a small white dot might occasionally be seen, marking a representative of Western civilization. But such a sight would require patience and sharp eyes, because of its rarity. Such spots generally indicate the location of some isolated cattle-station homestead surrounded by a holding counted in thousands of square miles. Like a contrasting speck on an enormous expanse of reddish-brown carpet laid down as far as the eye can see, until it merges with the horizon in a vignette of pale ocher and blue. Once, during the Ice Age, this part of the continent had been a large ocean, with accompanying rainfall, but now it was a gasping land of perpetual thirst. The dry continent. But it has a unique, awesome majesty when viewed from the comfort of a modern jet aircraft.

Ross Berger was grateful to have a window seat. He had been too long away from his Australian roots. He had already renewed acquaintance with his hometown of Sydney, but this was another part of the country that aroused a mystic longing. Maybe for too long he'd been like those small clumps of clouds far below, just drifting aimlessly. Moving wherever a chance wind took him. Searching? For what? He'd stopped asking himself that question a long time ago, because he had never found a satisfying answer. He was twenty-eight now, and maybe a resolution would always elude him. He shrugged it aside and thought instead of his dead brother.

The initial grief was past now, replaced by a numbed

acceptance. It had been worse for his parents, because they had been much closer to Mark, at least in a physical sense. But Ross's long absence overseas had not caused him to lose any affection for his younger brother. He'd always kept in touch, and they had spent time together during his brief visits back to Australia. But inevitably long separations had weakened the threads. But Christ, for Mark to die like that, and so young. Death had sent Ross searching back into past memories of early days with his brother. They had been inseparable through adolescence and early teens. The competition that sometimes creates barriers between brothers had been nonexistent. They had shared the usual scrapes, school successes and failures, the fumbling with giggling girls in the park. Only two years separated them, yet Ross had always assumed the mantle of leadership in those formative times. It had seemed a natural thing to both of them, and the years had run together with an easy blur in those uncomplicated times. Only in Ross's late teens had come a restlessness he couldn't control, a revolt against the threat of life dropping so easily into a routine of suffocating dullness. It had been an average middle-class home, his parents set rigidly into the traditional pattern of breadwinner and housewife. There seemed to Ross no great passion in the marriage, but more an attitude of passive contentment. And the usual middle-class fervor for education. No matter what sacrifices, it had to be the best schools for their sons. Ross hadn't wanted it. Vaguely he had yearned for freedom and excitement, without knowing how it could be achieved. His parents had watched his mutiny with concern, without understanding the nature of the problem. He recalled the anxious father-son discussions with a twinge of embarrassment. Of course life had a certain predictability, his father had argued, but it was important to obey the rules, and "get on." Ross rejected it as crap. He drank too much, he drove too fast, he did everything with a nervous reckless energy. At nineteen, the relationship with Mark changed for all time.

Mark never had to search. Never suffered the uncertain confusion of trying to find a path. He picked up a camera at sixteen and found a natural talent that gave him an unswerving certainty where he was going. Photography consumed every spare moment of his life, and Ross could only watch with envy. Mark's photography was something his parents could understand, take pride in, and it only heightened his own aggression. From this distance in time he could wince at his behavior. He had been screaming for attention. He drove his ancient car like a maniac. There were close brushes with the police. He didn't look back on that period of his life with any pride, yet had he really changed?

When he told his parents he was off to take on the world, he had viewed their conflicting expressions of concern and relief with contempt. Well, they had Mark and his grand obsession, so he'd figured he had no reason to stay around. He still loved his brother, and in a perverse way was proud of his talents, but he couldn't take living in his shadow. So he went, with foolish courage and an amoral indifference to how he kept alive. He worked as an extra in Hollywood. A deckhand on a tanker. Ferrying strange people with mysterious packages between Miami and Cuba. His swimming ability, learned in the surf of the Sydney beaches, saved him one night, when a powerful launch loomed out of the fog and cut his boat in half. He never found out what happened to his passengers, but he floated for four hours before a passing launch plucked him out of the sea. He carried a gun for a lost cause in Central America, and again it nearly cost him his life. He drove a taxi in London. Washed dishes in Soho. Escorted ladies clinging desperately to fast-vanishing youth in Paris. Was a lone courier to Yugoslavia. He had enjoyed that. No taint, no stain, the closest he had ever come to his school-boy dreams of high adventure. He never did find out what was in the package, but someone died for it. He knew he was on an endless, time-consuming wheel, repeating himself. Running, running, but only from himself. But it wasn't all loss. He learned how to hang loose, develop a presence, a highly personal style, the way he talked, held himself. It was an acquisition paid for in sweat and fear, by the way he'd lived his life.

He had the same sharp features as his brother, the same curious eyes, an identical darkness, but no need of a beard to disguise a youthful face. Lines of maturity had set early, and with his assured poise it made him an attractive man. There had been women, but only those eager to bond him with their bodies. He was as restless with them as with life, and none held his interest for long. They only offered predictability, so he was always moving on, moving on.

On his rare visits home, when his parents inquired what he was doing, he said searching, and laughed away their puzzled expressions. But he took pride in the developing stylishness of Mark's photographs, his growing reputation. He had urged him to go overseas, but Mark had insisted he wasn't ready. Maybe in another year. And his doting parents anxiously agreed, fearful of losing their anchor. They had never learned the art of letting go.

When Ross arrived back in Australia unannounced this time, his father had told him of Mark's big assignment. A brief to catch the soul of Australia with his camera, to go where he chose, and come back with the best portfolio of shots ever taken of the country. Ross had been impressed. Disappointed at missing his brother, but delighted the kid was doing so well. Then pride was abruptly canceled by grief. To find himself now flying to Darwin to identify his brother's body, because it was an ordeal too traumatic for his father's diseased heart. Ross had few plans to cancel. An offer in London of top money for some private army in Zimbabwe, but a one-way gamble he would have passed anyway. It was irrelevant now. Some fucker had filled his brother's body with bullets, and Ross wanted to know who. And why.

"There are some crazy people in this country," said the man beside him.

Not only in this country, Ross wanted to answer, but he held it back. He'd been too self-absorbed since takeoff to notice the man. Elderly, overweight, balding, large-framed spectacles dominating his face. He wore a beautifully cut suit that would be wrinkle-free when he disembarked in Darwin. It was a contrast to Ross's fawn canvas slacks and casual brown shirt.

The man folded the newspaper on his lap and tapped the lead story with a scowl. "People have short memories," he muttered. "Where would we have been without the Americans in the last war? Probably taken over by the Japs, that's where."

Ross nodded politely, an absent smile on his face. It wasn't a subject to excite his interest. It was a generation-gap thing. Japan meant cars, electronics, and economic success to him, not war. "I suppose so," he murmured vaguely.

"Look at this survey," the other continued. "We've got a general election in about three weeks' time, and there's overwhelming evidence that the opposition is going to win in a landslide. Walk it in."

Ross nodded again without comment. He knew of the coming election, but it had scarcely entered his mind since Mark's death. He distrusted politicians. It didn't seem to matter if it was a banana republic or a democracy; the ones he'd seen were all expert manipulators of fear and ignorance. Back stabbers. Truth benders.

"Perhaps they're due for a turn," he muttered disinterestedly.

The man turned in the seat and sourly studied him. "Then I hope to Christ they don't get it," he declared fervently. "You know they've said they'll close down all the American bases in this country if they're elected. Just kick 'em out. That's lunatic talk. Commie talk. Like committing suicide. We need the Yanks here. Maybe we don't know all that's going on inside those bases, but so what? We've got to trust someone, and better them than the Russians. This is a big country, and we haven't got a hope in hell of defending ourselves. We don't want to do anything to offend the Yanks. Boy, I tell you we really need 'em." He shook his head in disgust. "Yet if this poll is accurate, it's going to happen. I tell you, people are nuts."

Ross didn't need the conversation. "Perhaps we should think about trying to defend ourselves," he said, and turned his face to the window in a blunt attempt to sever the discussion.

The man ignored the rejection. "With our population?" he said scornfully. "In a country this size? Forget it." He tapped the newspaper with added force. "The media are half to blame. They're crazy too. All of 'em."

Ross didn't answer. Australia's security paranoia was something he'd almost forgotten during his long absences. The man was spoiling for an argument, and he wasn't in the mood to become involved. He dozed fitfully, dreaming of the dark-eyed, sexually voracious young woman in Honduras who had come close to insinuating herself into his bloodstream. Who had kept him in heat so long in Trujillo, it had almost cost him his life. Of Aldo, his body pockmarked with machine-gun bullets. He hoped he wouldn't find Mark's body in the same slaughtered condition.

The landing chimes and the clicking chorus of connecting seat belts jerked him awake. He saw by his watch it was ten o'clock. The jet was already low and into a steep, banking turn. Now the vegetation was more the rich green of the tropics, swaths of trees stretching out to the sea. The aircraft straightened, and the far-off cluster of buildings that was Darwin glittered in the morning sunlight.

The man in the other seat gruffly cleared his throat and pointed to the window. "Darwin," he said with a hint of pride in his voice. "I don't know if you're only coming for a visit, but I'll wager you'll never want to leave." He grinned and waggled his head. "It gets to you, boy . . . it really gets to you."

He was obviously a resident. Ross acknowledged the comment with a vague smile. He was suddenly aware of a sense of foreboding. He'd seen many dead bodies, but he wasn't sure how he was going to react to the sight of Mark. Perhaps a resurgence of grief. Of anger. And he must go and see the woman Lisa Marnoo, after he'd spoken to the police. He had liked the words of sympathy and compassion she'd used in her letter to his parents. Better than the insensitive phone call from the Darwin police asking for official identification from next of kin. If the woman had befriended Mark as she stated in the letter, then she might have something more personal to tell him than the police. Maybe it was his instinctive wariness of authority, but then, she was the one who had first identified Mark.

The wheels touched down with a shriek of rubber, and the thunder of the engines filled his ears. He closed his eyes in a brief attempt to compose himself for what he had to do. It was a glorious day. The sun shone benevolently out of a cloudless sky, providing a temperature in the mid-seventies. He had a reservation at the Asti Motel on Smith Street in the city, so he decided to check in first. He only half-listened to the babble of the taxi driver on the delights of living in Darwin. Or the Top End, as some of the residents called it. On the climate. On the friendliness of the people. On the dynamic recovery from the 1974 cyclone that had almost flattened the city. He answered in monosyllabic replies, but it did nothing to discourage the garrulous driver. After a time he just clammed up, nodding and smiling, but letting the words flow past without being absorbed. Besides, the sense of apprehension was growing in his belly. Mark's alive, vital face was so fresh in his memory, and he knew it would be wiped out by the expressionless look of death.

"How far is it to the hospital?" he asked, cutting across

the driver's long-winded oration of an area called Fannie Bay.

"You're not feelin' well, mate?" asked the driver with concern.

"No, I'm fine. I just need to get there."

The driver shrugged. "You wouldn't want to walk it from your motel, mate. Eight mile or so, over in Tiwi. Way over the other side of the airport."

"Then why don't you wait for me at the motel? It won't take me long to check in, and you can drive me over."

The man shrugged again, and grinned into the rearview mirror. "It's okay with me. You're the one who's payin', mate."

The motel was a modest three-story block grid of rooms. On a windowless wall was a painting of a large black palm tree superimposed over a red sun, with the name Asti Motel. But it was a pleasant room. Comfortable bed, long desk, television, everything coordinated in shades of pastel lemon. He had stayed in innumerable rooms like this, and variation was rare. He swept aside the curtains and glanced out the window. It was a pleasant view, across the bay to the peninsula on the other side. At another time he might have enjoyed leisurely appreciation with a cold beer. He opened his suitcase and changed quickly into a fresh shirt. Then he rinsed his face briskly under the cold tap and brushed his hair roughly into shape. He didn't figure on being in Darwin long, but it was hard to tell. After the identification, arrangements would have to be made for the body to be flown to Sydney for burial, but he had no intention of leaving Darwin until he had some satisfactory answers. He picked up a tourist map on his way past the reception desk, and went back out to the taxi.

He was only a young man, not a great deal older than Ross, but the composed solemnity of his expression made him seem older. The tan of his face was in startling contrast to the white coat he wore. When he wasn't tending to the dead, he must have spent considerable time on the beaches around Darwin.

After the warmth of the outside sun, Ross shivered in the musty coolness of the mortuary. But he knew it was as much his own apprehension as the chilled air. The attendant was strictly wedded to an official routine, because he took time satisfying himself over Ross's identification before he would show him the body. Then with a detached wave of his hand he invited Ross to follow him.

"Have you spoken to Mr. Lupane at the Darwin police station on Mitchell Street yet, Mr. Berger?" he inquired politely.

They passed into the room, their footsteps rapping hollowly against the floor, and Ross didn't answer for a moment. At the other end he could see the corpse laid out on a trolley, the covering sheet outlining the body, and it seemed to thicken his tongue.

"Not yet," he answered in a muffled tone. "I thought I'd come here first. That's why I sent you the letter."

"Yes, that was a good idea. I wish everyone was so cooperative. It gave us a chance to be ready for you." He coughed dryly and made an apologetic gesture with his hand to his mouth. "You will be seeing Mr. Lupane, of course. You know he's in charge of the case?"

"Yes. I wrote to him also. I'll see him after I leave here. He'll be expecting me."

The attendant nodded impassively. He spoke very quietly. He had introduced himself in such a faint undertone that the name had eluded Ross. They came to a halt before the body, and Ross stared down at the covering sheet. If he felt any consolation at all, it was the fact he was available to come instead of his father. The old man's heart would have faltered from the sight of all his expectations for Mark come to nothing. He wondered if his father would have felt the same if it had been him. It was a disturbing thought. Even here, could he still feel envious of Mark?

The attendant's hand poised tentatively over the covering. "I suppose they told you that the young woman, Lisa Marnoo, made the original identification?" he murmured.

Ross sighed with ill-concealed exasperation. The man had a maddeningly slow, almost ceremonial form of procedure.

"Yes, I'm aware of that," Ross mumbled. "But the police insisted on positive identification from next of kin. That's why I'm here."

The attendant's fingers frittered along the edges of the sheet. "Yes . . . of course . . . not that there's any doubt about the Marnoo woman's identification . . . no, none at all." He looked uncertainly into Ross's face and cleared his throat. "There is some deterioration, you understand. We're not responsible, we have excellent facilities here, but the body was in the water for some time before being found."

"Yes, yes, I know that also," said Ross patiently.

The man mobilized his face into a mournful smile and drew back the sheet. Then he took several reverent steps backward, clasped his hands behind his back, and quietly waited.

The silence was so intense, Ross was conscious of the rhythmic pat of his heart, the soft breathing of the attendant behind him. For an instant, recognition failed him. The attendant's warning about decomposition hadn't been an exaggeration, for there was none of the tanned glow he remembered, only sagging white flesh. He wanted to move closer, but his feet refused the request. His limbs tingled as if circulation had slowed, and a deep sadness chilled his flesh. He felt no surprise at the involuntary tears flowing out of his eyes. It was Mark. Not as he remembered him, but certainly his brother. As yet, there was none of the rush of anger he'd expected.

"Yes . . . yes, it's my brother . . . Mark Berger," he muttered.

For a moment the attendant fidgeted awkwardly, then stepped back to Ross's side. He reached toward the sheet, but Ross quickly put out a restraining hand.

"Show me the rest," he said hoarsely.

The man stared at him blankly. "The rest?"

"Yes. The rest of the body. Not just the face. I want to see how he died."

Did he really? Was he only searching for a catalyst to anger he believed he should feel?

"Well, if you think it's necessary," said the attendant.

"Yes, I do. I wouldn't ask, otherwise."

The man hesitated momentarily, then shrugged and pulled the sheet back to just below the waist. The mushy skin texture of decomposition was more apparent, as were the seven marks where the bullets had impacted into the chest. The attendant held the sheet back for several moments; then, as if even he found the sight offensive, he brusquely covered the body completely again. He coughed harshly, the sound echoing about the room. "Death would have been instantaneous," he muttered in consolation.

Ross didn't answer. He stood tight-faced, wondering what he'd say to his parents. "I can see that," he said dully. He'd seen wounds like that before, and it astounded him. Aldo had died like that in Trujillo. Modern firepower leaves no time for last prayers, but who the hell would have used a weapon like a submachine gun on his brother? No one had said anything about a submachine gun. Maybe the police had an answer for him.

The attendant eased away from the body and began to retreat toward the door. He made a tentative gesture for Ross to follow. "There are documents that require signing, Mr. Berger," he said apologetically. He spoke the words in a sanctified whisper. "And we'll need to discuss the arrangements necessary for your brother's body to be transported to Sydney." He paused at the door, waiting for Ross. "Of course, if that's what you want . . . ?" he added.

Ross nodded silently. He reached out and placed his hand on the still form in a token of farewell, then turned away and walked slowly to the door. He could feel a simmering anger now, probably brought on by the nature

of the wounds. He held it down. Better to let rage moti-
vate any future actions, not blow it away in one fiery
outburst. Christ, he'd understood it to be a straight-out
murder and robbery, but what sort of casual thugs carried
submachine guns?

"I will want the body sent to Sydney," he answered
morosely. "Will you people be able to arrange it for me?"

"Certainly," said the other. They passed out of the
mortuary and into the corridor. The attendant didn't look
at Ross, hands clasped behind his back, walking at a
respectful pace, eyes to the floor.

"How long ago?" asked Ross.

The man looked at him inquiringly. "You mean since
death?"

"Yes."

The other shrugged noncommittally. "It's a little difficult to say. All that period of immersion. Perhaps ten
days."

"Who found him?"

The man halted at another door, placed his hand on the
doorknob, and glanced blankly at Ross. "I think they're
the sort of questions you should put to Mr. Lupane at the
police station." He grimaced with a regretful smile. "My
only function is to take care of the body." He opened the
door and ushered Ross through ahead of him. "It won't
take you long to sign these documents, and we may as
well finalize all the arrangements for transporting your
brother's body while you're here. We're cramped for space,
as you can appreciate, and the body can't be kept here
much longer."

Ross stifled an angry response with difficulty. It wasn't
the man's fault, he had a job to do like everyone else, but
it made Mark sound as unimportant as an inedible carcass.
It was only a small room, with a tiny desk and two flimsy
wooden chairs, whose solitary window looked out onto an
expanse of green lawn. The attendant went to the desk
and sifted through some papers, while Ross waited by the

door. He thought about the Marnoo girl. It might be a good idea if he called her from here and tried to arrange lunch for after he'd spoken to Lupane.

"If you could just wait here for a moment, Mr. Berger, I seem to be out of forms. I'll get some from the front office," said the attendant.

Ross motioned to the telephone on the desk. "Is it all right if I make a call?"

"Certainly, help yourself." Then he was gone, the rapid pat of his steps fading down the hallway.

Ross took the girl's letter from his pocket, noted the number where she could be contacted at an insurance office, and dialed. He waited while the switchboard transferred the call.

"Lisa Marnoo," said a cool, modulated voice.

She sounded younger than Ross had expected. Very composed, but young. He tried to picture a face that complemented the voice. Mark always did have a good eye for women.

"Lisa, my name is Ross Berger," he began smoothly. "Mark's brother. You wrote my parents a very nice letter after my brother's death."

There was a pause at the other end of the line. "Yes . . . yes, of course," she said carefully. Then, with more confidence, "Mark told me so much about you. I heard someone from the family was coming up to Darwin to . . . see about Mark's body."

Some of the cool composure bled from her voice. He wondered how involved she and his brother had been. "Look, I don't think we should try to discuss this over the phone," he said quickly. "But I would like to talk to you about Mark. From your letter, you obviously got to know him quite well. I wondered if maybe we could have lunch today. I . . . er, I don't expect to be in Darwin very long, so if you could make it today, I'd appreciate it. And I'd like to thank you for your letter. It was a nice thing to do."

There was another hesitant pause from her. "I don't

know if there's anything I can tell you," she answered
warily.

"Well, I guess I wouldn't even be here if it wasn't for
you identifying him. The family owes you a debt for that.
Apart from anything else, I'd like to thank you in person."

"All right, then," she agreed suddenly.

"Well, I'm a stranger to Darwin. Where's a good place
for me to meet you?"

"Where are you staying?"

"At the Asti Motel on Smith Street."

"Oh, good. I work on Smith Street. Why don't you
come along to the mall. There's a place called Paspalis
Centrepoint, where there's a small café called the Little
Lark. I won't have a lot of time, but we can talk there."

"That sounds fine," he agreed. "Say around one o'clock?"
He made a quick decision against telling her he was going
to see the police first. That was something they could talk
about over lunch.

"I'll wait for you just outside the door," she said. "If you
can possibly get there a little earlier, then we'll have a
chance of a better seat. Say a quarter to one?"

"All right. I'll look forward to meeting you, Lisa." He
was about to hang up, when he realized he had no way of
identifying her. "How will I know you?" he asked.

"Do you look like Mark?"

"Well . . . I guess so . . . but without the beard."

"Then I'll know you," she concluded confidently. "I'll
see you at the café around quarter to one, Ross."

"Fine . . . I'll look forward to it, Lisa." He hung up and
contemplated the telephone for a moment. She sounded
very much in control.

The attendant bustled into the room then, a sheaf of
documents under his arm. He smiled absently at Ross and
placed the papers down on the desk. "It's really just a
matter of your signature on these, Mr. Berger," he murmured reassuringly. "Just some requirements of the law.
Then we'll talk about the transporting arrangements."

Ross nodded, and referred to his watch. He wondered how long he would be with the police. Maybe it had been a mistake to make a firm appointment with the Marnoo girl. He would just have to wait and see.

Afterward he phoned for a taxi, and waited outside the mortuary in the sun. He was glad he had come, because the experience would have broken his father, but he hated the knowledge that the sight of Mark's body would leave a lasting image in his mind, when there were so many pleasant memories he would have preferred. He had a heightened impression that everything about him was so alive, the birds, the trees, the people, even the steady beat of his own pulse. He shivered in the shadow of his own mortality. He'd loved Mark, and he despised the feeling, deep within himself, the sense of relief at the elimination of a rival.

Michael Lupane was a large man. Ross stood just over six feet, but he seemed dwarfed by the detective sergeant. The policeman was around forty, and once he must have had the physique to excel at any sport requiring muscle. Now his belly was swollen with self-indulgence, and the buildup of flesh beneath his chin would probably expand further with passing time. Large hooked nose, full-fleshed mouth, and heavy-lidded eyes surveying the world with disarming somnolence from under bushy ginger brows. They were probably an attribute that could easily lull a suspect into a false sense of security. Tinges of early gray sprouted from around his ears into close-cropped rust-colored hair. He looked very conservative, white shirt, subdued tie, dary gray suit. It was a marked contrast to the relaxed Darwin dress style Ross had seen. And there was a striking white pallor to his skin, also at variance with the Darwin tropical tan. Ross decided he was either a recent arrival to Darwin or rarely stepped outside his office. The neatness of the office said something about the man—the carefully arranged desktop, the books carefully stacked on the cabinet, the paintings of Darwin on the walls, the elaborate map.

His hands, like everything else about him, were huge, engulfing Ross's fingers in a powerful grip. His preliminary words of welcome were uttered in a voice that was slow and deep in his chest. In the Australian manner his mouth moved little, and the words had to force a passage.

He closed the door behind Ross, motioned him to a chair, then lowered his own hulk down on the opposite side of the desk. He lit up a well-used pipe, all the time glancing at an open file on the desk. Then he took the pipe from his mouth and smiled with a practiced expression of trust and reassurance. "First let me express my sympathy for you and for your parents in this terrible thing that happened to your brother," he began gently. He shrugged mournfully. "Human beings do ghastly things to each other. All we can do is try to keep it to a minimum."

Ross studied him bleakly. He was past the stage of soothing syrup; all he wanted to know was what had happened. And who had made it happen. "Do you have any ideas?"

"Well, a few." Lupane glanced across Ross's shoulder to the closed door. "The door being shut doesn't bother you, I hope?"

Ross looked at him blankly. "No. Should it?"

"Well, there's a little tension here at the station. I've only been here a short time . . . sent up from Sydney. Headquarters had the idea that since your brother was from Sydney, it might be worthwhile to have someone from there in charge of the case." He grimaced, with a confidential wink. "The local boys are rather upset at having an outsider brought in. I guess they see it as a reflection on their competence, but it wasn't intended like that. So . . ." He gestured to the door. "I have to be careful. The case is difficult enough, without stirring up resentment." He sucked noisily on the pipe for a moment.

"But then, that's my problem. This isn't giving you any information concerning your brother's murder."

"I don't care who's in charge of the case, just so long as you get the ones who killed Mark," Ross stated bluntly.

"Of course, of course," agreed Lupane hastily. "That's what we all want." He peered down at the file, his large fingers running over the typescript. "I don't know what you've been told, Mr. Berger, but your brother's body was plucked out of the sea by a fishing boat, just off the west coast of Australia. The pathologist figures he was probably in the water four or five days."

"Yes. They told me at the mortuary about him being found in the sea."

Lupane's eyes flickered in surprise. The pipe had gone out, but he still clasped it in his hand as if it were a source of comfort. "Ah . . . so you've already seen your brother's body?"

"Yes, I thought I'd go there first."

"That's fine," Lupane assured him. "I know they were anxious to see you as soon as possible. They have a . . . space problem there. You want the body taken back to Sydney?"

"Yes. It's being arranged now."

"Good. I'm glad you took care of it so promptly." For some reason the policeman's composure wavered briefly, but it showed only in his eyes, and was quickly gone.

"The west coast of Australia is a hell of a large area," Ross said.

"You're right," agreed Lupane. He turned to the map on the wall and pointed with the stem of his pipe. "He was found off a place called Cape Jaubert . . . see, down south from the town of Broome. Oh, it would be about a thousand miles up the coast from Perth."

"That's a long way from Darwin."

"Right. The skipper of the fishing boat took the body into Broome, and they flew it to Darwin."

"Why Darwin?"

Lupane shrugged. He turned back to the desk and dropped the cold pipe into the large seashell ashtray. "Why not? They had no way of identifying the body. The fishing boat was based in Darwin, and the skipper knew the police would want to question him, so it made sense to bring the body here."

"The fishing boat's back in Darwin now?"

"Yes, I believe so. Boat's called the *Kunarra*. Skippered by an uncommunicative old bastard called Pat Tanna. I didn't get much out of him, but I guess there wasn't much he could tell me anyhow."

"I suppose Mark must have been camped by Cape Jaubert," mused Ross, studying the map.

"Yeah, that's right. Old Tanna went ashore to have a look around after they found the body. They found a few empty film cartons . . . things like that. It made sense when we checked back in Sydney and found out he was a photographer."

"Then you knew about his around-Australia photographing assignment?"

"Yes, we found that out too." He paused, eyebrows raised, eyes fixed on Ross. "You knew about the Marnoo girl's initial identification? Your parents would have been told."

"Yes, I heard about that." Ross didn't say anything about her letter to his parents or the fact he'd already been in touch with her. He didn't know why. Lupane's attitude invited confidence, but he didn't feel comfortable with the man. "You had a look around Cape Jaubert yourself?" he asked.

"Sure. Flew down a few days ago, but it didn't tell me anything." He shook his head. "Hell of a desolate place."

"I guess Mark would have been buried in an unmarked grave if it hadn't been for Lisa Marnoo knowing him," observed Ross. "I understand they struck up a friendship when he was passing through Darwin taking photographs."

It was a mistake, but too late to correct. Lupane would

know that information could have come only from contact with Lisa Marnoo. A momentary flash of alertness shone in his eyes, like the abrupt flare of a struck match. "That right. You know about that also," he said casually.

"Mark mentioned something about her in a letter to my parents," Ross lied. Maybe it was just his instinctive distrust of authority that made him so wary.

Lupane nodded. "Apparently your brother and the girl became quite friendly when he was here. She read in the local paper about the body being found in the sea, and thought the description sounded like your brother. So she went to the mortuary, and sure enough, it was him."

"Otherwise you would never have known who it was?"

Lupane leaned back in the chair, and it creaked ominously under the redistribution of weight. "Right again, Mr. Berger. Not us, not you, no one. There was absolutely no identification on the body, and it was a million-to-one shot him being found in the sea like that. Just . . . luck, if you want to call it that. Old Tanna rarely takes his boat into that area."

"And when they found Mark was from Sydney, they decided to send you up here, Mr. Lupane."

The detective shrugged, with a self deprecating smirk. "Well . . . they figured I had a little more expertise in this sort of thing. I hope they're right, for both our sakes, Mr. Berger."

Ross fell silent for a period. Maybe he should try to talk to this Pat Tanna from the fishing boat. It sounded as if he didn't take to Lupane either, and he might be more open with him.

"There was no sign of my brother's photographic equipment or his Land Rover, Mr. Lupane?"

"Nothing's turned up yet, but I think you know we're pretty sure that's why he was killed. Some of that stuff must have been very valuable. Plus the Land Rover would make a nice haul for some punk. I don't figure your brother had enemies vicious enough to want to kill him."

He paused and appraised Ross with a challenging stare.
"Unless you know something about his personal life we
don't, Mr. Berger?"

"Well, I've been out of the country for a while . . . but
. . . no, Mark wasn't the sort of man anyone could hate.
Everyone liked him."

"Yeah, I figured that myself," said Lupane with a condescending gesture of his hands. "You get a lot of drifters
moving around the country. And up the west coast. Gung-ho
young bucks, with no brains, no money, no conscience,
and usually armed. I'd say some of them saw your brother
alone, in an isolated place, and reckoned he was easy
pickings."

"Then afterward they threw his body into the sea?"

"Sure. They'd probably be anxious to get away, and
they wouldn't go to the trouble of digging a grave. Not
with the Indian Ocean there as a disposal yard. The million-
to-one chance of Pat Tanna happening by wouldn't occur
to them. Why should it?"

Ross nodded, slowly digesting the theory. Was it that
simple? A piece of horrific bad luck for Mark to be in the
wrong place at the wrong time. But what about the submachine gun? Christ, how well he remembered Aldo being
hit by a burst like that.

"Would the sort of people you're talking about kill so
easily?" he asked tentatively.

"Like they were swatting a fly. It's happened before.
It'll happen again. Playing out some macho role they saw
on television." Lupane sighed mournfully. "It's a sign of
the times we live in, Mr. Berger. No one raises an eye-
brow at the violence anymore. What I need from you now
is an accurate listing of your brother's equipment. And all
the information on his Land Rover. We'll put descriptions
out all around Australia. If it's the type of random killing I
think it is, these young bucks are going to try to convert
that equipment into cash as quickly as possible. That's
when we'll grab 'em. You mark my words."

"Would the sort of young drifters you're talking about carry submachine guns?" Ross asked bluntly.

Once again he saw the flash of light in Lupane's eyes, yet so quickly suppressed, and the man shifted his bulk around uneasily in the chair.

"Submachine gun?" he queried softly. If he was disturbed by the question, it didn't show in the timbre of his voice.

"I saw the wounds on my brother's body. They weren't from a rifle or a handgun."

"You sound as if you're talking from experience, Mr. Berger," Lupane said easily. His eyes were wide and disarmingly frank again, inviting confidence.

"I've . . . seen a man killed like that . . . with a submachine gun."

Lupane nodded, his hands fiddling with the ashtray holding his discarded pipe. "Top Enders Welcome You to Darwin," it said along the side. "Well, we're not sure at the moment—" he began.

"You have the bullets?"

"Yes, we have the bullets." Lupane coughed and arranged a stern expression on his face. "We prefer not to involve relatives of the victim in that . . . nasty side of the business. That's our role. What you pay your taxes for, Mr. Berger."

"You must know what type of gun the bullets came from?" persisted Ross.

Lupane soberly consulted space before answering, then shut the door in Ross's face: "We have it in hand, you can be sure of that. I think that part of your brother's murder is best left to us. After all, we are the experts. I don't want you to concern yourself about it. Don't worry, we'll trace the gun."

Lupane's voice was honed to a sharp edge of authority. Ross knew he was being told to butt out, but he refused to be sidetracked. "Surely it's highly unusual for the . . . gung-ho young bucks you're describing to be carrying a submachine gun?"

Lupane contrived another sigh, like air gushing from a deflating balloon. "Believe me, Mr. Berger, anything's possible with these young thugs," he said heavily. "Anything at all. There are places in Australia where you can buy any sort of weapon you want. You name it, they've got it. Rifles, handguns, yes, even submachine guns. Yeah, it's unusual, but certainly possible. The possession of such a gun would make one of these hoodlums a real hero to his mates." He smiled frostily and extended his hands in a gesture of consolation. "Naturally you're upset about your brother. A young man like that, with all the world in front of him. A tragedy. But believe me, we know about these things. These drifters. I'm positive it's how your brother was killed. You can leave it to us, Mr. Berger. We'll get 'em. Most of these young guys aren't particularly smart. They'll try to unload the stolen goods, then we'll pick them up. That's the way it always happens. You'll see I'm right." He leaned to the desk in a brusque change of manner, placed a blank sheet of notepaper before him, and picked up a pen. "Could you tell me where you're staying, Mr. Berger, and how long you think you'll be in Darwin? I may want to contact you."

It was a blunt termination of any further questions. No matter how unlikely Ross thought it was for such young drifters to be armed with a submachine gun, Lupane was telling him the police knew better. But the interview left him with a strange sense of unease. He was sure Lupane knew his job, but he had the feeling the man was being deliberately evasive. And Ross had certainly disturbed him by identifying the submachine-gun wounds. But it was useless pushing Lupane any further, so he accepted defeat. For the time being.

"I'm at the Asti Motel on Smith Street," he said. "I guess I'll be here for at least two days. It depends on when they can get my brother's body on the plane."

Lupane wrote the address in a swift, untidy scrawl. "That shouldn't take too long." He looked up with a smile of dismissal. "I may think of something else I want to ask you. And don't forget those details about your brother's equipment. The sooner I get those, the faster we'll get these bastards."

"I'll have to get that from the insurance people in Sydney. My parents will know who insured him."

"Right . . . well, when you can. The quicker the better. Why don't you see if the insurance company can phone the information direct to me here in Darwin. That would speed it up."

"Sure," Ross agreed. "I'll call my parents tonight and get them to arrange it."

The office opened abruptly, and a man half-inserted his body into the room. He was of a much smaller build than Lupane, but the narrow, angular body and small head gave an impression of height. There were deceptive lines of age creasing his face, but he was probably only about thirty. It was a face that rarely smiled. He had the lean look of a perpetually hungry wild dingo. He was dressed in the same conservative-suit-and-tie style as Lupane. His small eyes darted warily from Lupane to Ross. "Sorry, Mike, I didn't know you had someone with you," he muttered apologetically. His voice was a flat monotone.

"That's okay, Paul," Lupane said quickly, as if welcoming the interruption. He pointed the pen toward Ross. "This is Mr. Ross Berger, just up from Sydney." The pen switched direction to the man at the door. "Mr. Berger, this is Paul Garcott, my right-hand man. He came up here to Darwin with me."

Ross offered a friendly nod and extended his hand, but Garcott merely responded with a curt dip of his head. "Ah yes, the dead man's brother. We've been expecting you," he said. Nothing more, no pleasantries, no sympathy.

"Yes, well, I think we've got everything straightened out now," said Lupane. "Mr. Berger was just leaving."

Lupane had certainly decided there was nothing more to be said for the time being. Admittedly Ross had found

it difficult to establish any rapport with the detective, but
he failed to understand the man's guarded resentment.
Surely he was entitled to ask questions?

Garcott's eyes stayed on Ross's face for a long time, as if
he was memorizing every pore in his skin. Ross felt as if
he was being dissected. Then, as if he was satisfied, he
turned back to Lupane. "Just wondering what you were
doing for lunch, Mike."

"Sure, I'll be with you in a moment."

Garcott nodded, and turned his unblinking orbs back on
Ross again. "See you," he said sharply, and closed the
door abruptly behind him.

Lupane stood with an apologetic twitch of his shoulders.
"Don't mind Paul." He grinned. "He's a man of few
words."

"Yes, I can see that."

Lupane extended his large hand across the desk. "If I
don't see you again before you leave Darwin, have a good
trip back to Sydney. And pass on my sympathy to your
parents."

He was a portrait of affability, as if he felt a sudden need
to correct a bad impression. They shook hands, and as if to
reinforce his change of attitude, the grip was more powerful than before. Then he picked up the pen again, studying it with a musing expression, as if he might have
forgotten something. For a disconcerting moment Ross
wondered if he might be going to ask him to lunch, and
mentally he swiftly concocted an excuse. He didn't want
to say anything about meeting Lisa Marnoo. Once again,
he wasn't too sure why. Lupane might offer some preliminary observations about the girl, but he wanted to make
his own judgment. And lunching with a cold fish like
Garcott seemed a repellent idea anyway. An invitation,
even if it was considered, never came.

"Well, thanks for your help," Ross said coolly. "I'll ask
my parents to hurry the insurance company for you with
those details."

"Thank you again," said Lupane. He lifted his hand in another brief gesture of farewell. "And I don't want you or your parents to worry about the investigation. We'll get the murderers. As soon as we get any results, you'll be the first to know." Reassurance beamed out of his face like a tropical sun. "We do know what we're doing, believe me, Mr. Berger."

"I'm sure you do," Ross murmured with an equal pretense of reassurance. Then he nodded and went out the door.

He stood for a moment outside the police station, blinking in the strong sunlight. He had found the interview irritatingly inconclusive. Combine his antipathy toward authority with an active imagination, and he could have misinterpreted Lupane's attitude. But he was positive the man had been disconcerted by the fact he knew Mark had been killed by a submachine gun. Why should that disturb him? He tried to shrug it away. Maybe Lupane was right, they did know what they were doing, and he should leave it to the experts.

It was pleasantly warm, the sky a canopy of brilliant blue, without a trace of cloud. A soft breeze with the smell of the sea washed over his face. His watch said twelve-thirty, so the lunch arrangement with Lisa Marnoo had worked out fine. He parked himself in the shade of the building while he studied the Darwin tourist map to orient himself. He found he wasn't that far from the meeting place. Up Mitchell Street, then down Knuckey Street to the Smith Street Mall. He began to walk, conscious that the city around him was moving with the onset of lunchtime. Wide streets, deep green vegetation, and the occasional handsome palm throwing shadowed fronds across his path. Whatever devastation had been done to the city by the 1974 cyclone, there was no sign of it now. People of all ages walked the streets in tropical garb of shorts and shirts or colored blouses. There was a sprinkling of aboriginal people, some with the black skin of the full blood, others with the lighter shade of a European mix. The pace was unhurried, casual. Ross passed a poster in a shop window, featuring a candidate for the coming elections. A toothy, confident face proclaimed another man of the people. It brought back the conversation with the man on the plane. The manipulators would be going at full blast over the next few weeks, and with luck he'd be out of the country by then.

He found the Centrepoint easily, just down from Knuckey Street. There was more bustle, the collection of shops a stimulus to increased activity. He halted abruptly when he saw the dark girl waiting at the entrance to the Little Lark Café, more from surprise at the unexpected than anything else. Or maybe stirrings of unsuspected racial feelings, but he hadn't considered the possibility of a part-aboriginal girl. He knew instinctively it was her, stunning in a white summer dress against the dark of her skin. Jet-black hair embraced a face that was a superlative combination of European genes joined with one of the oldest races in the world. Retaining the black eyes, yet straightening the nose. Reshaping the chin, yet holding the full blooming mouth of the country's original inhabitants. Perhaps five-feet-four in height, she held herself with an erect pride that made her appear taller, that attracted lingering glances from passing males. Then she saw him, and he knew instant recognition was mutual. She stepped confidently toward him, hand outstretched, her mouth open to the whitest smile he'd ever seen. He estimated she was in her early twenties.

"Lisa Marnoo?"

"Yes, and you just have to be Ross Berger," she said warmly.

It was the self-possessed voice that had intrigued him over the telephone, given added charm by her physical presence. He felt slightly dazzled. No wonder Mark had been attracted to her. He smiled with an attempt to equal her warmth, and took her hand. It felt cool and tiny in his grip.

"Is it that obvious?" he asked.

"It is to me. The way you stand, the way you look. Yes, you're very much like Mark."

"I'm a trifle early—" he began.

"No, that's fine," she interrupted. "So am I, but we can . . ." She paused and glanced down to where he still hadn't relinquished his grip of her hand. He released her with an apologetic grin, and she gestured to the café. "I saw a vacant table over in the corner on the far wall. It would be a good place to talk."

He nodded agreement, and she led the way briskly into the café. She was slim, yet full where it was right for a woman. Everything being normal, his mind would already be working on the best way to get a woman like this into bed. Screwing his way around the world was the only constant vocation to which he'd applied himself. Yet almost immediately he felt a sting of guilt because of Mark. And envy that he had had a woman like this. Maybe he'd never lay Mark's ghost. Ross followed as Lisa threaded her way around the tables. She moved in a purposeful style that spoke wordlessly of strength and determination. They settled down in the corner, and he saw she was right about the location. Even if the café filled, they'd be uninterrupted here. She had a lot of poise, but he could tell by the way her hands frittered at the menu, and by her uncertain smile, that she was nervous.

"I hope this is all right with you, Mr. Berger," she began, "but I never have anything more for lunch than a sandwich and a cup of coffee."

"Ross," he said. "Call me Ross. And if you don't mind, I'll call you Lisa."

"All right." She smiled.

"And this place is fine," he assured her.

She pushed the menu aside. She had nice hands, fine

and delicate, with a caressing touch. "When did you arrive in Darwin?"

She had a way of asking a question so that her eyes were directed with unswerving attention at his face. It had been a long time since any woman had made such an initial impact on him.

"Just this morning."

"This is your first time in Darwin?"

"Yes it is."

"People who live here think it's the greatest city in the world."

"So I've gathered." He grinned. "Do you?"

She shrugged without enthusiasm. "It suits me. I have . . . ties."

He wondered if that meant a man. He was finding it hard to think about her in anything but sexual terms, and that was crazy, because he was here to talk about Mark. To try to fill in gaps that Lupane had left. He concentrated his mind.

"You like your motel?" she asked.

"Yes, it's fine. Although so far I've only checked into the room. Then I went straight to the mortuary."

He watched her face for any reaction. For the first time she averted her eyes, staring down at the table, fiddling again with the menu. Then the waitress inquired for their order, and she softly asked for a sandwich and coffee. Ross doubled up on the order. He'd eaten on the plane, and food wasn't a high priority.

"You wouldn't have found that very . . . pleasant," she said soberly.

"No." He watched her taut expression. "It's tough with someone you've grown up with, loved, heard laugh and get a kick out of just being alive." The macabre image of Mark's decomposing body jumped into his mind. "Then you see them like that." He watched her silently for a moment, but she offered no response. "It must have been tough for you too," he added gently.

She sighed, interlocking her fingers, and her eyes returned to his face. "You might say that. I didn't know Mark long, but yes . . . it was tough."

He wanted to ask about her relationship with Mark, but he didn't. Maybe he didn't want to know. It was ludicrous, but if it was sexual, he had the feeling it would be like some restraining leash about his neck. It was incredible to feel like that after only a few moments with the girl.

"I just had to thank you for the letter you wrote to my parents. We owe you so much for the identification. Mark would simply have vanished without it."

She smiled acceptance, not with the brilliant flash of white, but a softer amalgam of warmth and sympathy. "I wanted to write because I liked Mark so much," she said simply. "Even though I knew him only two or three days, he was a terrific guy." She gestured toward the entrance. "I met him right here, at the mall. He was shopping, and asked my advice about something. From someone else it would have seemed like a guy on the make, but . . ." She smiled softly at the memory. "He was so open and friendly, it would have seemed like bad manners not to help."

The waitress bustled to the table, placed their order down, and left with a harassed smile. About them the café was filling fast.

They were both silent for a period, concentrating on the food. Ross made a pretense of eating. The fresh image of Mark's slaughtered body was scarcely a stimulus to appetite.

Lisa patted delicately at her mouth with a napkin, idly stirred at her coffee, then concentrated her dark eyes on Ross again. "It wasn't really a . . . relationship I had with your brother," she began hesitantly. "We had a lot of . . . fun together while he was here—"

"You don't have to tell me about that," he said quickly.

"No, but I'd like to," she said firmly. "We just hit it off, right from the beginning. I showed him around Darwin, he took me driving. It was mainly over a weekend, so we saw a lot of each other. I thought he was a little crazy at first, then I realized he got this terrific kick out of just being alive." She laughed, her eyes misty with remembrance. "We went out along the Arnhem Highway one day, and he took off into the bush chasing buffalo, in and out of the anthills, both of us bouncing around like crazy." She shook her head. "I hadn't laughed so much in a long time. He told me all about his photography, how he was going around Australia for this publisher. He was terribly excited about it. He was leaving to do some more photography along the west coast, and he promised to come back and see me again when he'd finished." She suddenly stopped speaking, and her mouth twisted into a cynical smile. He was surprised at the shades of suspicion and distrust he read into her expression. Then it was gone, like a mask slipping back into place.

"I'm sure he would have come back to see you," he said, as if he felt the need to defend Mark.

"Yes . . . yes, I'm sure you're right," she agreed tactfully. "I guess I missed him badly when he was gone." She sipped quietly at her coffee, staring vacantly into space. "He was good to be with," she mused. "He took some photographs of me out along Fannie Bay. I don't know what happened to them. I think he said he was going to send them to me." Her words dwindled away, and they shared a moment of reflective sadness.

"The detective Lupane told me how you saw the item about Mark in the paper," he said carefully. He didn't want this to become maudlin, not if there was a chance of picking up information.

She looked at him in surprise. "You've seen Mr. Lupane?"

"Yes. I went to the police after I'd identified Mark."

She shook her head and pushed her coffee and half-eaten sandwich to one side. "That's right," she said slowly. "I didn't want to go, you know. I thought about it for a day. I tried to convince myself it couldn't possibly be him. I didn't want it to be him. I gave myself all sorts of naive arguments that that sort of thing doesn't happen to friends of mine. I talked it over with my girlfriend—we're very close. She finally convinced me to do something about it, and came to the police with me. She'd met Mark too, and liked him very much. Of course, I didn't see Mr. Lupane at first. He came to Darwin a day or so after I'd identified Mark. Then both of us—my girlfriend and I, that is—had to go and see Mr. Lupane later."

"You knew he was from Sydney?"

"Yes. He came to see me several times afterward."

"About the identification?"

She nodded, and frowned, her mouth curved into an expression of distaste. He wondered if Lupane had the same negative effect on her.

"Oh, to talk . . . to ask questions," she murmured. "He told me that one of Mark's family would have to verify the identification as next of kin, and he mentioned a brother was coming . . . which of course was you." The lines of distaste deepened about her mouth. "I don't know that he really believed me. I know that sounds odd after they'd checked Mark's background in Sydney, but he kept at me with questions." She smiled nervously. "He upset me in the end."

"What do you mean?"

"Well, it's hard to explain, but . . ." Her hands fluttered with exasperated gestures in attempting to convey her meaning. "It's just that over and over he kept at me about whether I was absolutely sure it was Mark. Perhaps I could have made a mistake. Because the body had been in the water for so long, maybe it was only someone who looked very much like Mark. I couldn't understand what he was on about. Why he kept asking me."

"He accepted it in the end?"

"He had to. I knew it was Mark. I suppose my reaction when I saw Mark was something like yours." Her voice fell, and he had to strain for the words over the mounting chatter in the café. "You meet a person who's full of life, then you see them like that . . ." She paused, and closed

her eyes. He held back any further questions, waiting
until she regained composure, and glanced surreptitiously
at his watch. The lunch was going too fast, and he knew he
wanted to see this girl again. "I can't imagine who would
do that to someone like your brother," she added unsteadily. She took another sip of coffee and smiled at him
with her direct, appraising eyes. "I'm sorry."

"I understand," he murmured sympathetically. He wondered if he did. She was obviously too deeply affected for
her relationship with Mark to be the fun thing she claimed.
"What happened about Lupane?" he asked.

"My girlfriend was with me the last time he called, and
it would have been rough if she hadn't been there to back
me up. She's not the sort of person who can be pushed
around." She paused, and there was a note of warning in
her smile this time. "And neither am I, for that matter."

He could see that. Beautiful as she was, there was an
impression of strength. She was no delicate butterfly. And
what she was telling him about Lupane only added to his
unease concerning the policeman. Why wouldn't he want
to accept her identification? But maybe it was just the way
the man liked to work. "I guess Lupane was merely cautious," he said, without conviction. "Cross-checking just to
make sure."

"Maybe," she answered doubtfully. "That's what he said
himself. Then he apologized for troubling us, and never
bothered us again."

He shrugged it aside. Being sent up specially from
Sydney probably meant Lupane was under pressure to
perform, and the hounds in Darwin would be barking at
his heels if he made any mistakes.

"Does he have any idea who killed Mark?" she asked
quietly.

He clasped his hands and studied her solemnly. "Lupane
figures he has it all solved. Some drifters who happened
on Mark, saw he was alone, and killed him for his photo-

graphic equipment and Land Rover. It's evidently happened before."

"It sounds awful. Is he sure?"

"I'd say absolutely sure. That bothers me. He's so positive he's right, I don't think he's even considering alternatives. Whoever killed Mark was pretty ruthless."

"You think there might be something else?"

He hesitated. Bringing up the subject of the submachine gun would only upset her. He had nothing really concrete. Lupane could be right—maybe the drifters *could* have had a submachine gun. "No . . . not really. I guess it just sounds so . . . pat," he said lamely.

"It sounds horrible." She shuddered. "People can be so cruel, more like wild animals than human beings." The words were spoken with an intensity that seemed to have special meaning outside Mark's killing, as if that was the way she saw life.

Ross's curiosity was aroused, but he didn't question her. "Wild animals would be insulted, the way I've seen some human beings behave," he muttered. He motioned with his hand to the café entrance. "I guess there's some crazies walking around out there right now, but you'd never know by looking at them."

"Sometimes it makes me feel as if I want to just lock my door and never go outside," she said soberly.

"You've got to go on living." He shrugged. "You think about all the terrible things that could happen to you, and you'd never get out of bed in the morning." He studied her with an appreciative smile. "It would be a pity to lock that lovely face away from the world."

Her mouth trembled into a hesitant smile, as if she questioned the sincerity of the compliment. He felt a shaft of guilt. Christ, they were talking about the brutal murder of his brother, but it didn't stop him thinking about how great it would be to get this girl into bed. But this girl was special. As if to detract from his remark, she glanced at her watch, then at his uneaten sandwich.

"I guess I'm not hungry," he preempted her. "I had something on the plane, and seeing Mark didn't exactly inspire an appetite."

"I can understand that," she murmured, and referred again to her watch. "I'm afraid I'm going to have to cut this short, Ross. I took an early lunch, and they don't like it if you're back late." She ducked her head with a wry smile. "Jobs are scarce, so I have to look after this one." She shuffled about on the chair preparatory to rising. "I really appreciated you calling me and asking me out for lunch. I wanted to meet you, and I hope it helped talking about Mark. It certainly helped me. I hope Mr. Lupane catches the ones who did it."

He didn't want her to go. Christ, he had to see her again. His restraining hand reached out and stopped just short of her arm. "I was hoping we could have dinner tonight," he said quickly.

She looked at him uncertainly, and for a moment he thought she was going to refuse.

"I . . . I don't think there's any more I can tell you about Mark" she said.

"I realize that. But I thought we might talk some more about you," he said frankly. Maybe he should have been more subtle. She could take offense since they had just been talking about Mark's death. "I'm not going to be in Darwin long, and I'd like to get to know you better. When I read your compassionate letter to my parents, I figured you'd be someone worth knowing," he added persuasively.

She studied him. Maybe she'd had some bad experiences, for she was a cautious one. But it was impossible to read her thoughts behind the impenetrable darkness of her eyes. "All right, then," she agreed with a quiet smile. "That might be nice."

He ignored the reservations in her voice. "Great," he enthused. "Where can I pick you up?"

"Do you have a car?"

"I was going to rent one, but it didn't seem worthwhile for the short time I'd be here. But I could still do it."

"No, you don't need to do that. I can pick you up in my car."

"Look, why don't you come to the motel? They have a restaurant there."

She hesitated a moment, then nodded agreement.

"Say around seven?"

"That'll be fine. I'll look forward to it, Ross," she said with sudden warmth. She glanced again at her watch, and stood up quickly from the table. "Now I really must go."

Ross paid the bill and walked out with her to Smith Street. The sun was higher, and heat steamed off the sidewalk. She held out her hand again, accompanied by the same vivid smile that had first greeted him. He briefly shook her hand, taking care not to hold it too long this time. He felt the warmth of a shared experience, and he sensed she felt the same.

"I'll be looking forward to tonight," he said.

"So will I," she replied simply.

"I'll wait for you by the front desk."

She nodded, gave a brief wave, then turned and walked briskly down Smith Street. He stood watching her departing figure, taken once again by her manner of walking, striding out in a way that detracted nothing from her femininity, but put the world on notice she was to be treated with caution. He sensed she was a complicated mix. Beautiful, but armor-plated beneath the skin. And he noted the open glances she attracted from passing men. It didn't seem conceivable someone with her vital looks wasn't committed to a relationship. Maybe that was something he could find out tonight over a leisurely meal. He turned and walked slowly in the opposite direction. He wondered what it would be like with her. Once you penetrated the armor, there was the promise of an explosive passion. He wondered if that was the only reason he wanted to see her again. He couldn't shake the uneasy sense of guilt that he

was moving in his dead brother's footsteps with this girl. It
would be weird for her if it came to that, lying there
making comparisons with the ghoulish memory in the
mortuary.

3

There was a message waiting for Ross at the motel desk.
A man named Pat Tanna had called and wanted to see
him. He would be on his boat, the *Kunarra*, down at
Stokes Hill wharf all afternoon, and could Ross see him
there? He went up to his room, poured himself a beer
from the refrigerator, and stood at the window watching
the glittering blue of Port Darwin. He relished the familiar cold bitter taste sliding into his throat. Australian beer
was one of the things he missed when he was away, even
if there was a time it had nearly turned him into a drunk.
Pat Tanna. Lupane had told him about Pat Tanna, the
skipper of the fishing boat that had found Mark's body. It
was an interesting message, because he'd thought of con-
tacting Tanna himself. Maybe Lupane had arranged the
meeting. He shrugged the thought aside. That wouldn't
make much sense. He settled himself down in a chair and
leisurely finished off the can. A red-hulled freighter moved
slowly across the port, trailing a white gash in the blue
sea. It was only two-fifteen, so he had ample time to see
Tanna. He took the map from his pocket and located
Stokes Hill wharf. He'd call for a taxi when he was ready
to go. Perhaps he should have rented a car after all,
because he hadn't figured on all this moving around. Well,
he'd be gone tomorrow. He opened another can, thinking
of Mark and Lisa, the image of his brother fuzzing into
extinction, while Lisa swelled to fill his mind. It made him
feel like a prick, and he went and called his parents to

quell the self-denigration. The connection came through with the anxiety-ridden voice of his father, but he fended off all inquiries for details about Mark. He wasn't going to paint horror pictures over the telephone. He passed on Lupane's request for information on Mark's equipment from the insurance company, saying he'd call again when he had the departure time of the body for Sydney. His father's voice sounded flat and drained, like a man who had lost a reason to go on living. Ross was sorry he couldn't be a replacement for Mark, but that's the way it was. Yes, he'd seen the girl . . . yes, he'd thanked her . . . no, he didn't know how much longer he'd be in Australia. He cut it short, and had scarcely hung up when the phone rang again. It was the man from the mortuary. There was a holdup in dispatching the body to Sydney, and it wouldn't be on the plane until tomorrow night. He sounded terse, as if he was describing someone living in an apartment without paying rent. Ross noted details of the flight, then hung up. He decided against calling his father back immediately. The sound of his dead voice had depressed him, and he could easily call later tonight. He went downstairs and called a taxi.

It wasn't far to the waterfront. Stokes Hill wharf coiled out from the shoreline like a snake, forming a protective wall for the small bay. Not that the tranquilized waters of Port Darwin needed much protection.

Midway along the curve the pier widened abruptly to a broad platform furnished with all the docking facilities for oceangoing vessels. A ring of muddy yellow water stained the opposite shoreline like an unwashed collar, and beyond were the usual industrial inhabitants of a port area. Past that was a strip of green parkland forming a cleansing bulwark between the port and the city. Small boats nestled like wary chickens against the protective arm of the pier. The bay reflected the sun like a mirror, throwing off an eye-dazzling glare.

At the far end of the wharf, said the man at the entrance

gate, and the taxi took Ross out along the wide curve to the main docking area. The view back across the water accentuated the flatness of the city, giving the occasional tall building a monolithic quality. There was a solitary freighter moored to the wharf, the crane clanking the cargo onshore.

A gaggle of workers listlessly maneuvered freight about the wharf, the men dressed in shorts, bare-chested with their skin cooked to mahogany brown by long exposure to the sun. A lone man in white looked down like an overlord from the ship's bridge.

The driver braked to a halt by the second storage shed and gestured to the partly visible structure of a small boat at the end of the wharf. "That'll be the *Kunarra* over there, mate."

Ross paid him and stepped out onto the wharf. He walked across to the boat, the sharp breeze like a cooling fan on his face. An ancient utility truck was parked to one side, piled with cray pots and reels of thick twine. The purr of the taxi faded, and then there was only the monotonous clank-clank of the crane. Ross stopped at the edge of the wharf and stared down at the *Kunarra*. It had the look of a large oceangoing tug, only the bridge structure at the fore of the vessel reaching above the height of the wharf, the lower deck level with the halfway mark. The word *Kunarra* was just visible in peeling black paint on the funnel. The entire boat looked as if it were a stranger to a paintbrush. The deck was a tangle of rope and fishing net, but there was no sign of any crew. Ross hesitated at the gangway leading across to the corridor beneath the bridge, then saw the dark head of an aborigine emerge from the hold. The man clambered up onto the deck, clad in a grubby T-shirt that had once been white, and a pair of stained jeans. Ross waved to attract his attention, and the man stared blankly at him.

"Mr. Tanna," Ross called, gesturing to the boat. "Where can I find him?"

The man waved vaguely in the direction of the bridge, then began to untangle the skein of gear around his feet. Ross shrugged, pushed out cautiously along the narrow gangplank and onto the deck. Almost simultaneously a figure emerged from the bridge and clambered down the ladder to meet him. Pat Tanna was somewhere between sixty and the end of life, a thick-trunked gnarled tree that has relished competition with life and grown rock hard by the contest. Ross was reminded of his own grandfather just before his death. Identical grizzled features, white hair rarely touched by a comb, eyes the color of the sea and landlocked with countless wrinkles from constant squinting at the sun. Skin like weathered leather, that had endlessly burned and peeled until it formed into a protective hide. He was about five-feet-five in height, and he wore a black tank top, faded jeans, and frayed blue sneakers. He grinned engagingly at Ross, and all the sun-engraved lines in his face multiplied. He thrust out a knobbly paw. "G'day, mate . . . you must be Ross Berger. I'm Pat Tanna. Glad you could come." Voice and appearance matched, with the sound of a file drawn across raw timber. Ross took the offered handshake, and his hand was enclosed by a texture like coarse sandpaper.

Then Tanna swiveled about with an impatient jerk of his hand and led the way to a door. He threw it open with gusto, as if he felt the need to display physical prowess. "Come in 'ere, where we can talk, m'boy."

The door closed behind Ross as he stepped inside, and for a moment he was smitten by near-blindness, until his eyes adjusted to the gray light. What he finally saw matched the untidy confusion out on the deck. A small desk strewn with papers, a narrow bunk tangled with blankets, a dining table scattered with the leavings of a meal and embraced by two decrepit chairs. A safe, refrigerator, cupboards, all draped with magazines, newspapers, and various items of clothing.

Tanna ejected the clothes from one chair to the floor

with a grandiose sweep of his hand and invited Ross to sit
down. "Put your ass down there, Ross boy."

Ross gingerly edged himself onto the chair. "I received
your message, Mr. Tanna, and I—"

"Jes' call me Pat, Ross," interjected Tanna. "Every other
bugger in Darwin does, so you may as well be in it,
mate."

"Okay, Pat." Ross grinned.

"Let's start with a beer, eh? Nothin' like a beer when
there's talkin' to be done, Ross." He was like a man grown
impatient with the world trying to catch up to him. He
clumped to the refrigerator without waiting for an answer,
took out two cans, and threw one to Ross. Then he opened
the safe, extracted a small brown paper package, and carried it with him to the bunk. He dropped heavily onto the
rumpled blankets, placed the parcel carefully at his side,
then zipped open the can. He didn't take it down from his
mouth until it was almost empty. Ross drank cautiously,
watching and waiting, unsure what he was doing there.
Then Tanna lowered the can to his lap, scrubbed the back
of his hand across his bristly chin, and belched with the
rumbling intensity of an earthquake warning. "Shit, that's
good. Puts hair on your chest, Ross."

"I would have brought some beer with me—" Ross
began apologetically, but Pat cut him off with a wave of his
hand.

"Forget it, mate, forget it, this is my shout." He patted
the parcel at his side. "Besides, this is for you, boy."

Ross glanced curiously at the parcel. "For me?"

"Yeah, that's right." He lurched up off the bunk with
the parcel clasped in his hand, stumped across and placed
it on the table beside Ross, then returned to the bunk. He
took another long swallow of beer, then gestured with the
can to the parcel. Beer dribbled down through the white
bristles and onto his neck. "Go on, you can open it,
mate." He cackled deep in his throat. "Christmas has
arrived early this year."

Ross shrugged, placed his beer can on the table, and began to unwrap the parcel. It had been crudely done, great swaths of crinkled brown paper layered clumsily over the article.

Tanna leaned forward on his knees and squinted quizzically at Ross. "I guess you've see the copper Lupane?" he grunted.

"Yes. Earlier today. He told me you were the one who found my brother's body."

"And you've seen your brother?"

"Yes, before I saw Lupane."

A muted growl issued from Tanna's belly. It was either an expression of disapproval or the result of rapidly consumed beer. "Fuckin' awful business," he muttered. "An' I'm sorry about your brother."

It was a camera. Ross pushed the brown paper to the floor and picked it up. He wasn't a camera expert, but he recognized a quality piece of equipment. A thirty-five-millimeter Nikon with a long lens attached, like he'd seen Mark use. He turned it over, examining it from every angle. There was a small, almost hidden indentation on the underside of the case, with the initials M.B. Mark Berger. He held it tightly, with the eerie sensation it provided a form of physical contact with his murdered brother. He stared at Tanna in bewilderment. "Christ, it's Mark's camera," he exclaimed.

"That's what I reckoned," said Tanna soberly. "The initials tally, all right."

"Where the hell did you get it, Pat?"

"From one of my crew. Thievin' little bastard. Hasn't been with me long."

Ross swallowed hard, his eyes wide. "Are you telling me . . . one of your crew killed Mark . . . for this?"

Tanna vehemently shook his head, threw his drained can down on the bunk, and went to the refrigerator for another one. "No, nothin' like that, mate. This little prick wouldn't have the guts to kill a frog." He peered at Ross's beer on the table. "How about another beer?"

Ross shook his head quickly. He could see if he got started with someone like Pat he'd finish up in a boozy haze. He placed the camera reverently on the table. "Then where the hell did it come from?"

Tanna squatted down on the bunk and unzipped the fresh can. "The copper—Lupane—he told you I went ashore near the spot I found your brother?"

"That's right."

"Well, I took a coupla the crew with me. Had to, to handle the skiff. Bastard of a place to make shore there, Ross. Real bastard. Wouldna even tried if the surf hadn't been flat. Crikey, otherwise you'd be dumped on your ass in five seconds flat."

"Your crew member . . . this one you're talking about—he found it?"

Tanna banged the can forcefully against the wooden frame of the bunk and scowled into space. "Fuckin' right he did . . . only I didn't find out until much later. We split up when we went ashore, just searchin' around. Not even sure what we was lookin' for. I mean, your brother's body was only a few hundred yards offshore, so I figured he must have fallen off one of the cliffs or somethin' like that. We didn't find much. A few empty film boxes laying around. There was some tire tracks, but they were way back from the cliff edge. I figured the bloke we found— your brother—must have been doin' some picture-takin'. This sneaky prick I had with me evidently found your brother's camera among the rocks on the cliffs. Don' ask me how he hid it. I knowed he was wearing a wet jacket, so I guess he just stuck it inside and hoped no one'd notice. And no one did." He paused and gulped at the beer, his throat pulsing like a piston, until the can was empty. Then he patted at his stomach, and the sound of rupturing earth spouted from his mouth again. "I tell you, Ross, that bastard don' work for me no more. No sir. I like

my crew fair dinkum. Boongs, whites, Japs . . . it don' matter to me, as long as I can trust the bastards. I've been fishin' out of Darwin all me life, an' everyone knows Pat Tanna's on the level, and I'm gunna keep it that way."

Ross stared at the camera thoughtfully. At least it would be something of Mark's his father could have.

Tanna went to the refrigerator and took out another can. He had quite a thirst. "Only found out about it yesterday. Little bastard had been hidin' it until he figured it was safe to sell. He had the rotten luck to take it to the shop of an old mate of mine I'd talked to about your brother. He put two and two together, and got in touch with me. I fronted the little prick, and of course he folded like a pack of cards. That sort always does." He took a large draft of the third can, then laughed contemptuously, with a display of yellowing teeth. "He'll remember the size of me boot on his ass for a long time." He laughed again, louder this time, the sound booming around the small cabin. Then the third can went the way of the other two. There was a time Ross had taken a certain pride in his own speed of consumption, but he'd never seen anyone drink beer as fast as Tanna.

Pat took a spool of film from his pocket and threw it across to Ross. "That came out of the camera," he said. "The creep didn't have enough brains to figure how to take the film out."

Ross examined it with the same eerie sense of curiosity. They were probably Mark's last photographs—something else for his father. Then he experienced a sudden acceleration of his pulse. Christ, was it possible Mark could have photographed his murderers before he died? Not after he was shot—death would have been instantaneous—but perhaps before then. It was an exciting thought. "They'll be worth looking at," he muttered.

"Well, that's up to you, mate."

Ross placed the film beside the camera and silently

contemplated the idea. It was a wild shot, but possible. "Funny, the camera being in the rocks like that."

"Yeah. Maybe he hid it there."

"Perhaps. But why?"

"Maybe he figured those blokes who knocked him off . . ." Tanna paused self-consciously at the expression. "He reckoned they were goin' to pinch his stuff, and he managed to hide that one before they got him."

"I guess we may never know," Ross said mournfully.

"I wanted you to have it anyway, Ross. I'm sailin' out of Darwin tonight, and I'll be gone about a week. That's why I had to see you this afternoon."

"How did you know I was here?"

Tanna winked at him, and a chuckle rasped in his throat. "If you've lived in a town all your life, you've got all sorts of eyes and ears workin' for you. I heard. I wanted to make sure you got the camera."

Ross nodded uncertainly, and his eyes returned to the camera. "You know, you should have taken it to Lupane instead of giving it to me," he said bluntly. "He's in charge of the case. It really should have gone to the police, Pat."

Tanna leaned back in the bunk until his head rested against the wall. There was a wavering of focus in his eyes from the rapid consumption of alcohol. "Lupane's a shit," he stated with equal bluntness. "I've been around a long time, Ross, an' I can read a face pretty well." His eyes squinted with the effort of conveying shrewd appraisal. "Now, you . . . I'd say you've been around too, Ross, but you come across as true-blue straight. But I don' like the questions that bastard Lupane asks—or the way he asks 'em. Why do they want to send some smart-alec cop up from Sydney? The local blokes could do just as well— probably better."

"I don't think he impressed Lisa Marnoo too much either." Ross grinned.

"That's the girl who identified your brother?"

"Right. You know her?"

"That one I don' know, though I hear she's quite a looker. If Lupane pushed her like he tried to push me, then I can understand her feelings. Jesus, you would've thought I'd done in your brother."

"Perhaps I should take the camera to him," Ross said thoughtfully.

"Suit yourself." Tanna shrugged. "It's your camera now. I wouldn't give the bastard the time of day. What's he gunna do with it anyway? Hold it as evidence for the next six months? Or longer. You'd probably never get it back."

Ross picked up the film spool and jiggled it absently in his hand. "Maybe. I'd sure as hell like to see what's on this."

"You don't think you'll find the killers on there, do you?"

"It might be possible."

"You're kiddin' yourself, Ross, if you think the killers were gunna stand there and have their pictures taken first." Tanna snorted. "You take me advice, and hang onto that stuff. Givin' it to Lupane isn't gunna bring your brother back. You hang onto it as somethin' to remember him by."

Ross nodded hesitantly and placed the film back by the camera. He had no intention of arguing with Pat, but he'd think about it. The old fisherman was too well-intentioned for him to spark any rancor. Then he stood up. "I really appreciate what you've done, Pat." He motioned to the camera. "My parents are going to love having this as a reminder of Mark. They were very close to him."

Tanna lurched to his feet and leaned on the bunk for support. "Then you take old Pat's advice, Ross boy," he muttered emphatically. "Take it to your parents, an' the fuck with Lupane." He meandered unsteadily across the cabin and gripped Ross's hand. "I hope it all works out for you, mate. I hope they get the miserable bastards that killed your brother. Christ, he was only a kid."

"That's what makes it so tough," Ross said stonily.

"I know. That's the way it is, Ross. Jesus, I might get full and fall off the *Kunarra* tomorrow an' get grabbed by a shark. Who the hell knows?" He waggled his head, picked up Ross's beer can, and rattled it about in the air. "How about another beer, eh?"

After the old man had gone to so much trouble, Ross didn't know how to refuse, but he wasn't in the mood to go off on a bender, and he didn't want a thick head for his dinner with Lisa. So he drank slowly while the old man rambled on about fishing, and women, and aborigines who were getting in the way of the mining companies opening up the territory, and Darwin, which he repeated ad infinitum was the greatest city in Australia. All Ross could think about was the film. Maybe Pat was right: if he handed it over to Lupane, he might never see it again. Lupane wasn't the sort of man who liked to be proved wrong, and he wouldn't take seriously anything that interfered with his drifters theory.

"Well, I gotta go," Tanna said suddenly, peering at the ancient timepiece on his wrist. "I probably got a drunken crew spread aroun' Darwin, and I wanta make sure they're here for sailin' time."

Ross felt a sense of relief that the drinking session was over. He tried to picture a drunken crew, and a drunken captain steering the *Kunarra* out of Port Darwin. With an elaborate gesture he consulted his own watch. "I'd better be getting back to the motel myself, Pat."

"How you gettin' back, boy?"

"Well . . . ah, I guess I can pick up a taxi around the wharf. Or I could walk. It's not that far."

"We can't have that," declared Tanna emphatically. "I got the old truck out there by the boat. I'll drive you back."

The old man's condition made it a dangerous suggestion.

"Look, you've gone to enough trouble, Pat, and it's no trouble for me . . ." Ross tried to protest defensively.

Tanna had reached the point of stubborn determination where he considered a refusal a personal insult. "I insist, Ross boy . . . I absolutely insist. Darwin hospitality, you know." He pushed himself off the bunk, swept the brown paper off the floor, and flapped it clumsily about the camera. "Better cover that up, mate, just in case any of Lupane's snoops are hangin' around the wharf."

Ross could see there was no point in arguing with Tanna. He took over the wrapping of the camera until it made a reasonable parcel. But as soon as he was seated in the truck he knew he'd made a bad mistake. That his parents were in grave danger of mourning for a second son. The old man was obviously used to long beer sessions, because he didn't look incapably drunk, but the vagueness in his red-stained eyes betrayed a fuddled brain. He tromped the accelerator until the truck quivered as if afflicted with fever, and the aged engine protested with a shattering, clanking roar, as if threatening to tear itself apart. Then he rammed into first gear with a screech of grinding teeth, and the old truck shot forward like a rocket, targeted at the men working on the cargo farther down the wharf. Words failed Ross. As if through a range-finder he saw the listless men turn suddenly startled faces toward the onrushing vehicle, then galvanize into frantic evasion with the alacrity of instant athletes.

Ross closed his eyes, fiercely clenched the camera, and had a horrendous vision of himself stretched out on a slab beside Mark. He felt the truck swerve violently, then his eyes popped open to catch a blur of terrified faces rushing past the window, and a stream of venomous obscenities rained on him.

Then they were past and into the long curve of the connecting pier as if it were a lap of the Grand Prix, Tanna's bellowed guffaws filling the cabin. "That'll wake up the lazy bastards, eh, Ross," he yelled. "I'll bet they're shittin' their pants back there."

Ross had no possibility of answering. All he could manage was a sickly smile, his tongue fixed to the roof of his mouth like a limpet. Maybe Pat was a lousy driver sober, but drunk he was hair-raising. He considered it demeaning to slow for anything or anybody. Ross spread his legs on the floor, braced his body against the door, and forced himself to believe that after risking his life around the world, it was ridiculous to imagine he was going to perish at the hands of an elderly Darwin fisherman. They drove in the same breakneck manner all the way to the motel. Perhaps Tanna was one of those people who drive under a lucky star. He blithely ignored intersections, yet there were no collisions, not even near-misses. Whatever was engaging the attention of the Darwin traffic police, they were nowhere within sight of Pat. He declined to use the clutch pedal approaching the motel, and the truck hopped the last few yards like an inebriated kangaroo, then ground to a halt with a squeal of brakes. Only then Ross realized he'd been holding his breath for most of the journey, and he let the air out slowly, as if opening a safety valve. He clambered out shakily, then reached through the window to grasp Pat's hand. It was as much a gesture of relief at surviving, as farewell. There was a roguish glint in the old man's eyes, as if he reveled in the role of never-say-die hell-raiser.

"Thanks . . . thanks for everything, Pat," Ross muttered weakly. He held up the wrapped camera. "And a special thanks for this."

"My pleasure, m'boy. My pleasure." He shook a warning finger in the air. "You hang onto it, you hear? Remember what I said. Handin' it over to Lupane ain't gunna bring your brother back." He started the engine and rammed into drive with another screech of tortured gears. "Now I gotta find that bludgin' crew of mine." He grinned, with an exaggerated wave of his hand. "Look after yourself, boy."

He revved the guts out of the engine, then, as if responding to a starter's flag, took off with the same abandoned lack of concern, barreling down the road until he was out of sight. Ross gave an incredulous shake of his head and walked into the motel. He wondered how Pat had managed to survive to such a good age. But it had been a rewarding meeting. He owed him for the camera. And the film. He felt suddenly incredibly tired. He went up to his room, put the camera on the bedside table, showered, and dropped down on the bed. It was four o'clock. A few hours' sleep would refresh him for the dinner with Lisa. He spread-eagled himself on the bed, closed his eyes, and let himself drift. He would think about the film when he woke.

He was running along a blood-red beach with Mark. It was a competition, albeit a friendly one, both straining with clenched teeth and aching lungs to win. Then Mark won, and he stood proudly at the edge of the water, his arms encircling a naked Lisa, and they were smiling at each other as if sharing a profound secret. Then there was a far-off repetitious hammering sound, and his brother turned the same crimson color as the beach, then fell away from Lisa. He vanished. Ross couldn't see him anywhere. The water was stained red, the foam like flecks of blood washing about his feet. It didn't seem to matter. Now Lisa was at his side, with an easy exchange of loyalties, her body molded to him, her mouth to his ear, whispering obscenities. Now I want your cock, fuck me. And he felt guilt, when he should have felt passion, rendering his penis ineptly flaccid. Guilty as hell. He moaned in his sleep, and fought to destroy the dream.

Darwin wasn't exactly New York, but then the General hadn't expected it to be. Yet the Telford International Hotel gave him most of the creature comforts to which he was accustomed. If it was a long way from Sardi's, or Broadway, or the elegant shops of Fifth Avenue, then he reconciled himself with the knowledge it was for only a short time.

Of course Darwin had changed beyond recognition from those long-ago war days, when as a young captain he had fled Manila with MacArthur. Go to the top end of Australia, Leo, MacArthur had ordered him, and be a pair of watching eyes for me. He had hated it. He was a New Yorker to his boots, and he had stifled in the backwater, parochial atmosphere, suffocated in the humid, drenching rains of the wet season. He hadn't managed to get out of Darwin until Okinawa, and into the fighting just long enough to ensure valuable promotion for his future. But they were long-past days, not to be dwelt on, when there was so much to be accomplished now.

He was furious about the incident with the photographer. He didn't question the necessity of killing the man—that was irrelevant compared with what was at stake. But the mission should never have been placed in such a position of exposure. Arne Blucker had made a bad piece of misjudgment, and if the General had the time, he would have replaced him as chief of operations. God, Arne had gone through Vietnam with him, he should have known better. Known the importance of painstaking reconnaissance before attempting a practice exercise. A preliminary overflight by the helicopter would have seen the photographer. For Chrissake, how could Arne make an assumption that a barren stretch of coastline was also barren of people? In this day and age a man could turn up anywhere. He shook his head and poured himself a whiskey. Arne had been so efficient, so reliable. It only showed how quickly a man could rust in civilian life. Well, it was done, they'd gotten away with it, but he'd make sure such a thing never happened again. Not before the raid. They were fortunate the investigations in Sydney had confirmed the photographer's presence at Cape Jaubert as merely coincidence, that pure chance had taken him there on his photographic assignment. But Christ, even the helicopter crew had bungled their job. They should have made absolutely certain the body wouldn't drift free from the Land Rover.

He drank too quickly to overcome his irritation, and the whiskey burned into his stomach. There was an air of amateurism and incompetence about the operation that made him uneasy. They were good men, he was sure of it, but maybe the discipline of war was too far behind them now. He hoped they recovered it in full measure before the actual operation.

He hadn't told Halmen about the Cape Jaubert fiasco yet, but no doubt the news would filter back from the ship. All he could do was anticipate Halmen's furious reaction and offer soothing comfort that everything was now under control.

There was a polite knock at the door, and he stalked across the room to throw open the door with an angry flourish. The caller was taken aback by the display, and waited apprehensively for an invitation to enter. The man's heavy-lidded eyes darted warily past the General and about the room.

"For Chrissake, don't just stand there, Lupane," exclaimed Starker in exasperation. "Come inside, and tell me some good news for a change."

The big man nodded, and lumbered cautiously into the room. He stood patting at his brow with a handkerchief while Starker closed the door. His dark suit and tie were in marked contrast to the General's perfectly tailored casual shirt and brown slacks. He held himself like a tentative soldier awaiting the order to break ranks. Starker barely gave him a glance as he passed back to his whiskey.

"It's pretty warm out there," Lupane muttered.

"Would you like a drink?"

"Thank you, General."

He waited in the same hesitant attitude while Starker poured for him, his gaze alternating between the view out the window and the General. Starker made no attempt to

conceal his sour mood. The way he poured, the downturn
of his mouth, even the chiseled lines in his face seemed
deepened by his irritation. He handed the whiskey to
Lupane and motioned impatiently to a chair. He remained
standing. He didn't intend this to be an inquisition, but he
always employed the psychological advantage of forcing
the other man to look up to him. He held himself rigid,
one hand stiffly behind his back, the other clasping the
whiskey. He ignored the expression of resentment seeping
into Lupane's face. Inevitably, it always showed sooner or
later in their meetings. Martin Blandhurst had ordered
Lupane to Darwin, but he knew the man objected to
being under his complete authority. The hell with him.
Lupane would obey orders like everyone else. The General knew Martin had made big promises to Lupane, so
greed and ambition would keep him a willing tool.

"You have the photographer's brother under control?"
Starker asked tersely.

"Well . . . I don't know about under control." Lupane
shrugged. "Let's say . . . appeased."

"He came to see you?"

"Of course."

"And he saw his brother's body?"

"That's *why* he came here," Lupane answered, with an
inflection of sarcasm.

Starker frowned. The broad accent was sometimes difficult to understand, but he didn't miss the innuendo. He
disliked the Australian, and his obviously unfit body. He'd
learned of the Australian contempt of authority during the
war, and Lupane fitted the pattern. Starker distrusted
men who fought for personal gain instead of principle.
They could always be bought by someone who offered a
higher price. But then, Martin had told him this man was
the best he had. No matter what an order entailed, he
would carry it out. He must want the job Martin had
promised him very badly.

"Did you form any impression of the man?" he asked.

"Yes . . . he bothered me," Lupane said candidly.

"What do you mean, bothered you?"

"I don't know his background, but he's been around. The bastard asks awkward questions." He took a long swallow of the whiskey. "He knew his brother had been killed by a submachine gun when he saw the wounds in the body."

The General studied his glass, and the lines of his mouth nipped even tighter. "We should have thought of that possibility."

Lupane shrugged again. "Maybe. People look mostly just at the head of a corpse for identification. This bastard decided he wanted to see more."

"You satisfied him . . . about the submachine gun?"

"I think so. He's hard to read. Let's say I left him with the strong impression that the investigation was my business, not his. I think he accepted it."

"You think?"

"Well, I didn't give him much choice. I told him we were almost certain it was drifters around the coast who did the killing. I don't think he'll give us any trouble, but he might be worth watching."

The General irritably placed his glass down loudly on the table. He pursed his lips, studying Lupane. Out in the port a ship's hooter mournfully sounded farewell. He took a packet of cigars from the bedside table, selected one, and lit up. He didn't offer one to Lupane. "I want him out of Darwin as quickly as possible," he grated. "I'll feel safer with him out of the place. We don't want anyone around who asks awkward questions."

Lupane scowled, and swirled the whiskey about in the glass. "You might be right, but I can scarcely order him out, General. I've no grounds."

"Maybe not," replied Starker testily. "But surely you can apply a little . . . subtle pressure. There's a time limit on the body being kept in Darwin . . . the anxiety of his parents for a funeral . . . things like that?"

"Sure, sure," Lupane said sullenly. "I've been working along those lines, General. Arrangements have been made for the body to go to Sydney. I'm sure he'll go with it." He paused, with an ugly grin. "Don't worry, if I hear of him sniffing around, I'll quickly put his bloody nose out of joint."

"That's all I mean," said Starker with sudden affability. There was the soft fizz of burning leaf as he drew on the cigar. "It's possible he'll contact the Marnoo girl."

"It doesn't matter. She can't tell him anything." He smirked at the General. "Maybe he wants a share of the boong cunt his brother was into."

Starker's mouth wrinkled with disdain. Apart from anything else, Lupane was crudely crass. He ignored the sexual aside. "All right," he said crisply. "I'll accept your word on that." He felt more relaxed now, and some of the rigidity in his posture softened. He half-turned to the window, the cigar dangling loosely between his fingers. "We were very lucky to get out of this, Lupane," he murmured absently. "Very lucky indeed. It would have been a tragedy to have to abandon the operation, after all the months of planning."

For a moment Lupane made no comment. Starker watched him, concealing the contempt in his mind. Lupane really didn't give a damn about the operation, he had no commitment, but he would kill and lie for the bait Martin had dangled in front of his eyes.

"Who was the idiot who ordered the Cape Jaubert exercise anyway?" Lupane asked finally, as if he felt constrained to say something.

The General shrugged. "It doesn't matter now. Discipline has been applied to make sure it doesn't happen again." He lifted his arm in a theatrical gesture to note the time. "I . . . er, I have to make an important call to New York, Lupane. Thank you for coming here and giving me a report on Berger. I was anxious about it, but I don't think there's any more we need to discuss now. But keep in close touch. Anything you think I should know, I want to hear about. No matter how small or insignificant you may think it is." He paused, with a thin smile. The dismissal was delivered in military style, blunt and unassailable. He could see it ruffled Lupane, but there was nothing the man could do about it. Lupane banged his half-finished whiskey down on the table in a mild expression of disapproval, but by the time he stood up Starker was already standing by the door, one hand on the knob. Lupane moved with deliberate slowness to the door, then halted. "When's it going to be, General?"

"In good time, Lupane. At the right time. The fewer people know at the moment, the safer it is for all of us." He opened the door, placed a hand firmly at Lupane's elbow, and urged him into the corridor. "Thank you again for coming. It was much appreciated. And keep in touch."

Lupane went out into the corridor without a backward glance, to conceal the anger in his face. He kept moving until he heard the door click shut behind him. He squeezed irritably at the back of his neck. Fucking General was living in fantasyland, thinking he was still in the army, and everyone jumping when he clicked his fingers. Blandhurst had mentioned that Starker was educated in one of those highfalutin military schools, and it showed. Lupane hated intellectual snobs, and the General's manner of lofty condescension with those he considered beneath him was so typical of similar bastards he'd met. Blandhurst had the same sort of background, but he was too shrewd a politician to put on any airs with those he needed. And Blandhurst needed him, needed him badly.

Considering his own lack of formal education, he'd done very well. At his parents' behest he had left school at fifteen; there was no money to keep him there anyway. But he had discovered early that everything was possible with dedication. And acquired shrewdness. It hadn't given him time for anything else, because he had to run a lot

harder than the ones with their degrees. So there was no
wife. No family. He was uneasy with women. It was
simple with men, with rivals: push them aside, stand on
them, destroy them. But women confounded him. Even
the Marnoo girl had been the same. Like them all, she
saw through the bluster as a camouflage for his unease. In
unguarded moments he dreamed of a woman who would
respond to him with committed passion, but it never
happened. Sex he had to buy, with its mechanical lack of
satisfaction. So he had buried himself in the organization,
the long hours, the step-by-step recognition, ingratiating
himself with the right people by his effectiveness. And a
still tongue that could be trusted. It wasn't bad for a boy
from the wrong side of the tracks to finish up the trusted
confidant of a cabinet minister. Starker might grate on
him, but there was the consolation of knowing it was only
a passing phase. And if he performed well, then Blandhurst
had promised the top job in the organization was his.
Christ, how he wanted that. Not only because it would
push that prick Kaufman to one side, but it would show all
those bastards with their upper-class accents that he was a
force to be reckoned with. Blandhurst had to keep his
promise. The minister had made himself vulnerable by
entrusting him with so much confidential information, and
he couldn't risk going back on his word. No, head of
Intelligence was his for the taking now. This phony job
Blandhurst had set up for him with the Darwin police
would be over in a few days, and already he was relishing
the stunned expression on Kaufman's face when he learned
he was finished as intelligence chief. Lupane would grovel
at Starker's feet just to see that.

He went rapidly around to Palmerston Park to his car.
It was close to dusk, and early headlights flicked along
Gardens Road. He panted like a running dog in the humid
air. Christ, he had to discipline himself to get rid of this
belly. Maybe if he streamlined himself, it would help in
his search for a constant woman, someone like Lisa Marnoo.

There were nights he spent creating fantasies over that lithe brown body, the beautiful face, the wary black eyes. Maybe when he was finished playing hatchet man to the General, he would do something about her. He'd heard the boong women were easy into sex, and it might be fun pressuring her.

She wore a pale pink off-the-shoulder dress and a wide vivid-pink belt. If Ross had been entranced at their lunch meeting, now uncharacteristically he groped for words. "You look very lovely, Lisa." He knew immediately it was totally inadequate, but she accepted the compliment with a warm smile. Then he took her arm and led her into Fernando's Restaurant. Beige walls, brown chairs, white tablecloths set with pink napkins. At the far end a cocktail bar set against a bright yellow wall, with a solitary man drinking. There was only a scattering of people in the dining room, but Ross wasn't fooled by the studied casualness of their appraisal in passing. The women evinced envy, the men longing. Ross secretly gained pleasure from the reaction. They took a small table by the wall, and he felt the hard edge of the film spool rub against his leg as he sat down. That was a subject for later discussion. He ordered a gin and tonic for her and a beer for himself, and they both decided for the barramunda. The north was the home of the sweet-tasting fish, so it seemed an appropriate choice.

She held her glass delicately, glancing around the restaurant, and he drank slowly, watching her. He wondered if she was comparing him to Mark.

"I've never been here before," she murmured softly.

"Do you go out much for dinner?"

"No. Too expensive." She smiled. "I've a small kitchen in my apartment, so mostly I cook my own meals. Sometimes I go out with my girlfriend."

If there was a special man, she took care to avoid mentioning him.

"Where do you live in Darwin?" he asked.

She placed her glass carefully on the table, and once again he was subjected to that scrutinizing gaze. "I have a small apartment over in Alawa. Alawa Crescent. Although it's a trifle crowded at the moment. My girlfriend, Jo Santeze, moved in with me this afternoon. I arrived home to find her waiting on the doorstep, which was a bit of a shock. I thought I was going to be late getting here. I didn't like leaving her, she was so upset."

"What's the problem?"

Her face went suddenly bleak. "Man trouble. What else?"

"We're not all trouble," he commiserated. He wasn't too sure what plans he had for this girl, but he didn't want the conversation to take too serious a turn.

"Maybe not. But she was living with this man, and he'd been . . . well, knocking her around. They had a violent row last night, and he hit her again. It was the finish for her, she walked out." Lisa smiled wryly. "I think she'll stay with me only a few days, then she'll go south . . . Sydney . . . Melbourne . . . as far away from him as she can get. She's a bit of a mess. I insisted she take my bed. She's had a rough time, and I don't mind sleeping on the couch."

He wondered if it was a warning she wasn't available tonight. Or was the powerful sexual appeal of the girl playing games with his imagination?

"You sound like a good friend to have," he said.

Her fingers caressed the glass, a reflective smile on her face. "Maybe. She's been a very good friend to me. She's the girl I told you about, who helped me with the identification of Mark. So I owe her. And I don't like to see anyone ill-treated—especially by someone who's supposed to love you . . . or says he does."

"I can't imagine anyone treating you like that," he said gallantly.

It was a mistake. She studied him silently for a moment,

and he knew the remark was being assessed for honesty. Anything vaguely resembling bullshit wouldn't sit with this girl.

"I wouldn't take that from any man," she stated flatly. "No matter who he was."

He could believe it. Once again he sensed the steel beneath the shell of femininity. She could be tough as hell if she was pushed. They were both silent for a time, each self-consciously drinking.

"Mark would never have been like that—or you," she added suddenly, as if she suspected he might have been offended.

He shrugged it off with a grin. "Well, at least that's established between us. I don't beat up on women."

She was embarrassed and glanced about the dining room to hide her confusion. The lone drinker at the bar had been joined by an overlarge woman, her buttocks spreading over the sides of the stool. A man at one of the tables laughed loudly, and his companions looked across at Lisa. She turned back quickly to Ross.

"Someone you know?" he asked.

She shook her head with a frown. "Everything is arranged with your brother?" she asked abruptly. He sensed her tension. Maybe the man had said something to upset her, and Ross hadn't heard the words. But he didn't pursue it.

"Yes. There's a slight holdup, but he's being flown to Sydney tomorrow night."

"And you'll also leave tomorrow?"

He hesitated. Did he sense regret, or did he want it to sound that way? "I guess so," he murmured. "I haven't decided yet." He saw the waiter approaching with their meal, and he pushed his beer to one side. "I'd like you to come to Sydney and stay with my parents. I know they'd love to meet you." He paused, considering his next words carefully. "And it would give me a chance to get to know you better."

The invitation surprised her, or was it his desire to get to know her better? But the arrival of the meal forestalled her answer. The fish was beautifully cooked in butter, with salad and lightly sautéed baby zucchini. They ate for a time in silence; then she patted her mouth with a napkin. "Are you sure they'd want me to come?"

He was surprised by the tentative manner of the question. "After the letter you wrote them, they'd be delighted. And so would I."

She plucked hesitantly at her meal. "I don't know . . . I didn't know Mark that long and . . . we only met today."

"I can see why Mark was so attracted to you. Maybe we have like interests, but I would like the chance to find out more about you." He paused over the meal, watching her cautiously. Maybe he was moving too fast, with the memory of Mark still so fresh in her mind.

It didn't seem to bother her. "It was special, meeting you today," she admitted. "Because of Mark. In some ways you're like him, and in others totally different. But I feel . . . comfortable with you, like I did with him."

"Then you'll come?"

"I'll think about it," she said cautiously. She might feel comfortable with him, but basically she was wary as hell. He didn't quite understand, and he wondered if she had been the same with Mark. He was subjected to the same inquisitorial gaze again. "They don't mind a bit of color?" she asked hesitantly.

He stared at her. "Color?"

"Yes. My color." Her eyes flickered briefly across the room. "Some people up here don't care for it."

He glanced across to the people at the other table, then back to her unsmiling face. Was that what the laughter had been about? "Christ, no, they're not like that," he declared forcefully. Did he really know, since they had never faced the situation?

Her mouth formed into a half-smile, and she pecked

sparrowlike at the food. "I just thought I should ask. And if I did come, you mightn't be there."

"I'd make sure I was there."

"Mark used to talk about you all the time—his rolling-stone brother, he called you. Never staying in one spot for long."

He hunched over the table, eating slowly for a moment. It was another spike of guilt for him. He'd had no idea he was so much in his brother's mind. "Well, I've been around," he admitted vaguely.

"You don't like Australia?"

"Sure, but there's a lot more to the world than this country."

"Where do you go?"

"Where the mood takes me. England, South America, America, Europe."

He sensed her disconcerting gaze was focused on him again, but he didn't look up. He had declared open interest in her, so she obviously considered she had equal rights.

"What do you do there?" she asked frankly.

He offered a disarming smile. "Whatever I can find to earn money." He did some sharp censoring in his mind. He wasn't going to tell her he'd run drugs in the Gulf of Mexico. Or killed a man in Honduras. "I drove a taxi in London. Took out fishing parties in Florida. Things like that."

"I can tell you've been around. Don't ask me to explain it . . . just the way you are."

He knew that, but he pretended innocence.

"You sound a little like me, Ross . . . looking for something without knowing what it is. Did you ever find it? I certainly haven't around here."

He stared at her. Jesus Christ, was it that obvious? Or maybe she was just remarkably intuitive. He tried to laugh it away. "I'm not looking for anything, Lisa." He managed to smile. "I'm just moving . . . having a good time. That's all."

She pushed her meal to one side. "I figure someone who can't stand still in one place for longer than it takes to count to ten has got to be looking for something," she mused. She looked at him, a slow smile emerging on her face. "I'm looking, you're looking."

"If I ever find it, you'll be the first to know." He grinned defensively. "Tell me what you think you're looking for."

"Myself."

"I have a feeling you know yourself pretty well."

She laughed sourly. It was the first unpleasant sound he had heard from her mouth. She folded her arms and gently caressed her skin. "See, I'm in between. Not black, and not white."

"I think you worry about that too much," he said sharply.

Her eyes widened. "That's what Mark used to say."

"Then he was right. You're a very beautiful woman."

She ignored the compliment. "I never knew my father. All I know is that he was white. I doubt if my mother even knew him. Just someone wandering through looking for a one-night stand, and she obliged him. She wasn't even a full-blooded aborigine herself. There was some white blood in her that came from God knows where." She gestured vaguely to the wall of the restaurant. "I used to live out there, you know."

"Out where?"

"Out there—in Arnhem Land. With the Bunitj, my mother's tribe, on the aboriginal reserve. They took me away from my mother when I was five years old."

"They?"

"The government. They could do it. A neglected child." She shrugged. "Maybe I was, but they're always mighty quick to act where black people are concerned. They sent me to a special school to get educated . . . even to speak properly. I was bright. They taught me how to be a very efficient secretary." She placed her hand solemnly to her breast. "What you see is what they made of me. I never saw my mother again. I might as well have been an orphan. They had no right to do that. I used to cry myself to sleep in the beginning, wanting her so much. Then I stopped one day, and decided no one was going to hurt me anymore. As if I'd grown a skin as tough as a crocodile."

Ross offered a sympathetic smile. He could identify with the feeling of not belonging. And now he understood the hardened steel beneath the beautiful exterior. "Did you ever try to find your mother?"

"Yes, when I was independent I went looking for her." She gestured vaguely again. "Out there. She'd died years ago. I guess she wouldn't have known me anyway. Probably forgotten I'd even existed. If she had come looking for me, they would probably have warned her off. No one would ever have told me. But I found some relatives . . . a grandfather. They're still out there, and I go and see them sometimes. Especially my grandfather." Old anger stirred in her, and she shook her head. "Maybe out there is where I really belong. Sometimes I feel more comfortable with them."

His mouth tightened in a firm line of disagreement. "It wouldn't work. You know it wouldn't work, even if you wanted to go back. You belong here. You'll marry . . . have a family of your own."

She appraised him with a cynical smile. "You think so, eh?"

"Sure, why not . . . someone as attractive as you?"

"Most of the men I meet are only out for a good time," she muttered. "There was one once . . ." She looked at him with a hesitant plea for trust. "I honestly don't know why I'm telling you all this, Ross."

"Because I want to hear it," he assured her gently. He wondered if she had unburdened herself to Mark in the same way. Perhaps he was carrying on a family tradition of inviting confidences. The waiter arrived like a rustling

shadow to remove their plates, and returned just as smoothly
with coffee. She stirred thoughtfully at her cup, as if
trying to decide whether to go on. "Well . . . there was
this man," she began in a low voice. "And I really liked
him." She shrugged resignedly. "Well, *loved*, if you prefer. Then I heard through a friend how he was boasting
around the town about this . . . boong he was sleeping
with, and what a great lay she was." Her mouth creased
down into a bitter line, her eyes an unreadable blackness,
like dead stars that absorb all light. "I never found out
why he had to be such a bastard."

He placed his hand impulsively over hers. "I'm sorry,"
he said, "but we're not all bastards."

She stared blank-faced at his covering hand, without
giving any indication she appreciated his sympathy. Or
believed him. "That's what I liked about Mark—he was a
sweet man. Fun to be with, and he didn't have any
hang-ups about anything." She smiled at Ross and with-
drew her hands gently from beneath his. "I think you're
like that too, Ross, even if I don't know you as well as
Mark."

Not yet, he wanted to say, but he decided against it. He
had the old, cold feeling of standing in Mark's shadow
again. Maybe he had come to Darwin on a mournful
mission, but he felt compensated from meeting her. Was
he a "sweet" man too? Not when he thought about some
of the things he'd done, but he would try to be for her.
Whatever she had felt for Mark, there was already a
connecting chemistry growing between them that he would
do all he could to foster.

He felt the rub of the film spool in his pocket, then took
it out and placed it on the table. She looked at it curiously, and he told her about Pat Tanna and the camera.

"I agree with Pat Tanna," she declared adamantly. "I
wouldn't give it to Lupane."

He shrugged indecisively and grinned. Lupane must be
the most unloved man in town. "I'm not too sure." He

turned the spool over in his fingers. "Lupane's so convinced of his drifters theory. I'd love to believe there was
something on this film to jolt his mind in a new direction."

"Then why don't you have it developed," she suggested.
"That way you can be sure he takes notice. You hand it to
him like that, and it's likely to be thrown into a bottom
drawer and forgotten. He's not the sort of man who likes
to be proved wrong."

He smiled vaguely at her paraphrasing of his own thoughts
concerning Lupane's personality. "I'd have to have the
film developed by tomorrow . . . before I leave Darwin. I
couldn't get it done that quickly."

She leaned forward on her crossed arms, an artful smile
on her face. "I could have prints for you in the morning."

"In the morning?" he exclaimed in surprise.

"Yes. Jo, the girlfriend I was telling you about in my
apartment. She works as a printer for a photographer in
the city. If I ask her, I'm sure she'd do them for you right
away."

"That would be fantastic," he said.

"Matter of fact, why don't we go and see Jo now. She
might even do them for you tonight."

He looked at her uncertainly, and glanced at his watch.
It was only nine-thirty. "That might be asking a bit much—
especially with the trouble she's had."

"No, no . . . she'd love to do it. I know Jo. It would
help take her mind off her problems for a while."

He was still uncertain. "You're sure? She could be
asleep."

"She might be lying down, but with her state of mind I
doubt if she's asleep," Lisa declared firmly.

He was convinced. He had wanted to be convinced. "All
right, then, let's go and see her. It would be great if I had
something to push down Lupane's throat before I left
Darwin."

He went to the washroom on the way out. His vague
sexual plans for the evening had been supplanted by the

exciting possibility of seeing what was on the film. Maybe it was just as well. He had the feeling he wanted more from this girl than a casual night in bed. He urinated, then washed his hands in the basin. The owner of the sniggering laugh from the other table came in and weaved in the direction of the urinal. His dinner had obviously been washed down with more wine than he could handle. He came to the washbasin and placed his hands unsteadily on Ross's shoulders. He peered into the mirror, owlishly contemplating the dual reflection with a fuzzy smile. He looked in his mid-thirties, pugnacious features colored to a florid complexion by the sun.

"Tell you what, man," he muttered thickly. "I wouldn't mind bein' where you're goin' tonight. No sir. Stickin' it in that boong piece." He slapped Ross on the arm. "Just say the word, man, and I'll swap places with you." He giggled, then stumbled toward the urinal. Ross stood drying his hands, glowering at the man, feeling heat flooding into his face. The water was still running in the bowl, and without taking his eyes off the man, his fingers found the plug and blocked the outlet. The man stepped away from the urinal, clumsily zipped up his trousers, and shuffled toward the door. He winked at Ross, and waved an admonishing finger. "Now, you take it easy, y'hear—they can kill you, those boongs."

Ross seized him by the arm, spun him around, clamped his fingers at the base of the man's neck, ignored the abrupt gurgle of alarm, then thrust his face deep into the water. For an instant the man was immobilized by shock; then he struggled violently, arms and legs flailing, his hands scrabbling ineffectually against the basin. Water slopped out like a running tide, over the man's suit, over Ross's shoes. Ross held him there for a few seconds, then let go and stood back against the wall. The man staggered wetly from the washbasin, spewing water, cannoned into the opposite wall, and sagged to the floor. His hair hung dankly into wide and disbelieving eyes, mouth spouting like a blowing whale. He was at once sober. "You . . . you crazy . . . bastard, what the fuckin' hell do you . . . think you're doin'?"

Ross casually dried his hands, ignoring the fast-running beat of his pulse. "I didn't care for your words," he said flatly.

He left the man slumped against the wall like a piece of cast-up flotsam, pawing the water from his eyes, unable to comprehend what had happened. Ross felt blood tingling in his fingertips, but he went out the door without looking at the man again. He was angry to have lost control. It hadn't happened in a long time, not since a croupier had tried to cheat him in Soho. Perhaps he was under more pressure than he realized, but he would watch that it didn't happen again.

It was a silent drive to Lisa's apartment. She had noted with curiousity his wet shoes and trousers, but he'd shrugged it aside as a clumsy accident. The only comment he offered was on her car. Young women like Lisa usually drove inexpensive small four-cylinder cars, but this was a BMW.

"I wish it was mine," she answered. "I'm looking after it for my boss while he's in Sydney. He's nervous about leaving it at his deserted house while he's away. He likes me to drive it around."

He merely nodded. She knew he was watching her, but he found it difficult to take his eyes away. She handled the car with composure. Much as he grieved for Mark, he did want to bed this girl down. She had so much style, he couldn't believe Mark hadn't felt the same way. He was beguiled by all the strange thoughts in his mind. Could he really feel jealous of a dead brother?

It was only a small apartment, simply furnished. A nondescript collection of chairs and a table occupied the living room. Bare polished floorboards, and a few scattered rugs. An island bench divided the living room from

a tiny galley-style kitchen. A bedroom about the size of a
large closet led off the kitchen, with just sufficient space
for the sofa where Lisa was sleeping. The living room also
served as a part-bedroom, with a bed set up in the corner.
An array of tourist posters decorated the walls, depicting
Darwin, Arnhem Land, local wildlife, and aboriginal cere-
monies. At least the place was comfortable.

Jo Santeze was watching television when they entered,
and she rose quickly to her feet to switch it off. She wasn't
unlike Lisa in appearance, about the same build and height,
but her darkness had its origins in Rome, a first-generation
Australian of parents who had migrated from Italy. She
wore a red checked blouse, brief white shorts, and nothing on her feet. She was also approximately the same age
as Lisa, attractive, but not striking like her friend. Perhaps
it was the lack of makeup, her sallow complexion, and the
sadness in her eyes. There was an ugly bruise on the side
of her face. But she greeted Ross with warmth. Her at-
tachment to Lisa was obvious, and if helping Ross was also
helping Lisa, she was only too happy to oblige by developing the film. She took the spool from Ross and examined it
with an experienced eye. "These are transparencies, Ross.
Do you want prints as well?"

"Well . . . wouldn't the prints be easier to see?" he
asked hesitantly.

"Yes, they would. I can make prints from the transparencies. If you decided to take the prints to the police,
then you could keep the transparencies for yourself."

"If it's no trouble."

"No trouble at all." She glanced at her watch. "I don't
see why I couldn't do them for you right now. I often work
nights, so I have a key to the studio. You could have them
in two or three hours."

"I'd be really grateful."

"No worries," she said brightly. "I loved your brother's
work, and I'd like to see them myself anyway."

Her fingers caressed the bruise in a self-conscious gesture of remembrance, and he felt uneasy knowing what she had been through. "I could wait until the morning," he offered. "Is the studio far away?"

She gave him a wan smile and patted his arm. "Ross, I'm not going to do much sleeping tonight. Doing these will take my mind off my own problems. That's why I'd like to do them now."

"I'll drive you down," Lisa volunteered.

"Accepted," said Jo. She motioned to both of them. "Why don't you both come down and keep me company anyway? It's always a little spooky in the studio when it's deserted."

It was agreed. They went out to the car, and Lisa retraced the route back to the city. Perhaps Jo sensed the chemistry between Ross and Lisa, because she made an automatic choice for the rear seat. The night was warm, but was made comfortable by a light sea breeze. The moon was an illuminating globe in a cloudless sky. The silhouette of a jet thundered out of the sky as they passed the airport, landing lights probing for the runway. There was a shattering roar, then they were past, heading into the city along the Stuart Highway. Only Jo made conversation, in the short staccato sentences of someone afraid of silence. Where should she go if she left Darwin? Could Ross recommend a place to stay in Sydney? She smoked continuously, quick, nervous puffs. Ross held himself half-turned to the rear to answer her questions, and occasionally her fingers strayed to the bruise on her face. He felt sorry for her.

It was a small shop on Peel Street, with bold, bright red lettering the length of the window, announcing it the premises of Bruce Innes, Commercial Photographer. Lisa drove the car into the small parking space by the side, and they went quickly into the building.

It was cool inside, with a vaguely musty smell. Jo switched on the light, and they followed her through the diminutive reception area, then across a small studio, their footsteps echoing on the concrete floor. Past a tripod-mounted camera, lights, benches scattered with film cartons, rolls of paper suspended against the wall, light cables snaking along the floor, until Jo halted at a small door. "My office," she announced facetiously.

They followed her in. She tugged at a dangling cord, and the room glowed with a muted orange light. It was the darkroom, full of benches, developing baths, enlarger, boxes of photographic paper. In one corner was a glass-topped viewing box with two spindly chairs at the side. "If you two would like to put your bodies on those chairs . . . with caution," Jo said brightly, "then I'll get on with the business."

Already she sounded better than when Ross had first met her at the apartment, so the diversion obviously was good therapy for her. They seated themselves on the chairs while Jo went deftly about the processing with the easy familiarity of professional expertise. For a time she continued the same sharp, punctuated conversation as in the car, of life in Darwin, her friendship with Lisa, of how she'd admired Mark's work, not waiting for answers, jumping spasmodically from subject to subject. Then, like a winding-down spring, she trailed into silence, until there was only the sound of her shuffling movements and the soft stirring of the developer. Ross was very close to Lisa, almost touching, and he could hear the gentle thread of her breathing, the accompanying rise and fall of her breasts. He laid his hand over hers crossed in her lap, and she turned to him with a smile, making no effort to draw away. He had no doubt she liked him. He only hoped he did more than rekindle memories of Mark. They sat like that, not speaking, just waiting.

"Come and have a look at these," Jo called finally. She yanked at the cord, converting the room from orange to white light. She held up a strip of transparencies as Ross moved quickly to her side. "They're dry now, so you should be able to see something." He bent to peer over her shoulder; then she lowered the strip with an apologetic grin and moved across to the viewing box. "Let me lay them out on the box. You'll be able to see better there."

She laid the transparencies out on the glass top, clicked on the switch, and the white light flared into their faces. The dull strip of film immediately took on a magical glow of color. She handed him the magnifying glass, and he crouched down over the film, squinting from frame to frame. They were amazingly sharp. But some of the anticipation of thrusting a revelation beneath Lupane's nose dissolved. He didn't understand what he was looking at. A small freighter with a helicopter standing on a pad at the stern. A rubber landing craft moored alongside the ship. Shots of the craft moving across the sea, filled with black-clad men. The craft drawn up on the beach and the men leaping out as if engaged in some form of commando assault. Maybe a navy exercise, but hardly a reason for Mark being murdered. They were very dramatic, but they didn't seem to have any relation to Mark's death. Yet he must have hidden the camera almost immediately after he'd taken these shots.

"Some exposures are better than others," Jo murmured. "I can pick those out for you."

Ross passed the magnifying glass to Lisa and wiped at his brow. The heat in the tiny room only added to his sense of disappointment. What had he expected? A posed portrait of the killers standing proudly with submachine guns in their arms? "I haven't the faintest idea what they mean," he said mournfully. "Who these people are . . . if they had anything at all to do with Mark's killing. Could you do me some prints of the freighter and the men coming ashore in the landing craft? He tapped at the film, allocating the shots he wanted.

"I'll make the prints to a five-four size—like a postcard," Jo suggested.

"Okay, that'll be fine."

"And maybe I should do two prints of each," she added.

"Two prints?"

"Well, if you do decide to show them to Lupane, it's possible he might know a professional photographer would be using transparencies. That means he'll ask for the transparencies as well, because he's going to want to keep them. If I do an extra set of prints, then you'll have a set to keep for yourself." She shrugged, her teeth pressed doubtfully into her bottom lip. "It's up to you." She took the magnifying glass from Lisa and hunched forward over the film. "I guess they're the last photographs he took," she said. "I don't know what they mean either, but it would be nice for you to have a set as a keepsake."

"I agree with Ross—it does look like some sort of navy operation," Lisa said.

Ross was silent for a moment. Much as he disliked Lupane, it made sense to show them to him. He guessed they were shots Mark had taken as part of his assignment, possibly a short time before he was killed. Lupane would be better able to trace the navy operation and see if they had any additional information. At least it might set the detective off on a different tack.

"All right, if it's no extra trouble, Jo."

"No trouble at all."

They sat back on the chairs while Jo pored over the film with the magnifying glass, marking each selected frame with a white pencil. Ross felt bloody tired. Or perhaps it was merely lethargy induced by a sense of anticlimax. He guessed he had built himself up to the conviction the film would produce some shattering revelation to knock Lupane's fat ass out of his chair, and now he just felt slightly ridiculous. He glanced at Lisa with a weary smile. At least she had meant well.

"I really appreciate this," he murmured softly.

"I only hope they help in some way," she whispered.

"My God, these are sharp," Jo interrupted. "I'll have to run a few tests first, but it shouldn't take long."

"That's okay." He yawned. The sense of urgency was gone. Lisa leaned to him until her head rested lightly on his shoulder. Her hair felt incredibly soft and smelled faintly of perfumed soap. It was the first physical contact she'd initiated, and he wanted to believe it was more than the fact she was sleepy.

"You're getting tired," he murmured.

Her hair rustled against his face. "I could fall asleep right now," she whispered faintly. "Wake me when the prints are finished, Mark." It was a drowsy slip of the tongue that passed her mouth unnoticed. Perhaps in a way he was Mark reborn to her, and he should just accept it. He slipped a supporting arm about her and let her doze against his shoulder while he watched Jo go silently through the procedure of making the prints. It wasn't until they were ready that he woke her.

They examined the prints together, passing them from one to the other without comment, but they meant no more than what Ross had seen under the magnifying glass. Once again he was struck by the eerie sharpness of the photographs.

Jo didn't question him again over his intentions about Lupane, but she made up two envelopes, the transparencies and a set of prints in one, and the second set of prints in the other. Then she handed them to him with a smile tinged with fatigue. He knew neither of the girls liked Lupane—the policeman wasn't exactly his own favorite human being—but they made it obvious it was Ross's decision what he did about the photographs. And the only thing that mattered to him was doing what was best to have Mark's killers caught.

It was twelve-thirty by the time they arrived back at Lisa's apartment. The streets around Alawa were quiet and deserted, the daytime bustle replaced by dormant shadows.

Jo vacated the car and paused at the passenger-side window, her hands against the door. Her white face in the

streetlight emphasized the bruise, like an unwashed smudge
on her cheek. Ross hastily wound down the window, but
she shrugged aside his thanks with a weary grin. "Only too
glad to help, Ross," she said. "Listen, if I don't get to see
you again before you leave, have a good trip back to
Sydney. I hope the photographs turn out to mean something about your brother's death . . . whatever you decide to do about them."

He reached out and gripped her hand. "And I hope
everything turns out okay for you, Jo. Look me up if you
come to Sydney. Lisa will have my address."

She gave a brief nod of thanks, then turned and walked
back into the building. In the half-light she could easily
have been mistaken for Lisa, except for the walk. Perhaps
it was her personal problems, but her hesitant step had
none of her friend's arrogant challenge.

Lisa waited until she was safely inside, then accelerated
cautiously away from the curb. It was close to one o'clock
by the time she braked to a halt outside Ross's motel. She
offered a jaded smile, but didn't switch off the engine. It
ticked over sweetly, the only sound in the night air. He
reached across to the ignition key and turned off the
motor.

Her smile expired in unison with the motor. "I'm a
working girl, and I'm tired, Ross," she said firmly. "It's
late, and I've just got to get some sleep before morning."

The warmth she had offered in the darkroom was gone.
Maybe the physical contact he'd experienced in the studio
was something given only in the safe presence of a third
person. He didn't know if he wanted anything from her for
now, but she had interpreted his act of switching off the
motor as sexually provocative. Maybe it was. What she
had told him about herself meant she would always be
defensively alert, never easily taken.

He gave what he hoped was an understanding tilt of his
head. "Just thank you for a wonderful night, Lisa," he

said. He patted the envelopes on his lap. "And thank you for making these possible."

At once the tension was gone. "Are you going to take them to Lupane?"

His mouth twitched indecisively. "Maybe. I'll sleep on it and see how I feel about it in the morning."

He peered toward the darkened motel. He thought of asking her up for a drink, maybe to talk about the photographs, but he knew she wouldn't buy what sounded like a transparent suggestion. "Can I see you tomorrow?" he asked.

"If you like." He was encouraged by the alacrity of her response. "Do you know what time you're leaving?"

"Mark's body is being flown down tomorrow night, so I'll probably go down about the same time. I should be in Darwin most of the day."

"Then perhaps we could have lunch together."

"I'd like that." He considered for a moment. "I'll call you about midmorning. I'll have made up my mind about Lupane by then, and we can arrange a place."

She nodded agreement. He could see by her face that fatigue was no pretense, that she was running down fast. Her hands moved listlessly over the steering wheel, and she stared ahead through the windshield.

"Thank you for dinner, Ross," she said. "I enjoyed it very much." She looked across at him. "You're a lot like Mark in many ways. In others . . ." She smiled, but didn't elaborate. Christ, she was smart all right, smart as hell. Mark wouldn't have killed Aldo's executioner in Trujillo, run drugs in Miami, pushed the man's head down into the washbowl at the restaurant. It set him apart from Mark, and she was intuitive enough to recognize the difference. He leaned over and kissed her on the mouth, not hard, but gently probing. She offered no resistance, but he felt her move, then the gentle pressure of her fingers on his arm. He didn't push it. It was the only mark he wanted to leave on her tonight.

"When this is over, and if you have no objections, I'm going to see a lot more of you, Lisa."

He saw a flash of that expression again, the lines of her mouth twisted in cynical distrust. She had him categorized with the boong-lover she'd told him about, a passing thing with the risk of hurt. But he did mean it, and he would prove it to her in time.

"We'll see," she murmured. She signaled dismissal by starting the motor. "I'll wait for your call in the morning," she added.

He waited outside the motel until the lights of her car disappeared. There had been other women, more sophisticated, intellectual, but nothing like her. Hidden depths she would reveal only as her trust grew. Perhaps after all this time, she was what he was looking for. Not his first instinct as a passing screw, but something to build his life around. He shook his head and walked into the motel. It was going to be difficult to put her out of his mind, but during the night he had to reach a decision about Lupane.

4

Ross slept badly and rose later than he intended. It was nine-thirty by the time he had finished a hasty breakfast in his room. But at least the restless night had produced a positive conclusion about Lupane. Dislike the man or not, dislike his authority, he had to put that to one side and do what was best for Mark. And that meant showing the photographs to Lupane. It was ludicrous to imagine he could carry out his own investigation. Lupane had all the right connections, all the expertise. Ross didn't know if the photographs meant anything, but at least they might force Lupane in some way to look further then his drifters theory. The more Ross thought about it, the less likely it seemed for drifters to be carrying submachine guns. But there was no way he was going to shake the man's theory, and maybe the photographs would do it for him. As soon as he'd gulped down the last of his coffee, he called Lupane.

"Ross Berger, Mr. Lupane," he said courteously.

The distant sound of an office typewriter was the only answer for a moment.

"Ah yes, Mr. Berger," came Lupane's voice finally. "I expect you'll be leaving Darwin today. I understand all the arrangements are finalized about your brother."

"Yes, that's right." He cleared his throat nervously. "There's something else concerning my brother I'd like to talk to you about."

"Ah yes . . . another thought. What is it, Mr. Berger?" His voice was languid with uninterest. There was a soft scratching sound in the background, as if he were writing at the same time.

"I'd like to come and see you this morning," Ross said.

"You think it's necessary to come to the station, Mr. Berger? Couldn't you talk to me about it over the phone?"

"I'm afraid not. I need to show you something."

Lupane laughed unpleasantly. If it was intended as an irritant, then it was well delivered.

"I think it's important," Ross declared stiffly. "I believe everyone wants to see my brother's killer caught."

"Of course, of course, Mr. Berger." Lupane made an effort to inject more spirit into his voice. "All right, then, why don't you come into the station and see me in about half an hour. It won't take long, will it?"

"Not at all," Ross said coldly, and hung up.

He sat for a moment studying the phone, irritated by the policeman's arrogance. He deflected a sudden urge to change his mind. Fuck him, Mark was all that mattered. He made a brief call to his father about the arrival of Mark's body in Sydney, and asked that he meet the plane. It disturbed his father that Ross mightn't be back in Sydney in time to take charge of the coffin, but then, his remaining son had always been an enigma to the old man. Ross didn't say anything about Lisa Marnoo, that there was a thought nurturing in his mind of stopping over another night to see more of her. That would have been incomprehensible to his father, and he wasn't in the mood to confess he was smitten like a schoolboy.

Then he called Lisa. There was a renewal of warmth in her voice that dissipated the chill of their parting last night. "I have a lovely idea," she said enthusiastically. "I'm going to make up a picnic lunch and take you out to the East Point Reserve. We can sit there, eat sandwiches, look at the sea, and just talk."

"That sounds great," he said with equal zeal. His voice took on a more solemn note. "I'm going to show Lupane the photographs this morning."

"I expected you would. And I think you're right."

"It probably won't change anything, but it's worth a try."

"He's going to be upset about Pat Tanna giving you the camera," she warned.

"I realize that. I'll just have to be honest about it."

"I'm sure you'll handle it all right," she stated confidently.

He thought of hinting he might stay on another night, but changed his mind. It would be better to gauge her reaction if he told her over lunch. "Say I wait for you outside the motel around . . . one o'clock," he suggested.

"That'll be fine. I'll see you then, Ross." He put the phone down and savored the warm sound of her voice for a moment. She seemed equally anxious to see him, so maybe he had something going with her after all.

He picked up the envelope containing the prints and transparencies but left the second set of prints on the bedside table. Then he walked briskly down Smith Street and around to the police station on Mitchell Street. He knew he should have brought the camera, but for now he intended to try to hang onto it.

It was a cooler day. To the north, gray clouds tumbled across the sky to form bulbous threatening formations. Gusts stirred the palm fronds along the street into violent confrontation with each other. It wasn't a good day for a picnic lunch.

Lupane was at his desk completing some documentation when Ross was ushered into his office. He glanced briefly at Ross, nodded curtly to a chair, and continued writing. He was again attired in the conservative dark suit and tie.

Ross sat quietly, watching Lupane, fingering the envelope. If it was a tactic to make him feel an unnecessary drag on the detective's time, then it was successful. Ross was just concluding he'd made a mistake in coming when Lupane pushed the documents to one side and welcomed his visitor with a sardonic grin. "Well, now, Mr. Berger," he said casually, "I thought you'd be on your way back to Sydney by now instead of bringing me a solution to your brother's murder." He made no attempt to conceal the inflection of sarcasm.

Ross decided he wasn't going to be baited. "I'm afraid I haven't got a solution, Mr. Lupane," he said politely.

"I was hoping you might have something . . . startling, after your call." Lupane crossed his arms on the desk with feigned weariness. "My hands are tied until we get that listing of your brother's equipment."

"It's been taken care of," said Ross. "I called my father last night. You'll be hearing from the insurance company."

Lupane nodded with satisfaction. He clasped his powerful hands together, rubbing and squeezing tightly. Used as a weapon, they could do a lot of damage. "I appreciate your acting so promptly," he said with a condescending smile. He glanced meaningfully at the papers on his desk, then back to Ross

Ross leaned forward in the chair and placed the envelope in front of Lupane. The detective looked at it curiously, then at Ross. Ross cleared his throat with a rasping

cough. Explaining Pat Tanna giving the camera to him
instead of the police wasn't going to be easy.

"I saw Pat Tanna yesterday," he began tentatively. "I
received a message he wanted to see me, so I went down
to his boat at Stokes Hill wharf." He grinned. "He's quite
a character."

"You might say that," Lupane agreed dryly.

"He gave me a camera . . . one of my brother's cameras."

Lupane's insolent lack of interest abruptly dissolved into
surprise. As if to conceal his reaction, he shuffled the
papers uneasily about on the desk. "Where the hell did he
get your brother's camera?" he asked harshly. "The stupid
old bastard didn't mention it to me when I questioned
him. By Christ, if he's been withholding evidence . . ."

"No, he didn't find out about the camera until yesterday." Ross made a rapid explanation of Tanna's crew member finding it on the clifftop, and how it came into the old
fisherman's hands. "I don't think he intended keeping
evidence from the police," Ross lied with an apologetic
gesture. "Nothing had happened to the camera. Old Pat
just figured I would like to have it. Which was true
enough. I know my parents will appreciate it as a keepsake
to remind them of Mark."

Lupane's initial lack of interest was firmly shouldered
aside by resentment. His brows knit together and his mouth
set into a sour, disapproving line. "The stupid old goat
should have brought it immediately to me. He should
have known that. That camera is evidence, Mr. Berger.
Maybe important evidence. I don't know whether your
brother hid it in the rocks or not but that's for me to
determine. You should have told Tanna to bring it to me."

Ross shifted on the chair with embarrassment. He wished
he'd never had the film developed. "I don't think Pat
thought about it as evidence," he explained. "And neither
did I, at the time. I was simply grateful to have something
of Mark's."

"Where's the camera now?" Lupane demanded officiously.

"In my motel room."

"You didn't bring it with you?"

"It seemed unnecessary for now," Ross said uncomfortably. He knew now what Lisa and Pat meant about Lupane's grilling technique. Fuck the man, he should have just kept the photographs to himself. "The . . . drifters you spoke about must have missed the camera in the rocks," he added inconsequentially.

"I think I'm the best judge of whether it's necessary or not," Lupane continued aggressively. "It doesn't seem like a very cooperative act to me. You do want your brother's killers caught, Mr. Berger?"

Ross straightened in the chair. He decided not to let this bastard push him any further. "I wouldn't be here otherwise," he said brusquely "I don't think the camera is going to tell you anything you don't already know." He was on weak ground, and counteraggression was probably the best tactic.

It seemed to have an effect on Lupane. "I'd like you to bring the camera to me, Mr. Berger," he said in a calmer tone. "It certainly needs to be examined. I understand your feeling of wanting something of your brother's. Don't worry, you'll get it back."

There was a hostile silence, as if a respite was needed for the chill to subside. Lupane picked up the envelope and looked inquiringly at Ross. "This is something to do with the camera?"

"There was film in the camera. I had it developed."

It was difficult for Ross to define Lupane's expression this time, because he disciplined his reaction. It could have been added surprise or a resurgence of anger. "You had it developed?"

Ross held himself in tight. It was there again, the feeling he was being cross-examined. "For the same reason," he replied. "To have something of my brother's. They're probably the last photographs he ever took." What else could he say? That he had them developed to shove up Lupane's nose and disprove his drifters theory?

Lines of disbelief crowded into Lupane's face. "Jesus Christ," he exclaimed in exasperation. "Don't you think I would have had them developed anyway, Mr. Berger? That I'd be just as anxious to see them as you?" He glared at Ross and fumbled at the flap of the envelope. "I don't think you quite trust me, Mr. Berger. Or maybe you just don't like the police."

Ross ignored the accuracy of the comment. Things were difficult enough already, without getting into any hassles about his attitude to the police. He gestured hesitantly to the envelope. "I thought they would be just outdoor scenes . . . shots that went with his assignment. But I don't understand those photographs. That's why I decided I should bring them to you, just on the chance they might give you a new lead. That's all." He stared hard at Lupane in an effort to recover the initiative. "And because I'm so anxious to have Mark's killers caught," he added with emphasis.

Lupane hunched sullenly over the desk, the envelope in his hand; then he shrugged with a thin smile of offered peace. "Okay, okay, I take your point, Mr. Berger. We're all anxious. You brought them to me, that's the main thing." He frowned. "How the hell did you get them developed so fast?"

"Oh, a friend of my brother's," Ross supplied vaguely.

"I'd say you were talking about Lisa Marnoo," Lupane guessed.

Ross offered a noncommittal nod. There was no point in an outright denial. In the time he was in Darwin, Mark would have had little chance to make friends, so Lisa was the obvious choice. Lupane probed some more as he upended the envelope and shook the contents onto the desk. "There was a girlfriend, I recall . . . she came in here with the Marnoo girl several times . . . name of Jo something. Worked for a photographer as a printer, if I remember rightly." He smiled encouragingly at Ross. "I guess she did them for you, eh? It's always good to have friends."

Again Ross merely gave a wordless nod. It hadn't been his intention to involve either Lisa or Jo, but Lupane was persistent. Ross would say no more. Lupane had the photographs now, and that would have to satisfy him, without any further cross-examination. But Ross was grateful to Jo that he had his own set of prints.

"As you can see, the originals are transparencies," he said. "They're difficult to see, so I had prints made up to a larger size."

He was unsure if Lupane heard him. The policeman was crouched low over the prints as if afflicted with acute myopia, leafing them one by one through his fingers. His head was so low, it was impossible to see any reaction. Ross waited, the soft shuffle of the prints passing through Lupane's hands the only sound.

"It looks like some sort of navy operation," Ross volunteered helpfully. "Something Mark must have photographed only a short time before he was killed. It would be easy to check back . . . those people could have some important information or be able to help in some way." His voice trailed away at the lack of response. Lupane didn't answer. He went through the prints again, subjecting each shot to meticulous examination. Then he pushed the prints to one side, leaned back in the chair, and stared thoughtfully into space. His face was a carefully composed blank mask.

"Well, what do you think?" Ross prodded impatiently.

"Well, they're certainly . . . intriguing," answered Lupane. "Very intriguing. Frankly, I'm not too sure what they mean either . . . or how important they are. If it was a navy operation, it could give us a more exact time for the murder. Maybe even open up a fresh area of investigation."

Lupane's reaction was scarcely explosive. But then, Ross remembered his own initial disappointment, so maybe he had been expecting too much. Perhaps he shouldn't have bothered, merely gone back to Sydney with Mark's camera, and saved himself the trouble.

"I was hoping they might give you a new lead on your . . . drifters theory," he declared curtly.

Lupane straightened in the chair and offered an expansive gesture of appreciation. "Maybe . . . maybe. Don't get me wrong, Mr. Berger. Okay, I was upset about old Tanna and the camera, but I really appreciate you bringing these to me." He was suddenly surprisingly affable. "Like I said, they could lead us into a completely new theory. I'll get to work on it right away . . . believe me." He paused, reflectively stroking at his chin. "First thing to do is get in touch with the navy and see if they can back up these photographs."

Ross watched him doubtfully. He seemed a little out of character. Maybe he'd misjudged the man, because he didn't seem thrown by the fact his pet theory might need rethinking.

"What time are you leaving Darwin, Mr. Berger?"

Ross shrugged. "I haven't booked a seat yet, but I'd say late this afternoon."

"I wonder if you could do me a favor and stay over another night?"

Ross looked at him in surprise. "What for?"

Lupane dropped his hand heavily on the prints. "I'm going to get started on these right away, but I just might turn up something you could help me with. I don't know, something about your brother's background . . . something that might jolt your memory. It would help if you were here on the spot." He paused, with a cajoling smile. "I'd certainly appreciate it . . . and it *is* for your brother's sake."

The request immediately took Ross's mind on a tangent to Lisa. The girl had really gotten to him. Staying on in the hope of nailing Mark's killer seemed almost secondary to the fact he had a legitimate excuse to see more of her.

He grabbed at it. "Sure, that's possible," he said with contrived hesitancy. "Anything I can do to help. I've already arranged for my father to take care of Mark's body in Sydney." He smiled agreement. "Say I stay on until around midday tomorrow. Would you have something on the photographs by then?"

"I don't see why not." Lupane studied the prints thoughtfully for a while, shuffling them around on the desk, then looked to Ross with a bleak smile. "I really appreciate that, Mr. Berger." He eased his bulk out of the chair, and as if from a high tower he extended his hand to Ross. "And thanks again for realizing I had to see these." The syrupy words were a far remove from his original sarcasm, and once again Ross felt a spark of guilt that he might have misjudged the man. They briefly shook hands. "And I think we should have a look at the camera," Lupane added. He made a swift, reassuring motion of his hand. "I'll personally make sure nothing happens to it. Why don't you leave it at the motel desk, and I'll have it picked up. That'll make it easier for you." He was bending over backward with consideration. It was cool in the office, but Ross could see beads of moisture on his forehead. The man was hard to read. He had himself so much under control, yet the perspiration was a sign his mind was bubbling over like a pressure cooker. Was he so excited about the photographs?

"Call me at nine o'clock in the morning," concluded Lupane. "I should have something for you by then, and we can talk about it. Okay?"

"Sure." Ross moved to the door. Maybe nothing would come of it, but he was certain now he'd been right to come to Lupane. His mind was filling with the thought of being with Lisa tonight. "Until tomorrow morning."

Lupane lifted his hand in an exaggerated swirl of farewell.

Lupane held his position for a long time after Ross had departed from the office, until his arm dropped to his side like the lowering of a flag. The mechanical smile on his face bore no relation to the turmoil in his mind. His stomach whined as if his bowels demanded release. He swept the photographs into the bottom drawer, then padded out of the office and down the corridor to the washroom. He closed the door, ran cold water into the washbasin, loosened his collar, and stared bleakly at his reflection in the mirror. For a moment his stomach threatened vomit. He closed his eyes, tightly pressed his mouth, and leaned his head against the mirror. Christ almighty, he took pride in his self-possession, but how the fuck did he manage to act so normally when faced with those damning photographs? They could finish everything. Blandhurst's promises to him would go down the drain if they ever got out. More than that, he was so deeply involved himself now, he would sink like a rock. God, what if Berger had taken them to a newspaper? He felt the taste of vomit again, and he bent over the sink, sluicing cold water repeatedly into his face until the nausea was gone. He dried off, forlornly studying his face in the mirror. He was in trouble. Deep trouble. Blandhurst was in trouble. Starker was in trouble. The whole fucking plan was in trouble. He had to act fast, because so far only Berger and the two girls had seen the photographs. Starker would react predictably. Lupane had him figured for a bloody-minded old bastard who was only interested in taking the hill, and the hell with who got killed along the way. Whatever had to be done, someone like the General would have no trouble justifying it to himself. Who cared about a little blood, if it was for the cause? And Lupane had no doubt he would be selected for hatchet man. Well, he had known there were risks, but he was too far in now to afford any attacks of conscience.

  He walked unsteadily back to his office, closed the door firmly, and called Starker.

*   *   *

"I'm not leaving for Sydney until the morning," Ross said quietly. Lisa looked at him in surprise. He waited, hoping her reaction might have overtones of pleasure. They were parked in the car where Dudley Point overlooked Fannie Bay. The day had deteriorated further, and the sky was a roof of slate gray, muddying the deep blue of Beagle Gulf. The car shivered in the wind, and out in the gulf the surface was a pattern of broken white water. It was sufficient reason to stay inside the car. She had brought sandwiches and white wine, and there was no denying there was a simmering of magic building when they were together. Their conversation had been easy, if shallow, so far, until his statement about staying over. He knew from her expression she was debating the implication, and he didn't know whether to be pleased or annoyed. It was obvious she thought it was for her, and he let her off the hook. "Lupane asked me to stay."

He studied her smile, but he couldn't tell if she was relieved he had a legitimate excuse.

"Because of the photographs?"

"That's right." He described the interview to her, Lupane's various reactions to Tanna, to the camera, to the film. "Maybe I just wasted my time, but he said he was going to start inquiries immediately. Maybe we were a little harsh with Lupane. He didn't seem too thrown that he might have to do some rethinking about his drifters theory." He shrugged. "Well, I'll know in the morning." He was silent for a time. A gull alighted delicately on the hood of the car and expectantly watched them eating. Ross wound down the side window and threw a piece of bread to the bird. It snapped it up in midair and winged off pursued by squawking competitors. "Hell, those photographs have to mean something, Lisa. Even if it only gives him a fresh angle." He paused for a sip of wine, and all his doubts about Lupane came rushing back. "If he doesn't turn up anything, I might try a little nosing around myself when I get back to Sydney."

"He wouldn't have asked you to stay if he wasn't serious," Lisa ventured.

He knew she was right. Lupane would only make himself look foolish with an empty request. "Maybe I'm a natural pessimist," he grunted.

"You might be pleasantly surprised when you call him in the morning," she said brightly.

He realized he was starting to sound like a moody shit, and he moved off the subject of Lupane. "How's Jo after the late night?"

Lisa's mouth twisted in a wry expression, and she frowned. "Depressed. She didn't go to work, just moped around the apartment all day. I called in for her and told her boss she was ill. Which is true in a way. I think she should go south as soon as she can. I'll miss her, but there's no way she can straighten herself out while she's in Darwin. I'm a little scared the guy she was living with might come around to the apartment and make trouble." She grimaced. "That would be hard to handle, but there's no sign of him so far."

"She still has your bed?"

She looked at him warily. Suddenly everything between them had a coupling innuendo. He felt a shaft of irritation to be so unsure of the girl, but Christ, he wasn't going to force her into bed.

"Yes . . . yes, I insisted. I'm comfortable enough on the couch in the back room."

"I wish there was some way I could help her."

"It'll work itself out, I guess." She smiled warm thanks. "She liked you, and she'd appreciate the thought."

They completed the meal in near-silence. She watched the agitated movement of the sea, the hovering gulls, and he watched her, the way her throat pulsed as she swallowed, the soft darkness of her eyes. He thought of kissing her, then decided against it. Instead he composed words that would sound easy and natural. "I was hoping we could have dinner again tonight," he said casually.

She considered the question. "I'd like that, but I don't want to be late, Ross. Was she warning him again? Yet the invitation was so readily accepted. "It's just that I don't like leaving Jo alone for long at night. Not the way she is at the moment," she explained.

He offered a reassuring grin. "Promise. We won't be late. And there'll be other times."

He waited for that small cynical twist to her mouth, but it didn't come. Maybe she was starting to believe him. She was finally realizing he was more than just a clone of his brother, was someone to be reckoned with in his own right. He was sure now that his feelings were more than wanting something that had belonged to Mark. If it worked with her, maybe his stay in Australia would be longer this time. Perhaps forever.

Starker pushed the small table closer to the window and hunched forward over the prints like a predatory bird. He looked slightly schoolteacherish with his spectacles perched on the end of his nose, peering through the magnifying glass, carefully examining each morsel before proceeding to the next. Nothing showed in his face, and an occasional sorrowful shake of his head was the only reaction he permitted.

He knew Lupane, standing nervously in the center of the room, was watching him, and he could hear the sound of his heavy breathing, as if there were insufficient air in the room. Lupane cleared his throat with a harsh sound of breaking phlegm, wanting to speed a reaction, but the General took no notice.

"The photographs are incredibly sharp," Starker murmured softly. "The name of our ship, *Seaboro*, can be seen quite clearly."

"Yes, I saw that," said Lupane.

"That's a disaster, Lupane."

The other shuffled his feet nervously about on the car-

pet, and swallowed noisily several times, as if to indicate
the need for a drink, but Starker ignored the signal.

The General finally pushed the prints to one side, leaned
back in the chair, and placed a cigar with great deliberation in his mouth. Beneath the carefully acquired tan, his
face appeared slightly paler. Coming on top of the foolish
practice exercise at Cape Jaubert, he wondered what
Halmen would make of these. Well, he would not involve
New York. They had placed him in command, the arbiter
of life and death. It was his ultimate responsibility, so he
would do it. He lit up and expelled a small cloud of smoke
toward the ceiling. The thing to do in such a crisis was
create an atmosphere of confidence, show that ruthless
decisions would be made unhesitatingly for the safety of
all. He took the cigar from his mouth and absently studied
the ash for a moment. "No one else has seen them except
Berger and the two women?" he asked.

"I'm sure of it. The girl Santeze only developed them
last night, and Berger brought them to me first thing this
morning."

The General nodded. "Kill them," he said tonelessly.
"Kill them, and do it quickly." The committee would
admire such resolution. The cause was all that mattered,
and a few lives were irrelevant.

"We're close now, Lupane," he went on. "A time has
been set for the raid, and we can't afford the slightest
risk." He stared at an unseen horizon and scowled. "God,
this should never have happened. One stupid miscalcula-
tion like Cape Jaubert, and it sets off a chain reaction. My
God, can you imagine if Berger had taken those to another
authority . . . or, heaven help us, to the media? The ship
could be traced right back to New York. It was a calcu-
lated risk that no attempt be made to disguise the ship,
that it was better to be seen as a normal freighter, on a
normal voyage. But for Christ's sake, who could have
foreseen this foul-up?" He removed his glasses with an
irritated sweep of his hand and dropped them with a

clatter on the table. "No, it's . . . regrettable, but it would
be madness to let anyone who's seen these photographs
stay alive." He shook his head and glowered at the prints.
"Absolute madness," he repeated. "And even after the
raid, the potential for damage is still there. From what
you've told me of Berger, he's sure to make a connection
between the photographs and the uproar that's sure to
follow the raid. It could be dangerous for Martin." He
angrily flicked ash from his cigar. "We have absolutely no
choice, Lupane. The entire operation is at stake. Kill
them. Tonight."

Beneath the anger was a sense of satisfaction. Christ, it
felt good to be making command decisions again. It was what
he'd been trained for, what his life meant. It wasn't murder he was asking of Lupane, merely the destruction of
the enemy. He stood up, pacing from one side of the
window to the other, in a restricted parade-ground pattern. The wind outside was a high-pitched whine, and the
beginnings of rain pockmarked the glass.

"It's not going to be easy," Lupane said uneasily.

The General halted his pacing and skewered Lupane
with an unwavering stare. He couldn't permit any doubting troops. Perhaps Lupane needed to be reminded of
Martin's promises. "I don't expect it to be," he said coldly.
"But that is why you're here . . . why you have such a
personal stake in our success." He smiled thinly. "I'm
sure you'll reconcile what has to be done with your own
ambitions, Lupane." Then he added an extra needle. "You're
in this as deep as any of us now. We go down, you go
down with us. Right to the bottom."

Lupane flushed his tongue nervously across his mouth.
There was no turning back now. "I didn't say it couldn't
be done, I said it wasn't going to be easy. It can't look like
a clumsy triple murder. It's got to be handled right. This
sort of thing is Garcott's specialty."

"That's up to you. I understand you have great . . .
expertise in this area," encouraged the General. "But do it

fast. It must be tonight. To leave it any longer only increases the risk of them talking to other people about the photographs." He paused, and his eyes widened at a sudden thought. "My God, is Berger still in Darwin?"

"Of course." Lupane permitted himself a self-congratulatory smirk. "As soon as I saw the photographs, I knew it was essential to keep Berger here until I'd spoken to you. I gave him some bullshit about needing him around, and he agreed to stay on another night."

"Good, good," Starker said with relief. "That was quick thinking, Lupane. But that only makes it more essential for you to act tonight."

Lupane nodded morose agreement, and they both fell silent. The rain pattered against the window with increasing force, and the General shuffled his feet about in the mannerism he used to indicate a meeting was over.

"What about the photographs?" Lupane asked.

In answer Starker swept them briskly back into the envelope and handed them to Lupane. "Destroy them as soon as you get back to your office."

"Berger might ask to see them during the day."

"Why?"

"I don't know. He just might."

"Tell him you sent them off for examination. Stall him. I'm sure you can find a satisfactory answer. No. Destroy them. None of us can feel safe until you do."

Lupane offered no further objections, and slipped them into his briefcase. "You know, General, without these as evidence, it's only Berger's word anyway. And the girls'."

Starked eyed him suspiciously. It sounded very much like Lupane was trying to backtrack on his termination order. He tapped his forefinger meaningfully against his temple. "What they saw is still in their minds, Lupane. Maybe even the name of the ship." He drew his brows tightly together and stared balefully at his subordinate. "I'm not prepared to risk that—for the sake of all our necks. Is that understood?"

Lupane nodded sullenly. "I was just making a point, General." He hesitated. "You want me to discuss the . . . termination arrangements with you?"

The General pursed his lips thoughtfully. It wasn't an area he could make any contribution to, and probably the less he knew, the better. Not from any squeamish considerations, but he was only interested in Lupane carrying out the order, not how it was accomplished. He gave a firm, negative shake of his head. "From what Martin has told me, I think I can rely on you to do the job with a certain amount of . . . imagination. You don't need my help. Just make sure there's no mess . . . no loose ends. Understand? Give it a legal framework, it'll look better that way. You know what I mean?"

"You're not interested in method, General?"

"No, Lupane. I don't involve myself in method, only results."

"It doesn't matter to you if we strangle the girls . . . or shoot them . . . or knife them to death."

The General drew himself to full military height, placed his hands behind his back, and glared at Lupane. There was no mistaking the insolence of the man's tone, the implication that repugnance was the basis for his refusal. He had seen it in Vietnam. People like Lupane were only the shit. There were those who commanded, and the butchers. That was the natural order of things. "Do it," he said bluntly. "For Martin. For yourself."

Lupane picked up his briefcase, responded with a cynical sneer, and left the room without another word.

Starker eased himself back into the chair, and the taste of the half-smoked cigar seemed suddenly unpalatable. He sighed, put it down in the ashtray, and gazed out the window. Wind-driven clouds skimmed across the sky, and the sound of the rain drumming against the window only added to his depression. How, after so much meticulous planning, could things go so wrong? People could never be fully trusted. There was always an unsuspected idiot,

like a booby trap set on the path. He wasn't unduly
troubled by the three who had to die. He had a cause to
save. If a few more people had been ready to die in
Vietnam, he would have saved that cause too. Insubordi-
nate troops funking their patrols, who wouldn't fight. He
placed his hands into fists and ground them savagely together. Just thinking about that past gave him resolve.
First thing he must do was call Martin. Then perhaps his
wife. Maybe it wasn't wise, but there was thirty-five years
of loyalty there to be respected. Muriel never questioned
his decisions; whatever he decided was all right with her.
Except where their son was concerned. The boy no longer
existed for him, but he knew she was still emotionally
involved. How could three generations of military leadership produce a radical idiot? It was inconceivable to him.
How could anyone with a modicum of intelligence prefer
the peace-movement traitors to West Point? God, he had
done all the right things by the boy, applied the necessary
rigid discipline to prepare the boy to follow him. As his
father had done. He twisted irritably in the chair, soured
against calling his wife by the memory of his son. He
picked up the phone and dialed Martin Blandhurst's number. The misjudgment at Cape Jaubert had shaken Martin's confidence, and it was essential the General's friend
be reassured that everything was under control.

Midway up the eastern coast of Australia, in the Queens-
land sugarcane country, the small town of Beton sits con-
tentedly in the tropical sun. Beton is a sugar-mill town
designed to meet the needs of the surrounding cane growers. At this time of year the fields stand tall with green
swaths of ripening cane, almost ready for the burning
method that precedes cutting. The growers check their
machinery, transportation arrangements to the Beton mill,
and speculate on the cash value of their crops.
  Beton is like many small Australian settlements, the
highway like a vital artery through the center, straddled

on either side by merchants taking their lifeblood from the beat of the town. A friendly town where there's time to sit in the sun over a beer, offer bantering talk about crops, prices, and the latest delicious rumor concerning the sex life of the district's most famous son, Martin Blandhurst.

A mile west of town a gravel road turns north off the highway, with a pointing sign, neatly lettered white on black, that says simply "Sweetwater." Almost as an afterthought, there is a supplementary line of small type declaring it to be a private road.

Sweetwater is the home of Martin Blandhurst, fourth-generation Australian, descended from Samuel Blandhurst, come from London to seek his fortune, who first tasted the waters of the creek running through the property and aptly named the area Sweetwater. Cane grows there in rich abundance, surrounding the house like a magnificent green wall. But there is more than cane. Impeccable white fences enclose superb blood-stock racehorses. Fat, aristocratic cattle move ponderously from one clump of scientifically produced grass to the next. A long white-fenced driveway winds half a mile from the road to the house, the last few hundred yards through gardens of professional botanic splendor. The house itself has a sense of elegance and style, built in a time of colonial grandeur, not ostentatious, but with confident taste. Long, low, and white, with handsome lattice windows, beautiful natural timbers, and a wide covered veranda that encircles the house like a shading umbrella. The interior of the house is in perfect matching harmony. Hand-crafted furniture of graceful lines and polished timber, imported from England in a time long past. From room to room a sense of quality, from the paintings on the walls, the chandeliers hanging from the ornate ceilings, the draperies framing the windows. The modern intrusions of television and air conditioning are scarcely noticed in the all-pervading atmosphere of another era. Not the grand elegance of the great houses of Europe, but a superb adaptation to the harsher Australian climate.

Martin Blandhurst lived well. The property was expertly managed, so it took little of his time. Educated in the best schools, well-traveled, sophisticated, Blandhurst was a raconteur, gourmet, and art connoisseur, a former army colonel and now the senior and most influential cabinet minister in the federal government. He was sixty years old, his once-handsome face florid with self-indulgence, the narrow, shrewd eyes now heavily pouched, the lean nose somehow grown longer, a thin mouth spidery with lines, and a former strong chin merging with slack folds of skin. But he was well over six feet tall, and even with a spreading paunch, he was still active. His full white hair, still with the waves of youth and coiffured like a manicured lawn, was an indication of his fastidious sense of dress. On his occasional inspection tours of the property, he was always attired in impeccable dress. In a way, he was out of his century, the country squire, supremely confident that he is born to rule. In another age, not burdened with tiresome democracy, it would have been his natural right to guide the destiny of the nation. It was predestined that he follow his father into politics, and achieve high cabinet rank, even the prime ministership if luck was with him. At the moment he was responsible for the security of the country, and at least that gave him a sense of power.

He had no great philosophical creed except a ferocious determination to hold power. That was all that mattered, and it made him a feared politician. It was inconceivable that any but the natural ruling class should govern the country. To attain that objective, no political maneuver was too ugly, too vicious. Although he had great personal charm, politically he was the ultimate carnivore, and it never ceased to surprise cannibalized victims that a product of the best schools could be so adept at gutter politics.

He had been married to a beautiful, socially acceptable

woman who bore him three children, then departed to a more stimulating union with a wealthy lover in Europe. He pretended indifference, but the manner of her going had harmed him politically. He had always been a sexually active man, his range extending far beyond the matrimonial bed. There were rumors in the town of mysterious, beautiful women descending out of the night in Blandhurst's private plane on to the Sweetwater landing strip, and departing just as mysteriously after a few days. This brought knowing but not condemnatory winks from the men of the town. Such behavior, in a strange way, tended to be a political plus, because it humanized him, made him one of the herd with the same predictable appetites.

Blandhurst had met Leo Starker on a visit to Vietnam when that wretched war was close to collapse. It had been a meeting of compatible minds, with a common concept of a natural ruling class destined to govern at all costs. For days in the sweat of Saigon they talked of little else, for they both knew the war was lost. But it was the beginning of a powerful bond that grew over the years, with constant correspondence and visits to each other's countries. Absolute trust developed between them, and Blandhurst was loud in his approval of Starker's involvement with the Committee of Concerned Americans. He confided to the General that in time such an organization might be necessary in Australia.

When Leo tentatively asked his help with the raid, he almost pleaded for the chance to be involved. It was a perfect meshing of desires, the General to prevent the threat of closure to the American bases in Australia, and his own fierce determination to block fools and nonentities from winning the coming election. The few years they had managed to attain office still rankled like an obscentity in his mind, and any risk was worth taking to prevent that happening again. At least that's what he'd thought until the foul-up at Cape Jaubert. It had shaken him badly enough to seek sedation with any diversion.

So he was occupied when Starker's call came through from Darwin. He had met her at a Sydney function, thirtyish, well-groomed, part of the bored social set, and well aware there was a kinky prestige in being selected for Martin Blandhurst's bed. It was all accomplished with finesse and discretion. No questions asked, no favors expected, a mutually agreed time of availability when her husband was occupied with business. He never ceased to marvel at the abandoned carnality of some of Australia's refined social register. Remove them from the cocktail rounds, with their impeccable manners, nametagged clothes, well-bred accents, then inspire them with the appropriate stimulus, and they would outperform any of the ladies who charged for services rendered. Just watch her now, engulfing him with her mouth like a gluttonous magician, his erection disappearing and reappearing, disappearing and reappearing. Such enthusiasm. It confirmed his long-held belief that sex was all in the head, as much the result of fine breeding as anything else. He sighed and closed his eyes. It was a feeling to make the trauma of Cape Jaubert seem far, far away. And also the horrendous possibility of losing an election. He was sure Leo would resolve that for him.

When the phone rang he was so close to coming his hand groped heavily at the offending instrument as if to strangle the sound. He peered down at the woman's head moving like a rhythmic piston, and her eyes were turned up to him in questioning fashion. He gave a sorrowful shake of his head, twisted free from her, and picked up the receiver. He couldn't risk not taking the call, in case it was Leo. She shrugged, squatted up on her haunches, but left her hand still resting softly on his genitals. She had good breasts, and it was something for him to appreciate while he took the call.

"Martin, it's Leo Starker," came the familiar clipped voice.

There was a slight bump in Blandhurst's pulse. He

hoped it was good news. "Just a moment, Leo," he said. He placed a hand over the mouthpiece and offered a regretful sigh. "I'm sorry, my dear, but I must take this call in private." He offered a gesture of condolence. "There's all the rest of the night yet."

She formed a petulant shape with her mouth. "I must get back to Sydney tonight, darling," she whispered throatily.

He nodded impatiently. "Yes, I understand, but let's talk about it later." He pointed to the adjoining bedroom door. "If you could just wait in the other room for a moment."

She was peeved, but he couldn't help it. She shook her long blond hair about her shoulders, slid her magnificent body into her robe, and stalked from the room. He waited until the door was closed before he resumed the conversation.

"How are you, Leo? I hope you've got some good news for me," he began warily.

Starker was always direct. "I'm sorry, Martin, but I've had an unfortunate development here. I wanted you to know about it."

Blandhurst responded as if an ice pack had been placed on his stomach. For a moment his vocal cords seemed forzen.

"Hello, hello," the General said testily. "Are you there, Martin?"

"Yes. Yes, I'm here."

"I thought we'd been disconnected."

"No. For Christ's sake, don't tell me something else has gone wrong. The Cape Jaubert farce was enough. What do you mean by a bad development?"

"I'm just keeping you up-to-date, Martin, but everything is under control," rasped Starker.

Blandhurst listened, the frost spreading in his belly, while Leo told him of Ross Berger and the damning photographs. Unconsciously he drew the bedcovers tight about his body, seeking reassuring warmth. Sex evaporated from his mind, and his penis sagged into wrinkled defeat. Not since the war had he experienced such real fear. "My God," he gasped hoarsely when Starker had finished. "My God, Leo, if any of this could be traced back to me, I'd be finished. Ruined. I've supported you all along the line, Leo . . . committed myself .   . but this is a disaster . . . and with the elections so close now."

"The elections are why I'm here too, Martin," Starker commented dryly. "There's no need to lose our heads. It *would* have been a disaster if Berger hadn't taken the photographs to Lupane. But he did. That's the important thing. It means we can control the situation. I just thought it important you know everything that's happening."

Blandhurst twisted feverishly on the bed. Damn Leo and his consideration. If it was under control, then he preferred not to know. "But Berger has seen the photographs, Leo." He scarcely recognized the high pitch of his voice. "Maybe he doesn't understand them now, but it could be dangerous to the operation. And after the raid, he's sure to know. Nothing can change that. And if the name of the ship did register in his mind . . ." Fear choked the words in his throat.

"You sent me Lupane, Martin," the General said. "Is he as good as you claim?"

Blandhurst wrenched himself into a sitting position on the edge of the bed. The hell with Lupane. Christ, it was all very well for Leo to be so bloody cool. The General could disappear back to the States, but he'd be left holding the bag. His ear ached from the pressure he was exerting on the receiver. "Yes, Lupane's all I claimed," he assured. "That's why I detailed him from Intelligence to you, Leo. You know I promised him the top job in Intelligence if this worked out. He's a hungry man. He'd murder his own mother for that job. Anyway, he's in so deep now, it's his skin as well as ours. But the hell with Lupane. What about Berger?"

"I've instructed Lupane to take care of the problem, Martin."

"What exactly does that mean?"

There was a pause. Blandhurst could hear the General's heavy breathing, and he realized that for all Leo's composure, he was also feeling the strain.

"It's a military problem, Martin. You don't have to concern yourself."

Blandhurst silently considered the homicidal innuendo. It had come down to more killing. First the photographer, now his brother. The whole plan had seemed nothing more than glorious adventure in the beginning, and now he was deep in blood. Too deep to back out. What Leo had originally proposed as a marvelous election-winning gimmick to solve both their needs now made him feel like a Mafia chieftain. God, how had he, of all people, been naive enough to be sucked into this bog? And with all the information he'd entrusted to Lupane, was he going to spend the rest of his life in some form of blackmailed indebtedness? For once, had blind enthusiasm overruled his natural caution? He had no course but to go on now, with faith in Leo.

"Are you still there, Martin?" demanded Starker's impatient voice.

"The two women you spoke about . . . with Berger. What about them?"

"That's part of the military solution," the General stated coldly.

"I . . . I had no idea it was going to cost lives like this, Leo."

"Neither did I, but there's no going back now. I would have done this with or without your help, Martin. For the good of both our countries. You realize that. I have no alternative to a military solution."

"I don't want to know about it," insisted Blandhurst.

"You're wise. Leave it to me."

"You have a time for the . . . operation?"

"Tomorrow night. No doubt you'll hear about it . . . like the rest of the country. It will be a busy time for you."

"I expect so," Blandhurst said grimly. "Our man . . . from the Russian embassy—he's still safe?"

"Of course. I don't want you to worry about him, or anything else, Martin. He is safe, and well. When the time comes for the raid, the procedure has been well planned for him to be left behind as a corpse. Nothing will go wrong, old friend." His voice took on a more kindly tone. "You'll win your election. This will turn all your opinion polls upside down."

"Very well, Leo," Blandhurst said with resignation. "I know you well enough to have absolute trust. I'll try not to worry."

"I'll be in touch," Starker concluded briskly, and hung up.

Blandhurst was still holding the receiver in his hand when the woman reappeared at the door. He put it down slowly as she posed for him, an enticing smile on her face, hands resting on the door behind her. Her robe hung open provocatively. He scarcely noticed the perfect breasts now, the triangle of black hair so desired before. He looked through her, seeing only the imagined forms of Starker and Lupane coolly engaged in their butchery. He didn't want her anymore. "Get dressed," he said vaguely.

The sexual pose dissolved, her arms dropped to her sides, and the sensual smile vanished from her face.

"Dressed?" she echoed in astonishment.

"Yes. I'm sorry, but . . ." His shoulders twitched ruefully. How could he explain? Lust was gone, and it had nothing to do with her. "As soon as you're ready, I'll have you flown back to Sydney." Her expression moved from surprise to indignation, and he felt a spark of guilt. "I'm sorry, it's not your fault. Things have . . . changed."

A lifetime of sexual conquest had ill-prepared her for rejection. Color flooded her face, and her mouth opened as if to fire a volley of words to match the spite in her expression. Then she changed her mind, wrapped herself tightly in the robe as if shutting the gates for all time, and strode from the room.

Ross knew Lisa was going to come up to his room after dinner. He never actually posed the question, but the meal was charged with an atmosphere of sexual implication. He knew from the way she moved, the way she talked, that it was on her mind. And in a way it puzzled him, because he sensed she had made a decision more as a test, a challenge, than any eager desire. He might have offered a few asides about the view from his room, or a fatuous suggestion that he needed to talk with her further, when everything had been said. But he might as well have held his tongue, because she came without hesitation, and a strange ambivalence he didn't understand. It was as if she wanted to resolve a conflict in her mind, and it made him cautious of touching her. From what she had told him, it wasn't inexperience. He was sure she'd slept with Mark, and maybe that was the problem for both of them. But he was the one with her, not his dead brother; there was nothing more he could do about Mark now—that was in Lupane's hands. Whatever she had felt for Mark, he wanted her to feel it for him.

So he gentled her, not hurrying, trying to align himself to her uncertain pace, a kiss, an almost accidental caress, and she offered no rebuff, going with him, but there was a mechanical lack of emotion in her response. A separation of body and mind: take what you want, but you can't have the real me. At least not yet.

But he stubbornly persisted, when he knew it wasn't going to work, so inevitably he was disappointed. All the things that needed to be done were done, and she was easily compliant, matching caress with caress, feeling and stroking, but he could have been any man, any body, any cock. She spread for him, and he drove hard into her, trying to rouse her with vigor, but she answered with a beat that was more reflex than passion. In the end he was sure she faked orgasm, as if she wanted him out of her, relief from pretense. If it was all pretense, what was she doing here anyway? He gave her up. He pulled out of her, slid off her body and rolled over onto his back.

They lay silently for a while, dissatisfaction like a fence between them. He had wanted this to be the time he could say what he felt for her, but it was all shit now. He couldn't find words to break the silence, and it would have been ridiculous to try to whisper words of love. He thought of a cigarette, but he hadn't smoked in a long time. He wondered if she had any.

"I'm sorry," she whispered.

He didn't look at her. The sole light from the bathroom warmed the shadows of the room. He placed his hands behind his head and stared up at the ceiling.

"You wanted me too fast," she went on. "Maybe I wanted you too, but it's too soon. At least I think it's too soon."

Jesus Christ, it was Mark. He felt a sudden savage anger. Wasn't he ever going to get out of his fucking brother's shadow? "You didn't have to come," he grunted sullenly. "I didn't force you to get into bed, to spread your legs."

She read his tone, and she took time before answering. "I wanted to come. I wanted it to be right. You're a . . . nice man. Maybe something will happen. I'm . . . I'm frightened to let myself go yet. Give me some time. I don't want to get hurt again. Used."

"I guess I just haven't got as big a cock as Mark," he said bitterly, and was immediately repentant. He turned on his elbow to her as she sat up abruptly in the bed, staring angrily at him.

"Look, I didn't mean—" he began, but she cut him off.

"Jesus, it's not easy, you know, passing from brother to brother. How do I know you're not going to go back to Sydney and tell all your mates how you screwed this easy boong in Darwin? Maybe Mark was the same, for all I know."

"Christ, will you forget this boong thing? All I meant about Mark—"

She cut across him again. "I know what you meant. You know you've got a thing about your brother. Maybe you don't think him being dead is such a bad idea after all."

She forced him to swallow hard. He didn't want to believe that. She had pushed him into retreat, and it was his turn to apologize. "Now, wait, Lisa . . . wait." He held up his hands in a gesture of peace. "Don't let's get into this. I mean all I've said to you. I want you to come to Sydney, to stay with my parents. I . . . I think I'm falling in love with you. I'll give you all the time you want."

She swiveled her body away from him and put her feet down on the floor. Her dark skin shone with a velvet sheen in the soft light. "Thanks a lot."

"I mean it."

"Sure you do. You *think* you love me? Just long enough for you to screw me again."

"Don't be crazy. Of course I think. It's only been two days. You're not going to believe me if I say I'm madly in love with you. I was hoping it meant something to you."

"It doesn't," she said flatly.

He didn't believe her. She was angry, just using words.

She turned back to him on the bed. "What do you call love?" she questioned fiercely. She brushed her hands swiftly across her breasts, over her belly, and into her crotch. "Is this what you call love?"

"It's more than that. Christ, don't take all your hurt out on me, Lisa. It's not my fault you've had it rough. Give me a chance? I do love you."

"Go to hell," she answered furiously. "You've had your fuck, you don't have to soft-soap me with that phony shit." She stood up angrily, moved to the chair, and hastily began to dress.

He'd never imagined her like this, yet all the fire only

made her more beautiful. He watched from the bed,
stupefied into silence, aware of how badly he had handled
the situation. "I don't want you to go like this," he said
finally.

Suddenly, ridiculously, it seemed the most important
thing in his life she didn't go like this. "Okay, I said a
stupid thing . . . it's none of my business . . . but at least
let's talk about it."

"Leave me alone," she blurted. "Go back to Sydney. Go
back and bury your brother."

He slouched back in the bed and scrubbed his fingers
despondently through his hair. He couldn't get through to
her. She had been badly wounded in the past, and it had
made her more fragile than he realized. She was wary of
trusting anyone. The tough shield was part pretense. The
white dress he had so admired on their first meeting fell
into place, and she thrust her feet angrily into her shoes.

"After the funeral you can tell your pals about the boong
tart in Darwin, who was a lousy screw anyway," she flung
at him.

He eased himself off the bed and stepped tentatively
toward her. He had some unformed idea in his mind that
if he could touch her again, feel her, everything would
come right. "That's crazy talk," he said hoarsely. "For
God's sake, cut out the boong thing. I'm sick of the sound
of the bloody word."

"People like you don't let me forget it," she cried.

"That's ridiculous." He took several more cautious steps
in her direction, and she raised her hands defensively.

"Don't come near me, Ross. Believe me, I know the
score," she warned.

"I think you're the most fantastic woman I've ever met,"
he tried again. "I'm just trying to make you believe it."
He reached for her, and she hit him. Not hard, but with
the back of her hand, and it stung. She was at once
contrite, her hands clenched in front of her mouth, and for
a moment he thought she was going to cry.

He sat back on the bed and studied her solemnly. "You're mixed up," he said. "Crazy. But I understand why, I really do. Let's forget tonight. You leave if you want to. But I'm going to see you again. And I think you want to see me again."

Her expression was more confusion than anything else. She backed away from him toward the door. "I . . . I have to go."

"I'll call you tomorrow," he persisted.

She shook her head. "Got to go," she repeated. "Jo will be worried."

He could feel the flesh tingling on the side of his face where she'd struck him. "I *know* I love you," he said.

She paused at the door and stared at him for a long moment, and he thought she was considering coming back to him. Even if she left, he had the feeling he'd won, he was believed. He meant every word of it. Forget the blond dancer in Soho, the sex-crazy bird in Honduras, this was the first woman he'd wanted for all time. And he wasn't going to let go. If there had been something with Mark, then the hell with it. "Tomorrow," he repeated.

She shook her head slowly, her eyes wide. "Maybe."

"And for as many days after that as there are," he added.

She fled from the room.

He went to the window and watched her get into her car. He had a fleeting memory of old Pat Tanna, the way she revved the engine and took off down the road at a speed so uncharacteristic of her cautious driving. It was another confirmation for him. He couldn't ever remember wanting anything so much.

Garcott lit a cigarette and peered through the windshield at the apartment house.

"What d'you think?" he asked Lupane.

Lupane lifted his wrist to the streetlight and checked

the time. "We'll wait until three o'clock." He was on
edge, and it showed in his voice.

The car was parked about a hundred yards down the
road from the building. It had stopped raining, but the
streetlights glistened in the black sheen of the wet road.
Garcott shrugged and slumped down in the seat. "It's
three hours ago now since I saw her drive home. And an
hour since you joined me. She hasn't moved out of the
apartment. Jesus, she'd be sound asleep by now, Mike,"
he grunted. He inclined his head toward the building.
"We're goin' to be pushin' time," he warned. "After we fix
the Marnoo bird, we've got to get over to Wulagi to take
care of the Santeze baby, then get to the motel and wrap
up Berger." He drew hard on the cigarette and blew a
smoke haze at the windshield. "Three o'clock's fine if
everything runs smooth, but it doesn't give us any margin.
Know what I mean?"

Lupane unnecessarily checked the time again. It was
two-thirty. "I'll decide," he said bluntly. He was nervous,
and Garcott knew it. It was all right for a bastard like
Garcott, who didn't know what scruples meant. Who didn't
think any more about killing people than he would of
stepping on an ant. "You checked out the Santeze girl's
apartment this afternoon?" he questioned sourly.

"Yeah. Evidently the guy she was livin' with has moved
out. Which makes it nice and easy for us. We might have
had to take him as well." He sniggered. "From what I
learned about the way he's been beating her up, he's a
perfect fit to take the rap. I checked her work place, and
they said she was off sick for the day. We couldn't have
asked for it better. She won't give us any trouble." He
pointed with his cigarette to the apartment house, an ugly
grin on his face. "I'm quite lookin' forward to this one. I
haven't tried the boong stuff yet. I'm hard just thinkin'
about it."

In the darkness Lupane made no effort to keep the
contempt out of his face. Fucking animal. Garcott was

efficient, and necessary, but he'd never made it out of the caves. He would have been at home among the apes. This had to be done, but for this creep it was like looking forward to a party. He could have just left it to Garcott, but it was too important, and Starker would expect him to handle it personally. He had no intention of keeping his promise to take Garcott with him to the top of Intelligence if they pulled this off. He'd get rid of him somehow; there was no place for a psychopath where he was going.

"Starker approved the plan?" Garcott asked.

"No. I didn't tell him."

"I thought he'd want to know."

Lupane gave a short, cynical laugh. "Quite the opposite. The bloody-minded old bastard doesn't want to know. Doesn't want to dirty his own lily-white hands. That's only for idiots like us. He's probably fast asleep right now, without even a bad dream on his mind. He doesn't give a fuck who dies, just as long as he doesn't have to do it."

He looked at Garcott, but the man was scarcely listening. The creep didn't even know what he was talking about. This was the natural thing for Garcott, his bread and butter.

Lupane shuffled around on the seat and appraised the deserted street. It was a graveyard, and he sniffed contemptuously. He'd be glad to get back to Sydney. At least the place was alive.

It was beginning to rain again, and a pattern of droplets quickly obscured vision through the windshield. Perhaps Garcott was right: they were cutting it fine to wait. He opened the door and nodded to the other man. "Okay, we'll go now."

They climbed out in unison, pushed the doors delicately shut; then hugging the shadows, they paced quickly toward the apartment building. The weeping drizzle was an added concealing cloak. One house light at the far end indicated a solitary insomniac, but the remainder of the street was deep in sleep. They went silently into the entrance, each man knowing exactly what he was going to do. The lock on the apartment door was child's play for Garcott, and they were quickly into the room. They stood close together for a cautious moment, listening, waiting for their eyes to adjust to the darkness. The blind was drawn on the solitary front window, and the outline of the room was barely discernible. The soft, even sound of someone breathing came from the darkness. Garcott flicked on the pencil flashlight and swept the narrow beam around in a rapid circuit. Table, casual chairs, television, dividing cupboard to a small kitchen, and a bed in the far corner, the sleeping girl's hair black against the white pillow. Garcott switched off the light and put it back in his pocket. It seemed even darker than before. Lupane could hear Garcott's quick, palpitating breath, a man on the edge of anticipation, mingling with the sound of the sleeping girl. He shut his mind to what they were about to do. "You see her?" he whispered unnecessarily.

Garcott answered with a swift impatient flick of his hand. "Let's go," he muttered.

They moved silently across the room and halted at the bed. The dim shape of the girl's head was outlined by the pillow. Her arms were outside the covers and crossed over her breasts. Lupane stared down at her, not moving. He thought of his dreams, and how good it would have been to have had this girl, her wanting as much as him. Now he had to do this to survive. He moved with surprising speed, jerking the pillow abruptly from beneath the girl's head, thrusting it savagely over her face, then leaning forward in the same motion, seizing her wrists and clamping her arms back over the pillow, one on each side of her head in a form of self-locking device. Just for an instant there was no reaction from the girl, as if her mind was grappling to decide between nightmare and reality. Then, as if she grasped that it was horrendous reality, her body arched up in convulsive fear, her arms fought to free themselves

from Lupane's grip, and muffled sounds of terror came
from beneath the pillow.

"Quickly," Lupane muttered urgently. "For Chrissake,
make it quick."

Garcott was ahead of him. Already he had the covers
thrust back to the girl's waist, scrabbling eagerly up onto
the bed, hands gripping her ankles, violently levering her
legs upward and wide apart. It was like holding a caught
fish, each limb gyrating in a frenzied desire to be free. In
the semidarkness Lupane saw the pale tubular shape of
Garcott's erection jutting out from his crotch; then it was
gone, thrusting forward into the girl. For a moment the
brutal penetration halted her struggles, as if her mind was
still confused between nightmare and hideous reality. But
then, movement for her was almost impossible. Lupane
had his entire bulk pressed on the pillow, and Garcott had
her legs trapped tightly under his arms, savagely driving
at her, so the stifled sound of her cries was the only
resistance she could offer.

"Hurry," urged Lupane. "You son of a bitch, you're not
having a good time with a whore . . . get it over with."

Garcott ignored him. He was like a man on fire. Hours
of waiting in the car, primed with anticipation, left him no
answer but the guttural, lust-driven grunts emerging from
his throat. They merged with the scuffling sound of his
body thrusting at the girl, and the piteous cries filtering
from beneath the pillow. Then the scuffling increased to a
frantic tempo, and the grunts transformed into a long-
drawn moan of pleasure. The pumping action of his body
slowed, then halted. He released the girl's legs, and they
fell loosely to the bed, like dead things beyond struggle.
Then Garcott clambered back to his feet, the zipping
sound of his fly magnified by the sudden silence of the
room. The girl didn't move, her legs inert where Garcott
had released them, her body stilled by fear and exhaustion, an occasional muffled whimper still escaping from
under the pillow.

"I guess you could say she's well and truly raped," Garcott sniggered.

Lupane glanced anxiously about the room. "Come on, you bastard, get it over with."

Garcott fumbled in his pocket and moved around to the side of the bed. "Don't get you guts full of chickenshit, Mike." He sneered. "Everything's under control. What's the matter, you uptight because I was the one elected to screw the girl?" He giggled unpleasantly. "Maybe you wouldn't be able to operate in this situation, eh . . . is that it?"

"Just do it," he said coldly. The worst part was having to work with shit like Garcott. "Move," he ordered sharply.

Garcott pushed his hands into the gloves he'd brought with him, and took the knife from his pocket. He hesitated a moment over the still form on the bed, then raised the knife over his head and plunged it into her body just below the breasts. Once, twice, three times. The girl merely uttered a startled grunt, gave a slight jerk of her body, then lay slackly on the bed.

Garcott laconically wiped the knife on the sheet and put it back in his pocket. "She's had it," he announced to Lupane. He took off the gloves and put them in the same pocket as the knife. Lupane waited silently for a moment, then released the girl's wrists. At the last second, just before the stabbing, he had turned his head away, and he hoped Garcott hadn't seen him. It was important to hold his authority over Garcott, but the creep had no respect for anyone who didn't share his cold-blooded sadism. He bent forward and checked for any pulse in her neck. There was nothing. Her arms remained in the position he had held them, curved back over the pillow. His stomach rumbled in protest, and he tasted vomit in his mouth. He shuffled uneasily away from the corpse. For some macabre reason he could hear the sound of her voice, recall the image of her white smile.

He swallowed hard and fought to control his stomach. Vomiting in front of Garcott would be a dangerous admission of weakness.

Garcott motioned to the pillow over her head. "You don't need that anymore."

It was dark, but even in the dim light Lupane was repelled by the thought of seeing her dead face. "Leave it," he said harshly.

"Okay." Garcott stepped away from the bed, and moved slowly toward the door. "Do you want to stick to the same timetable? We go to Berger first at the motel, plant the knife on him, then arrest him for rapin' and murderin' this bird. Or should we go to the Santeze bird first and take care of her? I know you said Berger, but I was wonderin' if it might be easier to take the woman first. What with havin' to arrest Berger and charge him."

Lupane cleared his throat before answering. He wanted to be out of the room, away from what they had done to the girl. He swallowed away the curdled sourness of his mouth and forced an authoritative tone. "We stick to the original schedule. We take Berger first."

"How do you want to handle it? Do I take Berger?"

Lupane could tell by the sneering inflection that Garcott knew the answer without asking. Well, that's what he had a hatchet man for. Why should he have to pull the trigger when he had a goon on the payroll to do the job?

"We wait until we get him away from the motel," he said tersely. "We don't want any witnesses. It shouldn't be hard to find a place to make it look convincing he made a break for it. Yeah, you'd better be the one to shoot him. And make sure it's in the back, like I said—as if he was running away." He didn't mind about Berger. Not like the Marnoo girl. Berger was a smart-ass, and there was a certain amount of satisfaction about him getting his come-uppance. "I think we'd better drive around for a short time. Make it look right, as if Berger had time to get back to the motel and into bed after the killing."

"Is that goin' to leave me time to get to the Santeze girl?"

"We'll make the time. We'll have to." He pushed Garcott ahead of him toward the door. "And like I said, just disappear the Santeze girl. I don't want her body showing up for a while. It would only complicate this frame we're fitting on Berger. The guy who's been beating her up can answer for that one."

"I picked out a good place—over near the swamp."

"I'll leave that to you. I won't come with you to the Santeze girl's apartment." He took one last hesitant glance at the room. "If we want to fit that guy for the killing, you might have to . . . make it look good."

Garcott thwacked his fist into his hand, an obscene sound. He would enjoy that. "Don't worry, I'll make it look good."

"I'm sure you will."

Lupane eased the door carefully open and scanned the street. It still had the appearance of an abandoned city. The rain was heavier now, and the night was a medley of staccato drops and gurgling rainspouts. "I want to leave any investigation of the Santeze girl to the local people," he murmured as an afterthought. "So I don't want her body turning up until we're long gone from here. They'll know about the guy she was living with beating her up. They'll make it stick. That should please our friend at Beton. All nice and legal to keep Martin's hands clean." He took Garcott's elbow and urged him through the door. "Take it easy," he warned. "No need to hurry. Nice and casual, and stay with the shadows along the side of the street until we get to the car."

He saw the sneer on Garcott's face as he moved out, and felt a spur of irritation. Maybe he did sound like a timid rabbit, but they were playing a dangerous game, and for high stakes. He guessed no one was going to be peeking through windows at this time of night in this dead place. Garcott was too stupid to realize it, but it was their own necks they were saving, apart from anything else.

Lisa wasn't sure what had woken her. She had lain long without sleep after coming home, Ross on her mind, and even when she had finally succumbed, it had only been to a semiconscious state of dreaming. But the waking disturbance was hard to identify, except that it seemed to be composed of whispered, menacing words. It frightened her. She lay there straining her ears, while the rising beat of her heart diffused the sounds. It was a quarter to three by the luminous dial of her alarm clock. She debated if she should get up or call out and ask Jo if she was all right. She feared the violence of the man Jo had been living with, and her first thought was that he might have broken in to see her friend. Maybe to try to force her to come back to him.

She finally came to a decision, slipped silently off the couch, padded to the door, and peered nervously out into the darkened living room. Something was happening on the bed. She could just see the dim shapes of figures, hear the rustle of sheets and a hoarse grunting sound. And a muted whimpering, like a trapped animal. Her breath thickened in her throat. Was it what she feared, that Jo's boyfriend had broken in and was over there on the bed with her? Should she walk boldly into the room and confront him? But she recognized the pleasure sounds of a man in a woman, the same sounds she had heard from Ross, and it made her hesitate. It would be an embarrassment if there was a passionate reconciliation taking place on the bed. The breathless grunts terminated in a drawn-out moan; then there was silence. Still she hesitated.

"Come on, you bastard, get it over with," she heard a grating voice say.

She froze. The true meaning of rigid fear came to her, because she couldn't move. She recognized the voice, a man who had pressured her, to whom she had taken an

instant dislike. The detective Lupane. In her apartment?
At this hour? With Jo? Then she heard another sound, too
horrifying to identify, a sound she might have made herself by thrusting a knife into a thick-skinned vegetable.
Once, twice, three times. Then another voice, unfamiliar,
terrifying, coldly declaring, "She's had it," and the whimpering sound was gone. Lisa wanted to scream, but her
mouth was so dried of saliva she was scarcely capable of
sucking air into her lungs. Strength bled from her body,
her legs buckled, and she clung desperately to the door
for support. She hung there, her breath coming in gasping
puffs, listening with dazed horror to the men discussing
their plans for the night. Only the pain from her fingers
fiercely clinging to the door convinced her she was awake,
not caught in some terrifying nightmare. In spite of her
grip, she sagged slowly to the floor, until she was slumped
against the wall. She stayed there, staring blankly into the
darkness, every overheard word fixed with eerie clarity in
her mind.

She heard Lupane's final sentence about Starker and his
friend at Beton; then there was the click of the closing
door, and only the brushing sound of rain on the window.
She didn't know how long she lay there, her mouth wide,
gasping air, the thrum of her heart gradually subsiding.
There was no sound from the bed. She had to go to Jo, but
she dreaded what she might find. Whatever they had
done to her friend, there was no doubt from their conversation that they'd thought it was Lisa in the bed. God, but
why? They were going to cold-bloodedly murder all of
them. Fear enveloped her again like fever, and she struggled to control her trembling. She couldn't just lie there.
She had to get to her feet. There was Jo . . . and Ross . . .
God, she had to warn Ross. Somehow she made it to her
feet, staggered into the kitchen, and fumbled in the drawer
where she kept the flashlight. She was terrified by the
thought of switching on the overhead light. They could be
waiting out there in the street, just to make sure, and

what if they saw the light come on? There'd be no second chance for her. No ghastly piece of luck that had put poor Jo in her place. She flicked on the flash, directing the beam to the floor so no light splayed around, and groped her way unsteadily to the bed. She kept her back to the window so that none of the light would show outside, then cautiously shone the beam onto the bed. She moved closer, forcing herself to stare at the blood-soaked sheet gleaming in the light, Jo's arms hooked back over the pillow hiding her face, her legs spread loosely on the bed. Tears spilled down Lisa's cheeks and wetly onto her neck, but she made no effort to stem the flow. The bastards, the vicious bastards. For the moment an amalgam of pity and anger blocked the realization that but for chance it would have been her on the bed, her blood, her terror.

Gently she lifted Jo's arms back to her sides and removed the pillow. In a way she was prepared for the look of death, even the thin trickle of blood from the mouth, but not the staring, horror-filled eyes. Not from Jo, after all her love, all her understanding. It broke her. The flashlight slipped from her fingers to clatter to the floor as she stumbled against the wall with a retching cry and violently disgorged the contents of her stomach. Even as she crouched there, the muscles of her stomach aching, she knew she had to call Ross. Call him quickly, warn him. Lupane had spoken about driving around for a short time, but it wouldn't be long before they headed for the motel. Ross wouldn't have a chance, not with anyone vicious enough to do a thing like this to Jo. Or to her if they got the chance. But why? In God's name, why? She couldn't even try to answer that question, not now.

She levered herself weakly to her feet and scrubbed at her dank mouth with the back of her hand. Her nose caught the stench of her violated stomach, and for a moment she thought she would retch again. She ran her fingers distractedly through her hair, pressed her mouth into a tight, determined line, and dragged herself awkwardly toward the telephone.

Ross knew someone was calling him. He turned restlessly in bed, tangling the covers, trying to stifle the sound. It must be schooltime, and he hated rising early. Only his mother would be that persistent. She was calling . . . no, she was knocking . . . no, in some strange way she was ringing. He jerked upright in the bed as the jangle of the telephone brought him back to consciousness. He pawed the sleep from his eyes and switched on the lamp. He saw by his watch it was just after three o'clock. Who the hell would be ringing him at this time of the morning? He clamped the receiver to his face and slumped back on the pillow. "Hello," he muttered.

For an instant his partially wakened stupor prevented recognition of the answering voice. The thin, thready tone, on the edge of hysteria, defied identification. "Ross . . . Ross . . . it's me . . . it's me," repeated the voice.

"Who the hell is me?" he asked blearily.

"It's Lisa . . . Lisa Marnoo."

"Lisa," he responded dully. Comprehension came slowly, and he took another puzzled glance at his watch. Surely she didn't want to talk about their sex disaster at this hour of the morning, when it had already taken him hours to get to sleep because of her. Then he grasped at the terrified inflection in her voice, and it swept the sleep from his mind.

"Lisa, what's the matter—are you all right?" he asked with concern.

"Don't speak, Ross . . . don't say anything . . . just listen to me." Her words came in short, gasping bursts, as if she was having trouble breathing.

"Just tell me you're all right," he urged.

"Listen . . . I said just listen," she continued with the same breathless urgency. "You have to believe what I'm . . . going to tell you . . . and don't question me . . .

understand . . . not a word. Lupane . . . and another man have been here . . . at my apartment . . . they've just left—"

"At this time of the morning?" he said incredulously. "What were—

"For Chrissake . . . will you just shut up and listen!" She shrilled at him. "They've killed Jo . . . murdered her." She was forced to stop, her voice obliterated by strangled sobs, and he could only wait in shocked silence. "Oh God . . . it's horrible . . . poor Jo," she cried.

"I'm coming over," he said firmly.

"No . . . no . . . stay where you are," she protested wildly. "They made a mistake with Jo . . . they thought they were killing me. It was dark . . . they didn't know I was here. Oh Christ . . . I can't explain it all now, but . . . but they're on their way to see you, Ross . . . right now . . . they're going to arrest you for Jo's murder . . . frame you . . . then fake an escape attempt . . . and kill you too." She was forced to stop again, as sobbing took over control of her voice. He was trying to grasp what she was saying, take in a horror story that had him as one of the main characters . . . but made no sense. His brain cells scrambled into a traffic jam: Lupane a murderer? . . . Jo murdered? . . . Why try to kill Lisa? . . . Or him? . . . Or anybody? It was crazy. He had an instant, ludicrous flash that it was all some insane joke by Lisa, she was getting back at him for what had happened between them. He knew instantly it was nonsense; she meant every word she was saying. "Oh Christ," he said.

"Get out," she started up again. Her hysteria was still there, but she was just managing to keep it under control. "Get out, Ross. Get out of the motel . . . now . . . as fast as you can. I've seen what these monsters can do. Don't stop for anything. You've maybe got a few minutes, because they were going to drive around . . . just so they could claim you had time to get back to the motel after the

. . . murder. But don't stop for anything, Ross—luggage . . . nothing. Just get out of the motel."

It was insane, but he had to accept it. There was no doubting the fear being transmitted to him, the urgency of her warning. Even while he still held the receiver, he was reaching for his shirt, slipping his feet into his shoes. He felt no fear. It was like old times, an automatic response to a life-threatening situation that had saved him in the Gulf of Mexico, saved him in Trujillo. Get out. Run. That's what Aldo had said to him, except Aldo hadn't made it. Ross had a fleeting thought that he should stay and face them, since he was forewarned now. But that was crazy. He didn't even have a gun. If they had already killed Jo, he wouldn't have a prayer. What the hell it all meant would have to wait for later.

"I'll go the East Point Reserve where we had lunch today," he said urgently. "Can you come there?"

"No . . . no, listen, Ross, they'll see you if you start running around the streets at this time of the morning. Go out the back of the motel . . . wait around there . . . in the shadows. I'll come and pick you up in the car. I don't know how long Lupane will take to get there . . . how long he'll drive around . . . but maybe I can beat them to the motel. I'll have to risk it."

She paused, and he could still hear the stifled sobs in her throat. But she was more under control, as if the first impact was already passing. "If they see me, they'll kill me too, Ross. They think they already have, and I don't want to give them another chance. God, they're . . . maniacs."

He was into his trousers, zipping up the fly. "Okay, I'll wait for you out the back," he said. "Take care." Then he hung up. He made a supreme effort to quell the turmoil in his mind. A policeman suddenly turns into a homicidal maniac? He hadn't figured Lupane for that sort of psychopath. And who was the other man Lisa had talked about? He thought of the thin-faced sullen man he'd met in Lupane's office. Garcott. Maybe it had been him, not that it mattered right now. He threw on his jacket, pushed some money into his pocket, and was heading toward the door when he saw the photographs lying on the dresser. Maybe they had something to do with this? It made as much sense as anything else, and they were the reason for his last visit to Lupane. But Jesus, were they worth killing three people for? He swiftly picked them up, thrust them into his jacket pocket, and went rapidly out the door.

The motel was hushed with sleep. He went at a crouched half-trot down the corridor, his feet whispering over the carpet. He went down the stairs on the balls of his feet, taking them two and three at a time. He halted uncertainly at the bottom. For all he knew, Lupane might be already coming through the front entrance, and it would be lunacy to go past the reception desk. There had to be a rear exit. He turned and headed toward the back of the building, infected by Lisa's desperate urgency. He found a door, not at the rear, but leading out into the side street. It was unlocked, and he passed through into the recessed doorway, then halted in the shadows. The wind was like a draft of air from a heating vent, throwing rain in his face. He heard the sound of a car from the front of the motel, and he knew he had to move. He stepped out from the door, hands thrust into his pockets, shoulders hunched against the rain, and walked rapidly around to the rear of the building. It was sparsely lit by a solitary light from the side street, and he selected a place where he could merge easily with the shadows. He pushed himself tightly against the wall and waited. He didn't try to count the time. It could have been fifteen minutes; it seemed like fifteen hours. Even now the killers might be searching his room or prowling the building looking for him, and he had to control the constant urge to bolt, to put as much distance as possible between the motel and himself. He realized now the hastily conceived plan to meet Lisa at the back of the motel was too dangerous, but he had no option but to wait. And he had no chance at all without a car. The rain

soaked down, flattening his hair, making a running foun-
tain of his face. He scarcely noticed. He thought of Jo, the
dark sadness of her eyes, picturing her slaughtered like
he'd seen so many others. He thought of Mark. Of the
photographs in his pocket. Of the sound of Lisa's terrified
voice. But the reason for it all engendered nothing but
confusion.

He watched the headlights come slowly around the far
corner of the street like wary bugs cautiously feeling their
way. The vehicle stopped at the rear wall of the motel,
and he recognized Lisa's car. The door opened, and he
moved swiftly across the intervening space. He crouched
down and peered into the car. She was leaning forward
over the steering wheel, and even in the dim light of the
dashboard there was an expression he'd never seen on her
face before. An expression he recognized, that he'd seen
in other faces, in another time, another place. Like a
scorch mark from the hot breath of near-death.

"Are you okay?" he asked quickly.

She nodded, her eyes darting uncertainly at the windshield and beyond him to the rain-swept street. "I know a
place where we can go . . . where we'll be safe," she said
breathlessly. "Get in. We'll have to hurry. Lupane can't
be far away."

"You want me to drive?" he offered. "Just in case there's
some hard driving needed. You can show me the way."

She agreed with a wordless sense of relief and slid
across to the passenger side. She had on the same white
dress as when he'd last seen her, but no makeup, and her
hair was an uncombed ruffle about her head. He shut the
door and paced quickly around to the driver's side of the
car. He crouched down to enter, and the sound of the shot
and the whine of the bullet gouging across the roof of the car
joined in simultaneous sound.

Stupidly he thrust his head back into the air in startled
reaction, and stared in the direction of the shot. He immediately recognized Lupane's bulk, standing at the far cor-

ner of the motel. There was a car parked behind the
detective, lights on, and the starting thrum of the engine
burred on the sodden air.

"Stop right where you are, Berger," Lupane bawled.

Ross ignored the order. He thrust himself forward behind the steering wheel, slammed the door, and gunned
the motor. He had no time to look at Lisa, but he felt her
shrink down in the seat. If he needed any further proof of
Lisa's frantic warning, then Lupane had provided ample
verification with the shot.

"Which way?" he screamed at her.

She pointed a trembling finger at the windshield. "To
. . . to the end of the . . . the street . . . and turn left,"
she stuttered.

He snapped the car into drive, jerked his foot off the
brake, rammed down on the accelerator, and the tires
howled with the effort of trying to grip the wet road. He
was sure Lupane would expect him to attempt a turn in
the opposite direction, but there was no time for that, it
would make him an easy target. He had a better chance if
he risked the unexpected.

There was another flash from Lupane's hand, but no
sound of an impacting bullet. The tires grabbed, and the
car took off with neck-snapping acceleration. He spun the
wheel, weaving the car violently from one side of the road
to the other; then he saw the vehicle behind Lupane
beginning to creep forward into the corner to block his
path. It was a large, powerful model, and he knew the
BMW would come off second best in a collision.

"Hold on," he gritted to Lisa.

She shrank back in the seat as the gun flashed again,
and there was the thunk of the bullet striking somewhere
against the car. Then they were past the gesticulating form
of Lupane, almost into the corner, and the other car was
coming fast. Ross held course until the last minute, then
hit the brake hard and wrenched the wheel over. The tail
of the car caromed around on the wet road in a wild spin,

the rear bumper struck the near front side of the other
vehicle with a jarring crash, then Ross thumped the accelerator again. The wheels spun frantically, spewing water,
gripped with a shriek of rubber, then the car gathered
beneath him like a greyhound and raced into the night.
Driving for the drug mobs in Miami had taught him
something. He glanced quickly into the rearview mirror.
The image of the other car was already shrinking fast, one
light still on, but obviously not moving. Certainly not
chasing.

"Where?" he snapped at Lisa again.

She pointed ahead once more, her mouth moving, but
without accompanying words. He knew she had just gone
through the most terrifying experience of her life, but he
had no time for sympathy. Not now. He wanted to survive
just as much as she did.

"For Chrissake, Lisa, they're going to be after us in a
moment. Which direction?"

"Straight . . . straight ahead," she said. Her voice was
pitched unnaturally high, but at least she managed to
articulate. Her raised hand still wove unsteadily about in
the air; then she dropped it down on her lap. "This . . .
this is the Stuart Highway," she added. "It'll take us . . .
out of Darwin. Follow the road around past the airport."

He gave a savage grunt of thanks, then settled down
grimly over the wheel. He pushed the car hard, and it
responded as if sharing their desire to survive, the engine
purring with effortless power. They'd been lucky. It looked
as if he had damaged the other car just sufficiently to
prevent pursuit. Thank Christ he'd taken over the wheel.
He felt good. The burr of the wipers and the swish of the
tires over the wet road combined into a comforting sound.
He went through the intersection at the perimeter of the
airport without slackening speed, gambling on an absence
of traffic at this hour. The dark expanse of the airport came
up on the left, sleek silhouettes of jets at rest, isolated
pockets of light transformed into fuzzed baubles by the

rain. Streetlights fled past the windows, flicking the interior of the car with intermittent illumination. He took a quick glance at Lisa, hunched against the door. In the alternating light, her face had a wet sheen like the road ahead. The wetness of tears trickling unchecked down her face. She stared unseeingly through the windshield, her hands cast limply in her lap. He took one hand cautiously from the wheel and laid it comfortingly over hers. Just for a moment, to show he understood. He had wept for Aldo, and he knew the feeling. All the anger, all the shit, the hot words that had passed between them in the bedroom last night, were irrelevant now. But he didn't ask her about Jo. Not yet. Maybe it could wait until they got to this place, wherever it was they were going, but he wasn't going to push her. Best let her grief run for a while; the questions would come later. But he suspected she had no more idea than he what it all meant, why in Christ they were running for their lives, why Lupane wanted them dead as well as Jo. But he had to know where they were going.

"Where are we headed?" he asked gently.

She didn't answer immediately. Then she seemed to brace her shoulders and lift herself in the seat, as if she knew grief couldn't be allowed to interfere with survival. She dabbed at her cheeks with her fingers, but she still didn't look at him. "Out of Darwin," she whispered. She was under control, the high pitch gone from her voice. "This place—we'll be safe there. At least for a while. We can't stay in the city . . . not after what I saw them do to Jo. We wouldn't have a chance, Ross. Not a chance. They're . . . they're animals."

He nodded silently, but didn't press her about Jo. He would let her set her own time on that. "How far to this place?" he asked.

"Maybe a hundred and fifty or sixty kilometers," she murmured uncertainly.

His surprised glance went from her to the fuel gauge. It showed full, so there was no gas problem.

"We'll be safe there," she repeated, as if to convince herself. "At least until we work out what to do. It'd be too dangerous to go down the main highway to Katherine. That's probably where they'd be looking for us." Her voice trailed off into silence again.

The streetlights disappeared, the houses thinned and were gradually replaced by the broken outline of the bush. The rain beat against the windshield with a light pattering sound. Occasionally he glanced into the rearview mirror, but there was no sign of any following headlights. It confirmed his estimate about damage to their car. A main-road fork came up in the headlights, and Lisa pointed left. He noted with satisfaction the steadiness of her hand now.

"Left," she instructed. "Out along the Arnhem Highway."

He obeyed without slackening speed, and the car slewed into the turn with a whining protest of tires. He straightened with a flick of the wheel, and sent it boring into the darkness of the new heading. They went on for a time in silence. He gave the car no respite, squeezing for every ounce of performance. It was as if they were fleeing through the black emptiness of an uninhabited planet.

"The bastards," she mumbled at his side.

He didn't look at her, eyes fixed to the highway.

"The bastards," she repeated.

He knew she was ready to talk. The grief was still there, but garnished with a cutting edge of anger. It was what he expected from her; she would want to hit back, not crawl away and hide. Like him, she was a survivor.

"No human being should be treated like that," she muttered. "You've got to make them pay for Jo, Ross."

"Tell me about it," he said quietly.

She told him, in a flat voice drained of emotion, as if she had decided that was the way to retain self-control. Occasionally her voice cracked, and she would halt to regain

composure, but he let her go on at her own pace. And he
was chilled in a way he had never experienced before. A
touch of ice on his spine that forced him to hunch his body
as if seeking warmth. He was joined to her in a common
bond of anger. He might have disliked Lupane, but he
hadn't suspected him of being a monster. If he did get the
chance to face the bastard, there would be no time for
questions and answers, only the urge to kill Lupane first.
And he wanted answers. Why the hell were all three of
them on Lupane's hit list? What had they done? What had
they found out? What sort of policeman deliberately sets
out to murder three people? Ross grieved for Jo, but he
shivered at the realization that it was only chance it had
happened to Jo instead of Lisa. Lisa was right, he'd make
the fuckers pay. But Lisa didn't have any more idea as to
why than he did. The question kept hammering away at
his brain, with no hope of answer, as they raced into the
night. Why? Why? Why?

For twenty minutes Lupane and Garcott wrestled furiously to free the fender jammed against the front wheel,
then gave it up in disgust. And the confusion in Lupane's
mind was equally unresolved. Unbelievably, he had seen
the Marnoo girl in the car with Berger. He was positive he
hadn't been mistaken, her face had showed so clearly in
the streetlight as the car went past. It had been no error,
no trick of light. He had been so stunned by the sight of
that terrified face that his finger had frozen on the trigger
of the gun. His mind told him it was impossible, yet she
had been there. That sort of resurrection was inconceivable. The girl back in the apartment was dead beyond
doubt, so who in the hell was it they'd killed? He had
tried to clear his mind before saying anything to Garcott,
but that obviously wasn't going to happen.
He glanced morosely toward the motel entrance. A few
bleary-eyed people had emerged, disturbed by the shooting, only to be curtly ordered back with an authoritative

display of his credentials. The motel manager had been instructed to call a tow truck, but where the hell was it?

They both stood back from the car, staring helplessly at the snared wheel, feeling damp and foolish in the rain.

"Berger'll be bloody miles away by now," Garcott said savagely. "Where the hell did he learn to drive like that?"

"Does it matter?" Lupane answered sullenly. "Maybe the Marnoo girl was showing him."

Garcott opened his mouth, then snapped it shut again. "What's that supposed to mean?"

"She was in the car."

Garcott moved into the headlights to peer at Lupane, a baffled expression on his face. "What sort of a crazy statement is that? You know where the Marnoo girl is."

Lupane lashed out angrily with his foot at the bent fender. "She was in the car . . . sitting alongside Berger. I saw her as they went past."

"You're outta your mind. Your eyes were playin' tricks on you, Mike. She's not drivin' around in any cars . . . not tonight, or any other night."

"No, I wasn't mistaken. It was her."

Garcott laughed derisively. "Jesus, I can't believe what I'm hearing. You were there when I stuck the bird. You think she's goin' to get up and drive around in a car after that?" The rain on his face glistened in the car lights. "You were seein' things . . . you had to be." He stared uncertainly at Lupane. "I'm not in the mood for that sort of joke."

"I don't know who it is you stuck back in the apartment, but I can tell you for certain it wasn't the Marnoo girl," Lupane insisted coldly. "Maybe because it was dark . . . I don't know. Christ, it looked like her, but I can tell you now, we killed the wrong girl."

Alarm rushed into Garcott's face. "Are you . . . are you absolutely sure?"

"Absolutely." He nodded in the direction of the road. "She's out there now, Christ knows where, with Berger."

Garcott finally absorbed the revelation. He stared at the useless car with dazed eyes. "Jeez, what a foul-up." He was silent for a time. "What the hell do we do now?"

"We'll have to go back to the apartment and see who the hell it was on the bed. We have to do that, to try to cover ourselves."

Garcott mournfully considered the answer. "I guess so, but it's a crazy risk. Christ, it looked so much like the Marnoo girl . . . at least in the darkness."

Lupane shuffled his feet impatiently on the wet road. He would have loved to push the blame onto Garcott, but he knew it wouldn't stick. It was his own cowardice, his reluctance to look at the girl, to shine the flashlight in her face. He slammed his fist against the hood of the car. "How in Christ are we going to get there without a car? We're running out of time. We can't set Berger up for a murder when we don't even know who it is that's dead."

"We should have called a taxi," grunted Garcott. "Forgotten the car."

"And just go driving up to the apartment in a taxi," said Lupane with angry sarcasm. "That's a fucking bright idea."

"We might have been able to get another car at the station," Garcott said defensively.

Lupane shrugged it aside. He was stumbling with indecision. If he put out a call on Berger, then he would lose the chance to create a situation where he could kill both him and the Marnoo girl without questions being asked. Yet the longer he did nothing, the farther Berger got away.

Then Garcott voiced a thought that was already in his mind. "Shit," he said, "what's Starker goin' to say?"

Lupane considered the question. Starker's reaction would be bad enough, but what if it got back to Blandhurst? The politician was already upset by the Cape Jaubert foul-up, and another blunder might panic him. Lupane had the feeling he was in a crossfire. He feared giving Blandhurst the chance to renege on all the promises he'd made, yet his own survival was at stake now. Christ, something had to go right for him. He held his watch to the car lights, and saw it was three-thirty. Where in God's name was the tow truck?

"I'll handle Starker," he said to Garcott. "But I'll try to talk him into not telling Blandhurst. All we need is time. We'll get Berger . . . and the girl." He didn't know how, but they couldn't get far.

The deep-throated growl of a heavy vehicle came from the end of the street, and the tow truck sluiced into view. Lupane gave a sigh of relief. At least some action was possible now. Jesus, there was the Santeze girl to be taken care of yet. He'd almost forgotten about her. What were they going to do about that? He shook his head despairingly as the tow truck squealed to a halt behind the car.

The driver clambered out and lumbered toward them, his head tucked down against the rain. He was a brawny, taciturn young man, arms resplendent with tattoos. He stood for a while scratching his head, laconically surveying the damage. He was totally unimpressed by Lupane's identification.

"Well, are you going to hook it up or not?" Lupane demanded in exasperation.

"Well . . . it's up to you, mate. But I got a crowbar in the back of the truck, and I reckon I could free that wheel so you could drive the car." He looked at Lupane and shrugged his broad shoulders. "It's up to you. I can 'ook her up an' cart it off quick as a wink, if that's what you want."

To drive the car was exactly what Lupane wanted. "How long will it take?" he asked.

The driver shrugged again. He wore a black tank top and a pair of ragged denim shorts, displaying muscles adequate to move mountains if necessary. "Dunno. Let me give 'er a try."

It took him five minutes with the crowbar, and the

result might not have improved the appearance of the car, but at least it was drivable.

Lupane nodded with satisfaction. "Thanks a lot," he grunted. At least it was one break his way.

The driver thrust a small grubby business card into his hand. "You take it to that garage, mate. He'll fix it for you real fast, an' at a good price." The accompanying wink was more a leer in the glare of the headlights. "Special price for coppers." He paused expectantly, and Lupane reached into his pocket and thrust twenty dollars into his hand. The driver pushed the money into his ragged pocket and winked again. "Thanks, mate . . . glad to be able to git you movin' again." He threw Lupane an exaggerated salute with its implied disrespect. "See you around." He swaggered back to the tow truck and took off with a bellowing engine and a crash of gears, a parting gesture that he was beholden to no one.

Lupane was past him before he reached the end of the street, his foot pressing the accelerator to the floor, spraying the tow truck with a deluge of road water. The truck driver answered with a blast of his horn, which Lupane ignored. All he wanted to do was get to Lisa Marnoo's apartment fast, and he had shut his mind to thinking beyond that point. Once he knew the identity of the woman they'd killed, maybe it would help resolve the other problems. What had begun as a well-planned operation had blown into a comedy of errors, and all he could do was play it by ear and hope to Christ it all worked out for him. He tried not to think about having to report all this to Starker. And he wasn't exactly looking forward to reentering the apartment. He wasn't usually squeamish, but he had little appetite for examining Garcott's brutal handiwork.

Incredibly, it was the Santeze girl. In the narrow shaft of Garcott's flashlight, even though her features were ugly in death, he recognized her immediately. He remembered when she had come to the station with Lisa Marnoo, sharp-tongued bitch, hovering around the Marnoo girl like a protective mother hen. The expected queasiness didn't materialize. If Garcott had done his job properly, he would have found out she was staying with the Marnoo girl. Maybe they had made a mistake in the dark, but at least the Santeze girl had to go anyway. But this meant Lupane had to rethink everything.

He stepped back from the body and nodded curtly to Garcott. "Okay, I've seen enough."

Garcott snapped out the light. "You know who it is?"

"It's the Santeze girl."

"Well, what d'you know." Garcott sniggered nervously. "And I thought I was poking the Marnoo bird. Well, it makes shit of the plan to frame Berger, but at least we got one of them. What the hell was she doin' in Marnoo's bed?"

"We should have known about that," commented Lupane acidly. He stood silently in the darkness, thoughtfully combing his fingers through his hair. "The Marnoo girl must have been here . . . somewhere in the apartment." He gestured to the body. "When this was happening. It's the only thing that makes sense . . . the only way she would have known to warn Berger . . . to drive to the motel. She must have been in another room . . . heard us talking." His eyes swept bleakly about the darkness. After all these years, to betray himself with a moment of lily-livered conscience. He wasn't going to admit that to Starker or Garcott, but that's what had happened. It wouldn't happen again. But if Marnoo had heard them and told Berger, he was in more danger now than at any time since this fucking raid operation had gone off the rails. They knew about him now, and he would be in danger for as long as they were alive. He had to kill them. He had to.

He stalked across to the doorway, located the switch, and turned on the light. Garcott blinked in the sudden flare, his mouth slack with astonishment. "What the hell are you doin'?"

"It's okay now," Lupane stated curtly. He walked into the small kitchen and picked up the telephone on the island cupboard. Garcott watched in apprehensive silence.

"This is what happened," declared Lupane. "Earlier we got a call from the Santeze girl that she was scared of Berger . . . he'd been making aggressive advances to her . . . getting violent. She asked for protection, for us to warn Berger off. We came here, found her raped and stabbed to death. We went to Berger's room at the motel and found the knife. Berger escaped with the Marnoo girl. It looks as if she was part of it—one of those weird sex things that got out of hand." He began to dial. "Now we put out a call they're both highly dangerous and wanted for murder."

"They get picked up by anyone but us, and they're goin' to start blabbin' about what the Marnoo girl heard in this room. Maybe even about the photographs."

"Berger doesn't have the faintest idea what the photographs mean. As for what Marnoo overheard, who's going to believe a loopy sex murderer? It's a risk, but we don't have any choice. Not now. They must be as confused as hell about why we want them dead. They get picked up, we'll have to make absolutely certain we're the ones to go and bring them back to Darwin." He stared bleakly at Garcott, his brows drawn into a scowl. He was pushed in tight, and he had no option now but to gamble his way out. But he'd gambled before, and rarely lost. "All sorts of strange things can happen when people get taken into custody. You know that, Paul. Cars run into trees and people get killed. They try to escape and get shot. Sometimes they even succeed in committing suicide." He waited for Garcott's approval, the receiver still to his ear.

Garcott stared blankly at the body, his head bobbing slowly with understanding. "Not bad, Mike," he murmured appreciatively. "Not bad at all, considerin' we're

out on a bloody limb. But I don't think we should just sit
around waitin' for them to be picked up. If we can get to
them first, it cuts down the risk of them talking to someone else."

Lupane frowned impatiently as the call signal burred
repetitively in his ear. "Right," he agreed. "They can't get
that far out of Darwin—even a full tank isn't going to take
them that far south. They'll have to stop for gas. Yeah, it'll
be that much simpler if we can get to them first." He took
the receiver from his ear and stared at it irritably. "Bastards must be all asleep," he muttered. He blocked himself into a corner and waited. The plan didn't sound bad,
not bad at all. Berger didn't know his way around the
territory, so he'd be relying totally on the Marnoo girl. If
she had contacts to help her, then someone in Darwin
would know about them. It would be so much safer if he
and Garcott could get to them first, so much easier to
arrange an accidental killing. But he couldn't risk not
putting out a call. He couldn't rely on Blandhurst for
protection, not a politician. If things got sticky when it
came to blowing Berger away, he didn't have the slightest
doubt Blandhurst would try to disown him. Let him try it.
Maybe if worse came to worst, it wouldn't be that difficult
to shift the blame onto Garcott. He would think about
that.

"Darwin police station," came a sleepy voice in his ear.

"About bloody time," he rasped. "Lupane here. I want
to put out an urgent call to have two dangerous suspects
picked up for questioning on a murder charge. Here are
the descriptions. . . ."

5

Arne Blucker had had only a hazy concept of God until he met General Leo Starker, and at once a firm image crystallized in his mind. Someone above normal men, with a sure instinct for what was right and proper for the future of mankind. Some men are ready to lay down their lives for their country; Arne was ready to lay down his life for the General. It had been a long way from his small hometown of Albion, Iowa, to Vietnam, a long way from the great fields of wheat stretching like a corn-colored carpet to the horizon. But he proved a dedicated soldier, resourceful enough to find a niche on the General's staff. He worshiped the General's shadow, and Starker found him a useful tool. A staff officer who knew combat, knew how to lead, how to die if necessary. Someone Starker himself would secretly have liked to become.

Arne had wept with the General over Vietnam, shared his bitterness that they had been betrayed by the politicians. Then Arne had vanished from the General's life. Back to the wheatfields, then leaving a mousy wife, drifting from city to city, looking for a substitute for the high point that had been Vietnam. Then the General sent for him. The letter must have followed him all over the country, and he could scarcely believe the General wanted to see him after the passage of so many years. But it was like an order for him that he wouldn't contemplate disobeying.

"Arne, what are you doing these days?" inquired the General warmly when Blucker went to New York, all expenses paid.

"Nothing, General."

"I mean with your life, Arne. What are you doing with your life?"

"Nothing, General. I need another war."

"Another Vietnam?"

"No. A war I can win."

"I have one for you, Arne."

Blucker knew little about Australia. He had spent a leave in Sydney once, screwing teenagers who seemed to come at him in waves, but he knew nothing about the American bases in the country or of the North West Cape base on the west coast of Australia. Starker sent him back to his hotel room with a dossier to read:

About seven hundred miles up the west coast of Australia, a peninsula juts out into the Indian Ocean like a jagged tooth. It is known as North West Cape. For thousands of years it was the homeland of the Talaindji aboriginal tribe, until Jacobsz the Dutchman landed there in 1618 and marked the beginning of European domination.

North West Cape is the location for the largest and most powerful station in America's worldwide submarine communications system. Its official title is the Harold Holt U.S. Naval Communications Station, named after a former Australian prime minister, and its function is as a main link with U.S. nuclear armed submarines in the Indian Ocean and Southwest Pacific. As such, in the event of a major war, the station is a prime nuclear target, but essential to American security. Even though most Australians regard America as an essential ally, the base and others like it have always been the center of political controversy, primarily because of the secrecy with which they were constructed and the fact that their use and control are exercised by the United States, with only meager consultation with the Australian government. Once again, this is important for American security. There are Australian politicians we regard as security risks, and great care must be taken as to what information is filtered to the Australian government.

The base is dispersed over approximately eighteen thousand acres, and in three areas, named A, B, and C, all set along the flat eastern coastline facing Exmouth gulf, and including the township of Exmouth, with a population of some three thousand people.

Area A is the main transmitting station, and the skyline is dominated by Tower Zero, the highest manmade structure in the southern hemisphere. Grouped around Tower Zero are thirteen supporting steel towers, and the antenna itself is a great spiderweb complex of strung wire, the system covering something like a thousand acres. Buried in the ground beneath the antenna are hundreds of yards of bare copper wire, which comprise the ground mat for communicating with the submarines. There are various other structures at Area A, such as a naval pier, a power plant, fuel facilities, and the transmitting building.

To some Australians the lack of control of this base on their own sovereign territory is sufficient price to pay for the continuance of America as an ally in a world power struggle. For others, our enemies, such a loss of control is anathema. We regard the continuance of this base, and others like it, as absolutely essential to America's security, and have the gravest concern that a party predicted to win overwhelmingly in the coming elections in Australia has pledged to have the base dismantled.

Blucker absorbed the information with little idea of its relevance to him, and studied the accompanying map of the area and the position of the installations. He had no doubt the General would question him, so he made sure he had a good grasp of all the detail. Then he went back to the General.

"Interesting, eh, Arne?" said the General.

"Yes," replied Blucker vaguely.

"We have to make sure that base stays there, Arne. Change the course of those elections. Our government won't do anything except sit on their asses and make bleating sounds. It's up to men like us, Arne."

"Who are . . . us, General?"

"You love your country, Arne?"

"Of course."

"You want to get back at those bastards who betrayed us in Vietnam?"

"Don't we all."

"You trust me?"

"Absolutely, General."

"Then I want you to head up a raid on the North West Cape base, Arne. I know you're the right man. I've seen you in action. You can lead. You can be ruthless. You, with a few handpicked men, to make a surprise attack on the base and turn Australia on its ear."

Blucker stared in astonishment. "Raid our own base?" he asked suspiciously. He hadn't seen the General in a long time. Had he maybe been sucked into some loony political organization?

"That's right, Arne. And you'll be well paid—more money than you've seen in your life before."

"That sounds like some sort of crazy commie idea to me, General," said Blucker cautiously.

The General laughed delightedly. "You're right, Arne. You're so right." He stood up and motioned Blucker to follow him to the table. He opened a briefcase, laid out a sheaf of papers, then gestured to a chair. "Sit down, Arne. I'm going to take you through the entire operation. I know your loyalty, your dedication, that you'll do whatever has to be done. When I'm through, you'll be so anxious to get started, you wouldn't care if you weren't being paid a cent."

The night conspired with Blucker to produce a cloak of carbon blackness. It was the small measure of luck he needed. Gone were the stars and moon that had shone on the *Seaboro* all the way down the west coast of Australia. The sea, the ship, the sky merged in common darkness. The only light was to the east, where a few miles away the flash of the Vlaming Head lighthouse marked the position

of North West Cape. Klomf had done a good job of black-
ing out the ship.

Blucker stood by the rail watching the launching of the
landing craft. Every man moved with precision in the
darkness, knowing exactly what to do. He had them trained
to a razor edge. He felt no nerves, only determination.
The Cape Jaubert fiasco was behind him now, and the
shattering realization that he had let the General down.
He would more than make amends tonight. He should
have been prepared for the possibility of long years out of
combat rusting his judgment. It wouldn't happen again.
They would go in like the old days, do the job, and be
gone before anyone knew what had happened.

He didn't notice Ferrel until the man was almost at his
side, so effective was the black garb. The Kalashnikov
assault rifle hung loosely in the man's hand. "We're ready,
Captain Blucker."

Blucker nodded. The General had conferred the rank as
necessary to military discipline. He checked his watch. It
was one-thirty. "The documents have been inserted in his
uniform?"

"Yes, Captain."

"Wait here, Eddie . . . I'll get him," he said.

His footsteps rang sharp on the deck as he walked
swiftly to the cabin. The *Seaboro* rode gently on the soft
swell. He unlocked the door and went inside. The Russian
was seated at the small table, dressed in the same black
uniform as himself. He looked very pale, very frightened.
His tongue, pink as a cat's, nervously washed his lips
before speaking. "Why have I been forced to dress like
this, Mr. Blucker?"

"Captain Blucker."

"Then why have I been forced to dress like you, *Captain*
Blucker?"

Blucker put his hands on his hips, his face impassive.
He didn't dislike the Russian. He had gotten to know him
quite well since he'd been brought on board, but there

was no place for personal considerations. "We're going on a journey, Karsov."

"A journey? A journey to where?"

"On shore. For a short time."

"We're near land?"

"Yes . . . only a few miles away."

Karsov nodded slowly. He sat very upright in the chair, his eyes never still, wary, fearful. "What . . . am I expected to do? I've been told nothing since my . . . kidnapping in Canberra."

"Nothing is expected of you. I'll be close by your side all the time. There'll be others besides myself."

"You won't tell me anything?"

Blucker shuffled his feet impatiently. There was no time for idle conversation. "I'll have a gun, Karsov. If you make the slightest attempt to escape while we're ashore, I'll kill you." He scowled menacingly. "Do you understand?"

Karsov stared with ashen blankness. "Y-yes . . ." He faltered. "I understand."

"Good." Blucker jerked his thumb toward the door. "Then let's go."

No further words passed between them. Not on the ship, nor in the landing craft. Instructions were conveyed with a nod or a push of the hand. On the way to the beach, Blucker positioned Karsov at the nose of the craft, the nuzzle of his gun resting lightly against the Russian's back. It was important to instill fear, if the man had any idea of making a break. He glanced briefly about the ten other faces packed tightly in the boat. The muzzles of the Kalashnikovs grew like stalks above their heads. No one spoke. They were good men who wouldn't let him down. Or the General. The outboard burbled with a comforting sound, and ahead the white line of gentle surf murmured welcome. Everything was going for him; even the sea was cooperating.

They dragged the craft into the shelter of a rocky outcrop, then assembled in single file on the beach. Ferrel took the point, then Karsov, with Blucker immediately behind, prodding the Russian forward with his gun. The three men carrying the explosive charge were detailed to the rear. Once Karsov turned as if to ask a question, even in the darkness his face a luminous white, but Blucker roughly urged him forward.

They went quickly toward Point Murat, then at Blucker's signal halted in a tight group within sight of the transmitting base. The cry of a pied butcher-bird came keenly from the acacia trees on the ridge. Blucker crouched to his knees, ticking off the layout against the map memorized in his mind. It was all there. The naval pier, the transmitting building, windows alight, Tower Zero soaring up to disappear into the night sky, surrounded by its family of smaller towers. Light reflections from the windows shivered across the maze of antenna wires. The only sign of life was two men standing in the light of the transmitting-building entrance, holding carbines. Probably guards.

Blucker nudged Ferrel. "You got it?"

"Just like our maps, Captain. Every detail."

Blucker turned to the other men. "You all got it?"

They nodded wordlessly. He checked the luminous dial of his watch. It was two o'clock. "Ten minutes at the most," he muttered. "Less if possible. We assemble back here." He paused. "Your group ready with the explosive charge, Markovitch?"

"Yes, Captain."

"Make it look good. Like the real thing."

"We know what to do, Captain."

Blucker grinned at the sarcasm. They were right, it was telling grandma to suck eggs. It had all been said a hundred times. "Go," he said.

He seized Karsov by the shoulder and held him back as the others moved past. He had delegated Ferrel to lead the assault, but he would have loved to do it himself. He had to stay with Karsov; the Russian was the linchpin of the entire operation. He could hear the strained, asthmatic breathing of the Russian, thready with fear.

They both waited, crouched together, until the crackle of the Kalashnikovs began. Someone shouted, and Blucker saw the two men by the entrance fall, then the black figures of his own men rush through the door. Another man in a white coat appeared from the other side of the building and fled into the darkness, but he only made a dozen yards before someone cut him down. Then there was more firing from inside the building. He counted off the minutes, then pushed Karsov to his feet. "Move," he commanded harshly.

"Captain Blucker . . ." entreated the Russian timorously.

"Move."

They walked about halfway to the transmitting building. The firing was spasmodic now. Blucker wondered how many they had had to kill. He prodded Karsov fiercely with the gun. "Stop here." It was open ground, and he would quickly be found. They both halted, and he poked the Russian again. "Turn around."

When Karsov turned, his eyes were partly closed, his mouth set, like a man resisting passing out.

Blucker didn't want that. "Go back to the beach, Karsov," he ordered abruptly.

Karsov's eyes flicked wide open in surprise. "Back to the . . . beach."

"Yes. Wait for me there."

The Russian hesitated, and once again Blucker stabbed at him with the gun. "Move, fuck you. Move," he grated.

Karsov shook his head in a gesture of confusion, then moved away with halting steps. Blucker waited until he had gone about twenty yards. "Wait, Karsov," he called.

Karsov came to a halt.

"Turn around."

The man turned slowly, his arms still at his sides. He swayed as if having difficulty keeping to his feet. It would be better, Blucker decided, for him to look as if he had been hit in the first moments of the raid, facing the building. He gave him one burst, in the chest, and Karsov fell over without a sound. Blucker looked back toward the tower. Already some of the men were heading back toward him. He walked over to the dead Russian and dropped the Kalashnikov beside the body. It had all gone like clockwork. He had known it would. The General could forget about Cape Jaubert now.

It was two hours after the raid before the confusion at Area A finally settled. It had been like a disturbed ant's nest, people rushing hither and thither with no sense of purpose. In the end they just stood in hushed groups, watching the bodies being brought out. A seaman on a lighter tied up at the pier had heard the shooting, sensibly kept his head down until it was all over, then given the alarm. Armed patrols were being organized to comb the surrounding Cape Range, but from what had been seen of the raiders' ruthless use of firepower, no one was anxious to start before daybreak, when a helicopter could be used. There were seven dead in all, including the dead raider, and already his body was under intense examination.

Messages concerning the raid were soon being read by a startled prime minister in Canberra, and with equal alarm by the State Department in Washington. It was only when daybreak came that an important item was added to the cables. An explosive device had been discovered at the base of Tower Zero, but the timing mechanism had failed to detonate the charge. If it had gone off, the tallest structure in the southern hemisphere would have been reduced to steel splinters.

By daylight the *Seaboro* was well out to sea and heading on a steady southern course to Perth. Blucker was jubilant. For all the trauma of Cape Jaubert, meticulous planning had finally paid off. They had gone in, done the job, and made it back to the ship in incredibly short time.

Even their planning hadn't prepared them for such perfect timing.

Injured pride had been restored to men who had lived long in Vietnam's bitter shadow. Granted, the money was satisfying, but it was more than that. It was to have a sense of mission for their country again. There were dead men back at North West Cape, their own countrymen, but sometimes sacrifices had to be made. They had achieved something of which the spineless politicians in Washington were incapable. The General would be delighted.

The equipment, the arms, the helicopter, had all been dumped in the ocean. There would be probing flights out from the cape in the next few days, but their story was pat and well-rehearsed: the freighter *Seaboro*, out of New York, with a cargo of farm machinery and animal hides for Perth. All they had to do now was wait, enjoy the glow of contentment, while the storm burst.

II

Aftermath of the Raid

6

Head of Intelligence Max Kaufman thought about Lupane on the flight back from North West Cape. It disturbed him that Lupane could intrude into his thoughts after the disaster at the communications station. All those men massacred. The horrendous potential of the failed explosive charge. And above all, the bombshell revealed by the examination of the dead raider. In cooperation with the Americans he had that under tight security for now. But the political ramifications were mind-boggling, especially with an election coming off.

So he was irritated at his concentration being side-tracked by an asshole like Lupane. The report to Blandhurst should have been the only thing on his mind at the moment. But then, suspicion of his subordinate's ambitions was never far from his mind these days. He was Lupane's superior, yet he had been maneuvered into a position where he had lost control of the man. It was beyond his understanding how Lupane had wormed his way into Blandhurst's confidence. They were such opposites. What the hell did a sophisticated man like Blandhurst see in a thug like Lupane?

Kaufman was responsible to Blandhurst, but there was little he could offer but mumbled protests when Lupane was removed from his authority to perform some vague secret assignment for the minister. Bloody politicians. Nothing like that had ever happened to him before, but since Blandhurst had taken the portfolio four years ago, he'd run Intelligence with his own peculiar brand of administration. He knew Lupane resented him, saw him as a Brit interloper, but the hell with him. Lupane was nothing but a hatchet man, it was laughable to think a man like that would have ambitions to head up Intelligence. Yet he couldn't overcome the niggling suspicion Blandhurt was working toward that end. That he was about to be edged out. So he had been forced to protect himself. Valued contacts had located Lupane at Darwin, posing as a police detective, with that other psychopath, Paul Garcott. The subterfuge baffled him. But he managed to install a listening post in the Darwin police to feed back information about Lupane's activities. He had been intrigued by what he'd learned. The contact with Blandhurst's old friend General Starker. Lupane's involvement with the case of the murdered photographer. Now there was this concern over the photographer's brother, Ross Berger. He had no idea what it all meant, but sooner or later it would come out. As long as it gave him something with which to nail Lupane. Lupane could be brutally efficient, but he wasn't very smart. It hurt Kaufman's pride to be forced to adopt such tactics to protect himself from his own organization. After all, he had given Blandhurst nothing but unswerving loyalty, and it was a bitter taste to have his own minister plotting his downfall. Or so he strongly suspected.

Perhaps he'd been unsuccessful in concealing his dislike of Blandhurst, but he had an aversion to gutter politicians. And he had reason to believe that after the elections, with a new government, his position would be safer. But not now. The revelations of the North West Cape attack would change all that. He had no doubt the government would use it to swing the election their way. It had been done years ago with the Petrov affair, and he had no doubt it could be done again.

He ordered a Scotch from the hostess and determinedly pushed Lupane from his mind.

He was an extremely benign man in appearance, and he believed it was one of his main attributes for a lifetime of successful intelligence work. Pale blue eyes studied the world from behind myopic lenses. His round face was almost cherubic, dotted with a small nose and full lips.

Strands of sandy hair failed to disguise approaching bald-
ness. Stripped of his well-tailored conservative clothes, he
was a surprisingly muscled five-feet-eight. He was in his
mid-fifties, and his accent quickly identified his London
origins. MI5 and the coldest days of the cold war had been
a bloody training ground. He didn't talk about it, not even
to his wife. It was past. He was ambivalent about violence.
If it was the only solution to a problem, then he had no
conflict. He lived quietly in a Canberra suburb, sharing a
love of growing roses with his wife. He shared little else
with her. Early, she had learned of murky MI5 conspira-
cies, and now she preferred blissful ignorance. Even his
three children, now left home, thought of him only as a
well-paid public servant. No one knew of his addiction to
the stock market. An early successful plunge had led him
uncharacteristically into a disastrous buying spree. He was
immersed in debts that would have astounded his wife, his
colleagues, even threatened his position. The job was his
life jacket, keeping him afloat, and while he held it there
was minimal chance of exposure from his creditors. So he
faced financial disaster, apart from career disaster, if he
allowed Blandhurst to destroy him. He had taken over
Intelligence in Australia at a time when the organization
had acquired a comic-opera reputation. They needed someone tough, and he'd given them that. He'd been a survivor for a long time now, and he had no intention of letting
cretins like Blandhurst and Lupane blot his record, no
matter what it took.

For now he would report on the communications-base
raid and watch Blandhurst's knee-jerk political reaction
with cynical interest. The revelation about the dead raider
would be like an early Christmas present for the politician.

There was a car waiting at the Mackay airport to take
him to Sweetwater, and he held it off while he called his
contact in Darwin. Any tidbit was worth knowing before
he faced up to Blandhurst.

"There's something going on," said his man.

"What's that supposed to mean?"

"There were more meetings between Lupane and Starker. Lupane looks like the world's about to come to an end. He and Garcott have been chasing around all night."

"Chasing around on what?"

"Ah, now that's the interesting thing. There's a call out on Berger and a local girl, both wanted for questioning over a murder. The girl's called Lisa Marnoo. She's the one who originally identified the dead photographer."

"Who's been murdered?"

"A friend of the Marnoo girl, name of Jo Santeze. Pretty nasty one . . . raped, stabbed, you name it, they did it to her."

Kaufman fell silent. It made no sense. What the hell was Lupane, an intelligence man, doing chasing a murderer in Darwin? And where did Starker fit? Did Blandhurst know he was in the country?

"Don't take it as gospel," added his man cautiously. "But I've a hunch Lupane wants those people dead."

"You think Berger's been set up?"

"I don't know, it's just . . . peculiar. I mean, it's the sort of thing the Darwin police should have handled from the beginning. Lupane's been pretty heavy with the authority he seems to have been given."

Kaufman nodded to himself morosely. Blandhurst would have seen to that.

"And this thing of Berger being a murderer seems a bit crazy to me," his man continued. "Guy comes up here to identify his dead brother, and suddenly is supposed to go off half-cocked and kill this girl. Make up your own mind, but it's got a funny ring to me."

"Okay, thanks. Keep your ears and eyes open," concluded Kaufman brusquely. "I'll call you again tomorrow."

He hung up and teased petulantly at his mouth. Was his imagination running riot that all the shit going on in Darwin seemed to coincide with the raid on North West Cape? He shook his head immediately. It was a crazy thought. But whatever Lupane was up to in Darwin, Kaufman had to find a way to turn it to his own advantage.

No matter what pressure he was under, Kaufman always derived pleasure from visiting Sweetwater. The green countryside, the house, the gardens, the sense of gracious living. The aura of historical wealth glowed in the early-morning light, and as always, he was stirred with envy. Blandhurst was a shit, but he had certainly flowered in beautiful surroundings.

There was no one waiting to greet him at the door, but he was familiar enough with the house to go through the ornate living room into the study. Blandhurst was sitting on the chaise longue resplendent in a rich red velvet robe, a sheaf of papers beside him, coffee and sandwiches set out on a small side table. The room matched the rest of the house in exquisite period taste. A desk of authentic antiquity. On the walls an invaluable collection of early Australian art, names like Roberts, Condor, Streeton, that Kaufman had learned to appreciate himself. The large lattice windows made a magnificent frame of the outside gardens.

Blandhurst rose as he entered, strode toward him, and shook hands with all the warmth of a practiced politician.

"Thank God you came so quickly, Max," he said effusively. "It's quite a flight to come direct from the cape. You must be exhausted."

Kaufman smiled warily. He wasn't used to such concern. He followed the minister across to the chaise. "This is terrible, Max . . . unbelievable," said Blandhurst. "Of course I've already had discussions with the prime minister, and I have to get back to him as soon as I have your report." They sat down together on the chaise. "You'll have some coffee of course, Max?"

Kaufman dipped his head wearily. "Thank you, Minister."

Blandhurst rapidly poured two cups, allocating one to Kaufman. "Six dead, you said over the phone . . . shot to

death by these . . . raiders. All American navy personnel,
I presume?"

"With the exception of the dead raider, which made
seven dead in all. One of the guards evidently managed to
get off a few shots before he was killed, and he must have
hit the man. It was the only casualty the raiders suffered."

"Dreadful . . . absolutely dreadful," exclaimed Blandhurst
between cautious sips of hot coffee. "And I take it there's
no sign of these . . . murderers?"

"None whatever, Minister." Kaufman found the coffee
too hot, and placed it back on the table. The sense of
theatrical outrage was what he expected. He had no doubt
plans were already in hand to take political advantage of
the raid. "The area around the base has been thoroughly
searched by armed patrols. Planes, helicopters, navy pa-
trol boats are still out combing the sea, but so far . . .
nothing. It all seems to have been very well planned. Of
course everyone at the base is making wild guesses. There
is the possibility they were put ashore by submarine."

"Does anyone have any idea how many there were?"

"Well, the navy man who raised the alarm could only
make a hazy guess . . . maybe a dozen. If they were all
dressed in black like the dead man, they'd be extremely
difficult to see. They just cut down everyone in sight."

"What time was this?" The politician's hand holding the
coffee cup trembled slightly, and it surprised Kaufman.
He wasn't a man subject to nerves. Maybe it was excitement at the thought of the political capital to be made
from the raid.

"They hit the base around two o'clock in the morning. It
was all over in ten minutes."

"Amazing," said Blandhurst incredulously. "The area's
still under tight security?"

"Yes, but it's going to be difficult to maintain. Exmouth
is on fire with rumors. How can you keep anything like
this under wraps?"

"It's going to leak out, Max. You can be sure of that. I

think the government should make a statement as soon as possible. Get in first. We're in constant touch with Washington, of course. We need to synchronize with the Americans." Blandhurst was having difficulty sitting still, constantly shuffling about, fingers plucking. "I'll need more details for the prime minister, Max. About the sabotage attempt on Tower Zero. And specially about the dead raider. You only whetted my appetite over the phone."

I'll bet you want to know about him, thought Kaufman cynically. He stifled an incredulous laugh. "I recognized him."

"You recognized him?"

"Yes, Minister. I know that sounds incredible, but it's true. It was Alexei Karsov, the member of the Russian embassy staff in Canberra who disappeared five or six weeks ago. You briefed me to conduct an investigation. We never found out what happened to him, but I carried his photograph around with me for some time. I recall we were waiting for him to come out of hiding and ask for political asylum, because we assumed he was a defector. Well, he was the dead raider."

Blandhurst stared at him in astonishment. "My God . . . That means the embassy is involved in the raid."

Kaufman pursed his lips thoughtfully. He believed he knew Blandhurst, but there was something different here that he couldn't quite put his finger on. The minister's responses were slightly caricatured, almost rehearsed. Or did he suspect everyone these days? "I don't think that necessarily follows," he murmured.

"There has to be a connection, surely, Max?"

"Certain . . . documents were found on Karsov's body."

"Documents? What sort of documents?"

"Detailed plans for the raid, set out in Russian code . . . but one easily known to us. We had it decoded in an hour. And of course there was the weapon found beside the body. A Russian Kalashnikov assault rifle."

Blandhurst was spurred to his feet, excitedly pounding

his fist into the palm of his hand. "I knew it, I knew it. From the moment you called me, Max, I suspected it was an undercover Russian operation to put the North West Cape base out of action. Probably to cover up some she-nanigans they're up to in the Indian Ocean. My God, it's just as well they failed." He paced about in small circles for a moment, muttering, still beating his fist. Then he resumed his seat beside Kaufman. "I'm sorry, Max," he apologized. "But it's so obvious. The bastards. Well, they blew it. God, can you imagine the repercussions? Was there much information in the documents?"

"Plans for the actual assault. Objectives, like Tower Zero. Instructions from Moscow. But strangely, no details about how they actually landed at the cape. That surprised me."

Blandhurst offered a dismissive wave of his hand. "It doesn't alter the main facts. It's all the proof we need. Christ, we're not going to let the bastards get away with it. It's nothing more than an invasion of our country . . . an act of war. If that explosive charge hadn't failed to fire, the entire complex could have been wiped out."

"I don't think we should go off half-cocked for the moment, Minister," interrupted Kaufman cautiously.

"Half-cocked? Do you consider an act of war against our country not something to be outraged about, Max?" he asked coldly.

"The Russians are sure to claim the documents are forged."

"They can claim what they like. Together with Karsov's body they are conclusive proof as far as I'm concerned. All this nonsense about Karsov vanishing in Canberra. It was all obviously planned." The minister's florid complexion took on a purplish hue. He leaned forward and rapped his hand forcefully on Kaufman's leg. "This means the expul-sion of the Russian embassy, Kaufman." Somewhere along the way, Kaufman's first name had disappeared. Blandhurst didn't like reservations about his opinions. "So much for these idiots who are trying to tell the Australian people we don't need the American bases in this country. We need them more than ever now, Kaufman." His head bobbed like a ventriloquist's dummy. "More than ever. By God, we do."

Kaufman offered no opinion. He still had the strange feeling he was watching a carefully rehearsed performance. You could never tell with this man. Or was he so cynical he couldn't recognize old-fashioned patriotic outrage anymore? But the raid was an absolute political bonus for the government. It would win them the elections. He tentatively selected a sandwich, and took a delicate mouthful. Lettuce and cucumber. How like Blandhurst. "If . . . if I may make an observation, Minister, it all seems just a little too . . . pat for me," he said cautiously.

Blandhurst eyed him with dour impatience. "What on earth do you mean, too pat?"

Kaufman shrugged uneasily. Professional pride fought a short battle with toadying compliance, and won. Suppressing reservations was no way to hold his job, even if Blandhurst didn't want to hear them.

"Well, for a start, the documents on Karsov. It doesn't make sense to me he would carry them on the raid. Okay, they were in code, but why carry them on the actual operation?"

Blandhurst laughed with a patronizing tone of dismissal. "You've been on the trail too long, Kaufman. You're thrown by shadows that only exist in your imagination. Why wouldn't he carry them? Obviously the last thing he expected, with surprise on their side, was to get killed. I'm sure it never entered his mind he'd be unlucky enough to stop a bullet. I saw enough men like that during the war. You always think it's the other man who's going to get killed. No, I don't buy that."

Kaufman wrinkled his mouth in disagreement, but didn't pursue the point. "Then there's the fact of the explosive charge at the base of Tower Zero failing to fire. Merely a failure to connect a single wire. After all the planning that must have gone into the operation, it seems inconceivable to me they'd make such an elementary last-minute mistake. I simply find it hard to believe."

"Are you suggesting they went to all that trouble, killed all those people, and then deliberately rigged the charge not to explode? What sort of ludicrous nonsense is that?"

Blandhurst's mouth formed into a grimace of annoyance. It was obvious he had no intention of being deterred from a plum political opportunity.

"They were guilty of nothing else but incompetence, Kaufman. God, you should know how that can happen under stress. People do irrational things at such times. Maybe they were in too much of a hurry to get away. Especially after Karsov was killed."

The observation led Kaufman to another point. "And I fail to understand about Karsov," he persisted. "Didn't they know he had the orders on him? Surely they would have taken his body away with them?"

Blandhurst spread his arms with an indication of mounting exasperation. "Maybe last-minute panic . . . God, I don't know, Kaufman. Like I said, men do unpredictable things under pressure. You're head of Intelligence . . . you find the answers for me. Maybe Karsov wasn't missed until they got back to their base, or submarine . . . or whatever it was. It's irrelevant at the moment. All the evidence is there of a dastardly Russian attempt to put out of action an important military installation in this country. Innocent people have been brutally murdered." His voice rose with anger, and he was impelled to his feet again. Brusquely he consulted his watch. "That's what I intend to convey to the prime minister. He'll confirm our evidence with Washington and make a statement to the people."

He paused, and walked slowly to the window, hands thrust into his robe pockets. In the nearby fields, the green stretches of sugarcane stirred in the early sun. He obviously considered the discussion at an end, but Kaufman wasn't finished yet.

"I merely think we should be absolutely sure, Minister," he said delicately. "Because we haven't examined the most important repercussions yet."

Blandhurst turned irritably from the window. "What's that?"

"Have you considered the American response?"

"I'm more concerned with the Australian response at the moment."

"But, Minister, the Americans may also consider it an act of war against their country. It's their base. Their people who've been killed." He hesitated, and nervously cleared his throat. "Isn't it possible this could spark a nuclear war between America and Russia? The Americans aren't going to take this lying down. No way."

There was a period of silence while Blandhurst sullenly considered the question. "The raid failed," he muttered. "No one's going to blow the world up over a failed raid like this."

"I doubt the Americans will see it like that. People have been killed."

"No doubt we'll have a period of increased international tension. I'm sure the Russians will deny all involvement. You said that yourself, Kaufman." He shook his head with sudden decisiveness. "No, that's an extreme alarmist view, Kaufman." He turned to the window again. "I want a detailed report of the entire incident on my desk by this afternoon," he stated bluntly.

Kaufman scowled at the perfunctory dismissal. Blandhurst had shut his mind to everything but the political advantage to be gained from the raid, but he was crazy if he thought the Americans were just going to slap the Russians on the wrists. He felt slightly foolish. He had done neither his career prospects nor his relationship with the minister any good by expressing his doubts. He'd been around long enough to know doubt is the last thing a

politician wants on his mind when he's preparing to go for
the jugular. But the raid still had a phony ring to him. He
would quietly carry out his own investigations, and if he
proved Blandhurst wrong, it could be to his own advantage. He longed to ask questions of Lupane, of Starker,
but that was for another day, when he knew more of what
was going on in Darwin. "This afternoon . . . very well,
Minister," he agreed.

Blandhurst's eyes remained fixed on the green fields.
"The car will take you back to the airport," he said stiffly.
At the last moment, when Kaufman was almost to the
door, he turned with a forced smile. "Thank you again for
coming from the cape so promptly." The words were so
transparently insincere as to be insulting.

"Only doing my duty, Minister," Kaufman said, with
mock modesty. He gave a deferential dip of his head and
left the room.

Blandhurst stood unmoving by the window for a time
after Kaufman's departure. He'd been thrown by Kaufman's perceptive doubts, and he needed to recover composure before he called the prime minister. Kaufman was
an irritating smart-ass, the man had annoyed him from the
very beginning, and he was glad to be maneuvering Lupane
into the job. Admittedly he was nervous that Lupane was
privy to so much dangerous information, but he'd be
easier to handle than the devious Englishman.

But Kaufman's questioning of the raid had made him
apprehensive. He knew Kaufman. The man would burrow
and ferret if he had suspicions, and Blandhurst would have
to make sure any such investigations were stopped dead.

It had been a bad night for him, when it should have
been a cause for celebration. Leo had promised, and delivered. It had all happened. The raid, the blame fixed on
the Russians, a great diversion to win the elections, but
Christ, all those people murdered. The news of the deaths
had genuinely shocked him. The General had deliberately

lied, right from when they had first discussed the plan, and Blandhurst had been assured it would be achieved without bloodshed. Christ, it was laughable now. First the photographer at Cape Jaubert. The other three in Darwin. Now the Americans at North West Cape. He'd accepted that Karsov had to be killed, to make the Russian involvement believable, but the others? All right, the three in Darwin were an unfortunate result of the Cape Jaubert bungle, but Leo must have known the killings at the North West Cape were a planned part of the raid. How could a trusted friend lie to him like that? The risk of conflict between Russia and America had been taken into account right from the beginning, and discounted, but the unnecessary killings had increased the risk tenfold. Oh, Leo would make consoling sounds about necessary sacrifices, but could he trust Leo after this?

With such thoughts on his mind, it had taken a monumental effort of will to pretend surprise and anger at Kaufman's report. Would he have gone along in the beginning if he'd known how many would die? He shook the thought aside. It was done, no matter how unpleasant.

Now it was up to him to make the ultimate political capital from the raid, to win the coming elections. He was sure the prime minister would go along with him. They shared an equal passion for power. The prime minister would soon be retiring, and if the government retained office, then he himself would become prime minister. The thought was sufficient to wipe out any darts of squeamish conscience. He picked up the phone and dialed the prime minister's number.

The prime minister spoke to the nation on television. It was a practiced performance by the long-ruling patriarchal figure, the coiffured white hair, the heavy eyebrows emphasizing outrage with the skill of a trained actor, the image of solemn responsibility.

A dastardly attack has taken place against our nation, he

declared. A raiding party has attempted to destroy the vital American naval communications base at North West Cape. Six innocent Americans have been callously murdered. Fortunately the attack failed, and one of the raiding party was killed. He has been identified as a member of the Russian embassy in Canberra. Both we and our American allies are demanding an explanation from Moxcow, and the Russian embassy has been expelled from this country. So much for the stupidity of people who would destroy the security of this country by closing down the bases of our valued American ally. Every Australian can now see the folly of voting for people who are as much the enemies of this country as the Russians.

The leader of the opposition demanded equal time on television. His presentation was equally responsible, equally well-staged, his white hair as carefully coiffured.

My party's position in regard to the American bases in Australia has been grossly misrepresented by the government and the media of this country, he thundered. It has never been the intention of my party to close down the bases of our valued American ally. We are merely seeking a more . . . cooperative basis on which these functions are carried out. Of course we have no intention of completely dismantling these bases.

Strenuous denials of complicity in the raid were issued from Moscow and the Russian embassy in Australia. The man Karsov had been nothing more than a minor clerk who had fled from the embassy months ago after embezzling money, and the Australian government was guilty of harboring a criminal. Any documents found on Karsov's body were forgeries.

The United States called for an immediate emergency session of the United Nations, and the president put the country on red alert. The rest of the world held its breath.

*   *   *

When the news reached New York, Halmen gathered together the Committee of Concerned Americans. They had succeeded; it was irrelevant who won the Australian elections now—both parties were committed to retaining the American bases in Australia. But it was a restrained celebration of the success of their first operation outside the United States.

The representative of the military-industrial complex demanded some explanations. "As I understood the plan," he said tersely, "the raid was to do two things. To create the impression it was carried out by the Russians, through the use of Karsov, Russian equipment, and an explosive device that did no actual harm to the base. And to frighten Australians into voting for a party committed to retaining our bases in Australia. As it happens, the second part has been achieved before the elections by the about-face of the Australian opposition. But nowhere do I recall seeing in any document that the killing of American citizens was to be part of the raid. That, more than anything else, has inflamed the country. There are already hotheads saying the raid was part of a first-strike plan by the Russians, and now we should get in first. Nothing has been achieved if we are all to be incinerated. Who . . .?" He paused and glared at Halmen. "Who authorized Starker to kill these people? When we examined the risk factors, that was not one of the things included."

He sat down heavily, while Halmen eased his bulk into a standing position. He didn't particularly like the representative, and he hated to be questioned by anyone. His embarrassment took the form of a film of perspiration on his face. "No one authorized the General," he said hoarsely. "I'm afraid Starker has interpreted our brief with a trifle too much . . . enthusiasm. I don't believe there's any need for"—he gave the representative a scathing glance— "panic. We have succeeded in what we set out to do. There are members of the committee in powerful positions of influence within the government, and they'll make sure to

dampen down any fires that threaten to . . . incinerate."
He hesitated, breathing with difficulty. "As for the General . . . well, we'll have to wait until he returns to apply any disciplinary action."

7

Time blurred for Ross. The horizon lightened to the east, separating the outline of the bush from the sky. A straggling formation of magpie geese headed north through the slot of pale gray color. The car had not missed a beat since leaving Darwin. A collection of buildings in the style of early bush architecture came up on the right, and was quickly left behind.

"The Bark Hut Inn," muttered Lisa. "A tourist place." She pointed ahead. "About another sixteen kilometers there's a side track that runs up to Point Stuart on the coast. We turn up there."

He nodded, glad she had broken silence since her agonized description of what had been done to Jo. Maybe they'd know why one day. But he'd be relieved to get off the main road now that daylight was breaking. There was sure to be a wanted call out on them, and there was always the chance of being identified by a passerby.

"Let me know when we come to it," he said.

She turned to him with a flickering of a smile. It was a sign she was coming to terms with the night's horrors. "Yes, I will."

"Where are we going?"

"Remember the grandfather I told you I found when I went looking for my mother? He lives out here by himself . . . near the Wildman River. I know he'll let us stay with him for a while. At least until we can work out what to do." She paused, her eyes wide and questioning. "Do you have any idea yet—?"

He cut her off in mid-sentence. "None. I've been turning it over in my mind ever since we left Darwin. I have no more idea why Lupane wants us dead than why Lupane suddenly became a homicidal maniac." He shook his head morosely. "Christ, if it wasn't for you, I wouldn't be alive now."

She shuddered. "It was so . . . so cold-bloodedly deliberate . . . so planned . . . so terrifying."

Her composure wavered again. Ross waited awhile, then took Mark's photographs from his pocket and dropped the envelope down on the seat between them. She glanced at it questioningly.

"Mark's photographs," he said. "The copies Jo made for me."

She picked up the envelope and turned it over without opening it, then dropped it back on the seat. "You brought them?" she said in surprise.

"One of those spontaneous things." He shrugged. "I just shoved them into my pocket as I rushed out of the room. You know, it's the only thing that connects all three of us."

She gaped at him. "You think Lupane wants to kill us because of these photographs?"

"I know it sounds crazy. Even crazier when I hear you say it. But what else have we got? What makes a cop act like a homicidal maniac? He's got to be a hatchet man for someone else. Don't ask me who." He shook his head. "Maybe Mark was killed because he took those shots. It makes as much sense as anything else." He put the envelope back in his pocket. "Only Lupane knows the answer, back there in Darwin."

"God, you can't go back there, Ross," she cried in alarm. "That would be suicide. Maybe they've found out their mistake by now . . . killing Jo instead of me. But that's not going to stop them. Even if you tried to get to someone with authority over Lupane, it's only your word against his . . . and you know who they'll believe. First chance he got, he'd kill you . . . and me." She pushed herself back into the seat, hands clenched fearfully. "No, please, I couldn't face going back there."

He gave her a reassuring grin. "Don't worry, I'm not going to risk that. What we've got to do is somehow get to Sydney. Maybe I can find someone there to show the photographs to." He scowled. It sounded like a forlorn hope, considering their situation at the moment. "Maybe they'll mean something to someone else . . . perhaps a newspaper. But we stand a good chance of getting killed if we stay around here."

She nodded agreement, then placed her head wearily back on the seat and stared silently at the roof, dull-eyed, slack-mouthed. "There's a man I know . . ." She paused. "I haven't seen him for a while, but he could help us. He's a pilot who flies out of Jabiru."

"Jabiru? Where's that?"

"It's a mining town." She gestured vaguely. "Farther out in Arnhem Land. He flies a Cessna on a regular run to Mount Isa."

"That would be terrific. We could get a Sydney plane from Mount Isa. Do you know him well enough to ask a favor like that—even if he knew we were wanted by the police?"

"I think he . . . Yes . . . he might." There was a note of reluctance in her voice that he chose to ignore. It sounded like there might have been a problem with the man in the past, but they needed all the help they could get now. "We could trust him," she added with a frown. "He doesn't exactly have any love for the police himself. He's had a few brushes with the law."

Ross considered the suggestion for a moment. The man sounded ideal. "Would he expect money?"

She shrugged. "He might do it as a . . . favor."

"I've got a credit card in my wallet. Would he take that?"

"He might. Let's wait and see what he has to say." She turned toward Ross, her hand raised in warning. "We'd have to get to Jabiru somehow without being seen. We couldn't drive there in this car. It'd be a dead giveaway."

"How much farther is it?"

She pouted thoughtfully. "Maybe another hundred and twenty kilometers. No, let's go to my grandfather first. He'll be able to get us to Jabiru. He knows this country better than anyone."

Ross peered through the windshield. The dawn light was sculpturing the countryside into sharp detail. Birds winged over the treetops, and the road stretched into the bush like a black ribbon. The rain was gone. He reached forward and switched off the lights. "The pilot is a great idea . . . if he'll do it," he mused aloud. "It's the only idea we've got at the moment. And we'd better get off the main road before it gets any lighter."

She pointed suddenly. "There's the turn now, Ross . . . just ahead on the left. It's only a track, so you'll have to drive a lot slower."

He turned carefully onto the track. He felt desperately tired. In spite of a determined effort of concentration, his eyelids drooped, and the car weaved unsteadily about the track. He was grateful now for the increasing light. It was only a formed track through the sorghum grass, snaking around eucalyptus trees and clumps of cycad palms. Brilliantly colored rosellas flitted through the trees, and the cry of black cockatoos sounded harsh in the early-morning air. At the sound of the car, water buffalo lifted their large horned heads from grazing and watched with lethargic curiosity. The ocher earth shimmered in the sun. Past anthills towering like miniature castles above the car, they came to another side track. It was half an hour since they had left the highway.

"Turn to the right," Lisa directed. She shared his fatigue, her head resting against the door. "It'll take us across to the Wildman River."

He swung the car cautiously, bouncing across the gouged surface, fallen twigs cracking under the wheels. He drove at a crawl for another hour. Lisa was right: no matter how they got to Jabiru, they couldn't travel in the car. They were going to have to dump it somewhere, because it was a dead giveaway. At her instruction he braked to a halt by a small clearing. A crudely constructed hut of old bags and galvanized iron sheltered beneath a giant baobab tree. There were the remains of a campfire and battered cooking utensils scattered about. Parked on the opposite side of the tree was an ancient rust-colored truck that recalled memories of Pat Tanna's old vehicle.

"Pull in over there, Ross," said Lisa. "Just by the tree."

He dawdled the car into the shade of the tree and cut the motor. He wanted the car out of sight, just in case there were any searching planes flying around later. From the lower branches two snow-white egrets lifted their long elegant necks in alarm and took off with a powerful swish of wings.

There was a sleeping man sprawled on the ground beside the truck, head buried in his hands. A lean, nondescript dog emerged from the hut, uttered several halfhearted challenging barks, then slumped languidly to the ground. The man by the truck didn't stir.

They sat in the car for a moment, almost too tired to move. Ross motioned toward the man on the ground. "Is that your grandfather?"

She shook her head. "No, he doesn't own a truck. I don't know who that is. Grandpa's probably asleep in the hut."

In immediate proof of her words a man stumbled from the shanty, scrubbing at his eyes. He dropped his hands and stared blearily in their direction. He was an aborigine, thick beard and shaggy hair a matching white, heavily built with a swollen paunch. He was dressed in a pair of

tattered dungarees and a red checked shirt. He was bare-
foot. He looked at them without comprehension, then
reached back into the hut to produce a dilapidated stockman's hat, which he placed carefully on his head. Then he
walked with slow deliberation toward the car.

"That's him," said Lisa. "That's my grandfather. Come
and meet him, Ross."

She quickly opened the door and stepped out of the car.
The aborigine abruptly halted, a broad grin of recognition
spread over his face, and he held out his arms. "Lisa," he
called in a thick, gritty voice.

Ross followed her out of the car and stood hesitantly
waiting for an introduction while the two embraced.

Lisa broke away from the old man's arms and gestured
for Ross to join them. "Grandpa, this is a good friend of
mine, Ross Berger. Ross, this is Bill Weidja."

Ross took the old man's gnarled hand in a firm grip.
Lisa's grandfather could have been anywhere between
seventy and a hundred, with a face that bore all the
distinctive features of his ancient race. The heavy, pro-
truding forehead over deep-set black eyes, the wide splayed
nose, the full-lipped mouth, skin with the texture of dark-
stained weathered leather. Myriad wrinkles spread from
the corners of his eyes and down his face to disappear into
his luxuriant white beard. He smiled uncertainly at Ross,
and shuffled his bare feet about in the red earth. "Pleased
to meetcha, Mr. Berger," he grunted awkwardly.

"Ross. Call me Ross, Bill."

The aborigine ducked his head as if in embarrassment,
then turned back to Lisa. He peered momentarily up at
the sun. "You come pretty early, Lisa. Pretty early." He
scrutinized his granddaughter shrewdly. "You come all
way from Darwin." He spoke deep in his throat, running
the words together so that Ross had to strain for the
meaning.

"Yes . . . we've come from Darwin, Grandpa. We left
very early." She took him by the arm and began to guide

him slowly back toward the hut. Her legs had barely enough strength to carry her, and she leaned gently on the old man for support. "We'd like to stay with you for a short time, Grandpa," she said carefully. "There's been a little . . . trouble in Darwin."

Bill looked at her in surprise. "With you, Lisa? You never in trouble." His head waggled with concern. "You make it sound like plenty big trouble."

"Yes . . . big trouble. There are men in Darwin who want to harm me." She gestured toward Ross. "And Ross as well."

Bill shook his head with disbelief. "No. No, what fella would want harm to you, Lisa?"

"I can't explain it all right now, Grandpa. I just want you to believe me that these people will do us great harm if they catch us. It's important you understand that."

The old man stared anxiously at Lisa for a moment, then shrugged with a grin. "If you say, I believe, Lisa." He pointed to the hut. "You and Ross stay long time . . . long as you like."

Lisa gave a weary nod of gratitude. "Thank you, Grandpa. I knew you'd say that."

"Who owns the truck, Bill?" Ross interjected.

Bill glanced across at the truck, placed his hands on his hips, and shook his head in disgust. "Belongs that fella on the ground, my nephew Ted Jowalenga. He pretty sick fella . . . just sleepin' it off. Yeah, too much beer. He down from Oenpelli settlement." He made a disparaging gesture of his hand. "Bad place, Oenpelli . . . no good for aborigines. Just fightin' and drinkin' all time. Ted, he drink all time." He halted by the remains of the campfire and looked questioningly from Ross to Lisa. "I can get fire started. You plenty hungry, I guess?"

Lisa gave a weary shake of her head, then glanced at Ross for confirmation. He nodded in agreement. Fatigue had deprived him of any appetite, and he wanted nothing more than to lie down and sleep. But the old truck inter-

ested him. It could be a possible way of getting to Jabiru.
Lupane would hardly be looking for them in an ancient
crate like that.

"I'm absolutely beat, Lisa," he muttered. "I've got to
get some sleep before we can even talk about getting to
Jabiru."

Bill's white eyebrows lifted in surprise. "You want go to
Jabiru?"

Lisa stroked him affectionately on the arm. "We'll talk
to you about it later, Grandpa. Just for the moment, all we
want to do is sleep. It's been a long night. When we've
had a rest, then we can eat and talk about what we're
going to do." She offered a jaded smile. "All right?"

Bill returned a genial grin and indicated the shanty
entrance. "Sure. You both sleep in there. You in plenty
big trouble, then this fella look after you, Lisa. When you
wake up, we talk."

She managed a heavy-eyed smile of thanks, then gestured to Ross to follow her into the hut. He stopped inside
the single room and looked around. The rough building
materials only partially shut out the light. The interior was
indicative of Bill's sparse belongings. A collection of blankets was laid out in one corner on the earth floor. A few
clothes were draped over several old wooden crates. Another crate contained some canned food. An ancient kero-
sene lamp hung by a piece of rope from an overhead
rafter, and propped in another corner was a twenty-two
rifle that could have passed for a museum piece. There was
the soft drone of flies, already scavenging for their first
meal. The sun poking through holes in the walls formed a
variegated light pattern on the floor. Lisa went immediately to the crude bed on the floor and made space beside
her. Ross thought of the last time he had lain with her. He
was dog-tired, but maybe he should say something about
that, about the night, about the fact she'd saved his life.
He squatted down on one of the crates, ran his fingers
wearily through his hair, and owlishly studied her.

"Come on, Ross," she murmured. "I'm so tired I can't even think straight. I'm almost too tired to be frightened anymore. We'll talk about Jabiru to Grandpa later."

"I want to thank you for saving my life, Lisa," he said. "If it wasn't for you, I'd probably be stretched out in the morgue beside Mark right now. I owe you."

She propped up on her elbows and looked at him solemnly. "You saved mine, too. I could never have got here without you."

"About last night . . . in the motel," he said hesitantly.

"I wasn't fair. I lost my temper. Forget it."

"Maybe we can just start from scratch . . . just see what happens. I meant the things I said to you."

She dropped back on the blankets, closed her eyes, and nodded gently. "That's something we can talk about later. Just at the moment, all I want to do is stay alive, stay away from Lupane. You too." She patted the space beside her. "Come on, get some sleep."

He took off his jacket and threw it on one of the crates. "That old truck might be a chance for us to get to Jabiru. We're both agreed we have to dump the car. Do you know this nephew of Bill's—Ted Jowa . . .?"

"Jowalenga. Yes, I know him. I'll talk to Grandpa about it. It sound like a . . . good . . . idea." Her voice was already drowsy with sleep, her mouth scarcely moving. He stretched out beside her, his hands cupped behind his head. Every muscle in his body seemed to be crying out for release from tension. But maybe they couldn't afford this time. They should be running. But running where? It would be crazy to stay on the main highway in daylight. There was such a sense of unreality about all of it. He felt her stir beside him. She had saved his life; he must mean something to her. He felt closer her now than at any time during their frustrating sexual coupling. He encircled her shoulders with his arm, and she welcomed the embrace, crouching close to him. It was an expression of trust, perhaps even the beginning of love.

"Keep me alive, dear Ross," she whispered fearfully.

"I will," he promised. "We're going to be all right, darling Lisa."

She didn't answer, but he hoped she believed him. He held her tightly, her hair soft against his face. Her arm dropped slackly across his chest, and he felt the gentle pressure of her breasts. Even exhausted, he was sexually stirred. It seemed so right to be with her like this, she was what he wanted, and he hoped in time she would feel the same.

They slept. Once she woke him with a cry, mumbling Jo's name over and over, and he comforted her until they both fell asleep. When he woke again, she was gone, and his nostrils caught the tang of wood smoke mixed with the aroma of cooking meat. He sat up, yawned, tousled his hair, and consulted his watch. It was one o'clock. He stretched, and climbed to his feet. The hut had the temperature of an oven, the sun twinkling through the innumerable holes in the walls. The crackle of burning wood and the voices of Lisa and her grandfather drifted through the bag covering over the doorway. He felt better for the sleep, even hungry. He picked up his jacket from the crate, felt the shape of the photographs, and took them out again. Perhaps he took some perverse pleasure in the frustration he gained from looking at them. He went through them slowly once more, searching vainly for a clue he might have missed, something that would reinforce his feeling that they were a possible motive for murder. He examined the shot of the freighter again. There was a name there that would probably come up sharply under a magnifying glass. *Seaman* . . . *Seabird* . . . something like that. He should have picked it up before. It might be a good starting point for him if they could get to Sydney. But what was the meaning of the ship? Who were those mysterious men in black? He shook his head mournfully. And what about Mark's funeral? He didn't want to think about the lies probably being fed to his parents by now.

"Hi there, you're awake," said Lisa from the doorway. One hand held the tattered bag covering aside, and in the other was a steaming enamel mug of tea. Sleep had done wonders for her. But there was something in her eyes that sleep would never erase, that would stay forever, a wariness, a loss of trust, that he knew was for Jo.

He smiled. "You look better."

She extended the cup to him. "Grandpa's special. Billycan tea brewed over an open fire, with a special taste all its own."

He took the hot cup gingerly in his fingers and kissed her lightly on the forehead.

"I woke earlier, so I decided not to disturb you," she said.

He said nothing about her nightmares over Jo. The strong, biting flavor of the tea was a palliative to his mouth. "Some night," he ventured with a grim smile. It was a test, but he knew she could handle it.

"I'll never be able to forget what they did to Jo. Never," she said soberly. Sleep might have done wonders for her body, but nothing would ever obliterate the terror of last night. "I thought about something this morning that I'd forgotten last night," she added.

"What was that?"

She closed her eyes at the painful memory. "In the apartment . . . when they were leaving . . . after they'd . . . they'd finished with Jo." She opened her eyes again, and the shadows seemed even more pronounced. "Something Lupane said. I don't know if it means anything or not."

"Let's hear it anyway."

"I . . . I don't recall the exact words. It was something like what they'd done would please his friend at . . . Beton, I think was the word. It would keep Martin's hands clean." She shrugged. "I don't suppose it means anything to you either?"

Ross thought about it, sipping at the tea. "No," he

agreed finally. "It doesn't mean any more to me at the moment than the photographs." He pursed his mouth doubtfully. "Maybe it will someday." He pushed it to one side. "What we've got to think about is getting to your pilot friend at Jabiru. And quick. It's too dangerous to stay here."

"I mentioned your idea about the truck to Grandpa, and he spoke to Ted about it."

"Will he take us?"

She frowned uncertainly. "Ted never makes an instant decision. He's out there by the fire now. Why don't you come out when you're ready. Grandpa has some food cooked."

He nodded, and rubbed at his bristly chin. He could forget shaving for now.

Lisa responded quickly to the gesture. "There's an old tank around the back of the tree where you can wash," she said. "But don't go over by the river. You start splashing around by the bank, and you might finish up as lunch for a crocodile. I'll wait for you by the fire." She turned to walk toward the door, and he reached out suddenly to grasp her hand. She came to a halt and looked at him questioningly.

"We're going to be all right, Lisa. I want you to believe that."

She smiled at him faintly. "Yes . . . yes, I believe," she answered. Then she shook her hand free and went out the door.

It was a rusty half-tank, but the water was clear. It was a glorious day. The rain of the previous night was gone, and the dry soil had soaked all the evidence away like a sponge. A light breeze whisked the grass about his feet and composed a rustling melody in the branches overhead. He took off his shirt, splashed the cold water onto his face and body, then dried off with the threadbare piece of toweling hanging by the side of the tank. He had little doubt this was something Bill had put here for Lisa's visits. As he washed, Lupane was never far from his mind. He would even the score with that murderous bastard one day.

The others had already commenced eating when he reached the fire, and Bill wordlessly handed him an old enamel plate containing pieces of stringy meat. It could have been buffalo, wallaby, anything, but he didn't question it. There was another, much younger aborigine, about Ross's age, squatted on the other side of the fire, that Ross assumed was Ted. He was leanly built, with the same strong racial characteristics as the older man, except his hair and heavy mustache were coal black. Blood had congealed in an ugly wound on his left cheekbone. He wore a checked shirt similar in style to Bill's, tight-fitting stained jeans, and highly polished stockman's boots, with ornate stitching. The way he sat gave pride of place to the boots. He was smoking, and there were several cans of beer at his side. He looked across at Ross as Lisa spoke.

"Ross, this is Ted Jowalenga, a cousin of mine. He was asleep when we drove in this morning."

Ross stepped forward as if to move around the fire to shake the man's hand, but the aborigine merely waved a can of beer in his direction. "Good day, Ross," he called. "How'd you like a beer?" He was the younger generation, with little trace of the ancient tribal influence still apparent in Bill. He didn't wait for Ross to answer, but hurled the can across the intervening space, and Ross moved quickly to catch it.

"Man doesn't like to drink alone," Ted grunted, "and that old bastard won't drink with me."

Bill scowled at his nephew. "You behave, or you go back to Oenpelli plenty quick, Ted." He turned with a smile of support to Ross. "You drink when you want, Ross. Take no notice that fella."

There was an awkward pause as Ross squatted down beside Lisa. It wasn't a good start, when they needed Ted's help. He sought Lisa's eyes, but she deliberately avoided him, so he began to eat. The meat was tough and sinewy, but he was so hungry he scarcely noticed.

"You think you pretty clever, livin' out here on your own, don' you, Bill?" Ted sneered. He was obviously riled by his uncle's comment. He made a sweeping gesture with the can, leaving a trail of spilled beer. "The minin' companies find somethin' aroun' here, and it'll be the same as everywhere else. They'll stuff a pile of money in your pocket and boot you up the ass outta here."

"This home of Rainbow Serpent dreamtime," stated Bill woodenly. "Minin' companies no come here."

"Bullshit," Ted jeered. "You gettin' too old, Bill. The minin' companies don't give a fuck for your dreamtime."

"They no come here," repeated Bill slowly. "This sacred place of Rainbow Serpent. Minin' companies not allowed to destroy dreamtime. It where you come from, where all aborigines come from. All animals, sky, water, land. They all created in dreamtime." He gestured about him. "Our beginnings in all these sacred places. Don' you forget, Ted."

"Don' give me those old bullshit myths."

Bill ignored Ted, and there followed an uneasy silence. Ted finished the can, then opened another, and didn't lower it from his mouth until it was half-empty.

"You drink plenty too much beer, Ted," admonished Bill. "Plenty too much, that your trouble."

Surprisingly Ted took no offense, but contemplated the can for a moment. "Mebbe," he grunted. "But what else is there to do at Oenpelli? Watch television, play pool, listen to the jukebox, an' drink beer." His fingers traced tenderly at the congealed wound on his cheek. "An' fight. I don' know who the hell gave this to me." He nestled the can in his lap and slowly surveyed the surrounding bush with heavy-lidded eyes. Then he scooped up a handful of the red soil and let it trickle through his fingers. Longing sadness passed like a shadow across his face. "Wish I'd been born hundreds of years ago, that's what I wish. All

I'd be thinkin' about would be spearin' a kangaroo for me dinner, an' the dreamtime would take care of me life for me. All this'd be mine. No mining companies, no white man, just livin' at peace with the land." He put the can down savagely on the ground, as if he found the contents suddenly repulsive. He stared at the fire for a long time, then finally lifted his eyes to Ross and Lisa, picked up the can again, and his expression widened to a sly smile. "You two havin' a little trouble with the coppers, eh?"

"Something like that," Ross said offhandedly.

"Don' matter to me," Ted went on in a more conciliatory tone. "I don' like coppers anyway. Bill tells me you want to get to Jabiru." He motioned toward the car under the tree. "What about the car?"

"We can't go in that."

"They'd be watching for it, eh?"

"Could be. It'd be a crazy risk to take."

"Would you take us in your truck, Ted?" Lisa asked anxiously.

"You still might get picked up."

"Maybe," said Ross, "but there's less chance that way."

"An' what happens to me if you get picked up?"

No one answered. Ross put his plate down by the fire, and a swarm of flies descended on the remnants of the meal. Ted gulped at the can, waiting for a reply, beer coursing in small rivulets from the corner of his mouth, down his throat, and into his shirt.

"You take Ross and Lisa, Ted," Bill growled. "You plenty smart fella if you wanta be. Or you no come back here to me."

Ted glared across at the old man. "What sorta shit is that? I was goin' to take 'em anyway. I could put 'em in the back and cover 'em over with the piece of canvas." He grinned at Ross in a sudden change of mood. "What are you gonna do in Jabiru anyway?"

"There's a man I know, a pilot called Alec Redpath.

Everyone knows him as Red," interjected Lisa. "He has a regular flight across to Mount Isa."

"Figurin' on tryin' to fly out, eh?"

"It's worth a try. I'm hoping he might agree to take us. It's the only chance we've got." Her voice broke slightly, and a measure of concern showed in Ted's face at her suddenly apparent fear.

"They're really hasslin' you?" he asked in a more kindly tone.

"Some fellas want bad harm to Lisa," warned Bill. "Bad harm. She needs plenty help, Ted."

Ted shook his head and rested the can by the fire. "Yeah . . . yeah, I can see that. What happens if you get to Mount Isa?"

"We could get a plane to Sydney," said Ross.

"What are you goin' to use for money?"

Ross shrugged. "I've got a good credit card. We'll be okay."

Ted poked at the fire with a piece of stick, silently studying the flames. "Okay," he grunted finally. "We'll leave after you finish eatin'. The old truck don't go very fast, so it'll probably take us a while. If it don't break down, we'll make Jabiru about dark. I won't go back to the highway along the track, just in case we bump into someone. I know a way across country, an' it'll be safer that way."

"Thanks a lot, Ted," Lisa said gratefully.

"You on your own once we get there." Ted's tone was surly, as if his expressed concern was a weakness to be quickly suppressed. "I don' want any trouble with the coppers."

"We won't involve you, Ted," Ross assured him.

Ted merely grunted, finished the beer, wiped at his mouth, and motioned with the can toward the car. "An' you can't leave that hangin' around here with old Bill. What if the coppers spot it? That'd mean real trouble for the old coot."

Ross glanced across to the car, then looked questioningly at Lisa. Ted was right. It would mean trouble for the old man.

"It's not even my car," Lisa murmured.

"You get ready to go Jabiru," interrupted Bill. "I fix car plenty quick."

"What do you mean, Bill?" Ross asked.

"Place up Point Stuart I hide. No fella ever find."

"How you goin' to drive it, you old coot?" Ted demanded.

"I drive. I drive your truck plenty good." He turned with a confident grin to Lisa. "You show old Bill, Lisa. I drive okay."

"An' how are you goin' to get back? Fly like a cockatoo?" Ted inquired sarcastically.

"Easy walk. I come that track plenty times."

There was a hesitant pause. Lisa's eyes moved from Ross to her grandfather, then questioningly to Ted.

Ted read her unspoken query and shrugged. "Maybe," he said. "He handles the old truck pretty good. Is it automatic?"

"Yes. It'd be much simpler to drive than the truck."

Bill scowled around at the three of them. "I drive easy," he insisted. "You show, Lisa, and I hide plenty quick."

She shifted her gaze to Ross, and he offered the same noncommittal shrug. "Why not, if Ted says he can drive? It's too dangerous for Bill to leave it here, and I think we should get the hell away as soon as possible. There could be someone in Darwin who knows about your relationship with Bill, and if Lupane found out about it . . ." He left the remainder of the words unsaid, but it was sufficient to convince Lisa.

"All right." She smiled at her grandfather. "But you show him, Ross."

Ross scrambled to his feet. "Okay, Bill, let's go and have a look at the car."

The old man beamed a pleased smile on Ross. "This

fella not let you down," he said confidently. "I hide it
plenty good, Ross."

They walked slowly across to the car as Lisa watched.
The sun burned their shadows black into the grass. The
lean dog appeared from out of the bush and followed
panting in Bill's tracks. There was a constant traffic of
twittering, cawing multicolored birds through the trees.
Ross went through the motions of instructing Bill on the
car, but his mind was on Jabiru. He hoped to Christ Lisa's
friendship with the pilot meant something. He didn't want
to be trapped in Jabiru with nowhere to go.

Lupane received little satisfaction from the frenetic media coverage of the raid. All he could think about was
Berger and the Marnoo girl. He and Garcott had spent a
fruitless night, until fatigue had forced him back to his
apartment for a few hours' sleep. But he had ordered a
sullen, equally weary Garcott to keep digging. It was the
stupid bastard's own fault. He should have found out
about the Santeze girl staying with Marnoo.

Lupane had woken to a television newscast agog with
the biggest story ever in Australia. Sat and watched it all.
The shots of the base, the interviews, the threatening
denouncements from Washington, the denials from Moscow, the Australian politicians exchanging insults, the
solemn-faced commentators with their fears of war and the
now obvious madness of closing down the bases of our
valued American allies. Through it all was a sense of
patriotic near-hysteria. It had all happened. Starker and
Blandhurst had pulled it off. But Lupane was disconcerted
by the international repercussions. Hadn't the silly bastards thought about that? Surely they weren't crazy enough
to start a nuclear war? But because of the success, Lupane
was in, and Kaufman was out. It should have been enough
for him to break open a dozen bottles of champagne, but
all he could do was sit slumped in a fog of gloom. Where
the fuck had Berger and the girl gone? He could never be

safe while they were alive, no matter what job he held. Starker would be waiting for his report, but he intended to hold off as long as possible. Maybe Garcott would make some sort of miracle breakthrough. He was on dangerous ground. Starker and Blandhurst wouldn't tolerate failure, especially if it threatened themselves. He was going to have to bullshit to the General if he called. Christ, it was an impossible situation. He had all the roads south covered. Surely they wouldn't have headed into Arnhem Land. That would be a dead-end trap.

And where was Garcott? He should have reported back by now. Lupane postponed calling the station, made himself some coffee, and morosely watched yet another repeat of the prime minister's address. Mealymouthed old hypocrite. All he wanted to do was win an election. The telephone rang, and he let it go for a long time before answering. It could be Garcott with some good news, but it might be Starker, and he hadn't decided what to say to the General yet. Except lie. He would get those two, but he had to have some breathing space.

It was the General. "I was hoping you'd be in, Lupane," crackled the authoritative voice. "I called the station first, but they said you were getting some sleep after an all-night job." Even rigid self-discipline failed to suppress the note of jubilation in his voice.

"Congratulations, General," Lupane said quickly.

"Ah yes . . . thank you. I was sure you had heard."

"Who hasn't? I haven't seen any newspapers yet, but there's nothing else on television."

"Yes, everything went well. Very well indeed. Our friend in Beton should be delighted."

"Ah . . . I hope we're not all going to get blown away by nuclear bombs, General," Lupane said cautiously.

"No, that won't happen," the General stated blithely. "They'll hurl insults at each other for a while, then it'll all cool down."

He sounded very sure. Lupane let it pass. He hoped

the General knew more about that sort of thing than he did.

"There's a small item in the local newspaper you might be able to clarify for me, Lupane."

"Like I said, I haven't seen any newspapers yet, General."

"I think you may know about this. It refers to the murder of a girl in the Alawa area of Darwin. The name of the victim is Jo Santeze."

"Ah yes . . . I've been working on that case," Lupane answered warily.

"I had a feeling you might be. A man and a woman are wanted for questioning," probed Starker. The General was being a trifle cute. Did he think the phone was bugged? "I'd like your view concerning the people wanted for questioning," he added. "I mean, have they been detained, or . . . what's happened to them?"

Lupane swallowed away the abrupt dryness in his throat, and kept his voice steady. "I don't think those people are going to be found."

"You mean they've disappeared?"

"Not exactly. I just don't think they are *ever* going to be found. For questioning or anything else. I have a feeling they'll never be seen again." He tried to inject confidence into his voice. He was sure the General understood the implication.

"Good. Yes, excellent, Lupane. I understand. I just wanted some reassurance. I wouldn't like to think you might believe such a . . . disappearance wasn't necessary after our success. It was very, very necessary. We wouldn't want to leave any dangerous problems lying around for our Beton friend. He'll be relieved to hear your news. You've done well, Lupane."

"You intend to see our friend?"

"Yes. I'll let things cool for a couple of days, then I'll pay him a visit."

The door to the apartment opened to a gray-faced Garcott.

He moved into the room and dropped wearily into the chair by the television set.

"Well, you don't have to concern yourself about those two, General," stated Lupane confidently. For the moment he was off the hook. He would get those two in his own time, and neither Starker nor Blandhurst would know about it.

"Fine. I'd advise you to close down your operation here as quickly as possible."

"I intend to, General."

"Then I may see you at Beton. And congratulations yourself, Lupane. Our success is your success. I know there is a big job ready for you."

Lupane knew that their mutual dislike was too obvious for the words to be anything but hypocritical syrup. "Thank you, General, and good luck," he said woodenly.

"And to you too, Lupane. Thanks for all your help."

Lupane put down the phone with a sour grimace and turned to Garcott.

"What did the old bastard have to say?" Garcott asked.

"He thanked me."

Garcott stared at him. "Thanked you? For what? For letting Berger and the Marnoo bird off the hook?"

"Christ, you don't think I told him what happened? I . . . implied those two had been taken care of. He was only too happy to believe me. What the hell else could I do?"

Garcott gazed blankly at the television. Someone was declaring the armed forces in Australia should be placed on instant alert. Lupane irritably switched it off.

"We'll be in fuckin' trouble if they bob up somewhere else before we get 'em," Garcott warned. "Blandhurst'd take a dim view of that."

"I'm aware of that." Lupane scowled and jerked his thumb at the television. "I guess you've heard the news."

"How could I miss it? They're doing everything but write it in the sky." He laughed dryly. "In spite of all the foul-ups, they actually pulled it off. That means Blandhurst will probably become prime minister."

"Let's forget Blandhurst for now," Lupane suggested tersely. "Did you manage to dig up anything?"

"I think I might know where they are."

Lupane stared at him. "Well, for Chrissake, don't just sit there. Tell me."

"Something I picked up from the local people. Seems Lisa Marnoo has a grandfather—a boong—who lives in a shack out on the Wildman River. It's off the Arnhem Highway . . . oh, about a hundred and thirty kilometers out of Darwin. There was a driving-license problem some time ago, and she gave a reference for him." He shrugged. "In last night's panic it could just be the place she'd head for. Berger wouldn't know where to go."

Lupane nodded slow agreement. "Makes sense. You know how to find the place?"

"Yeah. They drew me a map."

Lupane stretched, as if flexing his muscles after a long sleep. He shrugged into his coat, checked his thirty-eight, then slipped it back into the holster. "Then let's get the hell out there," he muttered. "That's the only way we'll know if you're right."

Garcott climbed wearily to his feet. "Jesus, I'm nearly dead," he protested. "Can't it wait an hour or so? If they are there, they're goin' to stay put. We got 'em boxed in."

"We go now," Lupane stated coldly. "After the way I just had to bullshit Starker, I'm not risking them alive any longer than I can help."

"Then you'll have to drive," Garcott whined. "I'd have trouble keepin' the car on the road."

"Okay, okay," Lupane agreed impatiently. He trundled Garcott toward the door. "Just stay awake, because I'm going to need your directions."

Garcott stumbled through the door, propelled by Lupane's hand. "What do we do about the grandfather . . . if they're there?"

"He goes too," declared Lupane savagely. "Harboring fugitives is a criminal offense. It's not our fault if he accidentally stops a stray bullet."

They paced quickly down to the garage, Lupane urging the sullen Garcott ahead of him. He had to resolve this once and for all. The grandfather would go, and anyone else unlucky enough to be there with Berger and the girl. And if it was an isolated place, maybe they could do it without reporting anything. He was too close to cherished ambitions now to be cheated by squeamish conscience.

The old aborigine stood with his arm raised in farewell until the ancient truck lurched and spluttered out of sight amid the trees. He was concerned for Lisa, but he was sure Ross would keep her safe. But it didn't dull the sense of anticipation with which he went to the car. He had done well under Ross's short-term tuition. He'd never sat in, let alone driven, such a beautiful car.

The old truck had proved difficult to start, so they had gotten away much later than planned. It would be dark before they got to Jabiru, but it would be safer that way. Just so long as Ted didn't drink too much, because Bill knew he had beer in the truck.

He went eagerly to the car, shuffled into the driver's seat, and just sat behind the wheel for a time, running his fingers around the rim, examining the dials, pressing himself into the upholstery. It seemed almost a crime to destroy such a wonderful car. He wasn't too sure he'd give up his life to own beautiful things like this, the way the white man did, but it would be a temptation.

He started it the way Ross had shown him, the engine humming like the bees along the river. He put it carefully in drive, then circled the baobab tree several times, the dog trailing in the rear, barking encouragement. Then he set off along the track, hunched over the wheel, a smile of pleasure on his face. He drove cautiously at first, maneuvering around the gouged sections of track; then, as he gained confidence, he increased speed. He began to enjoy himself, Lisa's problems forgotten for the moment. It was so easy to steer, not like dragging at the wheel on the old truck. The bush seemed to take on a new dimension, in a way he'd never experienced before. The trees, the colors, even the occasional buffalo seemed stirred by a fresh magic. It was good to be doing something for Lisa; she had done so much for him. He came to the track that would lead him north to Point Stuart, and stopped. Before he turned, he peered south toward the Arnhem Highway. He saw another car, far down the track, blue in color and much larger, threading through the trees toward him. He had immediate alarmed thoughts for Lisa. Cars so rarely used the track, maybe these were the people who wanted to do her harm. He had a moment of indecisive confusion. He could turn back to the hut, but the truck wouldn't have reached the highway yet, and he might endanger Lisa. He headed the car north toward Point Stuart, jabbing too hard at the accelerator, and he nearly lost control as the wheels slewed into the turn. All the joy was suddenly gone. He drove faster than he should have now, crouched apprehensively over the wheel, broken branches and stones whanging against the underside of the car. Occasionally he attempted to glance into the rearview mirror, but he was fearful of taking his eyes off the track ahead. But every now and again he saw glimpses of the blue color as proof the car was following him and had not turned off toward the hut. He was almost to the Point Stuart fork at Jimmy's Creek when he became conscious of a new sound, not the splintering snap of a branch under the wheels, but a more ominous noise, like the report of his old rifle. Then there was the cracking detonation of something striking the rear window, and fear supplanted anxiety. They were shooting at him. He was right. They must be the people wanting to do harm to Lisa. They must have recognized the car, like Ross said they would, and given chase. He forced himself to glance into the rearview mirror. The other car was lurching crazily about the track, the driver obviously unused to the rough conditions, and even as he watched, it slammed into a small tree and nearly went out of control. Through his fear he felt a glimmer of satisfaction. If he could lead them far away from the hut, then he was really doing something to help Lisa. Something important. They weren't close enough to see who was inside the car, so he was sure they believed it was Ross and Lisa. They were bad people. He had no doubt of that. He knew his granddaughter too well to believe she could do anything criminal. Do harm to anyone. He risked a quick glance into the mirror. They had fallen behind now, and stopped shooting. He couldn't drive anywhere near as well as they did, but he could beat them with his knowledge of the country. He would drive up by the deep hole at Swim Creek, then turn off the track into the open country. He could lose them there, no matter how powerful their car. He pressed his foot a trifle harder on the accelerator, and the car gathered speed beneath him as he swept into the Swim Creek turn. But he was going too fast, his aged reflexes and inexperience with the car a dangerous combination. At the apex of the curve by the high point of the water hole, he swung the wheel too hard and put the car into a sliding skid from which he had no hope of recovering. The car slewed sideways out over the rock ledge, becoming momentarily airborne, and the old aborigine clung to the steering wheel, his eyes tightly shut. He hoped the bird of the night was ready to take him to the distant island where the spirit of his mother would be waiting to greet him. "This for you, Lisa," he whispered. Then there was a jarring crash, and the bird of the night enfolded him gently in her wings.

Garcott eased himself slowly out of the car and plodded across to join Lupane standing on the rock ledge overlooking the water hole. Already only the rear end of the car showed above the surface, and that was fast settling in a

profusion of bubbles. Neither man spoke as the car slid
from sight. Lupane had the thirty-eight ready in his hand.
On the opposite bank several crocodiles waddled from the
bushes and launched into the stream with a menacing
flurry of water. Just a brief flash of armored prehistoric
body and long, cruel jaws, then the powerful sweeping
tails took them quickly beneath the surface. There was no
sign of life from where the car had gone down.

Garcott motioned wearily to the thirty-eight. "You can
put that away. Looks like the crocs'll do the job for us."

Lupane nodded silently, but he still retained the gun.
Small waves spread out from the point of impact and
lapped softly against the shore. All life about the water
hole was stilled. Birds hovered cautiously overhead, and
across the water a small group of wallabies cowered in the
sorghum grass.

"A meal for the crocs," Garcott sniggered. "Well, at
least you won't have to lie to Starker anymore."

Lupane scratched doubtfully at his chin and slowly replaced the gun in the holster. "We should get the car
checked out."

"What the hell for?" Garcott asked. "No one's goin' to
get out of there. Christ, you're askin' for problems if you
involve the Darwin police. Jeez, leave it with the crocs, I
say. Just count it lucky my information was right—they
were here, and we were lucky enough to spot the car." He
gestured to the water hole. "I'm certainly not goin' down
to do any checkin'. And neither are you."

Lupane nodded hesitant agreement. Garcott was probably right. After the crocodiles had finished, there'd be
nothing left anyway. But he wished one of them had come
to the surface, if only for a few minutes before the crocs
dragged them under again. But getting divers out from
Darwin would certainly produce complications he didn't
want, questions he might find difficult to answer. He
thought of the Marnoo girl, her body, her smile, the way

he'd wanted her. He tried not to think of her being torn
apart by the crocodiles.

"Okay, we'll leave it stand for now, as if they're still on
the run," he said. "No report, nothing. They just disappeared. We'll leave the call out on them . . . and the
reward for information. It'll be a hell of a lot easier for us if
no one ever knows what happened to them. We never saw
this. Okay?"

"Sure thing," Garcott agreed. "I know it's the best way
to handle it. No questions, no complications, no official
explanations to make." He squatted down on a rock, draped
his arms on his knees, and yawned widely. "All I want to
do is get some sleep."

Lupane suddenly experienced an enormous sense of
relief. He was finally safe. They were all safe: Blandhurst,
Starker, himself. It was stupid to have regrets about the
girl, after all she must have overheard when they were
sticking Jo Santeze. She could have put him away, ruined
him. Now he had the immeasurable pleasure of looking
forward to the expression on Kaufman's face when he
learned he was out on his ass.

They waited a time, but the surface of the water remained undisturbed. Then Lupane rapped Garcott on the
shoulder. "Come on, let's get the hell out of here and back
to Darwin. I'm just glad it's all over." He hoped he was
right and that Starker and Blandhurst knew what they
were doing. It would be an infuriating irony to take over
Kaufman's job just as the world blew itself apart in a
nuclear war.

8

There were moments when Ross wondered if they would
ever make Jabiru. On the first part of the drive across
country they had shared the cabin with Ted in a bone-

shaking ride along rust-colored rocky escarpments, around lagoons, through timbered scrub, on a circuitous route that seemed to go on forever. But once they were back on the highway, Ted had insisted on concealing them beneath a dank-smelling canvas on the open tray at the rear of the truck. It was stifling, but both he and Lisa had borne it stoically, realizing it was safer that way. But not seeing, huddled together in slimy sweat, made the remainder of the journey seem interminable. Several times the truck chugged to a halt as the engine died, and they crouched, helplessly listening to Ted's curses as he coaxed it back to life. Sometimes the truck rocked gently with the slipstream of a passing car, but no one stopped them. Time dissolved into an endless procession of jolts, stops, starts, and sweaty discomfort.

When the truck lurched to a halt for the last time they were unsure if it was another breakdown, until Ted dragged the canvas clear and peered cautiously down at them. Overhead the night sky was sprinkled with white dust. They both sat up warily and looked around. It was like stepping from a steambath into the sharp air. To the right, in the distance, clusters of lights marked habitation.

"Where the hell are we?" Ross asked.

"Jabiru," Ted answered. "Bloody truck gave me a lotta trouble. Sorry it took so long."

Ross pawed at his face, and it was as if the skin had been doused with water. "Thank Christ. God, it was hot under that thing."

"Whereabouts are we in the town?" asked Lisa.

Ted gestured vaguely in the direction of the lights. "That way to the town." He turned and motioned in the other direction to several other pinpoints of light. "An' that's the airfield over there. We're just on the outskirts. This is where you wanted, isn't it, Lisa?"

"Yes, it is, Ted," she agreed.

Ted pushed the canvas into the corner of the truck, his head darting nervously about in the air like a kangaroo sniffing for trouble. "I don' want to stay aroun' here any longer than I hafta," he grunted.

No one moved for a moment. Ross held his watch to the moonlight and saw it was eight-thirty.

"Alec used to have a small office at the airfield," Lisa said. "I know most of his Mount Isa flights were at night, so I just hope he's there." She glanced hesitantly at Ted. "I think it's best if I go across by myself and speak to him. If he's there. Will you wait for me with Ross, Ted, until I get back?"

"I told you you'd be on your own once we got to Jabiru," Ted growled. "I don't want any trouble . . . not from the cops."

"I need a little time. Please, Ted . . . I won't take long. If Alec's not there, I'm not sure what we'll do."

"That's your problem." The aborigine scowled and scratched irritably at his matted hair. "I brought you like I promised."

"I'll be quick," Lisa assured him.

"What d'you expect me to do if he isn't there?"

"Nothing. Ross and I will just have to risk hanging around the airport until he shows up. All I'm asking you to do is wait with Ross until I get back."

Ted shook his head sullenly. "Okay, but you better be quick, or I'll leave before you get back. I wanta get back to Oenpelli tonight."

Ross jumped to the ground and lifted Lisa down beside him. Ted leaned against the cabin, glowering at them both. He left no doubt he considered he was making a bad error of judgment.

"It might be a good idea if I come with you," Ross suggested.

Lisa shook her head. "No . . . this needs to be handled carefully, Ross. Alec can be a little difficult, and I know it's best if I do it alone. There's a better chance he'll take us. You wait here with Ted."

He trailed his fingers down her arm to grasp her hand.

"Okay, if that's the way you want to do it. You know the guy. Just take it easy."

"Don't worry, I know how to handle Alec," she said confidently.

She stepped away, and he stood back beside Ted to merge with the shadow of the truck. She didn't look back until she turned into the corner of the airfield. By then the truck had become part of the jumble of shadows thrown by the bushes along the side of the road. She went slowly, grateful for the moonlight, until she located the narrow gravel path she remembered ran along the side of the field. She let her memory guide her, trying to quell the nervous quivering of her body. It seemed almost a permanent condition now, something that had taken hold when she'd lain in the darkness listening to her friend being slaughtered. How long had it been since she'd spoken to Alec? God, it seemed like a thousand years now. She hated the thought of having to go to him like this, when she recalled the anger of their last meeting. Alec didn't forget things like that. She had said harsh things to him, but he'd been equally cruel. She was banking on the hope that traces of what he'd felt for her once still existed. It was possible she might have to try to light that flame again to get Alec's help, and she would do it if it was necessary. It would have been impossible if Ross had come along, but there was a chance if she saw Alec alone. She grieved for Jo, had been terrified by the murder, but her reaction had been more than fear. She wanted to survive, to survive with Ross, and she would do whatever had to be done. She had to try. There was nothing but death for her if she stayed here.

It was only a tiny office, but just as she remembered. Two rickety wooden chairs on either side of a small paper-littered desk. Filing cabinet, a cork pinboard on the wall, stuck with maps and schedules. A single naked globe burned overhead. She went cautiously into the room, patting nervously at her hair, smoothing at her wrinkled dress, and halted at the desk. A man entered through the opposite door, a folder clasped in his hand, and stopped abruptly when he saw her. He was about thirty-five, with a wiry six-foot frame, moon-faced, and wore the strained expression of a man who stares perpetually at the sun. Thinning fair hair was brushed straight back over his head. He wore neatly pressed white shorts and a deep blue open-neck shirt. His narrow eyes widened in astonishment; then he moved uncertainly to the desk and put down the folder. "For Chrissake, Lisa," he exclaimed. "Lisa Marnoo. Where the hell did you spring from?"

"Hello, Alec," she said with a confident smile.

He leaned his buttocks on the desk, crossed his arms, and studied her. "Lisa. My God, Lisa." He shook his head in wonderment. "I haven't seen or heard of you for . . . what, a year?" He grinned, but there was no warmth in the expression. "I'd just about forgotten you existed, then you pop up out of nowhere."

She knew he was lying. There'd been too much heat between them for him to forget after a year. She hadn't. The way he spoke, the way he looked at her, she knew it was still there.

"Well, is this a social visit? A time for dropping in on old . . . friends?" The tart sarcasm in his voice confirmed she was right. "I've got a flight soon, but if you'd like a cup of coffee, or to talk over old times, I guess I can wait a few moments." His sarcasm took on a sharper edge. No, he hadn't forgotten. But if she knew Alec, it was more injured pride at being brushed off than love. Maybe this was going to be impossible for her. "Say, where the hell *did* you come from?" he asked.

She gestured vaguely, then decided it was pointless to hedge with social chitchat. She had to remind him of what it was like with them before the break. She ran her hands down over her hips, straightening her dress again, and she knew he was watching. He seemed to see the state of her clothes and her ruffled hair for the first time.

"Christ, you look as if you walked from Darwin."

She managed a nonchalant laugh and pushed at her hair. "I had a . . . little difficulty getting here to see you," she admitted.

He looked at her in surprise. "Was it that important . . . after all this time?"

"Well, I . . . I came to Jabiru because I need your help, Alec," she began tentatively. "I need it badly."

His eyes squeezed with suspicion. "I would have thought I'd be the last one you'd come to for help," he stated coldly.

She tried to smile, and placed her hands on the back of the chair for support. He didn't ask her to sit down.

"We . . . we did have something going for each other once, and I thought maybe you could . . ." She stumbled awkwardly, and he smiled. She knew that expression of old, reveling in her embarrassment, and she hated him all over again. ". . . for old times' sake you might be able to help me," she forced herself to add.

"You kicked me out, Lisa," he said bluntly.

"I . . . I was very upset at the time, Alec, you know that."

"You're still the best-looking boong I ever screwed," he said offensively.

It was a deliberate attempt to throw her. To revive all the past humiliation when she'd heard he was boasting about her in Darwin. She pushed a smile onto her face. Better to be a live hypocrite than honest and dead. "I'm still the same girl," she managed.

He wasn't fooled. "You must want my help pretty bad." He checked his watch. "Well, I can't be of much use right now. My Mount Isa flight is all set to go. You can hang around here if you like, until I get back, then we'll talk some more about your . . . trouble."

"I want you to take me with you," she said quickly.

He stared at her. "To Mount Isa?"

"Yes. Me, and a . . . friend."

Suspicion flared in his face again. "A friend?"

"Yes. He needs to get to Mount Isa too."

"Where is . . . he?"

"Waiting at the end of the airfield."

He silently contemplated her. Intuitively she knew he was stirred by the old attraction, and she swayed her hips along the side of the chair.

"This . . . friend mean anything to you?" he asked.

She accomplished a disparaging laugh. "Oh my God, Alec . . . no, nothing like that. It's just that we have a mutual problem."

He nodded slowly. It sounded weak, but she had the feeling he was trying to make himself believe her.

"Say, you're not in trouble with the police, are you?" He immediately canceled the question with a sneering grin. "No, I can't imagine sweet Lisa in trouble with anyone."

She wasn't sure how to answer him. With Alec's background, a hint of trouble with the police might help her. "You know how things can happen sometimes, Alec," she said with a conspiratorial smile. "I might be the same girl in some ways, but in others I've changed a lot. Just let's say it would be healthier for me and my friend to be far away from Darwin for a while."

He looked at her for a time, doubt still unresolved. Then he moved abruptly away from the desk until he was standing very close to her. She kept her eyes steadily focused on his, a half-smile on her lips. His breath was hot and quick against her face. Then he moved his hands in a slow, exploratory circuit, up her arms, over her shoulders, across her breasts, down her stomach, and into her crotch, probing, pushing, feeling. She didn't resist, despising herself, her eyes half-closed. Survive, she whispered silently to herself. Survive. Survive. The image of Jo's body was so fresh, anything was possible.

"I never did quite get over you," he said unsteadily.

"I was never very far away."

He still held her. "What are you going to do in Mount Isa . . . if I take you?"

"Stay awhile." She shrugged. "My friend is going straight on to Sydney. I . . . I hope I won't be too lonely."

He released her, sat back on the edge of the desk again, and studied her with that peculiar intentness she remembered. She didn't dare take the smile from her face.

"All right," he said suddenly. "Wait at the end of the runway. I'll be taxiing out there for takeoff in about twenty minutes. You and your . . . friend be waiting for me."

It was so typical of Alec. With his erratic streak, he could just as abruptly have turned her down. Her tongue roved quickly back and forth over her mouth, and she began to back toward the door. "Thank you, Alec," she said huskily. "You won't be sorry. Believe me, you won't be sorry."

"Maybe." There was a faraway look in his eyes. Then he shook his head. "Just make sure you're ready and waiting for me."

She went quickly back down the path, occasionally stumbling in her haste. She felt unclean, but it wasn't the sort of dirt that soap and water could take away. It was done, and she just hoped Alec meant it, that he didn't change his mind. He had a weird sense of humor, and maybe he was merely stringing her along. He was capable of it. What she would do about Alec when they got to Mount Isa was a worry. No doubt he would turn ugly when he found out she had no intention of sharing his bed, but Ross would have to handle him for her. That meant Ross would have to learn about the sexual tactic she'd used. How would he react? She knew what he felt for her, and a similar feeling was building for him. She shut her mouth tightly and quickened her pace. He wanted to survive too. She wouldn't tell him, at least not yet. Maybe if luck was with her he would never have to know. But on the flight she would treat him like a stranger, with no hint of emotional involvement. Ross wouldn't understand, but if Alec was going to turn ugly, she preferred it to be in Mount Isa, not in midair.

Alec remained by the desk, moodily contemplating the door long after she'd gone. He wasn't sure why he'd agreed to take her. Christ, he still had the hard-on from standing close to her. Even after the angry way it had ended between them, she could still turn him on. Just the smell, the feel of her. She was a hell of a looker. Memories of the nights he'd spent with her flooded back. So he'd shot off his mouth a bit around Darwin about how good she was in bed. She should have been flattered instead of getting so all-fired upset. Shit, she was only a boong anyway. Remembrance of those final words stirred him uneasily. Just seeing her again was instant wanting, and she knew it. Christ, he hated to be conned. Maybe he'd been too impulsive.

He picked up the phone and dialed. "Listen, Mac," he said when the connection answered. "I'm just getting my flight together for Mount Isa. Make a few discreet inquiries for me in Darwin about a woman called Lisa Marnoo, will you? Just if there's anything on her with the police. Give me a call in flight if you get anything. Okay? . . . Thanks." He put the phone down with a grunt of satisfaction. He couldn't quite trust himself with Lisa. Maybe he could have resolved the problem by not picking her up at the end of the runway, but the thought of having that body again was too much of a temptation to be missed. It was hard to believe, but if there was something on her, then at least he'd have a lever to use.

Even when he was taxiing down the runway, he was still unsure if he was going to stop and pick her up. He peered through the windshield at the patchwork of black shadows along the perimeter of the field, but he couldn't see anyone. His mind was crowded with past images of Lisa pulsing under him, and they made his decision. He turned the Cessna at the limit of the runway and pushed open the door.

They came breathlessly out of nowhere, scrambling through the doorway and into the rear seat, mouthing guttural thanks. He didn't say anything. It was difficult to see the man's face in the dim light, but that could wait. He opened the throttle and sent the plane boring down the runway, then lifted smoothly into a sky sown thick with diamonds.

He went rapidly to his ceiling, leveled off, switched on the interior light, and looked back with a grin. The light took them by surprise. Lisa was in one corner of the seat, the man in the other, and she had one hand out as if restraining him in that position. The man tried to take her hand, and she wrenched it free to pat nervously at her hair.

He could feel the anger spurt into his face, and he switched off the light before the color betrayed him. "Everyone okay?" he asked breezily.

She gave a short, nervous laugh. "Fine, thank you, Alec. Everything went perfectly. I was a little anxious waiting for you."

"Didn't you think I'd come?"

"Of course," she said quickly. She motioned to the man beside her. "Alec, this is Ross Berger. Ross, Alec Redpath."

Ross leaned forward to offer his hand, but Redpath responded with a casual wave.

"We really owe you for this, Alec. I don't know how we could have got to Mount Isa without you. Lisa's lucky to have a friend like you to help us out."

A friend? He burned. So that's what she'd told Berger. He took time answering, wary that the volcano bubbling in his stomach would show in his voice. "That's what friends are for," he said. He concentrated on the controls, scarcely trusting himself to speak. "Why don't you two try to get some sleep. I'll let you know when we're coming into Mount Isa."

The Cessna rode easily on untroubled air. The landscape below was an irregular checkerboard of sharp black and white. The faces inside the cabin were cast in the same honed shadows. Alec struggled to get his fury under control. Jesus Christ, he'd made a fool of himself. All his judgment swept away by the overpowering urge to plant himself between the boong bitch's legs again. Betrayed by memories of her mouth, her skin, her cries, her belly heaving against his. She'd conned him. All her insinuations of loneliness and sexual availability in Mount Isa had been nothing but bullshit. He was absolutely sure of it now. She'd lied about this Berger character. Oh, nothing like that, Alec, he mimicked savagely to himself. He felt like an idiot. Maybe they sat behind him now like two prim innocents, but he'd been around, he knew the signs, you could amost feel the heat between them. What was she planning to do when he landed at Mount Isa, kiss him off and say: Thanks, sucker, but someone else made a down payment on me first.

He stared sullenly at the shimmering tropical sky and pondered on how he could fix the bitch. No one took him for a ride without paying for it. He should know by now his penchant for snap decisions often turned out sour. He fumed about it for half an hour, then Jabiru called him.

"This is Mac, Alec," said the voice.

"Yeah, what is it?" he snarled.

"About that inquiry you asked me to make concerning Lisa Marnoo?"

Resentment had deadened the memory of that last-minute request. He pressed his earphones tight and glanced surreptitiously into the rear seat. They were still propped into opposite corners, eyes closed, seemingly asleep. "I have that cargo on board," he murmured.

There was a surprised period of silence. "When the hell did that happen?"

"Never mind about that. What about the . . . cargo?"

"Well, seems like she's wanted by the Darwin police for

questioning over a pretty sticky murder. She's running with some guy called Berger, also wanted for the same murder."

Redpath's first reaction was to discount the information. Surely Mac had somehow got it all wrong. Lisa wanted on a murder charge simply didn't compute. Had she changed that much in a year? Maybe she'd been sucked into something over her head by the jerk beside her. "Can you describe the cargo?" he asked.

Mac fed back an accurate description of Lisa, and Alec shook his head in disbelief. It had to be the Berger character.

"What are you going to do about it?" inquired Mac. "Seems there's a reward out. You could make yourself a few bucks, Alec."

Redpath thought about it. Well, at least he'd be paid for making an idiot of himself. It was a nice twist to pay the boong bitch off. "I want you to contact the right people in Mount Isa to be ready to pick up the cargo," he said carefully.

"You mean the police?"

"They're the ones I had in mind."

"Okay . . . I'll get right on to it." There was a pause. "Don't forget I was the one who tipped you off, Alec. You might spread that reward around a little."

"Sure, sure," he grunted, and tuned out.

He settled back and let all the anger bleed out of him. He was a great believer in an eye for an eye. Or two. Someone tries to get at you, then you pay 'em back double. He squirmed at his own gullibility, but there was some compensation in the thought of the expression on her face when he touched down and she saw the coppers waiting. Shit, she was only a boong anyway. Jail was where she belonged.

The drunk was sprawled untidily in the opposite corner of the cell. Ross ignored him. He wondered where they had Lisa. After their arrest at the Mount Isa airport, they'd been brought straight to the jail, and he hadn't seen her since. He wondered how she was handling it. She was a fighter with plenty of spirit, but she'd be terrified at the thought they were sending for Lupane. He stood up from the bunk, wandered to the window, and stared morosely outside. In the distance the stack of the Mount Isa silver lead mine pointed like a finger at the midday sun. Bloody Redpath, why had the bastard agreed to fly them in the first place, if he was only going to turn them in? There was something between Lisa and the pilot he hadn't fathomed yet. Some past anger that called for an evening of old scores. She'd been like a wildcat at the airport, with a fury he couldn't have imagined, maybe a combination of fear and anger, but she would have torn Redpath apart if the police hadn't restrained her. Redpath had just stood by the plane laughing, an ugly, sneering sound. Ross shrugged irritably. Maybe he'd never know. She'd quieted down in the car, and scarcely broken silence all the way to the jail. At least she'd accepted his comforting touch then, not like in the plane. He didn't understand that either, holding him off like a leper. But he wasn't going to question her. Whatever there had been between her and Redpath once, she would tell him if she wanted to. She had spoken only one sentence, repeated at intervals during the car journey, like a sorrowful admission of defeat. I'm sorry, Ross. I'm sorry, Ross. A whispered apology, over and over, no matter how much he tried to console her. "We're not beaten yet," he'd said when they were separated at the jail. She hadn't believed him, going with a wordless shrug and an attempted smile, as if resigned to the face of Lupane killing them. He didn't see how he could believe it himself. Lupane and that other homicidal maniac, Garcott, were probably already on their way from Darwin with some murderous scheme for him and Lisa to have a fatal accident on the journey back.

The hell with them, he wasn't going like a bleating lamb

to the slaughter yard. The Mount Isa police had been lethargically uncooperative, but there had to be some way to obtain legal protection for the trip back to Darwin. If they could just manage to survive until they got there, they might have a chance. When Lupane arrived, he'd decided to stage some form of wild protest, shout, scream, whatever it took, so that everyone within earshot knew Lupane intended for them to have an accident on the way back to Darwin. If he had enough witnesses, it just might force Lupane to cancel his plan. That's the only thing he'd come up with so far after a sleepness night.

He slumped down on the bunk again, his shirt clinging wetly to his back from the heat in the cell. The drunk snuffled loudly, rolled to his other side, and began to snore. Ross put his head down and distractedly scuffed at his hair. He couldn't afford to panic, lose hope. A humorless laugh squeezed out of his throat. The craziest thing of all, he still didn't know why Lupane was so viciously intent on killing them.

He glanced up at the sound of a key turning in the door. A large balding policeman with a forest of black hair showing above his open shirt front opened the cell door and motioned to him. "You've got a visitor, Berger," he said laconically. "Follow me."

Ross stood tentatively to his feet. It had to be Lupane. He had it all figured out what he was going to do. Maybe it was going to take a couple of police to hold him down, but Christ, he'd make sure everyone knew what he was screaming about.

But it wasn't Lupane. He was shown into a small room, bare floor, small table, several angular chairs, and a barred window looking out to a nondescript street. Lisa was already seated on one of the chairs, and she looked at him with a wan smile. She'd combed her hair, and some of the old spirit showed in her face. Ross ignored the middle-aged man standing by the window and moved across to gently kiss her. She welcomed his mouth eagerly, with no

sign of her aloofness in the plane. The man coughed
awkwardly, and Ross straightened to look at him. He was
obviously a city man, conservative clothes and a clerkish
appearance. Ross had never seen him before. He offered
no gesture of welcome, but stood with his back to the
window, hands clasped behind. He looked in his mid-
fifties. There was an expensive-looking briefcase resting on
the table.

"My name is Kaufman, Mr. Berger," he began. He
spoke with quiet authority, in a clipped London accent.
He gestured to the vacant chair. "Won't you sit down?"

Ross complied to a request that was more like an order.
The man's name meant nothing to him.

"No doubt you were expecting Lupane," Kaufman said
bluntly. The words were delivered with an open desire to
shock.

Ross was nonplussed for a moment. He glanced cautiously at Lisa, then back at Kaufman. It didn't make sense
for Lupane to send someone else to pick them up. "You're
not from Lupane?" he asked.

"No, I'm not."

"Then what do you know about Lupane?"

Kaufman laughed shortly. He had a way of doing it so
that his mouth scarcely moved. "Only that he seems to
have an obsession about wanting to kill you people."

"You're from . . . Darwin?"

"No, I'm not from Darwin either." He smiled benignly.
"I want you to stop worrying about Lupane right now.
You're safe with me. Lupane can't harm you now."

Breath hissed from Lisa's mouth like air from a balloon,
but Ross didn't look at her.

"Then who are you . . . Mr. Kaufman? How do you
know about Lupane? About him wanting to kill us?"

Kaufman didn't answer immediately. He opened the
briefcase, took out an envelope, and dropped it on the
table. It was the envelope containing Mark's photographs.
The police had stripped Ross of all personal possessions,

including the photographs. Ross looked warily at the envelope, then back at Kaufman. He wasn't ready to trust this man yet. He could be part of some devious scheme Lupane had worked out to throw them off guard.

"I've been looking at these photographs the police took from you," said Kaufman. "I'm fascinated. You know what they mean?"

"I haven't the faintest idea," muttered Ross. "But I suspect they have something to do with the reason Lupane wants to kill us. Don't ask me to explain it." He shrugged. "Maybe I'm wrong."

"No, I don't think you are wrong," said Kaufman. "These are the photographs your brother took?"

Ross nodded silently.

Kaufman opened the briefcase again, took out a newspaper, and held it folded in his hands. "You haven't seen a newspaper, been near any news source in the last forty-eight hours?"

"We've been too busy trying to stay alive to read a newspaper."

Kaufman opened the newspaper and thrust it toward Ross. "Read it," he stated crisply. "The front page will suffice. You also, Miss Marnoo." He stood back, folded his arms, and turned profile to the window. Shafts of sunlight made transparent wisps of his thin, sandy hair.

The room fell silent, save for the rustle of the newspaper in Ross's hands. A high-pitched siren wailed outside, as if signaling a work break. It was all there on the front page, the screaming headlines of the North West Cape raid, photographs, denouncements, editorials.

Ross stared at Lisa, then at Kaufman, and some of the darkness lifted in his mind. "My God," he breathed.

"Exactly," said Kaufman tersely. "Although I doubt if he can do much for us at the moment."

"It all fits," Ross said in astonishment. "The description of the raider, the uniform he was wearing, matches Mark's photographs exactly." He shook his head. "Maybe it was an accident, a coincidence, but somehow Mark must have photographed them . . . maybe when they were rehearsing for this raid . . . perhaps off Cape Jaubert. He must have been seen taking the shots . . . and they killed him. It's the only explanation."

Kaufman plucked thoughtfully at his chin. "I'd say something like that probably happened."

"You're telling me Lupane knew all about this raid . . . was part of the planning. That he's a Russian agent. He's trying to kill us because we saw these photographs . . . he was frightened we might have found out what they meant." He stared down at the newspaper again. "Christ, no wonder he wanted to kill us. I had no idea it was something big like this."

"And it seems he still feels you're both too dangerous to be left alive," Kaufman said. "If not to the actual raid, then to himself."

"Is Lupane a Russian agent?"

Kaufman shrugged. "I don't know. I don't think so."

"Then what the hell's his part in all this?" demanded Ross angrily. "And yours too, for that matter."

Kaufman took his time answering. He sank into the remaining chair on the other side of the table and pushed the briefcase to one side. "Just let's say I'm responsible for protecting the security of this country . . . Intelligence, if you prefer the word. Naturally I'm deeply involved in the investigation of the North West Cape raid. Lupane is my . . . chief subordinate."

Ross stared at him blankly. He had the feeling of being at the center of a maze. "Lupane's in Intelligence? You knew what he was doing?"

Kaufman made a shushing motion of his hands. "Not at all. Believe me, I had no idea what he was up to." He coughed with an air of embarrassment. "What you might call something of an . . . organizational problem." He gave Ross a bleak smile. "Well, let's say I had some suspicions . . . but nothing like this. I had . . . contacts keeping an eye on Lupane in Darwin. That's why I'm here instead of Lupane. He never received the message from the Mount Isa police that you were here. My . . . ah, contact managed to sidetrack that information to me. Lupane doesn't know about your arrest . . . at least not yet."

Ross felt Lisa stir uneasily beside him, and he laid a hand over hers. "Yet? What's that supposed to mean?"

Kaufman displayed a carnivorous smile. "I want to be absolutely sure I can get your total cooperation."

Ross scowled. The man's appearance was obviously deceptive. He looked like a clerk, but he spoke like a fox.

"Cooperation in what?"

"In that you'll have to trust me for now."

"I can't think of one bloody reason why I should trust you," said Ross truculently. "I've found it hard to trust anyone since this all began, including the fuck of a pilot who turned us in to the police."

Kaufman fiddled with the earpiece of his glasses. "You have to trust me. What have you got to lose?"

"Our lives."

"Only with Lupane."

"And maybe with you."

Kaufman betrayed the first signs of impatience. "I'm an extremely busy man, Mr. Berger, and as you can appreciate, the North West Cape raid has put me under considerable pressure. Politicians, newspapers. I dropped everything to come to Mount Isa as soon as I got the word you were here, but I haven't a lot of time. You can talk to me, or you can talk to Lupane. It's up to you."

Ross hesitated. Maybe it was a bluff, but he resented being threatened. Would this innocuous-looking man really turn them over to Lupane, knowing it could cost them their lives? He cast a questioning glance at Lisa, and she twitched her shoulders.

"Maybe he's right. What have we got to lose?" she said.

"The lady makes sense, Mr. Berger," interposed Kaufman.

"Lupane's job with the Darwin police is only a cover?" asked Ross.

"I believe so." The intelligence man's lips set in a stern line. "I need an answer, Mr. Berger."

"If it's a cover, some high-placed bastard must be protecting him."

Kaufman sighed. "Your answer, Mr. Berger. Then we can discuss those questions."

It was hot in the room. Ross swallowed hard, and his throat felt like dried parchment. What he wouldn't give for a beer. "All right, what do you want to know," he conceded guardedly.

"Everything."

"What do you mean by everything?"

"From you, every detail since you set foot in Darwin. From Miss Marnoo, everything that happened between her and Lupane. Everything either of you can tell me about the killing of Jo Santeze."

"That'll take time."

"I'll make time."

Kaufman listened impassively while they went through it all. The conversations with Lupane, the chance that had put the camera in Ross's possession. Then it was Lisa's turn, and she went through without faltering until she came to the killing of Jo. She handled it well, even if she found it impossible to recreate every macabre detail. It was only when she repeated Lupane's words on leaving the apartment after the murder that Kaufman's attitude of detached observer changed. His eyes widened, and he hunched over the desk, hands tightly clasped.

"Would you repeat that please, Miss Marnoo?" he asked huskily.

"Something about pleasing his friend at Beton . . . keeping Martin's hands clean," she said again.

Kaufman blinked rapidly, like a man awakening. "Thank you," he murmured. Blankness came into his face, as if he'd abruptly drawn a blind over his mind. He remained outwardly attentive while Ross outlined the final hours that had brought them to Mount Isa, but his thoughts were obviously elsewhere.

Ross concluded, and the room fell silent again. Kaufman stared into space, his fingers picking at his mouth. His pale skin, now suffused with color, was the only indication of an inner excitement. Finally he stirred in the chair and placed a hand over the photographs. "Lupane has no idea you kept a copy of these for yourself?"

"I'm sure he doesn't. I gave him to understand he had the only copies."

Kaufman grunted with satisfaction, his eyes hooded. "Good, good," he muttered. He lifted the envelope and rapped it with a light drumbeat against the desktop. "I want to keep these for the moment, Mr. Berger. There are some items there that interest me greatly. Especially the ship."

"The photographs are very sharp," said Ross. "The name of the ship would come up clearly under a magnifying glass. *Sea*-something."

"Yes, I saw that."

"I'll get them back?"

"Of course. But later."

Kaufman seemed more relaxed now. He leaned back in the chair, fondling the envelope, the blue eyes behind the thick lenses set with a reflective glaze.

"What happens now about us . . . about Lupane?" demanded Ross.

"Like I said, Lupane doesn't know you're here. I'll keep it that way. I want you both to come to Sydney with me."

"Can you do that?" questioned Ross doubtfully. "The police here are holding us on a murder charge."

Kaufman replied with a nonchalant twitch of his shoulders. "Some calls have been made from Sydney by . . . influential people. I think the police are suitably impressed. Yes, I can do it. We should leave as soon as possible."

"Are we to consider ourselves as prisoners?" asked Ross.

Kaufman permitted a thin-lipped smile. "I wouldn't go that far, Mr. Berger. Let's say you're under my protection for the time being. I think we can have more talks, maybe even learn some more from each other. I'm sure both of you want to help in any way possible to get at the truth. For the country's sake."

The words were delivered in honeyed terms, but there was no mistaking the underlying steel. They could trust him, or take their chances with Lupane. And that was no chance at all.

"Is there going to be a war?" asked Lisa.

"Who knows, Miss Marnoo? Only a war of words, I think." He dropped the photographs back in his briefcase. "They took an awful risk of that with the raid. I can't help feeling that someone may have miscalculated about that possibility along the way." He stood. "I think we can move now if you're ready."

Ross nodded, stood slowly, and helped Lisa to her feet. She glanced at him with an uncertain smile. There was doubt for both of them, but also relief that this seemed a chance to stay alive. Kaufman was an unknown quantity, but they had to go along. But warily. There was no way they were ever going to trust any of them.

Lisa and Ross were taken by stony-faced men to a small seaside town called Terrigal, some hundred kilometers from Sydney, and installed in a small, comfortable cottage overlooking the sea. Then left to themselves. Everything was at the house, new clothes, provisions. They were told nothing except that Kaufman would be in touch with them in a few days. Plus an added warning to communicate with no one. That was almost impossible anyway, with the cottage sited on an isolated clifftop, and no telephone. Inadvertently, it was a haven for them. There was an intimacy about the house that engendered a healing mood. They wound down, and fear gradually subsided. Whatever

Kaufman wanted from them was for the future, and they tried to make a lifetime of the few days.

The house contained only a motley collection of old furniture, but it sufficed. A small balcony provided a beautiful view of the green cliffside running down to a winding belt of white sand lapped by the blue Pacific. Of course they weren't really alone. They didn't fully trust Kaufman, and he returned the feeling in kind. To step out the door, to stroll on the beach, was to immediately invite the appearance of distant figures, who never approached any closer, but always made sure they were provocatively visible. Where they came from, where they stayed, Ross and Lisa had no idea. Kaufman had promised protection, but doubtless these men were also warders. They learned to ignore them.

There were personal concerns—Ross for his parents and Mark's funeral, Lisa for her grandfather—but they were beyond resolution for now.

They were alive, and it inspired an intense spark to live for the moment, caught up in the exhilarating sense of immortality that follows survival. Whatever was to come, here and now was all that mattered, with no place for past fears, past hang-ups. Barriers, real or imagined, melted away. They made the tiny house a place of love, of commitment. Hushed nights clasped in each other's arms, where pleasing and being pleased were the only importance, touching, feeling, the moans of ecstasy and orgasm merging with the muffled drum of the surf. Perhaps it had a desperate edge, that this might only be as temporary as life itself, but that made it more moving. And Ross's whispered words of love joined with Lisa's whispered words of love, and he was finally believed. If sometimes in the night she still moaned for Jo, then he was there to comfort her, soothe her back to sleep. For a short time at least, love subdued fear. They walked the clifftops arm in arm, enjoying the keen wind, and rediscovered joy in small forgotten things of childhood. A seashell, a piece of driftwood, sunset drawing a scarlet haze over the world. Lupane, Kaufman, Jo, were still in their minds, but the delusion that this was forever made it a poignant time in their lives.

Australia may have made an occasional international headline with sporting prowess, films, and bushfires, but for the first time the country was center stage in world tension.

"This is a deliberate attempt by the Soviet Union to subvert the security of the United States," stormed the American ambassador to the United Nations at the emergency session. "To hurl the world into a catastrophic nuclear war. The free world can only guess at the devious mischief Russia intended in the Indian Ocean, which necessitated the destruction of the North West Cape base. The United States will not tolerate such contemptible international lawlessness."

"Never since World War Two," raged the Russian ambassador to the United Nations, "has a country lied so much to its people as have the governments of Australia and America. We absolutely deny any involvement in the North West Cape raid. It is obviously a monstrous deception to attempt to blacken the name of the Russian people."

The insults and accusations continued. But no one was pressing any buttons, and already it was evident that the only war to evolve was one of ferocious words.

In Australia the election opinion polls had undergone a convulsive about-face. It was now apparent the government would retain office by an increased majority.

After three days Kaufman came to see Ross and Lisa. They watched from the balcony as the car stopped outside the house. One of their mysterious guardians materialized from the surrounding trees, deferentially spoke to Kaufman for a few minutes, then waited in the car while the intelligence man entered the house. It was late afternoon, and as if to heighten their foreboding, the sky was a menacing shade of slate gray, the horizon obscured by a misty rain.

They settled down in the living room after a perfunctory greeting, Kaufman with his inevitable briefcase. Little was said but trivia over their living conditions, until coffee was made. Everyone was cautiously polite. Kaufman had reprieved them from execution, and doubtless he was there to ask payment for the debt.

He opened his briefcase, took out several large photographs, and laid them down on the small table. He motioned for Ross and Lisa to examine them. "I want you to tell me if you know either of these men."

They peered at the photographs. Both men were about the same late middle age, both distinguished in appearance, one in military uniform.

Ross pointed to the civilian. "I've been out of the country for a time, but I know this man. He's been in public life for a long time. A politician. A minister in the government. Blandhurst. Martin Blandhurst."

"I've seen his picture in the newspapers," added Lisa helpfully.

"Well, you're right, it is Martin Blandhurst." Kaufman nodded. "What about the other man?"

Both of them shrugged. "The face means nothing to me," said Ross. "The uniform looks American, but I don't know him."

Kaufman turned to Lisa, and she gave an equal disclaimer.

"General Leo Starker," declared Kaufman. "An ex Vietnam commander. Now retired from the United States Army. Did either of you ever see him in Darwin?"

"He was there?" asked Lisa.

"I have reason to believe so. Possibly there may have been more chance for you to see him, Miss Marnoo."

They both considered the picture further, then slowly shook their heads.

Something clicked in Ross's mind, and he glanced quickly

at Kaufman. "Martin," he said. "Keep Martin's hands clean."

Lisa's eyes widened in response. "That's right," she echoed in astonishment. "Our friend in Beton." She turned to Kaufman. "The words I heard Lupane use in the apartment. What does Beton mean?"

"Beton is the name of the district where Martin Blandhurst lives."

Ross stared at him. "Christ, are you telling us that a cabinet minister in the government is mixed up in the raid?"

Kaufman offered no answer. He shuffled the photographs on the table, like a chess player contemplating his next move. "I'm not going to say that at the moment," he murmured warily. "Make any accusations at all. I have to do what's best for the country—no matter who gets hurt. No matter how high-placed are the people involved."

"But it is Blandhurst. Lisa heard Lupane use his name."

Kaufman fell silent again. His fingers drummed lightly across the image of Blandhurst's face.

"What about my brother's photographs?" asked Ross.

"As I imagined, they were extremely useful."

"Did you find out anything about that ship?"

Kaufman pawed reflectively at his chin. "Like you said, your brother's pictures are exceptionally sharp. The name of the ship came up very clearly in enlargement. Name of *Seaboro*. Our . . . friends in America were able to trace it for us, back to an organization closely associated with General Starker, called the Committee of Concerned Americans."

"My God, how many top-level people are in this?" exclaimed Ross. "I can't believe someone like Blandhurst is a Russian agent."

"I'm sure he isn't." There was a long pause, as if Kaufman was waiting to let the significance of what he was saying take hold. "The General has been in Australia for the last few weeks," he continued. "Basing himself in

Darwin. I have information he's been in close contact with Lupane. And the General is also a long-standing friend of Martin Blandhurst."

There was another silence. Ross took a deep breath and let the air out slowly as the import of what Kaufman was saying gradually penetrated. Lisa cast a puzzled glance from one man to the other.

"An Australian cabinet minister," Ross said slowly. "An American general . . . an American ship." He shrewdly appraised the intelligence man. "Maybe you've got an explanation, Mr. Kaufman, as to why—but I've got a hunch it wasn't the Russians who raided the North West Cape at all. But it was done to make it look that way. The Russian who disappeared from the Canberra embassy . . . the way all these people connect up." He shook his head. "Why the hell would they do a crazy thing like that?"

Kaufman leaned back in the chair and stared out to the ocean. The rain was closing in like a fog. His coffee was cold on the table. "I have my suspicions, but nothing I can prove right now." His eyes flicked back to Ross, and then to Lisa. "You two people are the only ones who can help me get at the real truth."

Ross knew it was coming. The sales pitch had been made; now Kaufman was going to ask for the order. He wondered how high the price was going to be.

"I don't know how we can help you. It sounds out of our league to me. Cabinet ministers. Generals. And these bastards are playing for keeps. They'll stomp on anyone without losing a night's sleep. A young girl in Darwin was butchered just because she accidentally saw some photographs. Only luck saved Lisa. And me. Those bastards sit back safely in their untouchable heaven and make sure it's everybody's ass except their own. You too, for all I know."

"You're wrong there," said Kaufman. "But if you believe that's the way it is, then you can help change it, Ross."

He slipped easily into first-name usage, inviting confidence. Lisa was for the moment a bemused onlooker, absorbing every word.

"What do you want me to do?" Ross asked cautiously.

"I want you to call Martin Blandhurst at his home in Beton."

Ross blinked. "Just like that?"

Kaufman produced Mark's Cape Jaubert photographs from the briefcase and dropped them on the table. "Tell Blandhurst you have a set of your brother's photographs, and now you know what they mean. You know he's involved in the North West Cape raid, and you'll sell him the photographs for a million dollars."

Ross laughed scornfully. "If I want to commit suicide I'll find an easier way than that. You're asking me to put my head in a bear trap."

"Not at all. If you think it through clearly, you'll be quite safe." He picked up the prints and juggled them in his hand. "These are only copies I had made from your originals. You only have to tell Blandhurst the originals are being held in a safe place, with instructions to be forwarded to the newspapers if anything happens to you. He won't dare lay a finger on you."

He passed the prints to Ross for verification. They were poor copies, with loss of quality and color, but adequate as proof.

"You expect me to take these to him . . . show him?"

"Yes. At his house in Beton."

"Why there? Why can't I ask him to come here . . . or meet somewhere on neutral ground?"

A crafty smile curled Kaufman's lips. "It's more convenient. I have a contingency plan all set to plant a bug in the house. It can be done. And more important, I'm informed that General Starker has arrived at the house. That falls right in our lap. Two birds in the one nest is too good an opportunity to miss." He stalled the doubt in Ross's face. "Don't worry, it's all been carefully thought out. I'll have a listening post set up somewhere near the house when you're there. I'll have everything that's said between the three of you down on tape."

Ross stirred in the chair and glanced uneasily at Lisa. Kaufman made it sound so plausibly safe, but it was a hell of a risk. The attempt to kill them, what had happened to Jo, to Mark, were ample proof these bastards were absolutely ruthless. Why should he put his head back in the noose?

"What if Blandhurst won't buy it . . . if you're wrong about him, and he denies everything and tells me to get lost? Or worse, calls the police in?"

Kaufman smiled like an overfed cat. "He might, but I'm almost sure that won't happen. The connection's too strong—the ship, Starker, Blandhurst, Lupane, your brother's photographs. They're in it up to their necks." He nodded confidently. "They'll be shocked to hear from you. Maybe they think you're already dead. You'll put the fear of God into them, Ross."

Ross frowned. No, he was sure Lupane would still be looking for them. "What happens afterward?" he questioned.

"Let me worry about that. All I want for now is proof."

Ross gestured to Lisa. "I mean about us?"

"This is your ticket to freedom. Lupane'll be finished and no longer in any position to do you harm. I know you haven't killed anyone. You just go on about your lives." He glanced meaningfully from one to the other. "Whatever you want to do."

It was too pat. Ross studied him with cynical distrust. What was in it for Kaufman? The way he'd pressured them in Mount Isa with threats of Lupane showed an equally ruthless streak. Would he apply the same pressure now if they turned him down?

Lisa gave voice to all his reservations. "You got us off the hook, Mr. Kaufman . . . and we're grateful. We might be dead now if it wasn't for you. But I think this is crazy. These people are killers. The first thing Blandhurst will do when he gets Ross's call is send for Lupane. You can find a way to get your proof without us."

"It'll take too long, Miss Marnoo. I want it now, and I want it quick. They're talking nuclear war in the United Nations."

She shook her head stubbornly. "You can still get it without us. Don't do it, Ross."

Kaufman scowled. "He has to. You both have to." He glowered at her. "You're part of this too, Lisa."

She ignored him and turned to Ross. "You saw what they're capable of in Darwin, Ross. They're not going to be bluffed by anyone." She made an agitated gesture toward Kaufman. "I don't think this man gives a damn what happens to us, as long as he gets his proof."

"You seem to have recovered from your fear of Lupane remarkably quickly," Kaufman declared coldly.

It had the effect of momentarily silencing Lisa. Her tongue flashed nervously over her lips, and her eyes sought Ross for support. "I haven't forgotten Lupane," she said curtly.

"I'm glad to hear it." Kaufman directed his forefinger like a pistol, his aim wavering from Ross to Lisa. "I'm sure you've both had a very . . . pleasant time here at the house. He sneered offensively. "Maybe even forgotten you're both wanted in connection with a brutal murder in Darwin. I can still just walk away from both of you. Anytime. Just leave the North West Cape raid the way it is. Plenty of people would be just as happy to leave the blame with the Russians. But I think more of the security of this country than that. I'm going to dig these traitors out, no matter who they are. And you're going to help . . . both of you. Or I'll put you both back on Lupane's hook so fast you'll bleed before you know what's happened. Lupane can do what he likes, and you can both go to hell." His bland face was transformed by spleen. "I'm not bluffing. The stakes are too big. I'll squash you from sight if I have to, if that's the way you want it." He paused, breathing heavily.

Ross said nothing for a moment. The love idyll of the last three days shriveled and died. Then: "Maybe Lisa's right—you *don't* give a damn," he said bitterly. "You're just shit like the rest of them."

"I don't care what you think of me," Kaufman stated bluntly. "You've got the same choice I gave you in Mount Isa. A chance with me, or no chance with Lupane."

Ross slumped sullenly in the chair. That was no choice at all. "If I do it, Lisa stays here."

"No. You both go to Beton."

"Fuck you, Kaufman. Lisa's out. It's dangerous enough for me without dragging her into it."

"I've told you it'll be perfectly safe," declared Kaufman in exasperation. "It'll be more convincing if you're both there. More shock value. More chance of Blandhurst being thrown off balance. I want every word that can be squeezed out of him for the tape."

"I don't need Lisa," insisted Ross.

"The hell with what you want—that's the way it's got to be."

Ross lapsed into a petulant silence. He had no cards to play. No room for bargaining. Kaufman's demand was stupid, illogical, but he had no means to fight it.

Lisa leaned over and placed a consoling hand on his shoulder. "Thanks, but don't worry about it, Ross. I don't mind."

He didn't believe her. She was strong, but he wondered how she'd react if she had to face Lupane again, with the memory of what he'd done to Jo still so vivid in her mind.

"Don't forget your brother, Ross," said Kaufman in a quieter tone.

"My brother?"

"Yes. These people I'm asking your help to nail—they're the ones responsible for killing him. That's important. Surely it's an added incentive to do this for me."

Ross stared dourly out the window. He hadn't forgotten Mark. The rotting body in the morgue. But he'd wanted to settle that score in his own time. His own way. "If I was sure it was them, I'd take care of it."

"Down an alley . . . one dark night." Kaufman sneered. "Then you'd really be up on a murder charge." He made a placatory motion of his hands. "This way, you can be sure, really sure."

Ross shrugged. Maybe. He needed no more proof where Lupane was concerned. "When do you want me to call Blandhurst?"

"Now. I want a meeting set up for tomorrow night."

Ross glanced about the room. "There's no phone here."

"You can use the phone in my car. I know he's at the house now."

"How do we get to Beton?"

"I'll arrange that. By air to Mackay, and there'll be a car waiting for you. You'll need to push Blandhurst hard. Threaten. Let him know you've found out they're all involved. Starker . . . Lupane." The myopic eyes behind the thick lenses were riveted on Ross's face. "You can do it, Ross." Now wheedling assurance was added to intimidation. "We've checked you out. You've been around. You know how to handle a man like Blandhurst. All pomp and confidence on the surface, but chickenshit underneath. You've seen his kind around the world."

Ross looked at him with distaste. He preferred the threatening Kaufman to this sucking-up version. "I'll need a gun."

"You won't need a gun. I'll give you all the protection you'll need. I don't want to risk any shooting. I want these people alive. I keep telling you Blandhurst won't dare lay a finger on you. You'll merely be setting up a business deal. I'll take care of the confrontation."

"I'd feel safer with a gun."

"Forget it," stated Kaufman flatly. "I won't take that risk."

As on every detail, the intelligence man was inflexible. They did it his way or took the consequences. Ross shrugged. He had to go with it, but he'd watch every step of the way. He looked at Lisa and tried to smile encouragement when he saw the old fear in her eyes again.

Kaufman swept the photographs of Starker and Blandhurst back into his briefcase and stood up. "You're right about one thing, Miss Marnoo. Blandhurst is sure to bring Lupane into it after they get your call." He gave a contented smile. "That's a good thing. We'll have them all in the den at the same time. It should make interesting listening." He lifted a warning hand. "Just one point. I'm sure I can trust you," he said with heavy irony, "but don't deviate from the plan in any way. We'll be watching you." He contrived a menacing smile on his bland face. "For your protection, of course." He moved toward the door and motioned to Ross. "Now, let's get that call made. I'll fill you in on a few more details on the way down."

Ross climbed wearily to his feet. It seemed as if he'd been running for a thousand years. From Mark, from his father, from himself, from Lupane, and now this bastard. Lisa gripped him fiercely by the arm as he passed, and he patted her hand. Nothing could take away the three days they'd had together in the house.

Kaufman settled down in the corner of the back seat and mentally isolated himself from the other occupants of the car on the run back to Sydney. The others knew better than to intrude on his silence. It was dusk, but already the moon was reflected in the Pacific. The light carved his face into white marble. All the instincts he'd developed over the years told him he held all the cards. If he made sure he played them right. He had a lot riding on Berger, but he was sure the gamble was justified. Berger would do anything to protect the girl, and gallant knights on white horses were easy to manipulate. The meeting had been set at Sweetwater for tomorrow night, and it had been diffi-

cult keeping the gloating out of his face when Berger had
recounted Martin's stunned reaction to the call. He'd seen
Blandhurst flounder before when he'd lost the initiative,
and by God he'd be floundering now. He'd always known
Blandhurst was a ruthless politician, but this was something else. There was much he still didn't know, but he
could scarcely believe Blandhurst would place himself in
such a vulnerable position. Maybe the plan had gotten out
of hand. He could imagine the panic when those photographs came out of the blue just before the raid. No
wonder they were in such a murderous frame of mind.
Starker wouldn't quibble about a few lives, from what he
knew of the General. He was sure the raid was more than
just a contrived gimmick to win the election. Christ, how
many had they killed? And the risk of promoting a nuclear
confrontation between Russia and the United States was
enormous. Nothing would be more guaranteed to enrage
the Americans than the killings at the base.

When he had it all down on tape tomorrow night, he
would come to his own decision on how to resolve the
problem. He had to keep it out of the media. He would
have Blandhurst in the palm of his hand if everything
went according to plan, to manipulate in any way he
wanted. He would destroy Lupane. And maybe Starker.
But the General was a problem. A dangerous problem.
According to his information, this Committee of Concerned Americans to which the General was connected was
under close surveillance by American intelligence. If Starker
returned to America only to be exposed, revelations might
come out about the raid that would threaten the chance of
Kaufman's gaining a hold over Blandhurst. That was a
worry that needed considerable thought. And the same
concern applied to Berger and the girl. He'd had to take
them into his confidence to make the blackmail plan feasi-
ble, but could he possibly risk them wandering free around
the country with what they knew when this was all over?
They would have the same hold over him as he would

have over Blandhurst. It would be like sitting around on an unexploded bomb. Lupane was disposable garbage, but sufficient conscience still survived that viewed with repugnance the necessity of eliminating innocents. But he could never be safe while they lived. It could be an ideal world, Lupane finished, a hold over Blandhurst to guarantee him immunity for life, maybe even resolve his financial difficulties with a generous loan. And there was no harm in letting the world go on believing the raid was planned by the Russians. Provided the world didn't blow itself apart with a nuclear conflict, but he was sure now it was merely going to fizzle into a war of words. Already they were backing off. But it was an irresistible vision of the future for him.

He sat squashed into the seat for the next half-hour, hands thrust into his pockets, trying to resolve the problem. He couldn't risk personal involvement in any killings. The car turned onto the main highway, and the traffic thickened, the glare of oncoming traffic like starbursts in his glasses. Finally he sighed, opened his briefcase, took out the original prints of Mark Berger's Cape Jaubert photograpahs, and placed them in the lap of the man beside him. He had regrets, especially where the girl was concerned, but making unpleasant decisions about other people's lives was something he'd grown used to now. When it came to the crunch, he had to do what was necessary for his own survival. His companion glanced at the envelope, then questioningly at him.

"The option we discussed yesterday, Brett," he murmured. "I don't believe we have any other course but to go with it. See that they get to Lupane the way we agreed."

9

There were decisions that had to be made that day concerning the running of Sweetwater, and although Blandhurst somehow managed to issue instructions, it was as if his mind were groping through a fog. There were cattle to be readied for market, the impending purchase of new property, and the Beton mill was requesting that his sugarcane be cut. They were behind schedule, and his manager had declared rather testily that the cane would have to be burned off that night.

To all such requests the cabinet minister acquiesced with a numbed tilt of his head. He moved like a man in a state of shock, and his uncomprehending staff could only conclude that the impact of the North West Cape raid, plus the strain of the elections, had produced a physical reaction. Those all-night meetings in Canberra would sap the energy of a much younger man than Martin Blandhurst. Then there had been the arrival of General Starker. Even the most casual observer would have noticed the strained relationship between the once close friends.

If Blandhurst was aware of his staff's concern, he gave no sign. But he was relieved to reach the sanctuary of his study when all the necessary decisions had been made. Yet it did nothing to ease his state of acute anxiety. He went immediately to the gracious colonial sideboard and poured himself a long Scotch, ignoring Starker using the telephone at the desk. He drank deeply, and slumped down on the sofa as Starker hung up.

"Well, I finally got hold of Lupane," announced the General. "He's coming straight up from Canberra. He gave himself a few days' leave after he left Darwin."

Blandhurst absently swirled the whiskey about in his

glass. "What did that incompetent idiot have to say for himself?" he muttered sullenly.

The General strode to the window and stood at attention, hands clasped behind his back. "We can question him further when he gets here," he replied curtly. "The fool's practically incoherent at the moment. The fact is, he lied about Berger and the girl. He claims he *thought* they were dead. He should have made absolutely certain." The disciplined composure suddenly broke, and he pounded a fist angrily into the palm of his hand. "He lied. He lied. He put us all at risk, Martin. I can't believe anyone could be guilty of such a dereliction of duty. The cretin jacked off on us." He pointed a quivering finger at Blandhurst. "The man deserves to be shot for such an unforgivable deception."

The words jolted Blandhurst from his morose shell. He angrily thumped the whiskey glass down on the small table by the sofa. "For Christ's sake, Leo, is killing people the only solution you've got for everything?" he blurted out. He waved his hands as if making frantic signals in the air. "No more, Leo, you hear? By Christ, no more killing. I won't stand for any more of it. My God, Lupane isn't the only one who's been lying." The impeccable parliamentary debating voice was distorted out of recognition. He was a bad color, his florid complexion tinged with a purplish hue. He hadn't slept since Berger's phone call the previous day, and it showed in his face.

"We're not going over that again, are we?" snapped the General.

"We wouldn't be in this ghastly mess now if the killing hadn't got out of hand," accused Blandhurst. His mouth trembled, like an enraged child denied its own way. He picked up the whiskey again, and the glass quivered in his hands. "Maybe Lupane lied, but no more than you did, Leo," he stated thickly. "How you bloody well lied to me. Oh, I went along with the Karsov thing. I was prepared to go that far, but God, then there was the photographer because of the insane rehearsal decision at Cape Jaubert. Then the raid itself. We'll just fire off a few shots to make it look good, you told me. Christ, how many men were killed? You damn near started a nuclear war."

Starker shrugged. "It has to come sometime. Why not now? I merely did what I considered necessary to make the raid look convincing."

"That's crazy talk. You knew from the very beginning what was going to happen, Leo. You took advantage of our friendship. Used me. I don't see how our friendship can mean anything after this." His words became more indistinct, until the phlegm in his throat clogged him into silence.

"You're going to win your election, Martin," said Starker coldly.

Blandhurst grimly studied his whiskey. "The price is too high for me," he mumbled unsteadily. "Too high. I'll never be able to sleep easy while this Berger character is around with his blackmail threat. God, he could finish me. Absolutely destroy me."

"If that killing had been successful, if Lupane hadn't blown it, we wouldn't be in this situation now," observed Starker sardonically.

Blandhurst was silent for a period. He took a deep, quivering breath in an attempt to regain composure. "You used me," he repeated bitterly.

The sun through the window formed a glowing outline around the General's body. He studied Blandhurst, his mouth ugly with contempt. "You wanted to be used, Martin," he said acidly. "Christ, how you wanted it. You were obsessed to win an election. You were ready to do anything I asked, just so long as you could pretend you didn't know how it was done. Didn't dirty your own lily-white hands. You know I only asked your help because our aims meshed. You to win an election, me to keep the bases in Australia. I would have done it just the same way, with or without your help. Christ, I've known so many

politicians like you. I thought you were different once, but
you're all the same. You think you can keep a clear conscience if someone else does the hatchet work. Well,
you're not clear. You're swimming in the mud with the rest
of us. You can blame the fucked-up incompetent Lupane
for Berger's blackmail. I don't know how he got onto us,
but he has, and that's the reality to be faced. I was all set
to leave for home until Berger's call, but I have to stay
now. He's as dangerous to me as he is to you." He paused,
breathing heavily. "I don't know if our friendship's over.
I'll give you time to think about that. But by Christ, we'd
better work together over this Berger crisis." He made a
quick, impatient flick of his hand. "Now, how do you
intend to handle Berger when he arrives tonight?"

Blandhurst scowled. Leo was crazy, he should have
seen it years ago. If things got too tough, he would simply
wash his hands of Berger and return home to bask in the
congratulatory glow of his precious committee. "Agree to
pay him, of course. What the hell else can I do?"

"Why don't you let me handle Berger?"

Blandhurst squinted suspiciously. "Killing Berger isn't
going to resolve anything. You know his safeguards. That
would be a disaster."

"You'll just write him a check for a million dollars?"

"No, he wants cash. I explained this is only a preliminary meeting. He says he'll arrange a transfer somewhere
else."

Starker folded his arms and moodily contemplated the
floor. "We underestimated Berger. I know Lupane destroyed the prints in Darwin. Berger must have had another set of prints made at the same time." He shook his
head mournfully. "This could threaten the entire committee, Martin. That ship could be traced right back to
Halmen." His mouth twisted with irritation. "We'll play it
by ear when he arrives. Lupane will be here by then.
Together we might be able to figure out a way to handle
Berger. Although I'd hardly expect your incompetent as-
sistant to have any ideas."

"The hell with Lupane," declared Blandhurst furiously.
"I said I'd pay the money. I meant what I said, Leo. No
more killing."

Starker raised his hands in an exaggerated gesture of
compliance. "All right, all right. Pay the fucking money.
Spend sleepless nights for the rest of your life, wondering
when Berger's coming back for more. It's your funeral."

The study lapsed into a frigid hush, the men avoiding
each other's eyes. Finally, as if he could no longer tolerate
Starker's presence, Blandhurst strode stiffly from the room.
He went across to the living-room window and stared out
at the green swath of ripened cane. The friendship was
ashes. He couldn't imagine how he could ever recover
from the sense of betrayal. He could see his manager
talking to a group of men at the bottom corner of the
canefield. He loved Sweetwater. It was his inheritance,
his life, and in a moment of insanity he'd put it all at risk.
God, he'd been a fool. He'd pay off this Berger character
and hope to Christ he stuck to his part of the bargain.
Then Leo could get the hell out of his house and back to
the States. He didn't ever want to see him again.

Ross and Lisa disembarked at Mackay, and there was a
car waiting for them, as Kaufman had promised. The drive
to Beton was done mostly in silence. Occasionally, to
reassure Lisa, Ross gently touched her folded hands. Always
she responded with a pale smile but no words. Only once
on the plane had she put her thoughts into words. "I know
this is the way it's got to be, Ross, and I won't let you
down. I can face Lupane, I can face anyone, as long as
you're standing beside me." He had been moved, because
he knew she was frightened. And the flutter in his own
stomach betrayed a smiliar emotion. Maybe it was going
to work, but being forced to trust Kaufman bothered him.

Ross had sympathy with the chill he saw growing in Lisa
as they drew closer to Sweetwater. It was a game they
played, trying to conceal their fear from each other. Once

again he cursed Kaufman's intractable demand that they both go. Well, when they got to the house, he was going to leave her in the car. The hell with Kaufman. Besides, it was safer to have someone waiting ready in the car outside the house, just in case anything went wrong inside. Kaufman wouldn't allow him a gun for insurance, so he was entitled to some margin for safety.

She looked good. Someone with taste had bought the dark slacks and jacket, set off with the bright yellow blouse, but it failed to disguise the foreboding in her face.

Ross was sure they were being watched, but it was skillfully done. He saw nothing on the plane. On the long stretches of highway, a car would slide up behind them and hang there for mile after mile until Ross became convinced it was one of Kaufman's eyes. But inevitably the car would accelerate past and race down the highway until it vanished from sight. So he was never sure. But he still wished he had a gun.

It was close to dark when they passed through Beton, a few ragged strips of deep red cloud still low on the horizon. Through the town, the tips of the canefields along the highway were flecked with crimson. But all the color had gone from the sky by the time the headlights picked up the turnoff to Sweetwater. The buildup of tension inside the car was more powerful than any words could express. Ross turned into the drive, and the tires crackled over the loose gravel. A single weak porch light gave only a vague impression of the grandeur of the house. The place was in darkness save for several brightly lit windows at the side. He pulled in short of the entrance, behind several other parked cars, and cut the motor. Beside them, the house was almost concealed by the shrubbery growing along the side of the drive, and the night breeze stirred the leaves with a soft rustling sound. He wondered how far away Kaufman was, where he had his listening post set up.

"I want you to stay in the car," he said quietly.

She stared at him, her mouth slightly open. "It's okay," she murmured. "I can handle it, Ross."

He marveled at the steadiness of her voice. "I know that. And I know Kaufman's instructions. The hell with him. I prefer to have you here waiting in the car, just in case something goes haywire inside. I don't trust Kaufman. I don't trust any of them." He shook his head firmly. "No, I want you to stay right here."

She shrugged agreement. He was sure she was relieved, but it was difficult to read her expression in the dim light of the car.

"What if they're watching us?" she asked.

He bit anxiously at his lower lip. "I've got a hunch we've had a tail ever since we left Sydney. If we've come this far, I guess they figure we'll go the rest of the way." He was silent for a moment, scanning the bushes along the side of the drive. "When I get out, I want you to drop down out of sight on the seat. I'll go up to the entrance through all this shrubbery. If we are being watched, they won't be able to tell if we both got out of the car or not." He glanced to her for confirmation. "Okay?"

She tried to smile, but it was more of a grimace. "Okay." She put her hand on his arm. "If you want me to come, I really can handle it," she assured him again.

He grinned at her. She had guts. "Just be ready for a fast takeoff," he muttered. He opened the door and eased himself out into the bushes, keeping low.

"Come back to me, Ross," she whispered.

He went swiftly, threading through the shrubs, then hugging the wall of the house, carrying the sound of her caring voice with him to the entrance. The doorway was only dimly lit, and he sought the deepest shadows. It was Starker who opened the door to him. Ross recognized him at once from Kaufman's photograph, but the picture failed to convey the intense military bearing of the man. Even out of uniform, it hung on him like an identification tag. The General offered no conversation, merely a penetrating stare and one crisp word. "Berger?"

"Yes." He felt like he was on a high, every nerve

primed. It was always the way with him. He might sweat like crazy at first, but once he was involved, the adrenaline started pumping.

"Follow me," said the General curtly.

Ross went quickly in the General's wake, his eyes flickering briefly over the handsome surroundings. Whatever else Blandhurst did, he knew how to live well. They were all waiting for him in a room furnished like a study. Blandhurst was also unlike his photograph. The features were the same, but the smooth composure was gone. He sat awkwardly on a sofa, eyes evasive, hands fluttering nervously, even the beautifully tailored suit rendered shabby by his unease. He looked older, and a bad color. Lupane and Garcott, the cold fish he'd met at the Darwin police station, were standing on the other side of a desk. It was confirmation that Garcott was the one who'd helped Lupane murder Jo. Ross knew he had to make it look like a hard-nosed business deal, but he failed to keep the hostility out of his face.

"Well, Berger . . ." Lupane sneered. "Still managing to stay alive."

"Hello, scum," Ross answered.

Garcott scowled and shuffled forward as if to move around the desk, but Lupane restrained him.

Starker coughed forcefully, closed the study door, and positioned himself by the desk. "Okay, let's forget the compliments," he said harshly. "No one wants to prolong this unpleasant meeting. Let's get down to business."

It seemed that Starker was going to be spokesman. Ross glanced toward Blandhurst, but the politician appeared to be concentrating on his fidgety hands.

"That's all right by me," Ross agreed tersely. He reached into the inside pocket of his jacket, produced an envelope, opened it, and dropped the copies of the Cape Jaubert photographs on the desk. "You've all seen them before. I wasn't crazy enough to bring the originals with me, but those copies are good enough proof." He glanced at Lupane

with a sneering grin. "You see, I had the foresight to have
another set of prints made for myself in Darwin, before I
turned the others over to you, Lupane. Just as well,
seeing you turned out to be a fucking butcher." He squinted
belligerently around at the others. "General Starker, I've
learned a lot about you. I've done some digging in the last
few days. I know where the *Seaboro* came from, about the
organization you're connected to in New York, about your
connection to Blandhurst here. I'm sure Blandhurst passed
our telephone conversation on to you. I'm not going to tell
you how I know, but you're all up to your bloody necks in
the North West Cape raid. I don't know your motives, and
I don't care. Maybe you're working with the Russians,
maybe not. All I'm sure of is that if the information I have
went to certain authorities, you'd all spend the rest of your
lives in jail." He knew he was carrying it well, his voice
steady, with no trace of fear. "I'm sure none of you wants
that. As I said over the phone, I'm offering the original
prints for sale at a million dollars—in cash. And don't try
anything smart. The warning I gave over the phone still
stands. I walk out of here tonight, or the original prints go
straight to Sydney's most influential newspaper, together
with all the other material I've gathered. It'll finish you,
Blandhurst. And you, Starker." He turned malevolent
eyes to Lupane. "And you and your psychopath friend."

Ross paused, thrust his hands into his pockets, and
waited. No one denied anything. He was sure Kaufman
was hunched over his recording machine, mouth wet with
anticipation. No one spoke for a time.

"You've been a very busy young man," Starker said
heavily.

"Where did you get your information?" Blandhurst asked.

"That's my business. It's irrelevant as far as you're concerned. All you have to do is agree to pay the money. You
know what the photographs mean."

There was another period of silence. A sliver of anxiety
touched Ross's spine. There was something not quite right,

that he failed to identify, about their reaction. Granted, Blandhurst looked as if the world had crashed about his shoulders, but the others were too composed, too unmoved, for men who faced the prospect he'd just delivered. It could have been Starker's military discipline holding him in check, but there was a gloating malice on Lupane's and Garcott's faces that he didn't understand. He decided to cut the meeting short, get out. If they agreed to pay the million dollars, that was ample evidence of guilt for Kaufman.

"Keep the copies," he stated. "Look at them all you want, it's not going to alter anything. I'll leave it a couple of days, then I'll be in touch with you again, Blandhurst, as to how and where I want the money paid."

He began to back uneasily toward the door, a confident smile still planted on his face. Warning bells were jangling now, and he was glad he'd left Lisa in the car.

Starker spread the prints across the desk and raised a hand to halt Ross. "Don't be in such a hurry, my greedy friend," he said mockingly. "I grant you these photographs are very important . . . one might almost say embarrassingly important as far as we're concerned. But without the original prints it would be impossible to make the New York connection that involves us all in the North West Cape raid. Without them your claims are nothing more than rather ridiculous unsubstantiated accusations."

Ross contrived a dismissive shrug. "So what? I've got the original prints. They'll nail you to the wall."

Starker glanced across at Lupane, then back to Ross. "You're bluffing, Berger," he grated. "You're greedy, you're a fool, and you're bluffing."

With a supreme effort Ross held the malicious smile. All the warning signals kept flashing, but with no indication where the danger lay. "You think I'm bluffing, then try me," he jeered. "Chance your luck. Maybe I won't get rich, but it'll be a pleasure to see you all go down the tubes after what you did to my brother."

Apprehension finally betrayed his voice, and he knew from their expressions it also showed in his face. There had to be something Kaufman hadn't told him. He was mentally groping, trying to make contact with the threat. He began to back again toward the door, but Starker lunged forward and seized him by the arm. He savagely wrenched his arm free. "Are you crazy?" he cried vehemently. "Do you want to finish up in jail?"

Starker looked again at Lupane, who stepped to the desk as if on cue and dropped a sheaf of photographs on the top. They were another set of the Cape Jaubert shots, and Ross saw at once by the quality that they were original prints.

Lupane laughed derisively. "You asshole, Berger. You stupid asshole. You haven't got any original prints. The General's right, this is all nothing but a crazy bluff." He motioned to the photographs. "Okay, you did get another set of prints for yourself in Darwin, but this is them."

Ross stared dazedly at the prints. It was a trick. They were trying to throw him off balance. He gestured contemptuously at them. "Go to hell, Lupane. You think I'm a fool. They're the prints I gave you in Darwin."

"No they're not. I destroyed those days ago. These came to me from Mount Isa. I heard all about your flight there. How you got away from the police. These prints were found at the police station where you left them, and they sent them on to me. This million-dollar blackmail is nothing but a try-on, Berger. Maybe you got these useless copies made in Darwin, but you haven't got any original prints now. You've got nothing to sell, you stupid asshole."

"Bullshit!" Ross shouted. He tried desperately to cover his confusion with anger. Lupane had to be lying. There was only one set of original prints in existence, and Kaufman had them. "I'm leaving," he said angrily. "You crazy bastards can make up your own minds. I'll give you twenty-four hours, then you either come through with the money or get used to the idea of spending the rest of your lives in jail."

"You're not going anywhere, Berger," Lupane said coldly.

"Go to hell." But he didn't move any closer to the door, because suddenly Lupane had him covered by a gun.

"Check him," Lupane ordered.

Garcott moved around the desk and expertly ran his hands over Ross. "Nothin'," he announced laconically. He pushed an ugly grin close to Ross's face. "You must be outta your mind, you stupid shit, to try somethin' like this. You must think we're a pack of idiots."

Ross had the feeling his mind was clogged with glue. How in Christ could any prints come to Lupane from Mount Isa? He needed time to think his way out, but he didn't have any time. He tasted the bitter wash of fear. Somehow he had to try to regain the initiative. He made one more attempt, directing his words toward the silent Blandhurst, making a supreme effort to keep his voice steady. Any chance lay with the politician, his face an equal mirror of fear and confusion.

"Listen, I do have a set of prints, Blandhurst," he declared urgently. "You're out of your mind if you don't believe me. You want a name like yours dragged in the mud?" He gestured furiously toward Starker. "Tell these maniacs. Are you just going to sit there and let them destroy you?"

Starker ignored him. "Take him outside," he ordered Lupane. "Somewhere away from the house in the car." He scowled menacingly. "This is your last chance, Lupane. I don't want to see this fool again. My God, you do it right this time or you go down with the rest of us. After all, you are dealing with a wanted murderer. The law's still on your side."

"What about the girl?" Lupane asked.

Starker turned to Ross. "Where's the Marnoo girl?" he demanded.

"A thousand miles from here where you can't touch her."

Starker looked at him doubtfully. "You're probably lying.

Never mind, we can pick her up later . . . wherever she is. You're the important one, Berger. She's nothing without you."

Blandhurst came abruptly to life, like a sleepwalker suddenly awakened. He lurched forward off the sofa, consternation on his face. "No . . . no . . . no . . . now wait a minute, Leo," he said hoarsely.

"It's the only way, Martin."

"My God, I said no more killing, and I meant it. For Christ's sake, he could be telling the truth. Hasn't that occurred to any of you? I'm not prepared to take that risk. I'll pay the money." His voice whined on the edge of hysteria. No longer a bon vivant, a connoisseur of expensive women, just a panicky old man desperate to survive.

"No, he's lying." Starker was adamant. "I know men, Martin, and I know this one is lying. He tried to make himself some easy money, and he got found out. It's as simple as that. He doesn't have any prints."

"Goddammit, Starker, I told you I'm not prepared to take that risk. Let that man go." His voice screeched out of his throat in unrecognizable form. "I absolutely demand you let him go."

For a moment no one moved. Blandhurst's fingers dragged like a claw at the General's arm. The two men glared long at each other, the stone-faced martinet and the florid, terrified politician, and the final frail strands of friendship dissolved.

The General placed his hand firmly into the other man's chest and pushed him forcefully back onto the sofa. "Sometimes risks are necessary, Martin," he said sternly. "And this one is necessary. We've got more to gain than to lose. This is the only thing to do."

Blandhurst sprawled on the sofa, limbs askew like a broken doll, and glowered helplessly at the General. "You arrogant bastard, Starker," he blurted. "Get out of my house."

"I will when I'm ready, Martin," Starker replied coldly.

"You're too weak for me. I guess you always were. You bend, and you break. You'll thank me for this later, when you've had time to unscramble your mind." He motioned swiftly to Lupane. "Get Berger out of here, Lupane. I'll handle things here."

"Stay where you are, Lupane," Blandhurst demanded. "You kill that man and you can forget everything I ever promised you. Forget about taking Kaufman's job. Forget about working in Intelligence."

Lupane hesitated, glancing indecisively from one man to the other. "The General's right," he pleaded. "We leave this bastard alive, we all risk going down."

"Not if I pay him the money."

"I'm talking about your life, as well as mine, Lupane," Starker countered. "That's the real risk. Forget about everything else. We can't afford to leave this man alive. It's safe. You know as well as I do he's lying about the prints."

Ross could see Lupane was going to decide for the General. Lupane might have reservations about going against Blandhurst, but he'd decide for his own neck.

"Starker's conning you, Lupane," he tried desperately. "I'm not lying. He wants me dead for his own safety, not yours. He'll go back to the States, and you'll all be left holding the bag."

"Killing you will put us all in the clear," Starker persisted. "You don't matter, Berger. Haven't you understood that yet? You're a frightened, greedy little man caught up in something too big for you. We'll squash you, and no one will give a damn." He gestured angrily at Lupane. "Now, I'm telling you again, get him out of here."

"I tell you—" Ross began, then Lupane pushed him violently toward the study door. Maybe he figured he had a score to settle anyway, and vengeful spleen made the final decision.

"Outside, Berger," he ordered viciously. "You're the only one around here that's lying."

Blandhurst said nothing, slumped beaten on the sofa. Lupane jabbed Ross with the gun, and he stumbled into the living room. He had a chance. Kaufman would have heard everything. He didn't know how far away the listening post was, but Kaufman would already have men heading to the house to save him.

He was going out the front door, Lupane and Garcott on either side, when it suddenly hit him. In spite of his precarious situation, it forced a bitter laugh. Of course there was only one set of prints. Kaufman had arranged that phony Mount Isa story and gotten the prints to Lupane. He'd been set up. He knew too much. Kaufman wanted him dead as much as these bastards. And he wanted Lisa dead too. That's why he'd been so insistent Lisa come with him. The bastard would have his tapes, and these idiots had been sucked in to do murder for him. Ross shook his head numbly, feeling a fool. He was on his own.

The countryside was mantled with frosted moonlight. In the distance the field of cane stood like a snow-tipped wall. Somewhere Ross knew he was going to have to make a run for it. A bullet in the back trying for life was better than waiting for the end like a docile rabbit. He hoped to Christ Lisa saw them and kept down out of sight. At least she had a chance. And he wasn't going to give up. Not yet. He'd beaten Lupane once, he could do it again. He still had the same eerie alertness that had accompanied him to the house. He would make his try when they began to push him into the car. Lupane was hugging close, and he could feel the gun in his back. He drooped his shoulders, hung his head, and let his feet drag with the gait of a man accepting the inevitable.

They went to the car parked immediately in front of his own, and Garcott opened the rear door. There was no sign of Lisa.

"Get in," said Lupane. The repellent grin on his face was an obscenity. "I'm going to enjoy this, Berger. Get real pleasure. You shit all over my chances with Blandhurst, and the last thing you're going to hear is me laughing."

The abrupt sound of Ross's car firing into life took them all by surprise. Just the momentary whir of the starter, then the instant roar of the engine perpetrated by someone slamming the accelerator hard to the floor. Then the car launched forward as if from a catapult. There was only a few yards separating the vehicles, yet the moving car gathered sufficient momentum to impact into the rear of Lupane's car with stunning force. The open door struck Lupane in the back, cannoning him forward into Garcott. One flailing arm struck Ross, sending him sprawling to the ground.

Ross knew it was Lisa, knew it was a beautiful, crazy attempt to save him, when she could have hidden safely out of sight. He came up off the ground running, seeing Garcott already on his hands and knees, the glint of the gun as he threw a wild shot. The bullet ricocheted off the side of the car. The night air vibrated with strangled curses as Lupane struggled to regain his feet.

The engine of Ross's car coughed into silence. The hood was jackknifed out of shape, and a jet of white steam hissed into the air. It took Ross only a fast glance to see the impact had locked the two cars together, then he rolled swiftly over the misshapen hood, the starter motor whirring frantically beneath him. Behind him Lupane was screaming obscenities, intercut with answering oaths from Garcott. Ross wrenched open the door of his car. Lisa was hunched over the steering wheel, her fingers on the key, the starter motor spinning in a hopeless repetitious whine.

She turned to him, mouth hanging open, her eyes wide and as luminous as the moon. "I can't get it started again, Ross," she cried in anguish.

"Leave it," he shouted urgently. "It's too late. Get out." He didn't know where they were going, but to stay by the car was to die. He half-dragged her out of the door. There was another car parked ahead, but even if they could get there, it was probably locked. Then the option was canceled by Lupane's bulk shambling into view around the other side, one hand grasping at the car for support, the gun in the other snapping off a shot in their direction. They both ducked instinctively, but the bullet went wild.

"Run," Ross gasped. "For Chrissake, run."

They bolted, Ross leading, both crouched low, heading for the deep shadows of the trees along the fence line. The dual crack of Lupane and Garcott shooting followed them. Ross could hear Lisa gasping beside him, but he had no spare breath for encouraging words. At the end of the line of trees an open field stretched to the right in an unbroken swath of moonlit grass that would expose them like coal on snow. To the left was the tall stand of sugarcane, and beyond that the craggy outline of a timbered hill. Ross tried to judge the distance as they ran. Maybe they could lose Lupane and Garcott in the cane, and if they could get through to the timbered hill, they had a chance.

Ross grasped Lisa's arm as she stumbled, ignoring the hoarse sound of her labored breathing, not slackening pace, veering away from the last of the trees across a few yards of open grass. He glanced back to their pursuers, and they were coming fast, arms gesticulating; then he heard the crackle of gunfire again and the whisk of bullets zipping close through the grass. Birds fled from their night roosts in the overhead branches, wings flapping, cawing in alarm.

"Into the cane," Ross called urgently.

They blundered into the tangled wall of cane without stopping, Ross frantically battering a pathway, ignoring the thick, pliable stalks that gouged scratches on his skin, the leaves that snapped back with stinging force. It was like hacking through impenetrable jungle with bare hands. He lost track of low long they went on, aware only of the searing agony of sucking air into his lungs, not feeling the pain of his lacerated flesh. He didn't stop until the weight of Lisa's hands locked about his arm dragged him to a halt, with the realization he was almost carrying her.

She released her hands and sank down at his feet, her

shoulders heaving, the sound of her breathing a high-pitched, straining whine. "I've got to stop . . . Ross," she gasped. "I've . . . got to. I can't go any further . . . or I'll drop."

He crouched down and put his arm around her, his fingers anxiously at her mouth, trying to blanket the sound of her sobbing breath. It was dark in the cane, the stalks enclosing them tightly, the leaves overhead a moon-tinted canopy. They stayed there, not speaking, trying to recover breath. He was awash with sweat, and he knew by the touch of her skin she was the same. Night creatures scuttled about their feet, and he tried not to think of the deadly snakes that so often hunted in the cane. Behind them, coming closer, was the sound of someone else beating his way through the cane. Ross drew her tightly to him, pressing her head to his chest, trying to quell the sound of his own breathing. His heart thrummed like a betraying drum that could be heard for miles. "Be still," he hissed. "Absolutely still."

Someone went past only a few yards away, a black, indistinguishable shape energetically punching a path through the stalks. It was impossible to tell from the rasp of the man's strangled breathing who it was. It could have been either Lupane or Garcott. Gradually he passed, like a transitory shadow, the threshing sound fading, leaving only a track of battered cane.

They waited for a time, still crouched, regaining breath, their hearts slowing. To be running again for their lives from Lupane was like an endlessly repeating nightmare.

"Which way now?" Lisa asked unsteadily.

Ross moved into an upright position and pulled Lisa up beside him. "It's hard to know," he whispered. "But I think I've been following the line along the edge of the cane. If we head back the other way, it should take us out near the timbered hill." He gestured in the direction of the man who had just passed. "He's headed into the center. If we can get out of here while those two psychopaths are in here blundering around, we might have a chance." He grasped her hand and began to force a path back in the other direction. They had barely gone a few yards when a new sound came sharply through the cane, a new smell mingling with the dank aroma. Ross stopped and glanced suspiciously up toward the tips of the cane. The moonlit sheen was gone from the topmost leaves, replaced by an orange glow, and the sky swarmed with bright red sparks whirling in the air like disturbed fireflies. The acrid tang of smoke filtered through the stalks, the precursor of a crackling roar, sweeping toward them like an onrushing wind. Even as they watched transfixed, the sky above turned the color of flame.

"Oh my God, Ross, they've set fire to the cane . . . they're trying to burn us out," Lisa cried.

"Lupane couldn't have started it—that'd be crazy . . . not while they're in here themselves."

It was irrelevant who had fired the cane; Ross only knew they had to get out, or be fried. He started up again, threshing a path through the cane with an inspired frenetic energy, disregarding the pain in his hands, the taste of blood on his mouth. He'd seen cane burn before, and he knew it would go like wildfire. They both began to cough as the smoke thickened, swirling about them like a fog, reaching for their lungs. He wasn't going to burn. Not for Blandhurst, or Starker, or Lupane. And not for a bastard like Kaufman. He'd beaten animals like them before, and he'd do it again.

Manic strength such as he'd never known before flooded into his body, and his hands became like scythes chopping at the cane. He was screaming, his mouth open, but the sound drowned in the clamorous voice of the fire. He could vaguely feel Lisa's hands around his waist, and he knew he was dragging her with him, but she seemed weightless. The feel of her, and what she meant to him, gave him enough strength for both of them. The heat of the flames was like a searing blast against his back, as if they were standing before a vast furnace, all the world a violent, garish red. The smoke turned his eyes to dribbling founts, partially blinding him, and sparks showered down like hellfire rain.

Then they were out, unbelievably free, staggering from the inferno and dropping into the sweet wet grass surrounding the canefield. Ross didn't know how long they lay there. Pure, cleansing air filtered back into his lungs, and the trembling gradually went out of his limbs. He reached out his hand and touched Lisa sprawled beside him. He eased himself up into a sitting position, seeing by the glow of the flames the blood on his hands. Lisa rolled to her side and crawled to him through the grass, her eyes like black ashes, riveted on his face. He took her in his arms, cradling her like a precious child, stroking her hair, listening to her sobs, and he felt as if nothing could ever harm him again. They sat there, daubed yellow by the flames, and he rocked gently to comfort her.

Then he saw Lupane emerge from the cane farther down the field, and he only guessed it was Lupane by the bulk of the figure, because the man was a torch. A stumbling candle of flame from head to foot, arms gropingly outstretched like a man suddenly struck blind. Then he fell over in the grass, and twitched there, burning, the grass hissing under him. Ross didn't move, didn't alert Lisa, kept her head down in his arms. Away at the far end of the cane another human torch emerged that could only be Garcott, blundering around in frantic circles like an animal driven insane with pain; then he too collapsed into the grass. It was another horror, to all the other horrors, but at least Joe could rest easy now. And Ross felt a corrosive hatred that someone could take hold of their lives as if they were bothersome insects to be squashed as irrelevant.

He released Lisa, stood up, and gently helped her to her feet. They looked like two escapees from hell, hair disheveled, clothes torn, dried blood on their hands and faces. It didn't matter. They were alive.

"Wait here," Ross instructed quietly.

He walked down by the side of the smoldering cane to the figure in the grass. Smoke wisped into the air from the body, and small patches of blue flame still flickered over the clothes. Ross scarcely recognized the blackened corpse, but it was Lupane. There was a gun still clutched in his bloated hand. He reached down and pried it free. It felt warm in his hand. He checked to see that it was loaded, then slipped it into his pocket. He would need that, for Starker, or Blandhurst, or Kaufman—he didn't care who came first. At the far corner of the cane, in the light of the flames, he could see several figures who looked like workmen, standing watching the fire. He didn't go on down to Garcott, but walked slowly back to Lisa.

"Lupane?" she breathed.

He nodded. "He's not a pretty sight."

"And Garcott?"

"The same thing. He's farther down."

She closed her eyes and shuddered. "For Jo," she said.

"Yes," he agreed. "For Jo. And Mark." He took her hand and led her in the direction of the house. "They obviously didn't start the fire. I saw what looked like some workmen at the end of the cane. I think we just happened to be here at the time they'd decided to burn it off."

There was a small stream at the dark side of the garden, and they stopped to wash off the blood. The cold water brought the cutting edge back to Ross's mind. He felt incredibly calm. Or maybe it was just a dispassionate cold-blooded urge to even the score with Kaufman. He told Lisa what had happened in the house.

She listened impassively, her face dazed with exhaustion; then she gave a short virulent laugh. "Even Kaufman. We can't trust anyone, Ross." She looked across to the house. Several lights still burned, but there was no sign of anyone outside. "What are we going to do, Ross? God, it's hopeless. How are we going to get away from this place?"

He thought about it for a moment. "We can do two things," he said flatly. "We can wander around the countryside like this and eventually get picked up by the police. We're still wanted in Darwin, and it'd be so easy for Kaufman to disown us or even make another attempt to kill us." He jerked his hand in the direction of one of the parked cars. "Or I can try to break into one of the cars and see if I can get it started. That won't work either, because we'll still probably get picked up."

She shook her head mournfully. "I'm so tired of running."

"We'll be running for the rest of our lives if we let them get away with it." He took the gun from his pocket and showed her.

"Where did you get that?" she asked dully.

"From Lupane. It gives me a chance."

"A chance for what?"

"To go back inside the house."

She stared at him as if she'd misunderstood the words, and wearily brushed hair from her eyes. "You'd be crazy to go back in there."

"I'd be crazy not to." He urgently grasped her hand. "Listen to me, Lisa. Everything we hope for from each other means nothing if we've got to spend the rest of our lives hiding in corners. If they learn we're still alive, they'll shift hell to find us. If I go in there and get the prints back at least it'll be a form of insurance to guarantee our safety—I'll take them to a newspaper with what I know, and it'll blow them all away." He shook her hand with an edge of desperation. "Don't you see that? It's useless just running. We haven't got anywhere to run."

She was silent for a time, then moved her head slowly in agreement. "Yes, I see that." She leaned against him, and he put his arm around her. "It's some sort of miracle we've survived so far. I couldn't bear it if anything happened to you now."

He kissed her, and she smelled of ash, and smoke, and fear, and he loved her more than ever for her courage. "I have to do this," he whispered. "I owe you . . . over and over. You saved me in Darwin, and you saved me here. This'll give us a chance."

"But what about Kaufman?" she asked suddenly. "Where's he now?"

"I'd say on his way back to Sydney with his precious tape under his arm."

"But won't the tape finish Blandhurst and Starker?"

"I don't know. I've no idea what the devious bastard will do with it now. All the shit he gave us about doing what was best for the country. He set us up to be killed. If the good of the country was what he had in mind, then why is what we know so dangerous to him?" He shook his head vigorously. "No, trusting Kaufman with anything is a good way to get killed. We need those prints back, and I'm going to get them."

She gave a shrug of resignation. "Then please be careful."

He pointed to a clump of trees at the end of the drive, not far from the front entrance of the house. "Wait for me there," he said. "And don't worry. Blandhurst and Starker aren't going to give me any trouble. Other people do their killing for them. They're nothing without Lupane and Garcott."

He went with her to the trees, whispering more reassurances. Then he took a circuitous route around to the side of the house, heading for where he'd seen the lighted windows, clinging to the shadows, running swiftly at a crouch. He felt only a gathering anger now, and it was like an anesthetic to his aching muscles, his torn skin.

He saw no one, heard nothing. If Kaufman did have watching eyes around, they were gone now. He edged up to the window, gun gripped in his hand, and peered cautiously inside. Kaufman was there, propped against the desk, his hand resting on a small tape recorder. Starker and Blandhurst were sitting in opposite corners of the sofa, the politician ashen-faced, gripping the arm as if to prevent himself from sliding to the floor, the General rigidly erect, his eyes fixed disbelievingly on the tape recorder. Ross could see the prints, still on top of the desk. There was a briefcase at Kaufman's feet. The lower panel of the window was open, and he knelt below it, listening. No one in the room was speaking, all concentrating on the medley of voices on the tape. He was taken aback to see Kaufman. Why would he confront them with the tape immediately? The tape came to an end, and Kaufman switched it off. For a time no one spoke.

"How dare you bug a meeting of your own minister?" Blandhurst finally managed to say.

It was a ludicrous question, and Kaufman laughed easily. "You can't be serious, Minister?" he said mockingly.

"It'an act of . . . of gross disloyalty," persisted Blandhurst weakly.

"So is treason, Minister," said Kaufman derisively. "As for loyalty from me—as you so quaintly put it—how could you expect any such thing? You plotted to push me out for a thug like Lupane. A thug. Did you really believe you could place a hoodlum in this important position? That I would just stand by and let you do it?"

"Is that all that concerns you—your own miserable skin?" His eyes glazed, and he struggled to remain upright on the sofa. "You . . . you've destroyed me, Kaufman."

"How could you possibly . . . how . . . you and Berger?" Starker faltered. The usual authoritarian voice wavered like strung wire.

"That doesn't matter for now," said Kaufman sharply.

The General's intractable spine finally gave way, and he slumped forward, elbows draped on his knees, and stared morosely at Kaufman. "You did all this . . . destroyed something so important to both our countries . . . just to get at someone like Lupane." He shrugged dispiritedly. "It's a wonder you didn't bring Berger in here with you to gloat."

"I don't know where Berger is."

There was a puzzled silence.

"You heard on the tape . . . my orders to Lupane. Don't you have Lupane under arrest?"

"No. I haven't seen Lupane."

"You didn't stop him from killing Berger?"

"No. I thought it in . . . all our best interests not to interfere."

The General unfolded into an erect position again, dull eyes suddenly revitalized with curiosity. He glanced quickly at Blandhurst, then back at Kaufman. "In all our best interests?"

"Yes." Kaufman rested his hands on the tape recorder. "Let me explain. I don't see any reason why this tape should go any further than this room. It'll be in my care, of course. In a safe place. The Americans are beginning to calm down in the United Nations. There's not going to be a war. The world will make up its own mind. Those that want to blame the Russians for the raid will do so. The others . . ." He smiled sardonically. "They can think what they like. I intend to leave it that way." He nodded toward Blandhurst. "You're obviously going to win your election, Minister. I'll continue as your head of Intelligence . . . and perhaps special adviser." His fingers rapped against the recorder. "Of course, this is the end of Lupane. You understand me, Minister?"

"He knows a hell of a lot," Blandhurst muttered.

"He won't dare open his mouth when he hears what's on this tape." The mocking smile came again. "I'm sure we can find some faraway place for Lupane."

"You let Berger die?" said the General.

"No. You ordered him killed, General. Not me." Kaufman sighed theatrically. "Sometimes these unfortunate decisions are necessary. What he knew could have made life dangerous for all of us."

Starker uttered an incredulous laugh. "You . . . you set him up. You sent those prints to Lupane." He shook his head. "Christ, when it comes to being criminal-minded, we've got nothing to teach you, Kaufman."

Kaufman merely offered a noncommittal shrug, then frowned. "The Marnoo girl was supposed to be with him."

"I guess it makes sense you'd want her out of the way too. Well, he didn't bring her with him."

"Yes he did. I had them checked all along the way. She was with him on the plane, in the car at the airport, and when they turned into the Sweetwater drive." He stared reflectively into space, his fingers pawing at his chin. "She's not so dangerous as Berger, but still a worry. She knows everything he does. She has to be around here somewhere." He lapsed into silence, his brows tightly drawn. "You chose a hell of a night to burn off your cane, Minister."

"My manager insisted. Besides, I had no idea something like this was going to happen. I understood I was making a quiet arrangement with a blackmailer." He glowered at Starker. "Until this fool let it get out of hand."

"And there's been a minor car accident in the drive. A car rammed into the back of another. Do either of you know anything about it?"

Both men silently shook their heads.

"It has to mean something," Kaufman mused.

"Ask Lupane when he gets back," suggested Blandhurst.

"I don't intend to be here when Lupane gets back."

"What's the cost?" asked Starker curtly. He scented he was off the hook, and his normal bearing had returned.

"Cost?"

"Yes. For your . . . cooperative attitude."

"Mutual interest doesn't require payment, General. Go back to the States. To your committee. Bask in the glory." He turned to Blandhurst, as a snake contemplates a meal. "And I'm sure the minister and I can look forward to a long and successful . . . partnership from now on. I'm sure he can find a much bigger role for me to play in government."

Blandhurst glared malevolently from the sofa, but said nothing. There was an awkward silence while Kaufman placed the prints and tape in his briefcase. "I want to get out of here before Lupane gets back," he stated briskly. "And I need to get back to Sydney tonight. So let's wind this up." He snapped the case shut and stood away from the desk. "If you don't mind, I'd like a few private words with the minister, General?" Starker hesitated, sniffing the air suspiciously. "A few domestic problems that will need arranging, that's all, General."

Starker nodded tersely. "Very well."

"And have a good trip back to the States."

The General didn't reply. He strode from the study and closed the door firmly behind him.

Kaufman waited a moment, then took Blandhurst confidently by the arm, eased him from the sofa, and walked him to the window, Ross flattened himself into the shadows along the wall.

"There are several things." Kaufman's tone was mockingly subservient. "Tell Lupane nothing about this. The girl has to be here somewhere. When Lupane finds her, it's best if he still thinks he's operating to the General's orders. He'll act accordingly. Lupane's . . . destruction can come later." He paused, his fingers tightly into the politician's arm. "The other problem concerns the General. And that's a big problem. I have information that when he returns to the States there's a considerable possibility he'll be arrested. His committee has evidently been under surveillance by American intelligence for some time. I don't know if they can prove anything, but we can't risk waiting. With what he knows, that would be incredibly dangerous for us, Minister. You understand?"

Blandhurst gawked at Kaufman uncertainly, his mouth agape. "The committee has powerful friends in the government . . . in the Pentagon. They'll protect him."

"We can't risk that," continued Kaufman. "You owe him nothing, Minister. I heard the tape. He betrayed you, used you. He's no friend, never was."

"What are you going to do?" quavered Blandhurst.

"You don't have to concern yourself at all. When does he leave for the States?"

"I . . . I don't know, probably tomorrow. I don't want him staying here."

"Of course not. He has a car?"

"Yes. He hired a car and drove up from Brisbane."

"He'll be driving back alone?"

"Yes . . . I expect so. He certainly wouldn't expect me to accompany him . . . not now."

Kaufman smiled coldly. "Call me when he leaves. Understand? That's all you have to do. Everything will be arranged. Neither you nor I will be involved, Minister." There was no mistaking Kaufman's tone, that the reversed roles of master and servant had already been established.

Ross had heard enough. He had more than enough confirmation of everything he'd suspected about Kaufman, and he burned. The bastard was even more treacherous than he could possibly have imagined. The hell with the other two. Kaufman was the one he wanted. And the prints. And the tape.

He ran silently back to the corner of the house, then around toward the entrance, once again using the shrubbery along the wall as cover. He positioned himself in the bushes at the edge of the drive and waited. He strained his eyes toward the clump of trees, but there was no sign of Lisa. Beyond, the canefield was one huge glowing ember.

It didn't take long. Kaufman came quickly out of the entrance and strode rapidly down the drive, his feet crunching on the gravel. The briefcase swung easily in his hand. Ross let him get past a few feet, then stepped swiftly from the shrubs and prodded the gun into Kaufman's back. "Just keep walking," he hissed. "Don't act surprised, don't turn around, just keep on down the drive."

Just for a second Kaufman missed a step; then even when he picked up the beat, his pace was slower. "Berger?" he questioned hoarsely. He half-turned his head, and Ross savagely increased the pressure of the gun.

"Who else, you double-crossing shit? Don't turn around, I said."

They walked on for a short distance in silence. Ross could almost hear Kaufman's mind ticking over. The intelligence man's feet dragged, and gravel sprayed from his shoes.

"Listen, Ross . . . I'm glad to see you. I really am. What's happened . . . where've you been?" His voice fluttered. "Why the gun?"

"Where's your car?"

"Down . . . down the drive a piece. This is crazy. For Chrissake, put the gun down. What's the problem? Let's talk about this."

Ross jabbed him again. "You treacherous bastard. I've just been standing outside the study window listening to your heart-to-heart talk with Blandhurst and Starker."

That silenced Kaufman for a time. He stumbled, and Ross could hear the sound of his throat gulping saliva. Then he tried again. "You've got it all wrong, Ross. What you heard was only for Blandhurst and Starker. Just so they could imagine they're safe while I get the tape to the prime minister. Christ, Ross, everything worked for us . . . we've got 'em on toast."

"Bullshit. Lupane's dead. And Garcott. Nothing would give me more pleasure than to put a bullet in your back."

They walked around the curve, and another car came into sight, parked on the other side of the drive. A man was leaning casually against the car, smoking.

"You set me up, Kaufman," whispered Ross fiercely. "Set us both up. You got the prints to Lupane."

"I don't know where Lupane got them," protested Kaufman.

"Liar. When we get to your car, tell your man to go wait in the house. To report to Blandhurst. He's to hang around and see if the girl turns up. You'll be gone for a couple of hours." He slipped the gun into his pocket. "You make one slight move to tip him off, and I'll kill both of you. I've got nothing to lose, Kaufman."

"Ross, you're upset . . . and you're making a terrible mistake," Kaufman pleaded.

"It'll be a bad mistake for you if you don't do what I'm telling you," Ross gritted. "I'm taking the prints and the tape in your case. I can do it with you dead, or alive. It's your choice."

"Will you please listen—"

"Shut up. Do it. When we get in the car, you take the wheel."

They stopped short of the car, and Kaufman's man straightened. It was dark on the drive, and Ross stayed back, clinging to the shadows.

"You ready to go, Mr. Kaufman?" asked the man.

"I'm going to drive, Frank. I want you to go into the house and see Mr. Blandhurst. Tell him I want you to stay there and see if the girl turns up. He'll understand." The instruction was delivered in a steady, unruffled tone. Ross recognized the signs, and it made him doubly cautious. Kaufman had some guts; he'd played the staying-alive game before.

The man hesitated, stared toward Ross, dropped his cigarette to the drive, and squashed it deliberately with his foot.

"It's okay, Frank. I'll only be gone a couple of hours. We just have to see someone, then I'll be back," Kaufman assured him.

The man finally shrugged obedience. "All right, Mr. Kaufman." Then he stepped away from the car and walked steadily up the drive toward the house. By the time they were in the car, he was out of sight. Ross pointed ahead. "Take the car up to a clump of trees at the end of the drive and stop," he ordered.

He pushed the gun into Kaufman's ribs, and was sullenly obeyed. Kaufman trawled the car slowly up the drive and stopped by the trees. Then he lifted one hand from the wheel in an imploring gesture. "If you would just put that gun away for a minute, Ross, I believe I can explain exactly what happened," he said beseechingly.

Ross ignored him. He carefully opened the door and stepped out, still keeping the gun trained on Kaufman. "Lisa," he called urgently.

She moved apprehensively out from the trees, and he gestured impatiently for her to join him. She came quickly, and stopped beside Ross, her eyes flicking questioningly from one man to the other.

"No questions now," he forestalled her. He jerked the gun toward the car. "I want you to drive. Out this side, Kaufman, and get into the back seat. Bring the briefcase with you."

It took only a few seconds for the interchange to take place, then Ross slipped in beside Kaufman and pushed him into the corner of the seat.

From behind the wheel Lisa turned confused eyes to Ross. "Drive where?" she asked.

"Back on the highway, and through Beton until I tell you to stop," he ordered brusquely. She hesitated a second, and he tried to smile. "Can you handle it?" he asked in a kinder tone.

She didn't answer, but merely slipped into gear, swung the car in a tight circle, and headed back to the Sweetwater road.

He didn't give her any more directions, and she drove with extreme care at first, as if wary of her state of exhaustion. No one spoke. Kaufman hunched into the corner, his mouth set, face turned stonily to the window. If he was concocting another plea, then perhaps he was waiting to see what Ross intended before it was offered. They turned back onto the main highway and picked up speed until the scattered lights of Beton appeared through the windshield.

"Go straight through," Ross instructed. "But slow. I don't want to attract any attention."

Lisa nodded wordlessly, and dropped speed. There was little sign of life. The shops were closed, and the sparse streetlights revealed only a few wandering stragglers. The beat of rock music pounded from the hotel at the end of the road, then they were through and into the silence of the open countryside again. Lisa pressed on the accelerator, and the car surged under them.

"I think I've got most of it figured," Ross murmured. "At least about the raid. Blandhurst to win an election, Starker and his pack of crazies in the States to keep the American bases in Australia. Clever, in a lunatic way, to make it look like the Russians. But I haven't worked you out yet, Kaufman. Maybe I never will. Perhaps the power you figured you'd have with Blandhurst under your thumb was enough incentive. You were going to have me blown away, and Lisa, and Starker. But then, I could never figure out what makes guys like you tick." He uttered a short humorless laugh. "Funny, you obviously hated Lupane's guts, yet you're so much alike."

The shot went home. Kaufman turned from the window and glared at him. "Don't compare me to that hoodlum," he said bleakly. He shook his head, then stared at Ross as if seeing his ragged condition for the first time. "I don't know what you've been through, or what happened to Lupane and Garcott. I couldn't care less about them. But you're going to have to listen to me sooner or later."

"The hell I am," declared Ross in sudden anger. "I'll give you the same chance you gave us."

Kaufman retreated into his silent cocoon again. If he felt any fear, he concealed it well.

They went on for another hour, Lisa holding the car at a steady speed, through a moon-sprayed black-and-white landscape. Now and then a pinpoint of yellow light blinked briefly through the trees, marking an isolated farmhouse. There was little traffic. Once or twice other cars slipped past, and they rocked gently in the slipstream. But mostly they had the highway to themselves.

They came to a place where the road snaked in a series of sweeping curves through a section of forest and the trees grew with touching closeness.

"Stop somewhere along here, Lisa," Ross instructed.

They were the first words spoken in a long time. She slackened speed immediately, and gradually eased the car off onto the side of the road. A rest-stop turnoff cut through the trees showed up in the headlights.

"In there," urged Ross quickly.

She swung the wheel in response, the car bumped gently over a shallow culvert, then she drove to the center of the small clearing and cut the motor. Kaufman shuffled uneasily in the seat, and for the first time Ross saw fear on his face. He knew that expression so well, had experienced it so often, and there was a certain satisfaction in seeing it on Kaufman's face.

"Turn the lights off," he murmured. Lisa complied, and the click of the switch seemed inordinately loud. The forest around sighed, as if in mournful requiem. He opened the door and backed out, still holding the gun on Kaufman. "Get out, Kaufman," he ordered.

Kaufman failed to move. His arms were folded tight about his body in a subconscious gesture of defense. "Now, listen, Berger . . . don't do anything crazy . . ." he muttered weakly. The precise English accent wavered, and the words expired in his throat.

Lisa swung around to face Ross. "I know this man's acted like a bastard . . ." She faltered. "But I don't want—"

"If he'd had his way, you'd be dead now, and so would I."

"Yes, I know, but—"

He cut her off with a curt wave of the gun. "I know what I'm doing. Just stay with the car." He glowered at Kaufman. "Are you going to get out, or am I going to drag you out?"

Kaufman's posture of injured innocence collapsed. Somehow he forced his trembling limbs through the door, a step at a time, and he would have fallen but for Ross's savage grip on his arm. How well Ross knew that fear induces weakness, threatens support of the body.

Ross pushed Kaufman ahead of him into the blackness of the forest. "Walk," he commanded.

They went into the darkness, Kaufman feeling his way, stumbling, sometimes falling. Ross tramped in his wake, offering no assistance, prodding him with the gun when he was slow regaining his feet. Shafts of moonlight probed through the overhead foliage. The only sound was the brush of their feet through the undergrowth.

"Stop here," Ross ordered after they had gone several hundred yards.

Kaufman's breath came in quick fluttery gasps. "Listen . . . listen . . . listen . . .," he pleaded. "For God's sake, killing me won't achieve anything." It was a voice scarcely recognizable from the crisp tone that had issued orders in the Terrigal cottage. "Anything's possible the way I've got Blandhurst . . . you understand . . . anything at all. We can work this together, Ross. I can make you rich. Blandhurst is unbelievably wealthy . . . you've no idea."

A beam of moonlight spotted Kaufman, throwing into relief the agony in his face. Ross didn't even give an indication he'd heard the words. "Take off your clothes," he ordered.

"My clothes?"

"Yes. Take them off."

"I don't . . . ?"

"Do it." Ross waved the gun in his face. "Now, and fast."

He waited, the gun held loosely at his side, while Kaufman fumbled out of his clothes and dropped them in a bundle at his feet. With his milk-white skin he looked a slightly ridiculous forest gnome.

"Give me your wallet," Ross growled.

Kaufman rumaged in the bundle, produced his wallet, and handed it to Ross. It was expensive leather, and soft to the touch. It looked as if there was about a hundred dollars in the folder. Ross took out the money, put it in his pocket, and threw the wallet back with the clothes.

"I need some money to get where I'm going—just expenses." He motioned to the clothes again. "Now your tie."

Kaufman found his tie and handed it to Ross. Ross backed him against a tree, locked his arms about the trunk, and secured his wrists tightly with the tie.

"Nothing would give me more satisfaction than killing you, Kaufman," he said coldly. "Shit like you can find all sorts of rationalizations to destroy people's lives, but it's still murder. Somehow I can't bring myself to shoot you in cold blood, and I guess that's my hang-up. But then I'd be in your league, and I haven't hit the bottom rung yet." He stood back and picked up the clothes. "All I need is a little time, Kaufman. It'll be hours before you're found, maybe not until tomorrow . . . if you're lucky. Don't come after me. I'm going to mail the prints and tape to a secret address, so putting your hounds on me won't get you off the hook. Those photographs and tape are going to a newspaper no matter what, either from me or from the friends I send them to. There's nothing you can do to stop it. You're through. And so is Blandhurst."

He picked up the clothes. "You'll have trouble trying to identify yourself to whoever happens to find you anyway, without these." He began to retrace his steps through the forest, without a backward glance at Kaufman.

"You mealymouthed bastard . . . you ridiculous idealist creep," Kaufman called out. "You think anyone will believe you?" Strength had returned to his voice with the surprise knowledge he was going to live. Ross kept going.

"You really think you can destroy anyone as powerful as me . . . as powerful as Blandhurst?" Kaufman shouted. His voice reverberated through the trees, distorting the words. Ross kept going.

"You crazy fool . . . do you have any idea how rich I can make you?" Kaufman screamed. Ross kept going. Even though the final desperate entreaty reached hysterical pitch, the sound was thinner, diffused by the forest. The shrill words continued, but they became too distorted to make sense. Then they became like the far-off cries of a bird in distress, until finally there was only the sound of Ross's own footsteps scuffling through the undergrowth.

*   *   *

He took the wheel. Lisa didn't ask any questions, but he felt impelled to answer the query in her eyes. "Don't worry, he's alive." He jerked his thumb toward the clothes on the back seat and grinned. "Alive . . . but cold."

She made no comment. He knew she would be patient until he was ready, because there was much she didn't know. He drove too fast, spurred by an unconscious urge to express freedom, hammering into the curves, screeching the tires, drawn by the headlights boring ahead into the night. He glanced at her, and she answered with that marvelous smile that had first captivated him in Darwin.

"It's going to be rough," he said.

She placed a hand gently over one of his on the wheel, and squeezed softly. It was a simple gesture, yet it spoke for the depth of feeling they shared for each other.

"It's been that way already," she whispered. "I don't care, as long as I'm with you."

Tension seeped from him, and gradually his foot eased off the accelerator. He didn't have to run anymore. She was right. Anything was possible while they were together.